The Ones We
Fight For

Katie Golightly

ISBN: 9798387331169

Cover Design by: Sam Palencia at Ink&Laurel

Editor: Maryarita Kobotis

Formatting: Kristen Hamilton at Kristen's Red Pen

To those who fight for their family, their friends, and their own mental health.

And to Crystal, Taylor, and Mackenzie. I found you in a dark time and you continue to help pull me out through laughter and absolute chaos.

PLAYLIST

Lovely by Billie Eilish, Khalid
Unwell by Matchbox Twenty
Saved by Nashville Cast, Lennon Stella
Landslide by Fleetwood Mac
Hard Times by Paramore
I Look to You by Whitney Houston
There's Still a Light in the House by Valley
Willow by Taylor Swift
Only Love by Ben Howard
Friends Don't by Maddie & Tae
Jealous by Labrinth
Rewrite the Stars by Jams Arther, Anne-Marie
Here Without Youby 3 Door Down
Anti-Hero by Taylor Swift
In the Stars by Benson Boone
Superposition by Young the Giant
Waves by Dean Lewis
Chronically Cautious by Braden Bales
Grow As We Go by Ben Platt
Into You by Cast of Zoey's Extraordinary Playlist, John Clarence Stewart

Don't Ya by Brett Eldredge
Heal by Tom Odell
I Found by Amber Run
Beyond by Leon Bridges
In Case You Didn't Know by Brett Young
Close by Nick Jonas, Tove Lo
Sex on Fire by Kings of Leon
Better Together by Jack Johnson
Love Like That by Phillip Phillips
I Will Follow You into the Dark by Death Cab for Cutie

Author's Note

Content/Trigger Warnings: Off-page death of family members (drunk driving/mention of drug overdose), discussions of alcohol abuse and past physical abuse, on-page anxiety attacks, depictions of figurative drownings, descriptions of vomit, and mentions of infertility.

If you are someone who does not like handling hard topics with comedy, then this book might not be for you. Laughter is a defense mechanism I use and will continue to use. My characters do the same. Humor is often a last-ditch effort to find a shred of hope in a situation, and I love that we have the ability to turn something on its head and laugh about it. That being said, this is a book about grief and finding love through the thick of it.

In addition to the entire novel being in the aftermath of the tragic loss of two loved ones, there is mention of past alcohol abuse, past physical abuse, and infertility, all of which can be triggering topics. This book heavily focuses on mental health, with an emphasis on anxiety, depression, and self-worth. All descriptions of dealing with these traumas are mine. I do not pretend to know everything about any one of these topics.

With regard to infertility specifically, I want to prime all readers to know, right from the start, that there will not be a surprise baby trope in this book for the character who can't have children. Please do not go into this hoping for a miracle baby at the end, because that will not be happening. It's not because I'm heartless—well, maybe—but because I personally struggle with this and want to give a voice to women who don't get that specific happy ending. Some women have one child and then find they can't have any more. Some women can't have kids at all, period. Either way, they deserve a voice and to fall in love, too.

If, by some stroke of luck, you are still reading this lengthy author's note, my last warning is the one you've all been waiting for. Like this slow burn romance, I saved the best for last. This is an open-door romance. The door has been ripped off the hinges, and you will waltz right in. There will be sex scenes that I describe in great detail on top of the many sexual jokes the characters make throughout and constant cursing. If you are not over the age of eighteen or don't want to read that kind of thing, by all means, put this book down. If you know me in real life, please put this book down. If you are defiant and plan on reading it anyway, at least do me a solid and pretend that you didn't.

This book was a labor of love for many reasons, but most of all because I finally decided that I could do it. Yes, it is dedicated to others, especially those who built me up, but truly, I wrote it for myself. I wrote it to prove I could do something special after the worst few years of my life. To prove that my spirit, creativity, and joy hadn't fizzled out completely. To prove that I could laugh again and make something sexy if I wanted to. In the end, if that's all I accomplished with this, I'll have done what I set out to do.

If you happen to be in the same spot I was, wondering if there is anything left of yourself, I'm proof that there is always something left. You only need the tiniest of sparks to start a fire. I've built my small, secluded campfire, and if I keep feeding it (hopefully not with the pages of this book), then it might just grow into a bonfire.

Prologue

WALKER

Shards of glass tumbled over the asphalt, shattering into pieces of starlight under the glow of street lamps. It would have been an alluring sight to behold if not for the horrifying scene Walker knew awaited him once everything stilled. As if to affirm his impending doom, a chunk of metal sparked as it skidded to a stop in the middle of the road, a tiny firework in the darkness. The parade of beautiful and eerie destruction was swallowed up by the fog mere seconds later, like it hadn't even happened.

And then, a cold, dead silence.

There should have been noise, the sound of screaming or the hiss of steam from an engine, but there was nothing. The hollow thrumming in his ears made his head throb as he kicked up his feet to sprint toward the accident. He moved like a slug, weightless limbs floating around him as he hit something hard and icy.

Water. He was underwater.

Confused, he turned to find that there were four sides to the tank, locking him away from outside, where they were waiting. All that resulted when he beat his fists and feet against the plexiglass was an echoing thud inside the chamber. His lungs finally caught on to his predicament and strained for air. No one looked up from the scene outside his enclosure as he watched the multi-colored lights on top of a distant car speed toward the accident, reflecting off the glass and blinding him. He searched for a pocket of air, just enough to fill his lungs so he could continue trying to escape.

There was none.

A gurney rolled out toward the street, pushed by a dark figure as Walker continued to kick the pane in front of him furiously. Watching in horror, he slowly drowned, only caring that his lungs were giving out because he couldn't get outside. Couldn't get to them. Fighting against the pressure in his chest and the inability to breathe proved fruitless. The pounding in his head was almost audible when he finally shut his eyes to block out the disappointment.

Eventually, everyone would find out how helpless he truly was.

The alarm blared beside the bed.

ONE

WALKER

Jolting upright, Walker smacked the alarm clock so hard it clattered to the floor. The need to breathe roused him from sleep more than the actual alarm did, and he inhaled sharply to confirm he still could. Rolling out of bed, he placed his feet on the ground, still catching his breath. The freezing wood floor was a shock to his unsocked feet, expecting the warmth of the cheap carpet in his apartment. At first glance around the room, he was inclined to believe he'd had a one-night stand—which he wasn't opposed to —until the disillusionment of his surroundings settled in.

Right. You're at your brother's house, which, I guess, is now your house.

The nightstand next to the bed did not contain any condoms for his supposed one-night stand. Given the five—yes, count them, five—children Walker's brother and sister-in-law had, contraception was probably off the roster. Two of the kids were adopted, but it didn't change the fact that there would be no sex in Walker's future.

After four months of basically taking over his brother's life, Walker couldn't quite shake the feeling of not knowing where he was in the morning. It wasn't like he hadn't woken up in some random woman's bed before, but this was different. The air of familiarity was all the more confusing until his memories finally came flooding back to him, filling him with dread, like they always did.

Sighing loudly, Walker bent over to pick up the alarm clock, which read 5:30 a.m., setting it back on the nightstand that was nicer than any piece of furniture he had ever owned. He was now one of those responsible adults who woke at the buttcrack of dawn to get everything done and used a coaster to prevent water rings from damaging an end table. As if God had decided he needed to get his act together in the most fucked up way possible, his devil-may-care, casanova attitude had come to a grinding halt at the ripe age of twenty-six.

The motorcycle of Walker's dreams was sitting in his brother's —no, *his*—garage, untouched. The long hair he used to run his fingers through was chopped off because it was too greasy from his constant state of stress. His niece, Piper, who had an affinity for changing her own hair at the drop of a hat, had finally declared that he looked like the main character from a bad '90s movie and given him a new haircut. He had to admit, it wasn't half bad. Piper herself was now sporting bleach blonde hair with the tips dyed black. It didn't quite fit her normally sunny disposition, but it was fitting for the time being. She was old enough to dye her hair whatever color she wanted to, especially after all the shit she'd had to deal with recently. If she wanted to shave her head completely like 2007 Britney Spears, he would cheer her on. Who even needed hair?

After taking a shower, brushing his teeth, and deciding he was too lazy to shave his short beard, Walker pulled out the one drawer in the dresser that he had emptied for his stuff and put on a pair of jeans and a black T-shirt. Considering his job mostly involved sitting in coffee shops and ghostwriting the latest crappy novel, the scruffy, tattooed look wasn't going to hurt anyone. It was his one callback to his previously rebellious and carefree life. For the first time in months, he was all set for what he hoped would be a day spent with his laptop, coffee, and some goddamn peace and quiet.

Slipping his phone into his pocket—an Android, because at the time he'd purchased a phone, he thought Apple phones were for sheep—he made his way down the stairs. The thought seemed so stupid and insignificant now that it almost made him laugh. The luxury of thinking minuscule things mattered or that he could still have some semblance of normalcy was ridiculous. His nieces and nephews were the only things that mattered anymore.

When Walker reached the kitchen, he opened the fridge, already grimacing before he peered inside. Grocery shopping jumped the line on his to-do list. His fridge back at his apartment usually contained several takeout containers that he'd left in there for entirely too long, to the point that when he did eventually clean it out, the contents looked more like a science experiment than a recognizable meal. When his brother, Cole, mentioned his unhealthy eating habits, Walker would just shrug and go into a monologue about the discovery of penicillin in mold. It was a medical accomplishment of epic proportions; therefore, what were a few rotting chow meins in the grand scheme of things? Cole would roll his eyes, then invite Walker over for dinner, where his sister-in-law, Paisley, wouldn't allow him to leave without taking all of the leftovers home with him. She wasn't subtle about wanting Walker to eat a real meal. If he refused, she would just threaten to drop it off at his apartment or ask whatever girl he'd recently dated (and never called back) to take it to him.

If there was one thing Walker knew about Paisley, it was that she won just about every argument she was a part of. Paisley had her shit together. She was the reason Walker ate at all when he was in middle school and high school. Despite the eleven-year age difference between Walker and his brother, they had always been close. They had to stick together because their parents were the kind of people who never should have had children.

After their mom died of a drug overdose when Walker was

two, their dad technically became his sole guardian. But, in all ways that did matter, Cole had raised Walker. Their father was too busy getting smashed in his favorite lounging chair to bother with the work of being a present parent.

Cole and Paisley's love story was something straight out of a bad romantic comedy, and maybe that was why adapting cheesy movies and TV shows into novels never really bothered Walker. He liked to pretend that his job was ass, but deep down, he liked the idea of a happy ending. Until recently.

Paisley was a foster kid without a single family member to her name. She got straight A's in school, and, despite having no support, forged her own path in life. No one was going to stop her. Walker had always assumed that Cole desperately wanted that for himself, and so, when he had met his future wife, it had been an immediate attraction. At least, on one end.

Back when his brother was vying for Paisley's attention, she had shut him down, insisting that, despite liking him, she wouldn't let him distract her from her goals. Cole picked wild-flowers because they were broke, offered to hold her books on the way to class, and said repeatedly that he would wait, however long it took, for her to come to her senses. Eventually, Cole weaseled his way in by literally bribing his chemistry teacher to be Paisley's lab partner, and the rest was well, *chemistry*.

From the moment she had married his brother, Paisley welcomed Walker into their tiny apartment with open arms. He was always grateful that she never once complained when he needed a place to go to get away from his alcoholic father. The tiny apartment they rented soon became a tiny house, and then, immediately after Cole and Paisley's interior design business took off, the massive house Walker was now the temporary owner of. Never in a million years would he have guessed that Cole and Paisley wouldn't be there for their own kids.

"I'm going to do my absolute best to return the favor, I prom-ise," Walker said in a hushed voice as he pulled out a few boxes of cereal and a jug of milk. "I'll restock the fridge before work, after I make sure they all get to school."

There was no one in the kitchen, but Walker often found himself talking out loud as if Cole and Paisley could hear him. It was possibly more for himself than anyone else—like if he said his tasks aloud, it would get him started on actually accomplishing them. Better late than never to stop procrastinating.

Pulling the coffee grounds down from the cabinet, Walker made his way over to the coffee maker and stared at it, eyebrows knitting together in concentration as he twisted Cole's wedding band around his middle finger.

"Want me to do that?" Colin, Walker's nephew and the oldest of the kids, came into the kitchen, already grabbing the coffee out of Walker's hand.

"I can do it." Walker shook his head.

"Let me rephrase that: the coffee you've been making for the last few months is disgusting, and considering that everyone is going back to school today, I think we all deserve something that doesn't taste like sludge," Colin said, pushing Walker to the side so he could prepare the coffee. Tall and lanky, his nephew wasn't aware of his own strength yet, and Walker had to stumble a little to catch his footing.

"Okay, it's not that bad!" Walker protested, but made his way over to the cabinet to grab the bowls knowing full well that his coffee really was that bad. The coffee machine was too fancy, and he hadn't quite figured it out yet. He was used to his average Joe coffee maker that he bought at an estate sale for five bucks. This one had too many buttons and gadgets. Why couldn't anything just be simple anymore? Coffee makers shouldn't come with a learning curve.

"What kind of sugary cereal are we eating today?" Cooper, Cole's youngest son, bounded into the kitchen and sat down on a barstool, reaching for one of the bowls.

"Reese's Puffs and Froot Loops," Walker answered, raising one finger in warning. "But I'm going grocery shopping today, and I'm replacing all of this with healthier options, so enjoy it while you can."

"You are going grocery shopping?" Piper made her grand entrance, and Walker's eyes widened in surprise. She was wearing something he knew his brother would never have allowed her to leave the house in, what with her midriff showing and shorts that seemed like they were a few sizes too small. Honestly, where was the rest of her outfit? She had to have been only half-dressed at this point.

Walker probably should have said something or demanded that she throw on a sweater, but he couldn't bring himself to. He wasn't her dad, nor was he even old enough to be her dad. There would probably be nothing more uncomfortable to discuss when she had witnessed him bring many scantily clad women over for family dinner night. Walker could already hear the word "hypocrite" ringing in his ears. Between the hair and the clothing, he figured Piper was just letting off some steam, and he ignored it.

"Yes, I am." Walker fixed his face with confidence. "I'm going to make a mental list if you guys tell me what you want."

"You don't need help?" Piper pried.

"Despite what you think, I am an adult who is capable of going shopping by myself." Walker rolled his eyes. It was barely true, but he would have to be a real adult now, and it wasn't like he'd never gone grocery shopping before.

"And I think I'm going to make dinner tonight to celebrate everyone's successful return to school today." This declaration was met with loud groans from every person in the kitchen. "I promise it's going to be g—"

A blood-curdling scream abruptly interrupted Walker's desire to prove to everyone that he could cook, and he jerked his head toward the stairs. His first thought was that his cooking wasn't bad enough to elicit that kind of a response, and the second was immediate panic. No one seemed even remotely distressed by the noise, but he took off in a jog anyway, making it up the stairs in four seconds flat. He found the source of the scream to be his niece, Pearl, who had a tweenager's typical flair for the dramatic.

"Pearl? You okay?" Walker knocked awkwardly on the bathroom door.

"Don't come in here!" Pearl shouted, as if the door wasn't locked to begin with. Walker could hear the cabinets and drawers in the bathroom opening and slamming shut inside.

"Okay, but are you—"

"Go get Piper!" Pearl yelled, frantically.

Confused, Walker turned on his heel and raced back down the stairs to comply with her request.

Several minutes later, after leaving the kitchen to console her sister, Piper came back downstairs without Pearl. Walker looked up with his eyebrows raised, and Piper cringed, looking mildly embarrassed. He narrowed his eyes on her, trying to deduce what the major dilemma was by reading her face.

"Um... can you go to the store?" Piper asked, effectively avoiding Walker's obvious need to know what the hell was going on.

"Is she okay?" Walker inquired, annoyed that he even had to pose the question.

"Yeah... but she needs... stuff. I found one in my room, but she's going to need more."

Walker stared blankly at Piper. Mind racing, he came up with no answers and threw up his hands in exasperation. Life was chaotic enough already without having to play guessing games.

Folding his arms over his chest, he enunciated his words in frustration. "And what, may I ask, am I going to the store for?"

Piper waved him away from the kitchen and Walker followed her into the foyer, wondering what was with all the secrecy.

"She needs tampons and pads," Piper said, dropping her voice lower so her brothers couldn't hear.

Fuck. Of course. How old was Pearl? Didn't that normally happen when girls were around... her age, yeah. Shit.

"Oh," was all Walker managed to say, unable to form the proper words.

"Now. She needs them now," Piper reiterated. "Mom usually stocked us up, but I guess I've used them all since..."

"Right, uh, okay. Give me a minute to figure this out." Turning around, Walker rushed back into the kitchen. "Colin, I'm gonna run to the store really quick. Can you make sure everyone's ready to walk out the door by the time I get back?"

"Yeah." Colin nodded.

"Okay, one... two... three... Pearl's upstairs... and..." Walker trailed off in the middle of counting all of his nieces and nephews, still unsure of the whereabouts of one. "Where's Carter?"

Colin just shrugged, and Walker let out a long sigh before jogging back up the stairs in search of the long-lost sibling.

Lo and behold, when Walker found him, Carter was still curled up on his bed with the covers over his head. Silently cursing himself for not checking on him earlier, Walker reached down to shake his nephew awake, suddenly feeling sorry for every time he had overslept and Cole had to forcefully pull him out of bed. Teenage boys were the worst, and Carter, in his first year of high school, wanted all of the freedom and none of the responsibility. Out of anyone, Carter was probably the most similar to Walker, even though he was adopted. Walker's own personality was finally coming back to bite him in the ass.

"I'm not going," Carter mumbled, reaching for the covers, his muscular limbs only visible for a second before he burrowed back down under the bedding.

"You have to."

"Can't I just skip one more day?" Carter complained, rolling over and squinting at the bright light fixture above his bed.

"No. The more you guys are away from school, the more you fall behind. Look, I know it's shit, but you have to go back at some point," Walker reasoned. "You gotta be an example for Pearl and Coop."

"That's what Perfectionist Piper and Correct Colin are for," Carter shot back.

"As much as I enjoy your use of alliterations, you still need to get off your butt, out of bed, and get ready. No time like the present to get back out into the world. We've all been wallowing, and now we need some fresh air."

The pep talk felt like it was more for himself than his nephew. It was what Walker had been telling himself every day he woke up to this never-ending nightmare. The thing was, with five kids all stuck in the hell that they were now in, there wasn't a whole lot of time allotted for Walker to wallow. He had too many responsibilities, and, out of anyone, he needed to be the strongest. How he would become the rock everyone needed to make it through, he had no idea, but there was no room for failure.

"Now, I have to deal with a small emergency and run to the store. Can I trust you to get up? Do I need to come back with a bottle of water to dump on you?" Walker cocked his head at Carter sternly.

"Yes," Carter grumbled.

"To the water or the getting up?" Walker questioned, amusing himself.

"Get out." Carter pointed at the door.

Pulling the covers off of his nephew, Walker threw all the bedding to the ground so Carter would have to comply, at least to re-cover himself, if anything else.

"Jesus, wear some freaking pajamas when you go to bed," Walker huffed, walking toward the door.

"Nah, I like to be free." Carter grabbed one of the sheets off the floor to cover himself as Walker shut the door behind himself and jogged back down the stairs.

"All right!" Walker shouted, bolting toward garage entrance. "I'm taking my bike. If I don't get back in time, Colin, you drive, and I'll bring Pearl's stuff to the office for them to give to her at school."

"No!" Pearl cut in, emerging from the living room. "Please don't do that!"

"Then I'll... bring it to you personally?" Walker tried again.

"Just make it back on time," Pearl begged.

"Right." Walker nodded and grabbed his motorcycle helmet off the bench next to the door, along with his riding gloves and padded jacket.

It was nice out, and the breeze felt good against Walker's clothes as he raced through the streets to the nearest store that carried feminine hygiene products. The weather was the only agreeable force working with him that morning. He should have thought about the fact that his nieces would need different things than the boys. His latest round of toiletry shopping woefully lacked anything feminine other than the vaguely fruity-looking shampoo that he'd thrown in the cart. His brother would have known.

Cole would have been prepared if it had just been Paisley, but that's not what had happened. It was a pipe dream to wish it had just been one of them. What Walker needed to do was focus his energy on attainable goals, such as researching everything he needed to know about raising five kids.

You can do that. It's just like the research you do for your books, except this is real life and there are no editors to fix your mistakes. No pressure.

When Walker rounded the corner, a mile out from the nearest store, he was halfway through making the mental checklist of items he needed to take care of.

Call to check up on everyone throughout the day. Look up some sort of a recipe for dinner tonight that doesn't suck. Get some writing done. Prepare for the rest of the week with a more thought-out schedule.

Paisley used to make elaborate color-coded calendars with hand-drawn calligraphy, and Cole's phone calendar was always synced to his wife's so they both knew where each one of their kids was at any given point in the day. Too bad Walker's artistic abilities were lacking and there wasn't another person to bounce ideas off of.

For the second time that day, Walker was broken out of his thoughts by a loud sound. This time, the screeching of brakes and tires. He looked up to find a car rolling through a red light and colliding with another, blocking the intersection. He was only a few yards away, his bike running at full speed. His heart rate picking up, Walker squeezed his brakes forcefully, praying he would stop in time.

It wasn't going to be enough. He was going to crash.

Panicking, he ripped his handlebars to the side, hoping to squeeze into the sliver of space next to the collision. Holding his breath, he felt the side of one of the cars brush against his leg as his bike maneuvered away from the wreckage.

By some stroke of luck, Walker successfully passed the cars and came to a full stop, heaving air into his lungs. He pulled off his helmet to breathe better, clutching his chest.

That was too close. You can't leave them. You can't be on this stupid fucking bike anymore. It's too dangerous, and if you die too, then what? They will be left alone.

Hopping off his bike and shoving the kickstand down with his foot, Walker made his way over to the scene of the crash in a fury. It didn't look like anyone was injured, so the blind rage he was feeling took over any obligation to further check on the well-being of the parties involved. He marched straight over to the luxury blue Lexus that ran the light and ripped open the driver-side door. The culprit looked up at him as he glared down at her.

"What the fuck is wrong with you?" Walker snapped.

"Excuse me?" the woman shot back, lifting her expensive-looking sunglasses off her head.

"Don't drive like an idiot. Red means stop, and green means go. You and your rich lady entitlement are going to get people killed. Are you drunk?" Walker set his hands on his hips, examining her. She didn't look drunk in the least. Her hair was perfectly in place, despite ramming her car into someone else's, and her outfit looked like it cost a fortune.

"How dare you!" Accident-Prone Lady jumped out of her car, and Walker took a step away from her, surprised by how aggressive she was. Even with the heels she was wearing, she had to strain to look into his eyes, but acted as though she was towering over him. "My brakes went out, asshole. I *tried* to stop. I didn't purposely run the light, so fuck off."

"Then maybe you should get your car checked out more often so you don't end up with pedestrians splattered on your windshield," Walker retorted.

"I didn't even hit you, jackass! All I did was fuck up my own car. It looks like this guy's big truck is completely fine." The giant, lifted diesel with thick tires and a winch installed on the bumper looked virtually untouched. "You didn't even think to check on me before screaming your invalid complaints? You must be next in line for the citizen of the year award."

"You look fine." Walker surveyed her with a roll of his eyes.

More than fine.

Walker had made sure that everyone seemed lucid and unharmed before he confronted her, but the fact that she felt entitled enough to demand his assistance pissed him off. She was probably just fishing for compliments.

"And *you* are obviously fine enough to berate random strangers about things you know nothing about," she snarled. Her features were the exact opposite of her mouth. Soft, brown wavy hair flicked over her shoulders in the light breeze, and her olive skin practically glowed in the morning sunlight. Everything about her was decidedly irritating.

"It's an acceptable reaction to almost dying." Walker frowned down at her.

She really wasn't backing down despite his clear height and weight advantage over her. Her deep brown eyes ripped through him like a scalpel dissecting him from head to foot. He involuntarily swallowed before regaining his composure.

"You know what? I don't have time for this." Whipping around, he stalked off toward his bike. Just before reaching his ride, he looked over his shoulder to find her looking after him, and couldn't help but to get one last stab in. "Hope you like the view!"

"Don't flatter yourself!" she shouted back.

Amused, he lifted his leg to straddle his bike, slipped his helmet back over his head, and started the engine, revving it an unnecessary amount of times just to be annoying before he peeled out.

Two

TALIA

Talia Cohen stared at her fender in frustration. Today was turning out to be a day from hell because of course it was. She had just bought the damned car two days before, and already the brakes had failed to do the bare minimum: *stop*. There was nothing quite like upheaving her entire life to move across the country just to have all her hopes and dreams of a fresh start shot to hell in a single moment. As far as signs go, this was a pretty big one. She should have stayed in New York. She should have sucked it up and continued to put her law degree to good use no matter how much she despised being a lawyer. Honestly, she should probably pack up her shit, sell what was left of the Lexus and the store, and run back to her old job with her tail between her legs, begging for them to take her back.

"Are you all right, ma'am?" the big trucker of a man interrupted Talia's soliloquy of self-pity, walking over to her. Cringing, Talia lifted her hands in front of herself as if to tame a wild beast.

"I'm okay. I'm *so* sorry about this. I swear I was trying to stop, but the brakes gave out, and then I couldn't—"

"No harm, no foul. This rig is customized to take a hit. You barely scratched the paint. It looks like yours is a little worse for wear, though," he pointed out.

Talia expected a burly man of his size to be frightening, but his demeanor was more that of a giant teddy bear. It was good to know that there were nice people in town, unlike Motorcycle Asshole, who seemed to think the entire world revolved around him.

"Yeah, I think I'm going to need a tow. Let me get you my insurance information." Talia moved back toward her car, and the man waved her off.

"Nah, no need. Like I said, she looks fine." He slapped the hood of his truck. "Let's get you a tow truck. Do you need a ride somewhere?"

Talia's first inclination was to refuse his offer. If she were in New York City and accepted, she probably would have ended up in the bed of his truck, bound and gagged until she reached whatever destination he found best to murder her. Her second thought was that she needed to stop watching so many serial killer documentaries. She was in the suburbs and had always been good at reading people. Plus, the likelihood she'd run into the Zodiac Killer on her first full day in town was slim. This guy was harmless. Motorcycle Asshole, on the other hand, was a menace to society, probably off harassing someone new or storming around proclaiming how morally superior he was to everyone else. She would never understand why God ever gave people with such awful personalities attractive bodies. His just gave him even more fuel to be a dick.

"A ride would be great, actually," Talia decided. "But I'm only a mile away, so I can walk if it's too much of a bother."

"It's no problem. I'm Marty, by the way." The trucker stuck out his beefy, weathered hand, and Talia shook it firmly.

"Talia. I would say nice to meet you, but given the circumstances, 'sorry to meet you,' seems more appropriate," she said with a sheepish glance at her feet. "I should probably get my car out of the road, and then—"

"Oh, I got it!" Marty tossed his hand in the air and walked over to the Lexus, bracing his palms on the hood.

"Oh, wow! I mean, I can try to drive it off to the side," Talia offered.

"Nah, you don't know if it's driveable, and that seems unsafe," Marty said. "Just throw it in neutral for me, will you?"

Talia obliged, and was surprised at how little Marty strained to get her car out of the road. In a matter of minutes, the Lexus was pushed off to the side, no longer blocking the intersection, and the man had barely broken a sweat.

As it turned out, Talia was correct in her assessment of Marty. When she hopped into his truck, she noticed a car seat in the back and a picture of who she assumed to be Marty's wife or girl-friend holding a baby hanging from the rear-view mirror. He smiled at the photo as he turned the ignition, the truck roaring to life beneath her. She could see the appeal of a vehicle large enough to bulldoze over a tree and felt oddly safe sitting in the cab.

"My daughter is six months old now. She's got me wrapped around her finger just like her mama." Marty grinned, putting his truck into gear and slowly letting off the clutch to pull away from the scene of the accident. "Do you have any kids?"

People always felt the need to ask Talia that. Or maybe it was just that she was more aware of it. It was a simple enough question, and at least Marty wasn't one of those people telling her that she wasn't getting any younger or demanding to know when she would have them. She hadn't dealt with all of her issues in regards to infertility, and inquiries surrounding the topic always put her in a sour mood. Reminding herself that Marty was only asking because he was enthralled with his own kid, Talia plastered on a smile and shook her head.

"Nope, no kids. Yours is beautiful, though."

It wasn't a lie. The baby in the picture, though she still had that newborn alien-esque look about her, was adorable.

"She is, isn't she?" Marty beamed with pride, soon breaking

out of his spell with a clear of his throat. "So, are you new in town?"

"That obvious?" Talia asked.

"There aren't any plates on your car yet."

"Right. Yeah, I actually lived here till I was seven, and then my mom and I moved to New York City."

"Move back for family?" Marty questioned, pulling onto a side street that Talia pointed for him to turn down.

"Not exactly. My dad lived here, but he passed away recently. He was the owner of Lydia's. That's actually where we're going," Talia explained. "I'm the new owner."

"Ah, so your father was Jeff Cohen, then." In the span of that single sentence, Marty's demeanor had changed from friendly to unbearably tense.

Talia bobbed her head, looking out the window to avoid eye contact. If Marty knew of her dad, then he probably did not have the best opinion of him. The only nice thing that her father had ever done for her was leave her his grocery store in his will. Originally, Talia thought he had left her with a mountain of debt, but, per the books she looked over, Lydia's was profitable. It was her first day on the job, and so far, nothing was going swimmingly. She had left everything on a whim to come here, so she sincerely hoped the store's affairs were somewhat in order when she arrived.

Determined to fill the awkward silence that always seemed to plague conversations involving her father, Talia pulled out her cell phone to search for a towing company. A few minutes later, she had arranged for her car to be delivered to the nearest mechanic shop, and Marty pulled into a parking spot outside her new place of work. She scrutinized the building warily. It needed a new coat of paint, but other than that, it wasn't in terrible shape. The classic brick she remembered from her childhood looked the same, sturdy and unassuming. A splash of color would certainly help counter its drab appearance, but the bones were good. A pressure wash, a touch-up of the lines in the parking lot, and some new windows, and it would have real curb appeal.

When Talia stepped down from Marty's truck, her eyes landed on the motorcycle parked out front. She let out an exasperated puff of air through her nose. It would be just her luck if that belligerent motorcyclist from earlier was inside. What, was he just waiting for her to arrive to scream more unwarranted assumptions in her face?

"Thank you for the ride and," Talia shifted her eyes back to where they came from, "everything."

"No problem, Miss Cohen. You have a great day now." Marty saluted her with a tip of his ball cap and backed out of the parking spot, leaving Talia to face her future alone.

Taking a deep breath, Talia trudged toward the glass door, which slid open when she stepped in front of it. Pleased that there was a motion sensor, she tilted her head to the side in admiration, hoping the inside held up to the same technological standard.

Although everything was visibly dated, the sectioning of the store was tidy, and the floors were clean. It was a stereotypical grocery store that lacked pizazz and had obnoxious fluorescent lights that gave it a sterile vibe. Cuter signage, softer lighting, and something other than white walls would help. Changing the cleaning supplies out for more natural options would fix the subtle bleach scent, too. Talia could do it—she could make this place scream "welcome to Lydia's" instead of "welcome to the emergency room."

Talia's mental checklist of all the updates she wanted to complete was interrupted by the sight of Motorcycle Asshole standing in line at one of the registers. He was holding a brightly colored box under one arm. She narrowed her eyes on it in curiosity, coming to the conclusion that it was a box of tampons. He was clearly trying to hide it, looking embarrassed to be purchasing something that didn't match his leather, masculine vibe. Unable to resist the compulsion to screw with him, Talia marched over to the register.

"Ah, is that why you're having a rough morning?" Talia asked as she approached, pointing at the box under his arm. Placing her hand over her heart in mock pity, she gave him her best sympathetic expression. "Is it your time of the month?"

Motorcycle Asshole glared at her, then scanned his surroundings to gauge if anyone had heard her comment. Talia had purposely said it loud enough to make sure that people would. His mortification was a mission accomplished.

"Very funny," he growled under his breath.

"You know, I might have been wrong about you." Talia cocked her head to the side, a wry smile playing across her lips. "You may be one of Satan's loyal subjects, but you're nice enough to run to the store to get your girlfriend tampons. Then again, cardboard applicators are basically torture devices, so that's a knock against you, too."

"What?" Motorcycle Asshole bunched his face in confusion and looked down at the tampon box. The bag of pads in his other hand, she noticed, were nighttime pads, thick and unflattering. His girlfriend was going to be sorely disappointed that she was about to wear a diaper that could easily be seen through clothes. Not cute.

"Everything you've got going on right now is wrong." Talia gestured to the products he'd chosen. "Cardboard applicators are for people who don't mind raking out their insides and leaving permanent scars, and those pads are for people with major incontinence."

It was an over exaggeration, but Talia couldn't help but want to piss him off. Instead, he just looked anxiously at her, at the items, and then back at her again.

"You're lying," he stated confidently.

Talia laughed out loud. "Yes, clearly, I don't know what I'm talking about. I've only been a woman for twenty-six years. That does not at all qualify me to know anything about it."

"Fine," he muttered. "What am I supposed to get?"

Surprised that he didn't blow her off and was genuinely waiting for a response, Talia pondered her options. In the end, showing him was the best recourse. Not only would it be a learning opportunity, but she would be saving some poor soul from having to use the piss-poor products this guy was about to buy. It was also a way to parade Motorcycle Asshole all the way back to the feminine hygiene section with his current items so more people would see. She never understood why men were so weird about periods, but she would be remiss if she didn't use his embarrassment to her advantage.

"Follow me." Talia motioned, gearing up to give him a little exposure therapy. Looking back over her shoulder, she watched him hesitate for a moment before ultimately abandoning his place in line and jogging after her.

"Do you even know where you're going?" he asked as he caught up to her.

The short answer to that question was "no" because the last time Talia had been in the store was almost two decades ago, but she was completely capable of finding tampons.

"I own the store, so I should think so," Talia replied curtly.

"Great," Motorcycle Asshole grumbled. She wanted to ask him what exactly his problem was because the word "great" shouldn't ever be uttered with such venom, but she let it slide. She would be more than ready to enact her revenge when they got to their destination.

Sure enough, she found the health and beauty section and made her way over to the wall of feminine hygiene products. Motorcycle Asshole trailed behind her silently, and she cleared her throat, looking over at him before loudly asking, "So, what size tampons does she need?"

"Size?" Aware she was deliberately tormenting him, Motorcycle Asshole averted his gaze from two customers passing by and shrunk his shoulders to make himself smaller.

"Yeah. There's super plus, super, regular, and light," Talia explained, keeping her voice loud enough so that anyone in the vicinity could hear them.

"I—I don't know!" he stammered. "Normal?"

Amused, Talia smiled to herself. Between the pink in his

cheeks and the way he was shifting his stance every few seconds, she knew she had the upper hand. Motorcycle Asshole may have exuded dominance earlier at the crash, but now she was the one wielding all the power.

"You don't know how big your girlfriend needs them?" she asked, hoping to fluster him even more.

"She's twelve... or eleven, so, no," he replied bluntly, the scowl on his face returning.

Talia feigned clutching her pearls. "Your girlfriend is eleven? Well, I have to inform you, that's highly illegal and gross."

"That's disgusting. My *niece* is eleven." His nose scrunching, Motorcycle Asshole gripped his period products harder, the packaging bending at his fingertips. "You know what? I don't need this. I'm just going to get the shit I picked out already."

He turned around, and Talia jutted her hand out to stop him, feeling a little guilty. Not about him, of course, but about his poor niece, who was probably horrified that her uncle was the one purchasing her tampons and pads.

"Here." Talia took the box out of his hand and grabbed some regular-sized tampons with plastic applicators, shoving them in his arms before proceeding to replace the nighttime pads with long underwear liners.

"How do I know you're not just trying to upsell me right now?" Motorcycle Asshole cocked an eyebrow.

"Oh, I am fully planning on pocketing the extra thirty cents. That will get me approximately one-third of a candy bar," Talia replied with mock enthusiasm.

Motorcycle Asshole rolled his eyes before turning to walk away without so much as a thank you. He only made it halfway down the aisle when he stopped and turned back to face Talia again.

"How much do you need for two?" he asked.

"As in two women?" Talia clarified.

"No, two hamsters," Motorcycle Asshole scoffed. "Yes, two girls. The other one is sixteen. Does that make a difference?"

"Probably not as far as the size goes, but I'd get at least another box of tampons if not also another bag of pads," Talia offered.

"And how long will those last?" He moved back beside her, pulling his phone from his pocket and snapping pictures of the two products she had suggested.

"About two months," she said. "But it really depends on flow. You aren't just going to buy more now?"

"If you recall, I'm on a motorcycle. This is the only thing I can fit in my bag. That, and I don't shop here if I can get away with it. I assume you're related to Jeff Cohen?"

"Talia Cohen," she nodded, feeling her heart drop into her stomach. Before moving to Archwood, Talia hadn't thought much about her dad's reputation or the circumstances of his death. She barely knew her father past early childhood, so she didn't associate herself with him. The problem she had failed to take into account was that other people surely *would* associate her with him. "I'm technically his daughter. And you are?"

"Walker," he replied coldly.

"As in Texas Ranger?"

"As in Hartrick."

Hartrick. Shit.

If her heart could fully stop, it would have. She knew that name.

"Oh." Talia swallowed, her mouth going dry. "So, you're related to—"

"Cole Hartrick was my brother," Walker interrupted, a flash of anger returning to his eyes. "*Was* being the operative word, because as I'm sure you're aware, your dad kindly took care of him and his wife." He raised the products in his hands with a little more force than was necessary. "These are for their kids."

When Talia first received word of her father's passing, she wasn't surprised or sorry for her own loss. The shock came from the sheer amount of destruction he had caused on his way out. Jeff had died how she always assumed he would: drunk. She thought it would be liver failure or overconsumption, but instead, he'd thrown caution and the safety of others to the wind and drunk drove himself right into the headlines of the paper. Along with himself, he took a married couple who had been on their way back home to their five children. Cole and Paisley *Hartrick*.

"Oh my God," Talia pressed her hand over her mouth. "I—I'm sorry. I didn't realize—"

"I should have just gone to a different store, but this was the closest one." Walker looked around in disgust.

Talia desperately wanted to disassociate herself from her father, but the fact that she had taken on his business made that possibility seem far-fetched. It also felt inappropriate to move the attention back onto her and her own issues. Walker obviously had enough to deal with. Instead, she just nodded as he turned to leave.

"Uh... you don't have to buy those. They're on me," Talia called after him.

It was the wrong thing to say. Walker flipped around furiously to meet her eyes, visibly pissed.

"I don't need or want your charity. I want absolutely nothing to do with you or your family."

Each word cut like a knife, and all Talia could do was gape at him until he marched away without another word.

When she finally found the strength to move, Talia tortured herself by second-guessing the period products she'd recommended, and pulled a bottle of Pamprin off the shelf.

Just leave it alone. Let him leave.

But she couldn't let it go. She remembered when she first got her period and how uncomfortable it was to ask for anything from her mom. She couldn't imagine having to ask for anything from her dad, let alone an uncle after the loss of both parents. If Talia could relieve any discomfort for the poor girl, she would.

"Walker, wait!" she shouted, ripping off her heels to run barefoot after him.

"What do you want?" Walker jerked his body back around.

Talia held up the bottle, shaking it a little so the pills rattled.

"I said I don't want your help."

"I wasn't offering to pay for it, just letting you know that a lot of girls need this for cramps." She set the bottle in his hand. "They're especially bad the first time."

"Thanks." He blinked, giving her a short nod. Walker glanced down at Talia's bare feet with an unreadable expression, then walked off toward the checkout.

Three

WALKER

Two hours: that was how long it took to go grocery shopping for a family of six. Walker was woefully underprepared to navigate aisles and aisles of products he hadn't even known existed. Each and every time he'd been to a grocery store before the accident, he'd always beeline for the basics: spaghetti, taco ingredients, Top Ramen, and canned soup. On top of that, he ran into at least four people he barely knew, all of whom felt the need to bring up Cole and Paisley and murmur their condolences. In retrospect, he should have worn earbuds or something to make himself seem unapproachable. While, technically speaking, the folks were nice, Walker would have rather gouged his own eyes out than spend five minutes of the time he was supposed to be using to find provolone cheese talking to Cindy-what's-her-name about that one time she went to the same PTA meeting as Paisley.

People never knew how to act around him anymore. Walker wished that meant everyone would just avoid him, but it seemed the opposite was true. Random passersby came out of the wood-work to tell him that they once went to a barbecue where Cole was also in attendance. At the end of the two miserable hours plodding around the store, Walker wanted to scream, "I get it, Jim. You want to feel connected to Cole and Paisley somehow by pretending you know them and therefore understand the loss we're going through, but the truth is, you're pulling all of your memories out of your ass, where you should have left them! For the love of God, spare me the theatrics and tell me where I can find the damn provolone cheese?"

Maybe he might have been a little on edge after one too many encounters with Jeff Cohen's daughter. Walker shook his head, scoffing to himself.

Who walks around without their shoes on? And why the hell did you look at her feet like there was something to see?

Walker didn't even like feet, because he wasn't a foot fetish person, but his gaze had easily slid down to Talia's coral painted toenails nonetheless. He ultimately decided it was a natural reaction to the fact that Talia was an objectively attractive woman. He had eyes. If someone showed up unannounced in town looking like a freaking model, people were going to notice. But Talia was also the daughter of someone Walker wished was still alive just so he could have the opportunity to choke him to death. So, all of those natural thoughts he was having needed to be locked up in a deep, dark corner of his brain and stay there.

Finally finding himself on a sofa at the local coffee house, Roaster's Republic, Walker added grocery shopping to the list of things he abhorred but would have to train himself to enjoy and Talia Cohen to the list of sympathizers who pretended to care but really didn't.

Roaster's Republic was one of the many places in town that had hired Paisley as their interior decorator, and it showed. The inside had a steampunk feel, with Edison bulb lighting and pipe shelves decorated with art from various local painters. The couch Walker always sat on was both practical and decorative. Not only did the brown leather match the general vibe, but it was comfort able enough that he could sit for hours on end working and never feel like his ass was about to fall off.

After the rush of morning to-go coffee orders was fulfilled, the crowd at the coffee house usually dwindled enough to where Walker could finally focus. He pulled out his laptop to retrieve the notes on his most recent movie watch, ready to bury himself in work. The only problem was that he couldn't, for the life of him, remember the beginning of the movie, and his notes were a far cry worse from his usual standard. Walker had been so easily distracted lately that his notes were barely legible. It didn't help that the novel adaptation he was writing was of a romantic comedy, which automatically made him think of Cole and Paisley. It shouldn't have, considering the guy in the movie was a total dipshit and the girl was one of those wallflower types. Walker was shocked to find that the script writers didn't pull a "the girl takes off her glasses and suddenly everyone realizes she's been beautiful the whole time," or a "she gets a makeover from her gay best friend who stereotypically doesn't have a real role in movie other than to be the gay best friend."

What was wrong with glasses, anyway? Walker actually thought glasses were kind of sexy. Especially reading glasses, because people had them for the sole purpose of reading and reading was an inherently sexy pastime. He didn't make the rules. And where was the movie about a gay guy who absolutely despised fashion and got annoyed when people asked him to dress them up? This man would strictly wear flannel and say, "put a shirt on, Karen, I don't give a fuck. Not every gay guy's favorite movie is *The Devil Wears Prada!*" when asked for a makeover. Why was there always a dress-up montage and never a friend rightly pointing out that changing your entire personality and appearance for a relationship was a red flag?

Walker often had entire dialogues in his head that he felt compelled to write out, despite knowing they would never leave his computer. If he didn't write them down, his brain would hyperfixate on the thoughts until they ran cold.

After fleshing out several pages of back-and-forth dialogue for the characters he'd created on the spot, Walker finally opened the blasted movie, reluctantly preparing himself to rewatch it from the beginning. Sitting back against the cushion, he took a long sip from his black coffee and did his best to focus as the stereotypical overhead shots of whatever locale the movie took place in panned across the screen with the credits.

"What do we have today?" Walker murmured to himself. "New York, San Francisco, or a small farming community?" It was always one of the three, or somewhere near a water source.

A bird's eye view of the Golden Gate Bridge popped up, and Walker smiled to himself. "San Francisco, it is."

"A vanilla latte, please."

The voice reverberated in Walker's ears, and he aggressively hit the spacebar on his laptop, popping one earbud out as he swiveled to look over his shoulder.

Of course. Of course she's here.

Talia Cohen, in all her heeled glory, was at the counter, inserting her card into the chip reader just how she kept inserting herself into his day. Secretly, though, Walker was grateful for her advice on proper period products and even more grateful for the last-ditch advice on medication. When he had arrived back at the house, Pearl was hunched over looking like she wanted to vomit. Thanks to Talia's meddling, he could actually do something about it, but Talia didn't need to know that. He wanted to continue pretending that the chocolate candy bar he'd bought Pearl in the spur of the moment at the register was the reason Piper had looked at him like a freaking superhero—Menstrual Man, if you will.

Nope. Dumbest thought to ever cross your mind. Much like deciding to go to Lydia's Grocery to begin with.

Walker's eyes traitorously swept over Talia's figure as she leaned over the counter to grab her latte. Pressing her hips into the corrugated metal siding, she took a long, deep sip with her eyes closed, which seemed borderline inappropriate to be doing in public. When she turned around, presumably to grab a seat, she froze, catching sight of him. Walker schooled his expression into one of vague annoyance to hide the fact that he had been staring.

"You following me around now?" He cocked his head with haughty disdain.

"Yeah, I just love being in the company of people who *want nothing to do with me*," Talia threw Walker's earlier words back. "I didn't realize being the daughter of an asshole barred me from getting a latte."

"Lattes, no. Lattes infused with booze, yes."

The blunt way it came out of his mouth made Walker inwardly cringe. It was a low blow. He knew virtually nothing about Talia. It wasn't like she herself had plowed into his brother's car. He did get off on getting under her skin, though, and he deserved a little entertainment in his life. The cheesy movie he was about to watch was not going to do it for him.

It seemed his comment had the desired effect. Talia crossed her arms over her chest, staring daggers at him. Then, without speaking, she put her coffee up to her full, annoyingly perfect lips and threw it back like a shot glass. She cocked her head to the side as if to say "bite me" and jostled his shoulder with one hip on her way past the couch. She chose the farthest seat available, but it wasn't a large coffee shop, so she was still in plain sight. Pulling a book out of her purse, Talia slipped on a pair of wire-rimmed reading glasses and opened a thick paperback novel to a spot near the back where she had doggy-eared the page.

So, she's into damaging books, then.

Destruction seemed to be a theme with the Cohen family. The irrational impulse to grab the current novel he was reading from his laptop bag and un-doggy-ear the spot he had marked the night prior was overwhelming. Instead, Walker pulled the sleeve off of his drink and fashioned it into a makeshift bookmark, since he didn't own any real bookmarks—added to the list of things he should obtain to become a real adult—and reached for his bag.

While Walker dug through the many gum wrappers strewn

throughout the large compartment to find the goddamn novel, his cell phone started buzzing in the side pocket. Forgetting the novel completely, he pulled out his phone, swallowing, petrified, at the caller ID. *Archwood High School*. His mind flicked through any number of possible disasters. Colin, Piper, and Carter all attended Archwood High. The hope that the school was somehow calling to request *Walker's* presence in the principal's office for something he had done back in the day crossed his mind. A ridiculous thought, but his thoughts tended to lean toward desperation since the accident.

"Hello?" Walker answered, clearing his throat and adding, "this is Walker Hartrick," to the end in case they had called the wrong person.

"Mr. Hartrick," a woman's voice replied. "This is Patty in the attendance office. I am just calling to confirm that you authorized Carter to be out today. He gave us an absence slip, but we don't have your signature on file yet."

It only took Walker a split second to realize what Carter had done because Walker himself had done it a hundred times when he was in high school. His own dad had been too out of it most of the time to sign anything for school, so Walker had taken it upon himself to forge permission slips, tardy notes, and the obligatory "my son will not be present today due to unforeseen circumstances having to do with a distant relative who has passed away." The attendance lady at the time, who Walker was pretty certain was the same one calling him about Carter, always knew he was full of shit but could never call him on it.

"Uh, yeah. He's just struggling with everything right now. We're going to do our best to make sure he's there tomorrow," Walker said, sucking in a deep breath to fight off the panic rising in his chest.

"Of course." Patty's tone dropped sympathetically. "I'll collect his homework from each of his classes and send it home with Colin."

"Thanks," Walker said. Running around to grab absent

students' homework was definitely not a part of her job description, but he appreciated people that picked up slack for him instead of making him relive everything through forced conversation.

"We do need your signature on a few documents down here when you get a chance as well," Patty added, her tone making clear that she was not a fool and did not, for one second, believe that Walker had signed off on Carter's absence.

"Right," Walker bobbed his head as if she could see him. "I'll come down by the end of the week. And, Patty?"

"Yes?"

"Do you have any clue where the kids hang out when they skip school? Not that that's what Carter is doing right now, of course."

"Well..." Walker could almost hear the wheels turning in Patty's head before she spoke again. "If I was looking for one, I'd probably find them near the docks, but, then again, you'd probably know better than I would, Mr. Hartrick."

"Touché." He felt the corners of his mouth pull up slightly at the implication that he had some experience with playing hooky. She was definitely the same attendance lady. He must have been such a pain in the ass when he was in high school, but at least, if nothing else, he was memorable. "Thanks again, Patty."

"Sure. Feel free to call us if you need anything."

After exchanging goodbyes, Walker dialed his nephew, unsurprised when his phone rang two and a half times and then went to voicemail. Carter was out somewhere, lucid enough to decline his phone calls. It was the closest Walker was going to get to proof of life. He wanted to be frustrated by it, but he had pulled the same stunts when he was a teenager, ignoring every time Cole called to berate him about missing class. Cole most likely got insider information on all of his absences from Patty, now that Walker was thinking about it. Exhaling loudly, he shoved his phone back into his pocket and started to pack away his things.

So much for being productive with work today.

"You should track his phone."

Walker's head snapped in the direction of the voice to find Talia looking over at him. When he didn't respond, she shrugged and went back to reading her paperback.

"You were eavesdropping?"

Talia tilted her face back in his direction, hitting him with an unapologetic glare. "It's like a ventriloquist act, the way your voice carries but your face shows barely any emotion other than a scowl. It's actually distracting me from reading, so if you could keep it down, that would be great." She adjusted her glasses on her face and turned back to her book.

Walker wished he could be offended, but he was more thrilled by the idea that he was annoying her in some way.

"It would be way easier if I was the puppet," he retorted. The idea of his brother or another responsible adult controlling all of his motions sounded better than sex at this point.

His response must have surprised Talia because her brows cinched together just as he planted his signature frown back on his face.

"Again, I don't need your help, though. Tracking his phone is an invasion of privacy."

Walker shoved his laptop in his bag, slung it over one shoulder and drained the rest of his coffee. He tossed the cup toward the trash can with a forceful flick of his wrist. To his aggravation, the cup rolled around the rim and fell to the floor with a weak thunk. With a grumble, Walker bent over to pick it up and dropped it through the hole. Refusing to look back, he forged ahead, figuring Talia was probably ready to pounce with some sort of snide comment about how he was not the next Kobe Bryant. Usually, he was good at basketball and all things that involved throwing an object through a hoop. It was her unnerving presence and captious eyes searing holes into the back of his head that made him miss.

The drive out to the docks was uneventful and fruitless: Carter was nowhere to be found. Walker took a moment to himself, looking out over the ripples of water as he stood on the dock. The minute of peace was all he needed to clear his head before he was back in his trusty soccer mom van.

When Walker first claimed the minivan after the accident, he was surprised by how comfortable the seats were and how spacious the interior was. He wasn't upset about the backup camera and stereo system that made him feel like he was live in concert when he played his depressing music, either. The manufacturers expected the owners of these vehicles to be hauling a hundred kids around, so they made sure you could fit just about anything in the trunk: sports bags, dead bodies, you name it. The amount of curtain airbags that would drop over the windows if Walker ever did get into an accident were astounding. If Cole had driven this car instead of the sporty Nissan that found its new home in a wrecking yard, he and Paisley might have made it out.

Walker settled into his new role as a minivan driver with ease, even more a reason to ditch his motorcycle. After Talia had almost sent him flying over his handlebars, he'd posted pictures of the Ducati to several online marketplaces and taped a sign to it that read "for sale by owner." The only thing the bike *could* do anymore was make him a few bucks.

After checking most places within walking distance of the school, Walker pulled into the parking lot of a local mini market. He peeled out in frustration just a minute later when he could see clearly through the glass doors that Carter was not inside. There was only one option left. Walker gritted his teeth and forced his wheel in the direction of the coffee shop. There were things that were more important than his pride, and Carter was one of those things.

Talia was still sitting in the same spot Walker had left her in. He needed her help, for Carter's sake. If she had just left, he could have made a strong case that he had at least attempted to get her assistance and avoided this, but he needed her. He strode over and dropped into the chair across from hers, and she looked up.

"How do you track a phone? And do not patronize me."

Walker raised a finger in warning. "I need to find my nephew, and I don't have time for the back and forth."

"Has he ever logged into his email on your laptop?" Talia asked, bending the corner of a page in her book to mark her spot and setting it to the side.

Walker yanked his computer from his bag and flipped it open. "This used to be his laptop before his parents bought him a new one. I got all the hand-me-ups when my brother's kids were done with them."

"Okay." Talia nodded and rose from her chair, moving around the table to sit beside him.

Walker stiffened at her close proximity. His throat felt dry, and he barely allowed a shallow breath to escape his lips, as if the sound of him breathing alone could set her off. It was best to avoid a Norman Bates in *Psycho* situation. There weren't any knives or showers in the vicinity, but Talia's book looked heavy enough to wield as a weapon. If any of them were ending up in the shower, he hoped it would be her.

Releasing the reins of control, he slid the laptop in front of Talia. His bicep brushed her chest on the way over, and he pulled his arm back before the prolonged contact became too much. She glanced at him, but, to his relief, didn't mention it as she stroked her finger over the mousepad and clicked around until she found what she was looking for.

"I assume Ladykillercarter02 isn't you?"

"Jesus Christ," Walker muttered, shaking his head in confirmation that no, he was not planning on killing the lady game anytime soon.

"Luckily, he left his password saved, otherwise you'd probably have to guess or login to whatever one he uses at home to track him from there. I do know how to hack it, but it would take me a while." Talia hit the enter key dramatically.

"You know how to hack computers? Isn't that illegal?" Walker set his mouth in a flat line.

"I get the drive to do illegal shit from my dad," Talia said offhandedly, then bit back her lip. "Sorry... that was a bad joke. I was a bit of a hacktivist in college. My dad has nothing to do with that, I was just trying to be funny."

"No, actually..." Walker chuckled lightly. "I like dark humor. Deflecting is a hobby of mine."

"Healthy," Talia noted, then pointed to the map on the screen. "He's on the corner of 5th and Pine."

Walker's face fell, and his blood went cold.

"Is that place significant?"

The laptop slammed shut. Walker snatched it off the table and crammed it into his bag. He should have guessed Carter's location from the get-go, but he hadn't realized just how much his nephew wanted to indulge in his misery. His feet pounding the floor, Walker only made it halfway to the door before he felt a hand on his arm. It felt like volts of electricity shooting through his body, even through the thick material of his jacket. He knew it was Talia.

"What?" he ground out.

Talia swallowed and dropped her hand, her eyes revealing an edge of panic. "Is he okay? Is your nephew okay? I need to—"

"He's fine," Walker sighed. "You honestly don't know the place he's at?"

"I haven't been here since I was seven, so I don't really know my way around yet. What's on 5th and Pine?" Her face lacked evidence of any knowledge, and her caring expression seemed authentic enough, but Walker wasn't in the mood to explain semantics.

"It's where his parents died," he replied hastily, turning to walk out the door. Talia didn't say anything further as Walker pushed through the exit, and he didn't hear her shoes clack against the wood floor back to her table. He wondered how long she stood in that same spot, watching him leave.

～

Sure enough, Walker found Carter sitting on the curb with his feet planted in the bike lane, staring blankly at the busy road. The Pine street intersection was a high-traffic area. It was similar to a highway, with a speed limit of fifty miles per hour. If you were on 5th, the speed limit was only twenty-five. The stoplight was added as a result of one too many accidents from people pulling onto the main road from the side street. Unfortunately, reaction time to a red light is a little delayed if you're several drinks in, or, in Jeff Cohen's case, *very* delayed.

Walker had sat on the same curb watching the lights turn a few times since the accident. If he could, he would go back in time and switch his brother's green light to red and Cohen's to green, allowing the man to sail through without harming anyone.

"Hey," was all Carter said when Walker pulled up to the curb next to him.

"Hey." Walker unlocked the door and waved Carter forward.

Carter climbed into the passenger seat wordlessly. The kid wasn't much of a fighter, even despite his rebellious streak. When the jig was up, Carter knew it, just as Walker had when he was younger and Cole had caught him doing something stupid.

Walker waited until they were back on the main road, headed in the direction of the house, before he spoke again. "You know I'm not one to judge anyone's life choices, but—"

"I know." Carter sighed.

"Running around town searching for you and asking a woman I dislike immensely to assist me in tracking your phone was not at the top of my list of things to do today."

"Was she hot?" Carter inquired.

"Not the point." Walker shook his head in admonishment.

"So that's a yes." His nephew gave him a cocky grin.

"We are going to address your whole Ladykillercarter007 email address later," Walker chastised, ignoring the musings of a teenage boy who seriously needed to learn how to think with his head and not his... other things.

"Oh-two, not double-oh seven," Carter corrected.

"That's not as cool as double-oh seven, but, again, not the point."

"At least I didn't use sixty-nine."

Oh, yes, thank fuck for small mercies.

Walker blew out a breath. "Carter, I need you to be serious for two seconds. You can't forge my signature on documents. I can't not know where you are, and you can't ignore my phone calls. It's not okay. It gives me that sinking feeling in the pit of my stomach that we could lose you too. Without even mentioning how dangerous it is, you can't be sitting on the curb where your parents died and expect me to think you're okay. " He tilted his head toward Carter and saw his Adam's apple dip in his throat.

"I'm sorry. I-I don't know why I did it. I just wanted to... feel them again? Like maybe I could tell if my dad was angry that I skipped school?" The tears started to slip down Carter's cheeks. He reached up to angrily wipe them away, turning his head to look out the window. "It's stupid."

"You are not stupid. If it helps, I can assure you your dad would have been pissed. Actually, I guarantee he's looking down right now and seething."

Walker laughed, and Carter looked back toward him, the hint of a smile playing on his own lips. "But... he would also say that all of *that*," Walker gestured in the direction they came from, "is not the way to feel him. I think you need to talk to someone."

"I'm talking to you right now."

"Not me. A therapist. A counselor. Hell, literally anyone who knows what they're doing better than I do."

"You aren't doing so bad," Carter murmured.

The urge to argue almost won out. Walker did not, for one second, believe that he was an admirable guardian. It was glaringly obvious to him that he wasn't anyone's knight in shining armor. But if his nieces and nephews needed to believe that he was somehow holding it together, he would give that to them. He

could pretend to have the kind of confidence and stability of
someone like their parents if that was what made his family feel
safe.

"Thanks."

Four

TALIA

It had been a week since Talia's last Walker sighting, which made it entirely possible they could never cross paths again. Archwood wasn't a big town, but it wasn't small, either. There were just enough people to go your whole life without meeting some that lived there while simultaneously running into everyone you knew all the time. And yet, even with no hint that she would ever see him again, Talia found herself dwelling on her conversations with Walker and the emotions that gnawed at her after.

Walker was a decidedly irritating person. Talia had given herself the mental pep talk to play nice so many times it was becoming borderline psychotic. His current stage in life was heartbreaking, to say the least, but it didn't give him free license to be a dick to her. If she could have chosen her family, she would have cast a different man for the role of her father forever ago. Walker could just ignore her and pretend she didn't exist, but instead he acted as if her only reason to get a coffee was to stalk him. Granted, she did offer to stalk his nephew, but he should have been grateful for her assistance, not bitter and rude.

Neshama sheli, you must learn to be the picture of kindness and grace.

Talia's mother always popped into her head at inopportune times, the ever-present angel on her shoulder. Lydia Cohen was the epitome of everything she preached, but in the end, all it had gotten her was a sorry excuse for a husband and a short life.

"No thanks." Talia shook her head. "If Walker's going to be an ass, two can play at that game."

"You going home soon? You do realize it's one a.m., right?" Amala, the store manager and Talia's one and only friend since moving to town, popped her head into Talia's office.

"Yeah, in a little bit. I'm balancing the books. Why are you still here? It's your day off tomorrow, or I guess I should say *today*." Talia blanched, realizing the time. She could have sworn that she saw Amala leave earlier when the store closed.

"I was craving a burger, and I saw your car still out front." Amala lifted one shoulder and patted her barely pregnant belly. "My husband's with Jayla, who will hopefully still be asleep when I get home, or there will be hell to pay."

Jayla, Amala's eight-year-old daughter, was a little ball of joy who had more confidence in the tip of her pinky finger than Talia had ever had. The joy in children was often something that dwindled with age and the wearing down of life. The longing Talia felt to witness that in a child of her own was still there, despite knowing it would never happen for her, at least not in the traditional sense of the word. She wasn't destined to be a mother, but that wouldn't stop her from surrounding herself with kids all the time.

Amala had already taught Talia how to put castor oil in Jayla's hair, and Jayla had taught Talia the newest viral TikTok dance when Amala invited her over for dinner one night. Talia enjoyed every second of it. Her dance skills weren't terrible, but her ability to do hair was. Talia could never braid her own hair, let alone someone else's. The craziest updo she ever did was a ponytail.

Jayla's hair ended up looking like a five-year-old or maybe a bird had braided it. Amala promptly redid it while they all giggled hysterically through tears over the lopsided mess Talia had created. But that, *that* was the moment Talia decided moving had been the right decision. She had something here in Archwood that New York City hadn't given her since her mother had passed. Maybe she *could* choose her family.

"I promise I'm going to leave soon, I just have to finish this." Talia held her hands up in defense, noting the motherly look of reprimand on Amala's face. "I swear."

"I'll tell you what, I'm gonna go get my burger and maybe a milkshake because I deserve it, and on the way back, if I see that your car is still here, I'm going to come back in here and pull you out by your ear."

"Geez. Remind me to call you if I ever need backup in a fight."

"Girl, it'd probably be me starting the fight on your behalf." Amala grinned.

Laughing, Talia promptly closed her laptop, well aware that if she didn't comply immediately, she would forget herself and work even later. The consequences would be worse than the gains from having balanced bank accounts.

"Sometimes I feel like you are managing me even though I own this store." Getting up from her seat, Talia slung her purse over her shoulder and followed Amala to the door.

"I manage everyone in my life." Amala lifted her chin. "My husband pretends he doesn't like it either, but who else is gonna throw out his holey underwear? If you can sit on the toilet without having to take your underwear off, they have got to go. This man's out here wearing undergarments that look like they've gone through a cheese grater, and I'm supposed to *not* manage him?"

"I promise you my underwear aren't holey—well, they're lace. Does that count as holey?" Talia reached for the door and pushed it open, shoving her key into the lock after Amala had followed her out.

"No, that just counts as *uncomfortable*. I only wear those when I'm expecting someone to take them off." Amala winked.

Talia snapped her fingers together and pointed at Amala. "And that's how baby number two was created."

"You got a hot date I don't know about waiting at home?" Amala shouted over her shoulder, making her way to her own car.

The word "hot" conjured up an image of Walker in Talia's head that she quickly batted away like a pesky fly. When she and Amala had discussed Talia's many unpleasant encounters with the man, Amala had been more than happy to talk shit about him, as any good friend would do. She'd also called Talia's bluff when Talia had attempted to back out of a line of questioning that involved descriptions of Walker's tousled dark hair, deep brown eyes, and rugged features. Any mention of Walker now—even jokingly—would ignite another conversation about his *supposed* sex appeal. Talia carefully sidestepped the dating conversation entirely.

"I've been here for two weeks. What do you think?" Talia unlocked the door to her rental car—the Lexus was still in the shop—and grimaced when she felt the dirt on the underside of the handle coat her fingertips. She liked things to be neat and orderly, and the old sedan was an ugly bright yellow color, faded from sun exposure. Unlike the Lexus, though, when you hit the brakes, it stopped on a dime.

"You didn't answer my question," Amala singsonged.

Talia snorted. "Nope, I'm going home alone. I'll probably try to finish the book I'm reading, because if I'm going to be awake at all hours of the night with insomnia, I might as well spend it with a fictional man."

"You know what also occupies time in the middle of the night? Copious amounts of great sex." Amala smirked as she opened her car door.

Talia let an easy smile bloom across her face. That bluntness was why she and Amala had immediately hit it off. Amala was unapologetically herself: loud, funny, and sincere. Meanwhile,

Talia had tried her entire life to be perfect for everyone else. She loved the way that Amala could peel back layers of vulnerability without even trying. There was something freeing about having someone to bounce ideas off of again.

"You're relentless." Talia dramatically threw herself behind the wheel, feigning the incapability to sex anyone up due to pure exhaustion. "See you on Monday. If you show up for work in the morning, I will kick your ass out!"

"Don't worry about me. I'm going to catch up on the latest trashy TV show and sit in my pajamas all day," Amala shouted back. "See ya!"

While Talia pulled out of the parking lot, Amala's commentary about impractical underwear echoed in her head. She became intensely aware of the lace riding up and scratching against her skin. Wiggling in her seat to try to dislodge the fabric from its position, she groaned in annoyance when she failed, leaving both hands on the steering wheel.

Damn. These things really are uncomfortable.

Truth be told, Talia didn't have much in the way of normal clothes other than workout gear and pajamas. She had dressed as a New Yorker for so long—that is, she was expected to dress up for work—that throwing on her pencil skirts and button-down blouses had become second nature. She didn't enjoy dressing that way, but it was a fact of life when you were on retainer for high-paying clients and taking meetings all day with men dressed in Armani suits.

If Talia didn't dress to the nines every day at her previous job, the men wouldn't take her seriously. Even with her professional outfits, she still had to prove over and over that she wasn't just assigned cases so the partners or clients would have "something attractive" to look at. That was the exact phrasing one of her colleagues had used when she had gotten a case over him once. It was one of the many reasons Talia had left New York City and why, on her last day of work, she had left a cactus that looked like a middle finger on her co-worker's desk. The attached card that said "You don't have to water this a lot. I know how much you love to put zero effort into everything you do." was just an added touch. Was it petty? Sure. Would she cherish the look on his face till the day she died? Absolutely.

There were only a few cars out on the road that late at night. The quietness that loomed over everything at that hour was peaceful—New York was never that silent. Talia didn't miss the nightlife of The City That Never Sleeps at all. She loved staying in and taking hot bubble baths while devouring her latest romance novel. She liked quiet coffee shops, even if they were accompanied by irritating men named after medical devices with tennis balls attached to the legs.

Five minutes out from her house, Talia spotted a dark figure along the side of the road. She slowed her car and narrowed her eyes warily on the spot. Deer wandered around town like they owned it, and she would be convinced the universe was out to get her if she got into another car accident. As she crawled closer, ready to slam on the brakes if necessary, the picture became clearer. It wasn't a deer at all. It was a girl, hunched over with her hands on her knees and vomiting profusely. Quickly maneuvering to the shoulder of the road, Talia threw her vehicle in park and took off in a hurried jog toward the girl.

"Oh my God, are you okay?" Talia asked, approaching who she now realized had to be a teenager. The girl couldn't have been over twenty, if Talia had to bet.

"I'm okay, jusss... really drunk," the girl slurred and rose to her full height, wiping at her mouth with the back of her hand and stumbling a little. Her blonde hair, with its tips dyed black, swayed with her unsteady footing, and her blue eyes were glossed over. Talia stepped forward and set her hands on the girl's shoulders to steady her.

"I can see that." Talia nodded. "Why are you out here by yourself?"

"It's a bit of a long story." The girl giggled, looking a little worse for wear. "It's not actually funny. I don't know why I'm laughing."

Carefully pulling the teenager away from the vomit puddle pooling in the gravel, Talia directed her toward the car without questioning it. It was far too late for someone to be wandering around drunk on the streets, and she doubted the girl was sober enough to care about stranger danger.

"Can you get in the car, or do you need help?" Talia shuffled her feet along the dirt, bearing most of the weight for the two of them.

"I think I can do it," the teenager hiccuped.

Not sure she believed her, Talia opened the passenger door and monitored the situation as the girl slumped into the seat, her body moving like she was on a boat, swaying with the waves. After carefully shutting the door, making sure all limbs were safely inside and buckled in, Talia made her way around to her own seat, attention still focused on her passenger.

"My name's Talia, and I will be your driver for the evening." She mimicked an overly friendly Uber driver.

"Piper." The teenager tilted her head toward Talia and gave her a sad look, bleached hair falling into her face a little. "I'm sorry. I'm usually not like this."

"Don't be sorry. I'm happy to help." Talia returned a smile. "You don't have to tell me if you don't want to, I'm fine with just driving you home, but if you want to tell me the long story, I'm a good listener. Either way, I'm gonna need your address."

"436 Juniper Ssstreet," Piper recited, head lolling to the side. "I'm so stupid. I shouldn't be drinking at all."

"We all make mistakes. It doesn't mean you're stupid. At least you're not driving."

Talia drove in the direction of Juniper Street, or, at least, where she hoped Juniper Street was. She thought she had passed a street with that name on the way to Amala's once, but she wasn't the best with directions. If all else failed, she'd get her phone to give her directions. Piper had stayed silent for a while, and Talia thought she might not speak further until silent tears started to fall down the girl's face.

"I threw his keys in a blackberry bush so he couldn't leave," Piper said, as if Talia had any clue who she was talking about. "He wasn't supposed to drink but he did anyway and was gonna get in the car, so I had to. Why would he do that when he knows?"

Talia pulled out the package of tissues she had stashed in her center console and handed it to Piper, thankful that she'd transferred most of the stuff from her Lexus into the rental car. She was always prepared for a mental breakdown or allergies.

"You did the right thing." Talia passively patted the girl's shoulder to offer comfort. "You probably saved his life or someone else's. Alcohol sometimes makes people feel invincible. The part in your brain that registers bad decisions gets... confused."

"He broke up with me," Piper said, her face downcast.

"Well, he sounds like a dick, and I think you deserve better," Talia responded.

Piper snorted and bobbed her head, a glob of drool trailing down the side of her mouth. "You're probably right. He knows about my parents and was still gonna drive."

"Your parents?" It took Talia a second to register the words, because Piper's speech was almost unintelligible, but the underlying current to the conversation seemed to have taken a turn.

Piper looked even more miserable, head hung low as what little color was left on her face disappeared. There was something Talia wasn't quite getting, but the uneasy feeling in the pit of her stomach made her want to join Piper in upchucking her last meal. If Talia was driving the girl home just to encounter an even worse fate with her parents, then she'd rather let Piper sleep it off at her house. There was a spare bedroom, and Piper looked close enough to her size to borrow clothes.

"Yeah," was all Piper said. "He's probably going to be so mad at me."

"Who is? Your dad?" Talia pried.

"You think if I sneak in through the window he won't notice? It's this house, right here."

Piper pointed past her at the most beautiful house Talia had ever seen. The large, two-story home was well-kept, but not in an in-your-face kind of way. The olive green paint, white trim, and black accents were simple, but classy. Assorted shrubbery and colorful flowers lined the yard in between lanterns that hung off small poles, lighting the way to the front door. It looked warm and welcoming. A place for a big, happy family. But Talia knew that looks could be deceiving. Anyone could've looked at the house she'd lived in with her parents when she was little and assumed everything on the inside was just as kosher as the outside.

Mind racing, Talia knew she had to expedite her decision-making process even with limited information. Judging a book by its cover or a family by its house was, no doubt, the wrong move. Trying to obtain pertinent details from a drunk girl was like wading through molasses. Eyes fixed on the black front door to the house, Talia nodded once and turned her torso to Piper, holding out her hand.

"Give me your phone," Talia ordered. "I'm going to put my number in it so you can call me if you need to, and then I'm going to walk you to your door to make sure you're okay when I pass you off to your parents. I don't think you're capable of climbing through the window right now."

"I don't have to worry about my parents." Piper handed over her phone and looked down at her feet, a flash of sadness passing through her hazy eyes. The queasy feeling hit Talia's stomach again as she tried to work out what Piper meant. Coming up empty-handed, Talia quickly plugged her number into Piper's phone and dialed.

"My number is the last one called, if you need me," Talia said, hanging up before handing back the phone. Getting out of the car, she made her way around to assist Piper.

Piper had slipped further into her drunkenness, even more unsteady on her feet than before. Talia wasn't a bodybuilder, but she was strong enough to half-drag Piper to the front door. Sucking in a deep breath to ready herself for whatever Piper's home situation looked like, Talia knocked. There was no immediate response, so she rapped on the door again before lifting her finger to hesitate over the doorbell. A scurrying sound inside the house made Talia drop her hand and pull Piper into a more upright position. The door ripped open on its hinges a minute later to the one person Talia never expected to see behind it. Her spine went ramrod straight, and her stomach somersaulted. Clenching her jaw to keep it from dropping in surprise, she swallowed the massive stone that had lodged itself in her throat.

"What the hell? Piper?" Walker stood in front of them wearing gray sweatpants. Shirtless. The black tattoos spiraling up his left arm like tendrils of smoke flexed as he rubbed at his bloodshot eyes, a red pillow crease slashed across his left cheek. A rush of comprehension and something else swarmed Talia's head.

"I shouldn't be drinking at all." "I don't have to worry about my parents."

"What did you do to her?" he growled, the sleepy look on his face replaced with anger. The cold edge to his voice quickly sucked away the heat developing in Talia's core.

"Besides find her on the side of the road vomiting her guts out and drive her home safely? Nothing," Talia snapped. Walker glared at her, his nose twitching in indignation, and Talia recentered her focus on what really mattered: Piper. "She's really drunk. I don't think she can walk."

"Oh, fuck me!" Walker groaned before his eyes widened a fraction of a second and squeezed shut like he was in pain. He ran a hand through his messy bedhead, a cowlick of hair standing firmly in place. The sleepy look would have been oddly cute to Talia if she didn't know he was a jackass.

Finally, Walker stepped forward and easily swept Piper off her feet, cradling her like a baby.

"I'm ssso sssorry," Piper slurred.

"We'll talk about it tomorrow. Let's just get you in bed. Uh..."

Walker met Talia's eyes again in slight panic. "Is she okay? How much was she throwing up? Should I be taking her to the hospital? What—"

"I think she'll be all right, but I'd monitor her. Do you want me to... I-I mean, I can help her get ready for bed. She's probably going to need a change of clothes. She didn't entirely miss her shirt earlier." Talia pointed to the wet spot on Piper's chest.

Walker grimaced. "Yes, can you? Otherwise, I'm going to have to wake up her sister to help her, and Pearl is only—"

"Eleven," Talia remembered, stepping into the house. If she recalled correctly, Walker also had a sixteen-year-old niece, which confirmed her theory that Piper was not of legal drinking age.

"Right." Walker nodded. "Uh... follow me?"

Talia pulled the front door shut and trailed behind Walker as he hauled Piper up the stairs like she weighed next to nothing. Talia did her best not to notice his extremely toned torso or the way his back muscles worked when he moved around a corner, but dear God. To deter her thoughts, Talia ran through the checklist of reasons she should not be admiring Walker's body.

He's a jerk. He's been nothing but rude to you from day one. He's clearly not doing so hot in the raising children department— but he is definitely doing hot in... other departments.

Walker flicked on the lights to a room Talia assumed was Piper's and walked over to the queen sized bed in the middle of the room, gently laying Piper down. Piper mumbled out another "sorry" right before lurching over the edge of the bed and vomiting on the wood floor at Walker's feet. Jumping backwards to avoid the splatter, Walker rammed into Talia. The room turned sideways as Talia's feet searched for the ground, only finding air. Closing her eyes, she prepared to hit the hardwood, only to be caught by a pair of strong hands. When she opened her eyes, she was clutching onto Walker's arms, which, apparently, he'd wrapped around her to stop her from plummeting to the floor. Frozen, Talia stared up at him in shock. His bare chest, sprinkled lightly with dark hair, was mere inches from her face. One tattooed arm slid to the small of her back as he blinked slowly at her.

"Sorry." Walker cleared his throat and took a giant step toward the door, away from her, and even further away from the putrid mess on the ground. Talia just nodded stupidly, wondering when she had ever been at such an utter loss for words before.

Say something, literally anything, to move past this extremely uncomfortable situation.

"I assume her clothes are in the dresser?" Talia asked breathlessly as she pointed toward the classy wooden one in the corner.

"Yep, that is where clothes are usually stored." It wasn't a snide joke so much as an uncomfortable filler. Walker shifted on his feet, darting his eyes between Talia, the dresser, and Piper like he was begging for all three of them to evaporate on the spot. "Um... I'll be right back with paper towels and something to clean that up." Walker pointed to the floor, his nose scrunching in revulsion. "I'll knock before I enter in case she's not decent."

"Okay," Talia agreed. She waited for Walker to leave the room before finally exhaling the breath she'd been holding since his body held her upright.

"What was that?" Piper was sitting up in bed and looking over at Talia in curiosity, temporarily articulate after her last vomiting session. Talia moved over to the dresser and guessed correctly on the first try that Piper's pajamas would be in the second drawer down. Teenage girls were predictable.

"You just threw up on the ground, Walker's getting something to clean it up, and I am going to make sure you don't go to sleep in your own vomit."

"I meant the weirdness between you and my uncle." Piper waved a heavy hand toward the door. "You guys know each other?"

"That's a stretch." Talia grabbed the first pair of pajamas she saw and shut the drawer quickly. "Lift up your arms," she directed. Piper slowly obliged, raising her weighted limbs above her head. Pulling the shirt up, careful to avoid getting any vomit on herself, Talia averted her eyes. She wanted to pretend it was because she was helping a drunk teen get undressed, but that wasn't why. Talia had no qualms about assisting Piper, especially after understanding her history. Anything she could do to help the girl out, she would. What she didn't want was Piper to notice her blush-stained cheeks or ask further questions about her acquaintance with Walker.

It was no such luck. People always said the first thing that came to their mind when they were sloshed.

"He totally wants to bone you," Piper announced as fact.

"I can guarantee you *that* is not true." Talia slid the new shirt over Piper's head and moved to assist in pulling the fishnets and mini-skirt down Piper's hips, hoping to God it was taking Walker a long time to get cleaning supplies so that he wasn't listening in on the conversation. "Your uncle does not like me at all. Can't say I enjoy his company either."

"Ooooh," Piper drew out her response and lifted her legs lazily so Talia could slide fuzzy pajama bottoms on. Dropping her legs, Piper scooted her bottom into them and slowly sat up, continuing her thoughts in a medium voice she clearly meant to be a whisper. "Did you already have sex with him and he didn't call you? He does that sometimes."

"No, I didn't, but I can't say I'm shocked that he doesn't call women back," Talia replied in slight amusement. A knock sounded on the door, and she double-checked to make sure Piper was fully covered before announcing they were all clear.

Walker opened the door, brandishing a spray bottle and a roll of paper towels as if Talia needed proof that he'd done what he said he was going to do. He was now sporting a white T-shirt with his sweatpants. She obviously hadn't been the only one who was uncomfortable with their bare-skinned shuffle situation earlier.

"I should be making you clean this up," Walker told Piper as she flopped onto her pillow. He stooped down, ripping off several sheets of paper towels and layering them on top of the puddle. When the liquid started to seep through, he gagged, tilting his head to the side to look away from it. He glanced up at Piper again, but she was already out cold and snoring like a banshee.

"God, this is gross."

"Oh, don't be a baby." Talia stepped forward and shoved Walker's shoulder. She instantly regretted touching him but pretended it had zero effect on her as she bent down beside him and took the paper towel roll out of his hand. Ripping off several more sheets, she swiped her hand over the mess a few times, absorbing all the liquid. Walker gaped at her for a moment before finally springing into action and spraying the spot so she could continue.

When everything was clean, Talia wrapped the bundle of soiled paper towels in even more sheets—even she wasn't immune to how gross it was. They both rose to their feet quietly so they didn't wake Piper and tiptoed out of the room, Walker slowly shutting the door behind them. In the hallway, he looked over at Talia without saying anything, leaning against the wall. His arms casually crossed over his chest, as if he had zero idea why she was staring at him and waiting for some sort of direction. The man was truly clueless.

"Trash can?" Talia held up the vomit-soaked rags she was still holding, and Walker cringed. "As much as I want to help, I'm not taking this with me."

"Right, sorry. Downstairs." He motioned for her to follow.

The kitchen was immaculate. The hood vent over the massive stove was something straight out of *Better Homes & Gardens*. The cabinets were dark blue, and the backsplash was a light gray stone color that went perfectly with the butcher block countertops and gold accents. The kitchen was sexier than Walker... *almost*. Talia did want to marry it and put several buns in its double oven, though.

Stepping on a lever near the bottom of the large island in the middle of the kitchen, Walker cleared his throat, pointing to the drawer on a slider that popped out to reveal the trash can. Talia quickly disposed of the paper towels and moved over to the sink to wash her hands. There was no point in waiting for Walker to show her to the bathroom. He seemed to be perfectly content with making her feel as unwelcome as possible.

The only sound in the room was the faucet as Talia scrubbed her hands clean. It made her skin crawl to know that Walker was there in the room but not saying anything. Drying her wet hands on a nearby towel, she turned back to face him, not entirely sure where he was standing. Sitting on one of the barstools, elbows on the countertop and massaging his temples, Walker studied her with a watchful eye, as if she was going to grab the salt and pepper shakers and make a break for it. For a second, she wanted to do just that. If he was going to look at her like a social pariah regardless, she might as well get some kitchen accessories out of it. In the end, she decided against it when she took in the tired shadows under his eyes and the way his hunched shoulders made him look weak and spent. Walker looked like hell. At least, as much as a person with fallen-angel features could look like hell.

"So." Talia took a seat next to him, pretending his gaze didn't make nerves shoot up her spine. "Give me your number."

Walker's eyebrows jumped, his mouth parting in surprise as his hands dropped away from his temples.

"Wh-what? Why?"

"Because I want to check on Piper's well-being in the morning. Her boyfriend just broke up with her, and I—"

"Boyfriend? I didn't even know she had a boyfriend. Is it that guy, Harden? 'Cause that kid is an asshole and I told her as much." One of Walker's hands balled up into a fist on the countertop as he slid his phone over to her with his other. "Put in your number. I will text you."

"She didn't tell me his name, but my best guess is 'yes' considering he was supposed to be the DD and ended up drinking to the point where Piper had to throw his keys into a blackberry bush to keep him from driving. He definitely sounds like an asshole."

Talia set the phone back on the island. Both of Walker's hands were balled into fists now, knuckles turning white as he stewed, barely giving his phone a second glance. "I don't think she still wants to date him after all that, if it helps." Talia bit her lip, unsure if she should be offering him any placative words. The torment etched into the lines of his face made her want to impulsively rub away the creases with her thumbs.

"It doesn't," he replied with a sigh. "So, you've done the whole drinking till you throw up thing before, huh?"

There it is. That's why you don't like him.

"I don't drink." Talia's tone turned ice cold. She was not her father, and at this point, she was fed up with Walker's propensity to behave like she was.

"I have once." Walker shrugged.

It wasn't at all what she expected his response to be, and she was somewhat alarmed by his openness. "It was the first and only time I've ever had alcohol. I drank until I blacked out and woke up in my own vomit. Cole didn't drink either. Our dad is an alcoholic, and I think he passed that lovely little gift on to us... or just me now, I guess."

"I would say 'same,' but clearly you already know that," Talia mumbled. "Alcohol ruins people."

"People ruin people," Walker corrected.

Talia could tell what he meant without having to dig any further. Her father had ruined Walker's life and the lives of five kids who now didn't have a mother or father. But she didn't know her dad from Adam. She wasn't even sad to hear that he was dead, other than the way he had died. Yet, Walker still seemed hellbent on blaming her for it. She could understand the desire to put blame on someone, anyone, just to make the pain go away, but it didn't mean she deserved it. She'd already put enough blame on herself recently for things she couldn't control. Logically, she knew she wasn't in charge of her body's incapability to bear children, but her self-deprecative brain said otherwise. If she was going to hate herself for something, it was going to be *that*, not her father's mistakes.

"I'm going to go." Talia stood up from her seat and stalked toward the exit.

"I do know that I'm failing, ya know. Trust me, I'm aware." Walker shot a miserable look over his shoulder at her, and she halted, feet frozen near the door.

People ruin people. Maybe Walker hated himself just as much as he hated her.

"I'm sure you're doing the best you can do," Talia murmured.

"It's not good enough." Walker got up from his stool and made his way past her toward the door, ripping it open for her. "Piper told me she was at a friend's house tonight, and I had absolutely no idea where she really was. Thank you for picking her up. If she threw up in your car, I will pay for it to be cleaned. I'll text you in the morning to let you know she's okay."

"Walker, I..." Talia stepped outside, hesitating to leave him in his depressive state. "I'm sure she was just upset. That's not a reflection on you."

"Piper gets straight A's in school and is normally a walking government ad telling people to say no to drugs. Now she's out getting wasted at parties with boys who obviously don't treat her with any kind of respect, so you'll have to excuse me if I don't believe you. Good night, Talia."

Walker waved stiffly, and Talia swallowed, giving him a microscopic nod of her head, knowing she wouldn't be able to convince him otherwise. She couldn't even convince herself that she wasn't the cause of her own misfortune.

"Good night."

Neshama sheli, you must learn to be the picture of kindness and grace, her mother's voice rang in her ears, again and again.

FIVE

WALKER

Walker jolted awake with a gasp, whacking his head on the half-wall he was leaning against outside of Piper's room. Shirt soaked through and sticking to his chest, he looked down at himself, shaking his head. If the memory of the dream wasn't enough, the wet spot on his sweatpants was proof.

Fuck. What are you, sixteen?

He had only touched Talia once. Once. And it had been to stop her from eating shit after he ran into her like a freight train to avoid Piper's nasty, chunky bile. Walker decided to dwell on Piper's vomit to cool his body's recollection of his fingers pressed into the warmth of Talia's back. He pictured Piper upchucking stale beer on repeat. It worked, and also made his stomach a bit queasy, until his brain reverted to how Talia looked bent over the kitchen sink, rubbing soap into her hands with her ass pointed at him like a homing beacon.

"Fuck, seriously?" Walker hissed, feeling his groin tighten again. His bones snapped and cracked as he hopped to his feet, taking a cue from his dick to be entirely too stiff. His back was definitely going to be tweaked all day.

Nope, you're definitely not sixteen anymore.

The word "sleep" was giving too much credit to what he'd actually done the night before. Between waking up at the slightest sound from Piper's room and his invasive and unwarranted thoughts about Talia, Walker only managed to get a few hours of shut-eye. He had checked Piper's pulse so many times in the middle of the night that it bordered on insane. He had never once checked in on his dad after a long night of drinking, and Walker couldn't imagine Piper was that shitfaced, but it didn't matter. The impulse to continually make sure Piper was on her side so she wouldn't choke on her own vomit was so over-the-top that the second Walker heard any movement in her room, it had him launching up from his spot on the floor in a panic and barging in to verify she wasn't dead. Cole and Paisley were counting on him to make sure their kids were okay, and so far he was doing a bang-up job. He needed to do better. *Be* better.

At least he hadn't been haunted by his recurring nightmare. Drowning every night was beyond exhausting.

Making his way to his room, Walker changed into clothes that didn't reek of lust and massive amounts of stress. He threw his clothes into the hamper and covered them with the towel from his shower the night before, hiding the evidence of his body's release. Normally, a sex dream wouldn't have been such a big deal, and he would have found it a nice respite from his nieces and nephews killing him with adolescent chaos, but having those thoughts about *Talia Cohen* just made him feel extreme amounts of guilt. Here he was, taking care of—and doing a shitty job at—raising Cole and Paisley's kids while simultaneously thinking about sleeping with the daughter of the guy that had killed them both.

Assuring himself that his lack of sexual activity and masturbation since his brother's death had caused last night's incident, Walker took a few deep breaths and added *having a go at himself* to his daily to-do list so he didn't end up in a padded room with no doors or windows. Dating was not an option. He simply didn't have the time and needed to focus on the one thing that did matter: getting his nieces and nephews through this nightmare.

It was 6:30 a.m., and although it was a Saturday and the rest of the kids were sleeping in, it was as good a time as any for Walker to start on all of the hard discussions he would have to deal with that day. Piper needed some sort of punishment for lying to him. What frustrated Walker to no end wasn't that Piper drank—he could understand the impulse to drown her problems in alcohol and had thought about it a few times himself—but that she didn't call him when she needed a ride. Whatever punishment he came up with had to be severe enough to make her understand that her behavior was unacceptable but also mild enough that, if she did do it again, she would at least call him.

As Walker opened the door to Piper's room, water and ibuprofen in hand, he flicked on the lights and received a groan from the heap of blankets on the bed. Amused, he made his way over to Piper and ripped the comforter off to let the chill of the morning shock her awake. Her eyes squinted up at the light, hand flying to her head as her very first hangover made its debut.

"Good morning, sunshine!" Walker said in a cheery voice that was intentionally louder than necessary.

"Walker! Please..." Piper winced. "Why are you screaming?"

"Screaming, huh? That is probably what I should be doing considering someone decided to have a little rebellious outing last night." Walker crossed his arms over his chest and stared down at his niece with eyebrows raised.

"I... I'm sorry." Piper sat up, body swaying a little, no doubt from the onslaught of overstimulating senses and nausea.

"Mind telling me what, if anything, was going through your head?" Walker sat on the edge of the bed and held out the glass and pills to Piper. She took them and downed both, a trail of water running down the corner of her mouth when she lowered the glass.

"I was just... I don't know. Harden wanted me to go and said that he would make sure I was safe. He said the best thing for me to do would be to let loose a little bit, and I thought he was right?" Piper shrugged her shoulders, red eyes heavy with regret.

"Harden," Walker said in an icy tone that gave the kid's name the amount of hatred it deserved, "is a douche. He doesn't deserve you and suggesting you should lose yourself in alcohol or drugs is quite possibly the worst advice to ever be given."

"I didn't do drugs!" Piper said quickly.

"And thank God for that, but—Piper." Walker looked at his niece sternly, with all the sympathy he could muster. "It's not the same for us as it is for other people. Our family has a history of alcoholism, which means that we have to be more careful. We don't have the luxury of throwing caution to the wind. You might find that you don't crave that feeling, but do you really want to continue to find out? Once was enough for me to know that I do crave it and that if I ever tested my limits with it again, it would send me down a path that would not be good for me. Your dad was the same way. It's why we never drank. It's not because we didn't want to have fun, or we were sticks in the mud, it's because we knew we both had addictive personalities and neither one of us wanted to turn out like your grandpa."

"And I guess it's probably also why you made sure no one brought wine to their funeral. I thought it was just because of how they," Piper gulped, "how they died."

"I suppose it was both." Walker nodded. "That, and I was worried your grandfather would over-indulge."

"He showed up drunk anyway," Piper pointed out.

"Yeah, but at least I wasn't enabling him."

Walker had at least been able to make sure none of the kids saw when he had to kick his own father out of the wake for bringing a flask. When Dennis Hartrick showed up to the funeral, Walker caught the familiar smell of alcohol on his breath, but he hoped his father would sober up by the time they moved everything to the house. That had been wishful thinking. Walker could still picture the look on his father's face when he made him leave after catching him sipping out of a flask as he stared at the family photos on the dining room wall. Cole was Dennis' son, and he needed to grieve, too, but not at the cost of hurting his grandchildren even more than they already were. Dennis practically begged to stay, but when Walker's stipulation to stay involved ditching the prized leather flask in his coat pocket, he left without protest. If there was one thing Walker could count on, it was his father choosing alcohol over his family. Every time.

"I can't afford to let alcohol into my life right now. Not when I have all of you to worry about. I'm sorry I didn't realize you were struggling so much, Piper, but you can't lie to me again. You scared the shit out of me last night. If anything like this ever happens again, you need to call me. If Talia hadn't picked you up, you could have been hit by a car or passed out in a ditch somewhere, and I would have had no clue. You can *always* call me, Piper. I don't care if you're strung out on drugs, if you've robbed a bank, or if you killed someone. Please, just call me."

"I'm sorry," Piper sniffled, tears starting to form in her eyes. "I didn't want to be a burden. I was embarrassed, and I... didn't want to add to all the stuff you have to do now. I knew it was a bad idea the second I lied to you, but I just wanted to stop thinking for a little bit. I'm so tired of thinking about them *constantly*." Her voice broke and more tears spilled down her face. "And then everything went to shit like I knew it would, and I just wanted to pretend it didn't happen."

"Piper." Walker set his hand on her shoulder, trying to hold it together himself. "None of you are a burden. I would drive across the country in the middle of the night to come get you if you needed me to. But when you're feeling that low, I *need* you to tell me. I'm trying really hard, but I'm not a mind reader. I don't know what the fuck I'm doing most of the time. All of this is... it's a lot, and I need to know without a shadow of a doubt that you're safe. We can't lose you, too. *I* can't lose you."

Piper sucked in a shaky breath and bobbed her head. "I'm sorry. I'll be more careful. I'll be safe."

A choked sob escaped her throat, and she leaned forward to

hug him. Walker kept his breathing steady and looked up at the ceiling to make sure gravity wouldn't let the tears building in his eyes fall as he squeezed her back. "I can help you with all the things you've been doing lately." Piper let go, giving Walker a small, forced smile.

"What will help me is if you focus on healing yourself." Walker shook his head, recentering himself. "Don't worry about me. I need you to one, never give Harden the time of day again—actually, no, I'm your guardian now, and I'm telling you that you are not allowed to see him again. If you pass him in the hallways at school, your only form of communication with him will be a middle finger, you got me?"

"Okay," Piper snorted.

"Two," Walker held up a second finger. "You are going to therapy. I will set up an appointment for you, which, given the date of Carter's, will be a month out because apparently this country's obsession with instant gratification does not extend to useful things. You know what, now that I'm thinking about it, I think I'll make therapy mandatory for all of you."

"Are you going to go?" Piper inquired with a tilt of her head.

"I don't have time, and I'm fine. Do as I say, not as I do." Walker pointed at Piper, then lifted three of his fingers. "Next is your punishment, which... I am not sure what that should be. Any ideas?"

Piper gaped at him. "You're asking *me* how I think I should be punished?"

"Yes," Walker decided. "You come up with something fair, and I will approve it. I get veto power if I think it's under-whelming."

Piper tapped her finger against her lips in thought, tilting her head back and forth. Walker waited patiently, hoping that whatever she came up with would be better than the blank slate in his head. The only thing he could think of was taking her phone away, but then he wouldn't be able to get ahold of her and she wouldn't be able to get ahold of her siblings, which would cause his anxiety to skyrocket.

"I think..." Piper finally spoke, slowly at first. "I'm grounded, for one, in addition to never seeing Harden—"

"Can we give him a rude nickname or something?" Walker interrupted. "May I suggest 'dickwad' or 'fuckwit?'"

Piper burst into laughter, falling back onto her pillows. He was happy that she found something amusing, even though he was dead serious about the nickname. It was the first time he had heard her laugh since her parents passed, and it gave him a modicum of pride that he had been the one to bring back her happy-go-lucky attitude.

Smiling back at her, he shrugged and doubled down. "What? Do you want to combine them? Does dickwit or fuckwad sound better?"

It had the desired effect. Walker watched his niece crumple into a heap of laughter, and he couldn't help but let out a laugh of his own. It wasn't even that he thought giving a teenage asshole a clever nickname was funny, but rather that everything else he was dealing with was so overwhelming, laughter was the only way to live with it. When the hilarity died down, he coughed loudly to clear his throat and wiped at his watering eyes.

"So, the punishment?" Walker motioned for Piper to continue.

"Right." Piper sat up and took a deep breath. "In additional to never seeing that *dickwit* again—"

"Ah, good choice." Walker grinned in approval.

"Thank you." Piper bowed her head dramatically in a sitting curtsey before straightening her spine. "I think I'm grounded from going out with anyone other than family. And... I have to do everyone's laundry for three weeks?"

"Yes to the grounding, no to the laundry," Walker said immediately. "How about instead of that, you go grocery shopping with me and cook the food for the next two weeks?"

And dear God, please do not go near my laundry

"That sounds like more of a reward considering the chicken parm incident," Piper snarked.

"Okay, it wasn't *that* burnt," Walker protested. "You also have to clean the bathrooms, and if you continue to dress the way you have been dressing I *will* have something to say about it." Piper opened her mouth like a stunned fish, and Walker held up his hand in a stop position to cut off whatever she was about to say. "And no, I don't care if you think I'm a hypocrite. You are sixteen and you need to be acting and dressing like you're sixteen. Your dad probably would have had my head for letting you leave the house in whatever the hell you were wearing yesterday. Not to mention, you haven't looked even remotely comfortable lately, Piper. You used to wear dresses and knit sweaters every day. It feels very off for everything to change so drastically. You can go back to dressing however you want when you're out of this house because you'll be an adult, but for now, you need to cool it on the fishnets and weird wrap shirt thing that was barely a shirt before I start getting calls from the school about it."

"I didn't realize that you noticed." Piper sighed. "I'll go back to my 'I'm a valedictorian who gets no action' attire. Harden just said I was dressing too... never mind."

"No action," Walker repeated. "That's exactly what I like to hear. And it's probably best that you didn't finish that sentence. I'm not above murdering Dickwit, especially if he suggested you dress differently than you normally do. *He's* going to start dressing with his underwear halfway up his asshole if he ever suggests that again."

"Okay," Piper chuckled, but nodded in agreement before gingerly massaging her temples with her fingers, obviously taken aback by how much it hurt to move. "Can I... sleep a little more?"

"I guess I can let you sleep for a few more hours. Set your alarm for nine-thirty and be ready by ten. And when you get up, take a shower and change your sheets. You smell like you bathed in beer and vomit." Walker waved his hand in front of his nose and stood up from the bed, grabbing the empty glass to refill it in Piper's bathroom before he left her to her own devices.

"Hey, Walker?" Piper called out as he was halfway through the doorway.

"Yeah?" He looked back over his shoulder.

"Thank you."

"It's just water, but you're welcome."

"Not for the water. For... being there." Piper smiled.

"Anytime," Walker choked, a tight pressure beginning to strangle his heart.

You weren't there. You weren't.

Being there would have meant knowing how badly Piper was struggling. It would have meant she could call him when she needed an out. None of those things had happened. Instead, the only reliable adult in Piper's life seemed to be the one person he didn't want it to be. Talia.

Walker shut the door behind him and escaped to his bedroom before anyone else in the house could find him in the state he was in. Collapsing against the wall of the room that never should have been his, he hiked his knees to his chest and covered his face with his hands, gasping for air.

"Piper's okay. She's okay. She's fine."

Nothing he told himself worked. The tears slid down his face, unencumbered by his desire to hold it together. He did not have time for mental breakdowns. He did not have time to allow his emotions to get the best of him.

"I'm sorry." Walker's voice was shakier than he would have liked it to be, so he set his jaw and body firmly before repeating it. "I'm sorry. I'll do better, Cole. I promise."

Stifling a sob, Walker decided that the tears that had just slid down his face would be his last. He rose from the ground on unsteady feet and pulled out his phone. Finding Talia's number, he typed out a message and stared at it for a long while, worried it would come across wrong. In the end he huffed out a "fuck it" under his breath and sent the message.

Piper is okay, other than her newfound hatred for bright lights and loud sounds. She's a regular gremlin. Can I buy you a coffee as a thank you? - Walker

Six

WALKER

Walker's foot tapped nervously against the ground. He wasn't sure why he was so anxious. The coffee arrangement was just to thank Talia for being there for Piper when he wasn't. Yes, Talia was really hot, a fact that he was doing his best to ignore, but the meeting was purely to establish that his behavior the night prior was maybe not as grateful as it should have been. He owed her a coffee. If not for helping Piper, then at least to relieve his guilt for the dreams his brain had conjured up last night against his will.

When Talia walked in, she was wearing tight black leggings, sneakers, and a band T-shirt. A ball cap sat on her head, with her hair pulled through in a ponytail. Adjusting in his seat, Walker swallowed and looked down at his hands, trying to control the heat spreading through his body. She wasn't even wearing her usual upper-class bullshit that was designed to make her body look like she fell out of a magazine dedicated to beautiful people, and yet something about her outfit made his mind launch into the gutter. He wanted a fistful of her hair in his palm and to mimic the tongue and lips Rolling Stones logo on her shirt all the way up her body.

At some point, Talia was going to notice that he was staring. Walker forced himself out of his seat and walked over to her, his muscles rigid. He came up behind her and tapped on her shoulder. His fingers retracted quickly, and he mentally kicked himself for touching her again.

"Hey," Walker managed to get out. Talia turned around and gave him a once-over.

"Hey," she replied. "Rough morning?"

"Do I look like I've had a rough morning?" Walker raked his hand through his hair and looked down at his outfit, self-consciously verifying that his shirt wasn't inside out and backwards.

"Oh, I didn't mean *that*. I just meant dealing with teenage drama."

Walker shifted his stance and brushed his sweaty palms against his thighs. "Right. It went better than I was expecting. Uh... do you know what you want?" He gestured toward the chalkboard menu. Talia bit her bottom lip in contemplation, a sight that was both oddly erotic and endearing. She looked so focused on her order that Walker almost laughed out loud.

"I don't even know why I'm thinking about this," Talia declared, as if she could hear his thoughts. "I always get the same thing."

"Can I take a guess?" he asked, playfully grinning at her.

"You think you can read me? I doubt it," Talia mused. "You probably drink plain old black coffee, though. No cream, no sugar, just straight-up so you can feel the caffeine shoot into your veins."

"Damn." Walker's eyes widened, and Talia smirked, like she knew she had gotten it right. "All right..." He narrowed his eyes at her way longer than was necessary for effect. He already knew exactly what she drank because he overheard her ordering the first day she showed up at Roaster's Republic. "You drink something hot... because I, uh, saw you drinking something hot the other day. I'm gonna guess a... vanilla latte?"

"Nope." Talia smiled and turned toward the barista. "Chai latte, please."

Walker blinked, biting back a response. If she got the same thing every time, she was flat-out lying. He wanted to demand answers, but it would reveal that he'd been paying attention to her order like a psychotic stalker. Instead, he stashed the knowledge that Talia was prone to fibbing in the back of his mind to deter any future thoughts about her naked and sprawled out on his bed.

"Black coffee, Mr. Hartrick?" The peppy redhead across the counter had Walker's order down pat after he'd come in almost every day for the last three months. He gave her a nod, embarrassed that he could never remember her name. Taking a glance at her name tag in the most nonchalant way possible, he confirmed her name before replying.

"Thank you, Harper. You can just call me Walker."

"Walker," Harper repeated in a low, somewhat sultry voice. Walker wasn't stupid; he had seen the way she looked at him, and she was definitely his usual type, but for whatever reason, he felt little to no attraction to her at all.

Walker turned to Talia and pointed at a table. "Did you want to... sit?" His original plan had been to buy Talia a coffee and get the hell out of there, but his mouth and body ran off without his permission. Unaware of the mental battle going on inside his head, Talia took a seat on the antique couch Walker normally sat at instead of the table he suggested, as usual, blowing all his boundaries to smithereens. Walker sat down next to her and folded his hands on his lap, unsure what to say.

"So, are you going to call me on it?" Talia asked before Walker could spark up a conversation.

"Call you on what?" Walker furrowed his brow.

Talia shrugged. "I lied. A vanilla latte is my drink, and you already knew that."

Stunned into silence for a moment, Walker blinked stupidly at Talia. He'd been caught red-handed, and yet he was more annoyed that he'd been bested at whatever game they were playing.

"Fine. Why did you lie? What is this? Some kind of weird test?" He inquired.

"I just wanted to see if you would say anything, like I'm now going to call you out on the fact that you already knew what I was going to drink and tried to pretend that you were just guessing."

"You're... fucking insane." Walker gawked. It was the only thing he could think to say because he was still reeling from the shock of her being able to read him like an open book. He was so used to being an enigma to women that Talia's blatant disregard for the cool man of mystery vibe he tried to embody delivered a definite blow to his ego. "How?"

"They used to call me a human lie detector at my old job." Talia grinned, clearly enjoying his discomfort.

"What job was that, exactly? Assistant to Sherlock Holmes?"

"Lawyer."

"Ah." Walker nodded. "That explains the clothes." Talia looked down at herself, and he wanted to slap himself for mentioning anything that implied he'd spent any longer than zero time thinking about her outfits. "Not the current outfit. The stilts you use as shoes and the sunglasses that scream 'get away from me, I'm a New Yorker who doesn't open doors for people.'"

"So you know I'm a New Yorker, too, then?" Talia pried.

"That was a lucky guess. You aren't the only one who can read people."

Their coffee orders were called out before Talia could respond, and Walker waved her off to signal that he would pick up both their drinks. It wasn't hard to figure out which one was his. One of the cups had a phone number scrawled out on the side, his earlier friendliness toward the barista clearly mistaken for flirting. Sitting back down across from Talia, Walker passed her her drink and waited for her to take a sip. She did and cringed, obviously forgetting she had not ordered her usual.

"But I thought you *loved* chai lattes!" Walker teased, the smirk on his face compromising his feigned innocence and giving away his inability to pass up an opportunity to poke fun at her.

"I don't know why, out of everything, I chose chai. I *hate* chai. Literally anything else would have worked," Talia groaned.

"Here." Walker held his drink out to her, and she cocked her head in curiosity. "I like chai, and they have cream and sugar on that stand over there that you can add to this. I haven't drunk out of it yet."

"You aren't worried about getting weird diseases from me?" Talia inquired, passing her drink over to him.

"Do you have weird diseases?" Walker lifted the drink to his lips and took a sip in defiance before waiting for her response. He actually despised chai with every fiber of his being, but it was too late to turn back. He would drain every last drop of that blasted drink just to prove a point. What point, exactly? He had no idea.

"Yeah, I do." Talia nodded as if it was of no consequence. "It's this weird parasite thing that eats holes in your stomach. I got it when I went on a trip to the Amazon. I've had several surgeries to remove the parts of my stomach that have died off."

Walker choked on the chai sliding down his throat before recognizing the playful smile on her face.

"You're fucking with me," he determined, shaking his head.

"Definitely. But it sounds like some shit you would get in the Amazon, right? They have fish that swim up your urethra, why not flesh-eating parasites, too?"

Walker made a mental note to never visit the Amazon.

Talia walked over to the coffee bar and poured some cream into her new cup. The stir stick she picked up didn't go into her cup, but instead between her lips, chewing on the end of it with her teeth. She didn't sit back down across from him, choosing to stand as he took another sip of his disgusting drink and did his best to not give her the impression that he wasn't enjoying it.

"So... I wanted to thank you again for helping Piper. It's been... well, it hasn't been easy. I really wished she would have called me because I would have picked her up if she did. She shouldn't have been walking home at all. Anyway, we had a discussion this morning, and I think we're on the same page now.

I'm scheduling a therapy appointment for all of the kids as soon as places open up tomorrow. Carter already has one set up after the whole skipping school incident, but... you get the point."

"You don't owe me any explanation, Walker," Talia said plainly. "I'm not holding anything against you like you are me."

"What is that supposed to mean?" Walker stared back at her, remembering just how infuriating she was.

"It means my relationship with my dad was nonexistent. I lived here till I was seven. My mom woke me up in the middle of the night to skip town and get away from him, so I do know what a horrible person he was, and I'm sorry I wasn't more of a positive influence on him, but I doubt my presence in his life would have been enough to save your family. My mom was the most wonderful person I've ever met, and even her presence wasn't enough to cure his narcissistic personality.

"The only nice thing he ever did for me was leave me his grocery store, which I should really be thanking the manager, Amala, for, considering the only reason that place turned a profit is because she was running it while he drank his liver into oblivion. So, please, whatever grudge you have against me, I can say without a shadow of a doubt that I don't deserve it. I have nothing and no one anymore. That is why I left my job to be here. So, spare me your niceties. I've got enough on my plate without dealing with you pretending to be nice all of a sudden. You don't owe me anything. I don't owe you anything, unless you want the store. I guess you have more of a right to it than I do, and—"

"Wait, wait, wait," Walker interrupted, setting his drink down and holding up both hands in defense. "I don't want your store, and I'm not holding anything against you." Talia cocked her head, calling his bluff. Walker closed his eyes, feeling like an asshole, and pointed to the couch beside him in defeat. "Please, just sit down."

When he opened his eyes again, he was half-expecting her to be gone, but found her to be sitting back in her original seat, giving him the benefit of the doubt he hadn't spared her.

"I'm sorry."

"You're sorry," she regurgitated, as if the words were meaningless.

"Okay, I'm *really* sorry?" he offered, his voice going up an octave. "I... *was* holding a grudge against you, but not for anything you did. Except for maybe attempting to kill me on my bike, but—"

"I told you the—"

"The brakes. Yeah, I know. I'm just a little more aware of my life recently. I sold the bike. I shouldn't have been driving that death trap anymore, anyway. I can't be even close to reckless with my life, or the kids... they could end up with no one, and I can't do that to them. You didn't do anything. All you've done is help me at every turn, and my attitude toward you has been less than appropriate. I apologize. I get bitter when I think about your father, and seeing you just... brings that to the forefront of my mind.

"My brother was the single most important person in my life, and I lost him. Sometimes I think it's all a dream and Cole and Paisley are just going to walk through their front door. You remind me that that will never happen. No one is ever going to care about me the way they did. That, and..." Walker shook his head in frustration, not wanting to admit the next part to Talia, but feeling compelled nonetheless. "You're better at being a parent than I am, and you don't even know the kids. I should be able to... never mind, this is stupid. It's not your job to make me feel better about being an inadequate guardian. And you know what? I lied again. I hate chai."

Walker stood abruptly, avoiding eye contact. He figured Talia was wearing an expression of hatred or victory, and he didn't need to see either. He had completely spiraled out of control with his confessions. Talia didn't need his entire life story, just a quick apology and a "thank you for your assistance."

Marching toward the door in embarrassment, Walker tossed the half-full cup of chai into the trash and pushed his way out to the parking lot. He was a glass house that Talia had seen right through or, rather, obliterated with dynamite. He stomped over to his car, frantically hitting the unlock button on the keyfob as panic rose inside him. How had Talia been able to completely expose him in under a few minutes? Was this who he was reduced to now? Someone who had mental breakdowns in his brother's bedroom and poured his heart out to complete strangers?

"Walker, wait!"

An arm latched onto the crook of his elbow, and he froze. Walker turned slowly to look at Talia, fearing that whatever she had to say would undoubtedly cut him to the quick or make him feel stripped down to his bare bones. "I need... look, I need a friend and clearly, you do, too."

Whatever he was expecting, it hadn't been that. Staring back at Talia, mouth parted but unable to form words, Walker just stood there, probably affirming that there was absolutely no reason she should want to be his friend. He couldn't even spit out a "yes," "no," or "maybe" in response.

"Okay, maybe that's not at all what you're looking for? At least take your drink back. The barista clearly wants you to call her." Talia let out a strained laugh and held out the to-go cup.

"Yes." Walker bobbed his head repeatedly, unable to control himself.

"Right, well, here." She shook the cup a little.

"No," he chuckled, the sound coming out more like a nervous cackle mixed with air. "I mean, yes, I would like to be your friend, and no, I don't want the coffee back. I don't have time for a love life. Also, you've now put your mouth on it too many times, and I think that would put me at a higher risk of getting your flesh-eating bacteria." Not a second later, there was a sharp pain on Walker's arm where Talia had socked him, surprisingly hard for someone so small. "Ow!"

"You should know if we're going to be friends that I fight back." Talia grinned.

"You should know my one rule for our friendship is that you

can't fall in love with me," Walker shot back with a cocky lift of his chin.

"Oh, trust me, you would have to do a hell of a lot more than just look pretty for me to fall in love with you," Talia retorted.

"So, you think I look pretty?" He gave her a lopsided smirk.

"Do you want me to hit you again?" Talia raised her fist, and Walker took a large step back.

"Not particularly, no."

"All right, then, it's settled. We are officially friends." Talia stuck out her hand like it was a full-fledged business agreement.

"Do people usually shake on shit like this?" Walker wondered, already taking her hand and giving it a firm jerk.

"*We* do."

She was stubborn as hell. He liked it.

"So, can I ask a favor?" Walker asked, dropping Talia's hand before he had the urge to linger in the handhold.

"Already? You move quick."

"Okay, it's not for me. Will you check on Piper? I can give you her number. I don't know if I'm the right person to help her with certain things, and her mom's gone. I wouldn't ask, but since you gave me such good advice on tampons and we're now friends..."

"We've been texting all morning." Talia held up her phone, revealing a back-and-forth conversation between herself and Piper.

"Oh." Walker blinked. "Does she know that..."

"That my dad killed her parents? Yes," Talia replied bluntly.

"Okay. Well, I guess I'll see you around, then?" Unsure of how exactly to proceed from there, he finger-gunned the air and clicked his tongue like an idiot.

"Yeah, you have my number." Talia waved and walked off toward what Walker assumed was a rental car thanks to her run-in with Marty's massive truck. At least, if she was going to ram into anyone, Marty was the best option. The guy was basically all smiles all the time, no matter *what* happened to him. Marty owned the local gas station closest to Cole and Paisley's house and was always way too chipper in the mornings for Walker's taste. His overly friendly vibe was just plain annoying. Walker was usually gruff and took a no-bullshit stance on most things, but Talia made him feel like he was about to give Marty a run for his money.

When Walker sat down in the seat of his mom-mobile, he couldn't stop the smile from plastering his face. For someone who was annoyed by peppy people, he was doing a poor job of showing it. Between laughing with Piper that morning, having an anxiety attack, and coffee with Talia, he needed a freaking nap. There was no way people were meant to experience such an extreme range of emotions all in one day.

SEVEN

TALIA

"Girl, you are playing with fire."

The accusation came with raised eyebrows and a slow, not altogether disapproving shake of Amala's head. Talia's short explanation of her newfound friendship with Walker had made Amala immediately suspicious. Talia couldn't blame her, either. Somewhere out there, a bullshit meter was flying off the charts with every Walker-related sentence Talia tried to pass off as cool and casual.

"I don't see how," Talia lied through her teeth with a small, secretive smile. Amala followed closely as Talia walked in the direction of her office in the back of Lydia's Grocery. "Also, why are you even here? You're not supposed to be working today. What happened to staying in your pajamas all day and watching reality TV?"

"I'm a mom. That was wishful thinking—I didn't even get to sleep in. The little brat woke me up at six a.m. blaring some awful pop song. Plus, you said you wanted to talk to me about something, and this is kind of like reality TV. I can live vicariously through your poor decision-making skills." Amala reached down to pick up a can that had fallen off one of the shelves and put it back in its place.

"No working," Talia scolded, smacking the top of Amala's hand.

"You took over half of my job. I don't know what to do with all this extra time now!" Amala whined.

"It was never your job. Jeff never did what he was supposed to, and you took over so everyone wouldn't lose their jobs when he inevitably ran the store into the ground. I've seen the numbers. I saw how much you had to allocate to his liquor fund every month." Talia walked into her office and motioned for Amala to sit.

"Well, Jeff never really marked anything out of inventory. He'd just come in, grab the things he wanted, and walk out. I had to account for it somehow. Between that and having the staff notify me when they saw him come in so I could figure out what items he left with using the security cameras, we made it work." As if it wasn't a big deal, Amala shrugged, unaware that to everyone who worked at Lydia's, she was a hero.

"Don't sell yourself short. I know how much of a pain in the ass it must have been. Speaking of, I have something for you." Talia grinned in excitement, pulling out a manila envelope and holding it out to Amala. "I was going to wait till tomorrow, but seeing as you're here..."

"What is it?" Amala narrowed her apprehensive eyes onto the envelope.

"You could open it, and that'll probably tell you," Talia said, shaking the envelope in Amala's face.

The envelope was snatched out of Talia's hand a second later when Amala conceded to her curiosity. Inside, the tabbed and marked packet waited for signatures. When Amala pulled the papers out, she stared down at them for several long seconds before her head snapped up in surprise.

"Are you serious?"

"Of course I am. Unless you don't want to. You were already

doing all the work for it. I just showed up out of nowhere and took over. You deserve it, and I wouldn't want to do this with anyone else." Talia smiled and reached out to grab Amala's hand, giving it a reassuring squeeze. "I am going to want to make some improvements, but those are all outlined in the ownership agreement that I had made by a third party so you know it's not biased."

"Biased? I wasn't even expecting five percent stake in the store, let alone fifty! I can't take this." Amala shook her head wildly and slapped the packet down onto Talia's desk. "You're not even making me buy you out of the other half!"

"You already paid for it with your blood, sweat, and tears. You have more of a right to Lydia's than I do, and I'm still taking the other fifty percent!" Talia argued and grabbed a pen from the holder on her desk, holding it out to Amala. "We'll be partners. Take it, Amala. This place will only be better now that Jeff Cohen has nothing to do with it. You and I, we can make this something even better than you already have. You deserve to own the whole thing outright, but I quit my job and moved here, so I have to—"

"You're insane," Amala cut her off.

"That's the second time I've been called that today. Walker's words were actually you're *fucking* insane, but close enough."

"He would add 'fucking' to it, considering I'm sure that's exactly what he wants to do to you," Amala smirked and grabbed the pen from Talia's outstretched hand.

"Okay, I walked right into that one, but I'm going to firmly reiterate that *that* will not be happening," Talia said defiantly.

"What won't be happening?" a low, masculine voice called out from the doorway. Talia's eyes went wide in alarm as she stared at the source of the interruption. Walker leaned casually against the doorframe, Piper beside him wearing more appropriate clothes than the day before. Amala looked over to the newcomers and then back to Talia, just about ready to break out the popcorn.

"Nothing. It's not important." Talia quickly side-stepped

Walker's question, hoping he hadn't overheard Amala's colorful presumptions.

Talia was still trying to wrap her head around why she had suggested a friendship with Walker to begin with. Rationalizing was the only way she could get around it. If they were going to continually run into each other, as the universe would have it, being friends would be beneficial to them both. Walker needed assistance with things he could never understand about his nieces, and Talia needed to know more than three people total in town. The arrangement wasn't so odd, and finding him attractive wasn't going to be a problem. Objectively, Walker was hot. Most women and men would agree. It was hard to miss. But Talia was confident in her ability to appreciate someone's physical attributes while remaining completely platonic with them.

"What are you guys up to?" Talia steered the conversation to something more suitably matched for the friend zone.

"We're grocery shopping," Piper announced cheerily.

"It's part of her punishment for playing fugitive last night," Walker explained.

"Also, you suck at shopping and cooking?" Talia tilted her head to the side, looking up at Walker.

"Dammit! How do you do that?" Walker threw up his hands in exasperation.

"Piper told me about the chicken parm incident," Talia laughed, rising from her seat.

"I don't know why everyone insists on calling it an 'incident.' They were only a little burnt, and who doesn't like burnt cheese?" Walker argued.

"Oh, I like burnt cheese," Amala cut in, raising her hand.

"Thank you!" Walker grinned and pointed a thumb at Amala. "I like her."

"This is Amala. She's married, has an eight-year-old, and is two months pregnant, so I think you're going to have to tone down the flirting."

"Shoot, missed my chance," Walker played along, winking at

Amala, who pretended to faint in her chair from the attention.

"Something tells me I am not at all your type." Amala glanced over at Talia with a rueful smile, and Talia fought the urge to smack her. Instead, Talia glared back, loudly declaring in her head and with her eyes what she was sure Amala already knew her response would be.

I'm not his type either. We're just friends.

Luckily, Walker didn't seem to notice any tension, too focused on the small gagging sound Piper let out, apparently not enjoying the conversation about her uncle's prospects.

"My *type* is someone who wants five mostly teenage kids who enjoy putting me through the ringer." Walker glared down at his niece, who cringed apologetically. Talia looked away, trying to convince herself that he did *not* look at her when he had said the words *my type*. Her mind was playing tricks on her again. "Unless Mother Teresa wants to pop out of her grave any time soon."

"Ah, so you're into old, deceased women, then?" Talia chimed in, thankful for the opportunity to keep the conversation light and casual.

"Oh, absolutely. Who doesn't want a woman who has random mints floating around in her purse and smells like Irish Spring soap?" Walker mused. Talia let out a loud cackle in response, and Walker returned a smile in her direction, beaming with pride that his joke had landed.

"Did you need help shopping? I'm off today, but Talia can assist you." Amala held her palm up, gesturing to Talia like she was offering her up on a silver platter. With a tick of her jaw, Talia made a mental note to lay into Amala later for her blatant meddling. Walker was a grown-ass man. He could go grocery shopping on his own.

"I mean... I was just saying hi 'cause I believe that's typically how friendships work, but sure, why not." Walker shrugged. "I don't know what I'm doing, and Piper only pretends she knows what she's doing."

"Hey!" Piper shouted in disagreement.

"On that note, I need to take this," Amala raised up the ownership paperwork, "to my husband so I can brag about my accomplishments and so he can feel like he's a part of my super important legal team that doesn't exist." She stood up and slid the packet back into the manila envelope before swiping a pen off the desk. "And I'm stealing this."

"Won't be stealing if you accept the proposal," Talia pointed out. She stole a glance at Walker, who was leaning on the doorframe again, watching them with interest.

"Let's do dinner later?" Amala followed Talia's gaze. "Walker, you are welcome to come if you like. Cooper is in my daughter's class. He's a sweet kid. I'm making jambalaya, so it'll be a celebration."

"So, you're taking half-stake in the store, then?" Talia pried at Amala before Walker could accept the invite.

"We'll see." Amala smirked, feigning an edge of mystery. Talia already knew she would take it. She was way too ambitious not to.

Now following the conversation, Walker stood up straighter and flashed a smile at Amala. "Congratulations! But did you miss the five kids part? I wouldn't want to impose."

"Pish posh. I may have just come into some money," Amala shimmied her shoulders. "I'll make more food. You're coming."

"Um... oh-kay," Walker nodded awkwardly as Amala excused herself, pushing past him and Piper and leaving without another word. Talia made her way around her desk, amused at the flabbergasted expression on Walker's face.

"There's no point in arguing with her. She's bullied me into going to her house for dinner three times this week. Shall we get started on your shopping list, then?"

"Shopping list... right." Walker grimaced. "And if I was just going to randomly look up recipes on my phone and go off that?"

"You don't have a *list*?" Piper's mouth fell open, as if her uncle's lack of preparation was an egregious and personal offense against her.

"Well, maybe you are the one who should have made one,

considering this is *your* punishment," Walker took on a mock-parental tone, pointing at his niece sternly.

Talia gestured to the two guest chairs in front of her desk. "I've got paper and writing utensils. Take a seat, and we'll plan all of this out."

A half-hour of bickering later, they had their list, complete with Piper's meal schedule. After Walker's adamant monologue that Pop-Tarts were their own food group and a brief spat over whether or not they should buy a coffee maker that didn't look like a time machine, of which Talia had been the tie breaker—*no, Walker, you don't need a new one, just read the directions*—Talia was feeling more comfortable in her friendship with Walker. He was surprisingly funny, and she actually found his random sparks of spontaneity intriguing. Prior to the accident, she imagined that there probably wasn't a more fly-by-the-seat-of-their-pants person than Walker Hartrick. His brand of random decision-making was something she was missing in her life. The most spontaneous thing she'd ever done was move from New York, and that had still been an agonizing decision for her, despite having no real reason to stay.

After her engagement fell through, Talia knew how things would play out. Her friends would feel the need to choose sides or feel obligated to trash on her ex, Clifford, in her presence, and that wasn't how she wanted things to go down. It was no one's fault that they didn't work out, but she couldn't very well be around him nursing her broken heart after three years of wasted time, nor could she allow the friends they had made together to feel like they couldn't be in his life. So, she had done the logical, practical thing and spared everyone from the drama of the aftermath. Even her brief respite into spontaneity had been a clear and calculated risk. Walker seemed to be the type of person who took risks and went on adventures at the drop of a hat.

In the end, Talia was surprised by how easy it was to up and leave everything. Her friendships had been mostly surface-level, a fact she only realized because of Amala, and now Walker, who was already weaseling his way deeper into her life than her friends in NYC ever did. She had hated every second she spent working at Braxton, Bell, and Whitman Attorneys at Law, despite being good at her job, and her mother passed away over a year before everything went to shit. If her mom were still alive, it would have been reason enough to stay, but after she passed, the only person tying Talia to the city was Clifford. And after much debate, he had decided that his life would no longer include her.

Despite the gut punch of knowing that she wasn't enough, Talia couldn't blame Cliff, couldn't even find it in herself to hate him. It would have been nice to have something to despise him for, but occasionally leaving the toilet seat up in their apartment or putting the empty milk jug back in the fridge did not constitute reason enough to hate him. It was too bad he didn't cheat on her with one of her friends or have some other irreparable flaw that she could declare as the real reason for their breakup.

Cliff had their whole life planned out for them from the second they met. That extreme amount of stability was what had attracted Talia to him in the first place. She and her mom had scrambled to make ends meet when she was younger, and she craved the kind of life that Clifford had—perfect on and off paper. It hadn't been a particularly exciting relationship, but she *had* loved him.

Walker was the definition of not her type, and Talia was fully planning on clinging to that knowledge so as not to be distracted by his charm and devil-may-care intrigue. There would be no falling in love with Walker Hartrick, because Talia had always been into men who had all of their ducks in a row. *Cliff* had his ducks in a row, and so would any future men in her life.

"Should we do this?" Walker stood abruptly from his chair, tearing Talia away from her thoughts. "I kind of feel like I could take on the world now that I have a list."

"Calm down, Han Solo," Talia chided, getting up from her own seat. "We have to prevent you from impulse buying, so we're going to the produce section first."

"Hey, I am not impulsive!" The ever-present scowl reappeared on Walker's face, and he folded his arms. An urge to do something or say something to bring back his smile welled up inside Talia.

"Yes, you are," Piper deadpanned.

"I have a retirement fund, and I regularly go to the dentist!" Walker stated with confidence.

"I'm glad. You're going to need to continue doing both those things so you can keep frivolously eating Pop-Tarts till you're old and gray." Talia set her hands on Walker's back and shoved him out of her office to get the ball rolling, trying to smother the sharp breath she took when she touched him again.

Eager to jump subjects in her thoughts right over Walker's body, Talia turned to Piper and loudly declared that she would get the cart before shuffling off to do so. For the rest of their time in the store, Talia focused all her energy on training Walker how to shop and directed most of the personal questions to Piper. Now that Piper wasn't spewing every drunken thought that came to her mind, she worked as a nice buffer. Talia gleaned all new information on Walker from the tiny morsels he gave while commenting on Piper's responses. Telling herself repeatedly that the lack of conversation with Walker was just due to their new friendship and testing out the waters, Talia hoarded a list of her own in the back of her head: things she was desperate to know about Walker Hartrick.

The entire time they shopped together, Talia had to stop herself from revealing all her secrets and telling her entire life story. What was it about Walker that made her feel like she had known him her entire life but could simultaneously never know enough about him? She didn't like being out of control, and she would be damned if he was the one to make her lose it. Everything about him felt equal parts exhilarating, terrifying, and frustrating. He was a thrill she couldn't quite ignore.

Eight

WALKER

The bright lighting above the mirror in Cole's master bathroom cast Walker's face in a glow that almost made him look refreshed, save for the dark circles under his eyes. He scrutinized his reflection and button-down shirt and tilted his head to run a hand along his newly trimmed beard. He reminded himself, yet again, that it was his bathroom now. There was no reason he should feel like an intruder for being in there, nor should he be so incredibly anal about not leaving any hair behind. He must have checked the sink four times before deciding that it was clean enough that Paisley wasn't going to turn over in her grave to yell at him about leaving his "face pubes" everywhere. It was what she had always called Walker's facial hair from the time he had started growing it in high school because she knew he hated it. The car accident was probably the one and only time in Paisley's life where she didn't have the upper hand.

Walker muttered a curse under his breath, changing his anger's course toward his sister-in-law and the powers that be. Paisley should have told God that he could shove it. That she and Cole were staying with their family, right where they belonged. It felt good for a moment to blame someone for their deaths now that he couldn't blame Talia. He'd already spent so much of his time hoping Jeff Cohen was enjoying hell that blaming someone new felt less taxing.

It was the oddest thing after they were gone—the things Walker expected to remember of them weren't what came to mind. Of course there were the good memories, the fond recollections of the types of people Cole and Paisley were, but then there were the little things Walker never would have imagined mattered. The realization that his sister-in-law was never going to insult his facial hair ever again knocked the wind out of him like a punch to the stomach. His brother wouldn't hound him about settling down anymore. No one would be bringing up the one girl Walker brought to family dinner more than once purely because he was bored and didn't feel like eating takeout again. Cole had taken it as a sign that Walker was finally getting serious about someone, so Walker had made sure to not make that same mistake twice. Girls came to dinner once, but after that, they never lasted long enough to leave a permanent impression on his family.

That specific girl, if he recalled correctly, ignored Cooper's questions so many times at the table that Walker found it reason enough to dump her. His nephew was only five at the time, so the questions were a little repetitive and annoying, but Walker always managed to find the time to answer each and every one. Cooper's curiosity was integral to his personality, and his investigative nature was definitely going to take him places in life (whether that be the FBI or a jail cell). If Walker was going to break his lone ranger routine, then it sure as hell wouldn't be with a woman who dulled the sparkle in his nephew's eyes. Once that light was gone, it was hard to get back, and Walker was determined to fight tooth and nail to make sure it would never be snuffed out of any of Cole's kids.

The last time Walker wore a collared shirt was when he interviewed for his current job. He had half a mind to take it off and replace it with his normal casual wear so it didn't seem like he was trying too hard. Amala was the first person to invite him and the kids over for dinner since Cole and Paisley died, and Walker wanted to make a good impression. One that would get Amala to invite them back. He'd been shut out from most of the world, holed up in the house for so long, that loneliness had become a constant. To say he was hard-up for adult conversation would be an understatement.

The friends Walker had before his life became chock-full of responsibilities were like him: living in bachelor pads, dating around, and enjoying a detached lifestyle. It wasn't like he expected them to host a dinner party that included five kids, but to have someone, *anyone*, care about whether his family was eating properly was nice. Plus, Amala was pregnant and already had one daughter, so she had to know something about the whole parenting thing. He ought to pick her brain.

As he made his way downstairs, straightening his shirt against his torso to rid any wrinkles—he wasn't fancy enough to get out the iron—Walker caught one look at Carter and pointed toward the staircase, shaking his head.

"Go change."

"Why?" Carter complained, looking down at his Barenaked Ladies graphic tee. "It's a band!"

"Somehow, I have an inkling that you only bought the shirt because it's an inappropriate name. If you can name one song by them, I'll let you wear that," Walker challenged. Carter thought for a moment and opened his mouth like he was going to name one before Walker cut him off quickly. "Too late. Go change into something nicer."

"Trying to impress Talia?" Piper came down the stairs in one of her usual outfits that didn't scream *I'm having an affair with a senator.*

"We're just friends," Walker replied coolly, hoping his voice didn't waver. He would be lying if he said he didn't want to look nice in front of Talia. The woman could wear a paper bag and pull it off, but he was fully intending to lie to his family (and himself) about his attraction to her. No one needed to know that his thoughts occasionally ventured away from platonic to taking her against any flat surface in the vicinity. Walker was far from a saint, but he'd be surprised to find any warm-blooded, single guy out there who didn't take one look at Talia's glowy olive skin, wavy hair, and full lips and not want to—

Be punched so hard in the nose that his face concaves.

The thought of other men thinking of Talia that way made Walker's blood boil. Jaw ticking, he unclenched his fists and refrained from thinking further on it. Talia was his friend, so of course he wouldn't want a bunch of men objectifying her. His body's reaction was because of *chivalry*. Sure, that chivalry happened to look a hell of a lot like jealousy, but it *wasn't*. Because he said so.

"Who's Talia?" Colin came down the stairs with Cooper and Pearl on his tail.

"A girl?" Pearl asked excitedly. She was just like her parents, lighting up at the mere idea of Walker having prospects. Of Cole and Paisley's kids, Pearl was the romantic. It was good to know that she hadn't completely taken her head out of the clouds after her parents' deaths. She was still in there somewhere.

"A *friend* who is a girl," Walker replied. "She'll be at dinner tonight, but I should probably tell you... um."

"Her last name is Cohen," Piper offered. The realization dawned on Colin's face immediately, but Pearl and Cooper didn't catch on.

"Technically, she's Jeff Cohen's daughter. She didn't know him and hasn't seen him in almost twenty years," Walker explained, feeling the need to defend Talia to the kids.

"She's really nice. She picked me up when I was drunk and took me home," Piper added, an edge of defensiveness playing into her voice as well.

"You got *drunk*?" Colin's eyes went wide, and his face flipped to anger. "After everything that happened? Why would you do that, Piper?"

Colin's reaction was the exact reason Walker had refrained from mentioning why exactly he'd grounded Piper. Colin was adamantly against drinking, even more so now due to the circumstances of his parents' death. Splitting his attention between the two siblings, Walker tried to find the right words to reign in what he was sure to be a heated argument.

"It was just one time, Colin," Piper snapped. "I'm not planning on doing it again."

"Alcohol ruins lives!" Colin shouted, coming to stand in front of his sister and pointing at her. "Are you trying to die, too? What kind of example are you setting for Carter, Pearl, and Cooper if you're out getting smashed on the weekends? Mom and Dad didn't even drink, and they *still* died. Do you even know the statistics for—"

"That's enough!" Walker yelled over Colin.

"I don't think it's nearly enough." Colin scrunched his nose in fury.

"Sit. Down." Walker aggressively motioned to the stool at the island, but Colin didn't budge. "You don't dole out the punishments. I do. Piper learned her lesson, and you screaming in her face isn't going to make anything better."

"I'm eighteen in four months. I'll be responsible for them soon enough," Colin said matter-of-factly.

"What?" Walker blinked. There was an extra layer of meaning to Colin's words, something that was flying over Walker's head.

"I'm not going to college. When I become everyone's guardian, I won't be able to go to school," Colin replied simply.

Walker's brain short-circuited. He hadn't once considered that Colin would think to take over as head of the household.

"No." Walker set his jaw sternly. "You are going to college."

"I already told Johns Hopkins that I wasn't attending next year. This is just the way it has to be." Colin's mouth formed a straight line. Walker's reciprocating snort was a mixture of anger, amusement, and pride at how much of a man Colin had become.

"Abso-fucking-lutely not. You're forgetting that I used to

wipe your ass. You'll call them back tomorrow and re-enroll immediately." When Colin opened his mouth to interrupt, Walker held his hand up in a stop and continued. "*I* am everyone's guardian, and I'm not leaving an eighteen-year-old to fend for himself and four kids. Your eighteenth birthday will be just that: an eighteenth birthday. A fun milestone in your life that makes you legal to vote and nothing more. I am no longer the fun uncle, Colin. I do not *want* to be. I am responsible for all of you, and I will not be passing that responsibility to you. Ever. All of you." Walker turned to face each of the siblings, Carter coming back down the stairs finally. "You will be living your life just as you would have if your parents were still alive because, dammit, I am your parent now, and I refuse, *refuse* to let anything stand in the way of the dreams that you had before they died. They would not want you to throw your lives away, and neither do I."

"Aren't *you* throwing your life away on us?" Colin asked, analytical as ever.

"No. I'm giving mine more of a purpose," Walker stated with zero hesitation. "Now, we've been invited by a nice family to have dinner, and we are going because we need to get out of this fucking house occasionally and be around people who are alive and well. So please, for the love of God, everyone get in the car."

The drive to Amala's house was a silent one. Walker churned over his speech in his head, wondering if he had said the right thing. He could have at least left the profanities out, but he had been too riled up to keep the occasional "fuck" from slipping out of his mouth, because *fuck* if he was going to allow Colin to forfeit his full ride to college, and *fuck* if he was going to let any of them put their dreams on hold. Over his dead *fucking* body.

When Walker pulled up to the curb outside of Amala's house, he threw the car in park and sucked in a deep breath, releasing it slowly as he closed his eyes.

"Can we just relax and have fun tonight? Do we think we can handle that?" Walker turned to look around the cab of the car, witnessing several heads bobbing in agreement. He turned to Colin in the passenger seat, staring out the window with a stony expression. "Colin? Think you can remove the shitty look on your face for a few hours and enjoy some food that doesn't involve me ruining another pan and burning dinner?" The joke worked, and Colin cracked a slight smile, conceding with a bob of his head. Everyone piled out of the car, and Walker sent up a silent prayer to Cole and Paisley to appeal to God on his behalf so they could have a pleasant, drama-free evening. He felt there needed to be a third party involved in his conversation with God considering the inappropriate thoughts he was bound to have about Talia that the big man in the sky would certainly not approve of. Paisley could talk a sleazy used car salesman into buying the car he was supposed to be selling her, so Walker was sure she could convince God that he wasn't *that* bad of a guy.

When they made it to the front door, Walker flattened his shirt again, cursing himself for not using an iron earlier. He raised his fist to the front door. Before his knuckles even made contact, the door whipped open by itself. Walker stared into the empty doorway in confusion until he noticed the tiny girl, no more than four feet tall with poofy space buns atop her head, standing below him with a wild look about her.

"Finally! I've been waiting! You're a whole two minutes late!" The girl reached out and latched onto Cooper's arm, yanking him inside. The rest of the kids exchanged a mutual glance of amusement and followed in after their brother. Given the girl's immediate recognition of Cooper, Walker figured she must be Amala's daughter, as if the attitude and the resemblance wasn't a dead giveaway to begin with. "Come on! Everyone's on the back porch."

They obeyed the girl's commands without question, following her through a sliding glass door onto a small wooden deck with a glass table, a dark green umbrella slotted into the hole in the center. The deck looked older but also freshly stained, judging by the bucket of wood finish perched on the edge of the railing. A large willow tree with a rope swing hanging from one of the thicker branches shaded one side of the yard. On the other side was a play structure that looked homemade, a bunch of nailed-together two-by-fours with a metal slide, complete with a sand pit. A family lived here.

Talia, Amala, and a tall man Walker assumed was Amala's husband were already seated around the table. The man looked extremely familiar, but Walker couldn't exactly place him.

"Did my daughter introduce herself, or did she just boss everyone around?" Amala stood up from her chair with a reprimanding glare in her daughter's direction. On cue, the tiny spitfire curtsied dramatically.

"Hi, I'm Jayla. Coop already knows me. Don't you, Coop?" Jayla smacked Cooper's back like he was an old friend, and Walker attempted to hold in his laughter when his nephew flinched.

"We both have Mrs. Rensie," Cooper affirmed quietly, looking terrified to contradict anything that came out of Jayla's mouth.

"It's nice to meet you, Jayla. I'm Walker." He crouched down to her height to make eye contact and pointed to the rest of the kids. "That's Colin, Piper, Carter and Pearl."

"Oh, I know," Jayla said confidently. Walker couldn't help the smile that broke out on his face. "Cooper talks about his siblings a lot. You guys are all named after the first letters of your parents' names, right? The girls are all 'P's and the boys are all 'C's?"

"How did I not notice that before?" Talia mused.

"It's very annoying when you're trying to call out people's names and they start with the same letters." Walker stood up from his crouched position and automatically took his seat next to Talia, drawn to her like a magnet. "I take it Amala accepted your proposal?" Walker smiled, noticing the manila envelope sitting in front of her.

"She did!" Amala's husband spoke up and stuck out his hand.

"I'm Roscoe, and I believe we've met before." Walker shook his hand, hoping there wouldn't be a pop quiz on where they knew each other from. "Don't sweat it, I'm not expecting you to remember. Probably don't want to remember anyway. I sure as hell don't. I'm a police officer."

"Oh," Walker choked, the memory coming back in an unpleasant flash.

Roscoe was the one who showed up at Walker's apartment to deliver the news about Cole and Paisley. When Walker had originally opened the door, he thought Roscoe was there because the downstairs neighbor was a crotchety old man who frequently called the cops when Walker's TV was a notch too loud or if he so much as dropped a broom in his kitchen. He only vaguely remembered the life-shattering conversation that ended with his fist punching a hole through the drywall next to his front door and collapsing to the ground in a crumpled heap. It was like some sort of sick joke.

Walker wasn't sure how Roscoe managed to get him off the floor, into his patrol vehicle, and over to Cole's house so that they could break all his nieces' and nephews' hearts. He recalled there being some sort of pep talk, but the only part he remembered was Roscoe saying *they need you.* In the end, that was all the ammunition Walker needed. He got everyone through day one with sheer willpower and tunnel vision.

"Beer?" Roscoe offered, holding up his own bottle.

"Walker doesn't drink, either," Talia answered for him.

"Fair enough. Tastes like piss water anyway 'cause Amala got the wrong kind." Roscoe shrugged, took a swig, and grimaced in disgust.

"Well, we never buy beer! Plus, the new girl we just hired at the store was giving me the evil eye for buying it while pregnant. She apparently thought I was going to sit in the parking lot on my break chugging a six pack!" Amala laughed.

"I mean, you did devour that strawberry milk I brought you the other day," Talia pointed out.

"Strawberry milk is definitely a gateway drug," Walker tacked on.

"You know, I tried to get her addiction under control before we got married, but I guess flavored milk is more important than me," Roscoe jumped in, sighing like his wife's fondness for lactose was the worst thing that could possibly happen to a marriage. "You guys want soda?"

Roscoe gestured to the remaining teenagers left on the deck while Pearl and Cooper were dragged away to the sand pit and wooden play structure in the backyard by the formidable Jayla. Walker leaned back in his chair, hands laced behind his head as he took everything in. Piper and Talia were giggling over something on Piper's phone. Roscoe gave his wife a teasing smack on the lips before dumping his beer over the side of the deck. Amala rolled her eyes at her husband then took a seat on his lap at the table, reminding Walker a little of the kind of marriage Cole and Paisley had, playful and adoring.

It was easy how everything fell into place. Out of everyone at the table, Roscoe had seen Walker at his worst, and yet Walker felt no judgment from the man. Instead, there was a quiet respect behind Roscoe's eyes. A silent conversation between the two of them that said *they needed you and you were there* and *I'm trying*. Walker gave him a microscopic nod of his head, and for the first time since the accident, breathing didn't feel like an Olympic event.

NINE

WALKER

Dinner was phenomenal. It was the kind of next-level cooking that Walker could only dream of doing himself. He'd only had jambalaya one other time, and it was nothing compared to the out-of-body experience he'd had eating Amala's. Piper hit up the chef for the recipe two bites in, and the prospect of eating the jambalaya again was already making Walker salivate.

"Tal, you know how I said I wasn't looking for any sort of romantic relationship?" Walker asked, grinning from ear to ear, the spices in his mouth still burning his tongue and clearing out his nostrils.

"Uh... yeah?" Talia drew out her words cautiously. Walker figured it either had to be because she was genuinely worried about the direction of the conversation or because of the impromptu nickname that slipped out of his mouth like they'd already been friends for years. *Nice one, genius.*

"I changed my mind. I want to date this jambalaya. Actually," Walker swung out his chair, got down on one knee dramatically, and mimicked holding out a ring. "I'm prepared to propose marriage. Tal, you can be my best man. Roscoe, you'll be the maid of honor. Fuck gender roles."

The second he said it, Walker cringed. He was such an idiot. Why the hell did he always do such stupid shit around Talia?

"Excuse me, I don't have a role in this wedding? I literally made the love of your life," Amala feigned offense, coming in to save Walker's ass from embarrassing himself further. "The disrespect!"

"I would *never* forget you! You're officiating, obviously." Walker sat back down in his seat, glancing at Talia to see if any part of his ridiculous routine had made her smile.

"Dearly beloved, we are gathered here today, yada yada, you may now kiss the... rice concoction." Amala gestured wildly to Walker's bowl, and he shoved a large spoonful of jambalaya into his mouth on command, closing his eyes for effect. Why not go full send on this terrible rendition of a *Whose Line Is It Anyway?* episode?

"It's time for my toast as the best man!" Talia tapped her fork against her aluminum soda can, the picture of class, and stood up from her seat, drawing everyone's attention to her.

Oh my God, she's actually rolling with this.

"From the time I met the two of you, I knew you were fated to be together. It's been wonderful to watch the jambalaya really delve into their relationship and into Walker's stomach. Here's to a really... spicy wedding night." Talia winked at Walker, and a piece of his new bride lodged in his throat, sending him into an unhinged coughing fit.

Despite the rough start to the night, Colin and Piper seemed to be enjoying themselves, laughing hysterically at Talia's speech and Walker's subsequent hay fever episode. Carter, on the other hand, sat silently in his chair, eating and ignoring everyone. Walker had attempted to rope him into a conversation a few times throughout dinner, but his nephew was completely uninterested. Other than the great T-shirt change fiasco, Walker wasn't sure what had Carter in such a sour mood. Crisis with the jambalaya averted and his breathing finally under control, Walker eyed Carter with concern. Usually Carter would be chomping at the bit to poke fun at his witless uncle.

"So, Carter, how's school going?" Talia asked, giving Walker a knowing look. Her telepathy skills were always a shock to his system. He'd never had the kind of connection with someone where he could communicate without words. And God, he wanted to show her how much he could communicate with body language alone. But that was not on the roster. Friendships didn't involve tangling in the sheets and... doing other things that Walker chided himself for even thinking about.

"It's fine." Carter's blunt and direct reply was enough to pull Walker out of his daydream.

"Mind telling me why you're being so rude?" Walker asked, raising his eyebrows.

"Mind telling me why you're flirting with someone whose father murdered Mom and Dad?" Carter shoved back his seat, and Walker shoved back his own, shooting a worried look over to Talia as Carter took off through the house, leaving the sliding glass door open like he was born in a damn barn.

"It's okay," Talia murmured.

"No, it's not. I apologize. He's just looking for someone to blame." Walker sighed, carding his hands through his hair in frustration. "I'll be right back."

They made it through the house and out to the street before Walker caught up. Carter was aiming to take off down the road, but Walker had no intention to allow him to get away with his behavior. He knew the kid's thought process because it had been his own when he had first met Talia. He had been wrong. Seeing his nephew hold the same grudge was a slap in the face and the payback he no doubt deserved.

"Carter!" Walker shouted to get him to stop, voice coming out harsh and flat.

"What? What do you want? Her to be my new mommy?" Carter wrinkled his nose furiously.

"I *want* you to go back in there and apologize. That was wildly inappropriate, rude, and not at all the kid that I know!" Walker glared.

"How can you possibly like her?"

"I am *friends* with her because she has been nothing but helpful. She is not a damned thing like her father. She didn't even know him, Carter!" His voice escalated, unable to hold it together.

"Well, she's related to him, so she must have some of his blood," Carter said coldly.

"Oh, is that how it works? By your account, both your dad and I should've had some kind of substance use disorder."

"That's not the same—"

"It is the exact same. Should I atone for all of my father's misdeeds? If she's responsible, then we all are."

Carter's gaze fell to the ground, and his voice grew more pained. "Do you think I'll end up like them?"

It took Walker a second to make the connection to what Carter was asking. When he did, he shook his head somberly.

"We make our own choices. If you don't want to be like your bio parents, you don't have to be. But your bio mom, she was brave for what she did. And I see a lot of that in you."

The word "brave" was an understatement. "Selfless" was more accurate. Carter's biological mother, Aliyah, knew from the second she found out she was pregnant that her baby wouldn't be safe in her world. The women's shelter Aliyah stayed at was a safe haven during the pregnancy, but it wasn't a forever solution. A closed adoption proved to be the best option after she met Paisley, who, at the time, volunteered at the shelter on the weekends. Soon after the adoption was finalized, Aliyah skipped town to get away from Carter's abusive biological father, who was none the wiser to her ever being pregnant. Carter would never be able to contact Aliyah because it could potentially put them both in danger, but Paisley and Cole made sure Aliyah's name was spoken often in their home as a pivotal person in Carter's life.

"What if I end up like *him*?" Carter's eyes pierced through Walker like daggers.

"You won't."

"I have all this... *anger* that I don't know what to do with." Carter looked down at his feet in shame. "Like I wish Talia's dad was alive so I could kill him. It's not fair that he's already dead, because I want to do it. That makes me like my father, doesn't it?"

"Being angry about injustice doesn't make you like him. It means you're grieving and that you care."

Carter stood in front of Walker, fists clenched for a few seconds before the tension released in his shoulders.

"I'd kill him myself if he was still alive," Walker admitted. "It would not bode well for the whole guardian situation, though, so it's better that he's already dead."

"I'm sorry." Carter swallowed. "I only heard part of your conversation with everyone earlier at the house about who she was, and I... clung to it." He averted his eyes, and Walker crossed the distance between them, setting his arm on Carter's shoulder.

"I did the same thing when I first met her. But then she helped me track your phone when you skipped school and brought Piper back to the house when she was sloshed and was adamant about making sure that your sister was okay, and I..." Walker shook his head, trying to clear the intrusive thoughts that kept popping up. He had to cut himself off before he went too far down a path that would land him in troubled waters, pining after someone who didn't like him that way and whom he could never be with.

"I see the way you look at her," Carter said simply.

Walker's knee-jerk reaction was to deny it, but Carter knew him too well. In a way, Carter was him. Lying to himself repeatedly about Talia was not working out well, but he knew he would continue to, even if it tortured him. She wasn't an option. He couldn't go there.

"It doesn't matter," Walker finally landed on an answer.

"Why?"

"Because I'm not going to, and will never, use my brother and your mom's death to find someone or to get laid. Jeff Cohen left her the store in his will. The only reason she even moved here, the only reason I met her was *because* they died," he said bluntly, knowing that laying it all out would be the only way Carter would understand. Carter nodded in immediate comprehension, and Walker squeezed his shoulders. "She deserves an apology, though."

Wordlessly, Carter stepped forward, Walker trailing behind him as they made their way back to the backyard. Eight pairs of eyes lifted to watch Carter when he stepped back onto the deck, shuffling over to Talia with an apology on his face. Talia glanced behind him at Walker, worrying her lip. Walker gave her a reassuring nod, then nudged Carter's shoulder to encourage him to start.

"I'm sorry. I shouldn't be blaming you for something your father did," Carter finally croaked, his voice coming out uneven. Walker focused on Talia's face and was surprised to find that even more sadness passed through her eyes. The urge to jump forward and pull her into his chest was so strong that his body went rigid with the need for it.

"Carter, can I tell you something?" Talia finally spoke up, her voice soft. Carter nodded silently. "It's not to make you feel bad, it's just so you know exactly where I'm at. When we... my mom and I, that is, when we left my dad, it was after he... hit me. The only time."

Walker's eyes went wide in alarm, unable to stop himself from lurching forward to take his rightful place by her side. She set her hand atop the table as an invitation. He took it without questioning it, firmly lacing his hands in hers for support. Carter slumped into the chair next to her, looking like the life had been sucked out of him, the sacrifice his biological mother made resonating more than ever before. Piper sniffed back tears on the other side of the table, and the furious face Colin wore earlier returned, this time for a different reason. Amala was unfazed, and it struck Walker then that she must have already been aware of Talia's past.

"Don't feel bad," Talia said quickly, shaking her head at everyone's reaction. "It was a long time ago. I just wanted to explain. I... he hit my mom a bunch of times before that, but I guess him hitting me was the last straw for her, and we left. The reason I'm telling you is because I want you to know that I *hate* him, too. My mother was everything kind and right in the world, and he put her through hell. Regardless, I want you to know that if me being in his life could have somehow stopped him from getting in that car that night, I would have done it. I would have stayed and endured everything so you could have your parents back, and I know my mom would be okay with me saying that she would have done the same. So, I am sorry. I wish I could've stopped him. I wish I could've done something to prevent this from happening."

Too many emotions swirled around in Walker's head, suffocating him. Anger, filling him up and pricking his fingertips with the violence he wanted to inflict on Jeff Cohen as he held Talia's hand tighter. Sorrow, both for Talia and her mother, a deep-seated pain for the way that the world worked. Shame for ever doubting what a wonderful person she was. Everything she said, she meant. Just as he would, Talia would have endured the unimaginable so Cole and Paisley's kids would never have to live another moment without their parents. Beyond every other emotion, affection settled into his bones. He was no longer warring with sexual desire alone. Fighting tooth and nail to deny that piece of their developing friendship was hard enough. Knowing her heart was also beautiful posed an even greater dilemma. She was the exact type of person his family needed. The kind he would have invited to family dinner more than once.

Before tonight, if Walker allowed his attraction to win out, he would have felt guilty, but he could have moved past it. His actions wouldn't have impacted everyone, just his own conscience. Now, he'd sucked his family into Talia's orbit. The second he crossed a line with her, things would get complicated.

When, not *if*, he inevitably failed, because he was a garbled mess of depression and anxiety without an added relationship, his nieces and nephews would lose yet another person. And he couldn't do that to them.

The conversation at the table took on a lighter note, but Walker was barely paying attention. He was vaguely aware of plans being made for Piper and Pearl to sleep over at Talia's for a spa night (which Jayla promptly invited herself to). When Colin pulled out a book, Talia let him go on and on about the latest studies on wildlife in the Sahara, and she genuinely seemed interested. It was magic the way she easily held conversations with the kids. Her laugh rang in Walker's ears like a sweet melody that turned solemn when he realized just how much his nieces and nephews had needed tonight. She felt like a glass of water after traveling in a wasteland for far too long. But she was really a tightrope over a canyon. If he swayed too far left or too far right, he'd fall and everything would come crashing down around him. There was no room for failure. No room for his family to lose even more than they already had. He wasn't allowed to fall in love with her, yet he couldn't help but feel like the ground was going to be pulled out from under him anyway.

You are completely and utterly fucked.

TEN

TALIA

The morning was never really underway without music, and that morning, the vibe was teenage angst. Talia blasted her playlist consisting entirely of the punk rock bands she used to listen to as a teenager, pretending to be rebellious while in reality being as strait-laced as they came. The angry songs about fathers abandoning their daughters and the world being absolute shit were her favorite. Scream-singing songs in the morning allowed her to present as the same organized person she normally did day-to-day. Plus, who wouldn't love to belt out a line that perfectly described how emo their internal thoughts were. Simple Plan's "Welcome to My Life" spoke to every person whether they had daddy issues or not, and Talia did have some of those. Fountains of Wayne spoke to the crushing feeling of having the hots for your girlfriend's mom (okay, she'd never experienced that, but it didn't stop her from whipping her hair around to "Stacey's Mom"). Then again, she'd probably be more inclined to Stacey's dad—see daddy issues. And Green Day? Well, that just made her want to throw on some heavy eyeliner and hide under a pile of blankets (in the best way possible).

Talia knew the next song by the first piano note. She was fully prepared to loudly proclaim the lyrics while pretending to have thick curtain bangs when the doorbell interrupted. Amala was supposed to pick her up so they could carpool to the coffee shop together, but she was about a half hour early.

The amount of space Walker was taking up in Talia's head lately was starting to unnerve her, and spending every morning at Roaster's Republic with him wasn't helping. Inviting along Amala as a buffer was the perfect plan. Amala had always been on team "please feel free to sleep with Walker and then immediately tell me about it," but she agreed to help reign in the sexual tension by tagging along to coffee that morning like some sort of weird chaperone. Hopefully having a tag-along would help Talia convince herself that she wasn't going just to see *him* every day. It was strictly because of her caffeine addiction.

There was no chance of a romantic relationship with Walker. He was still grieving, for heaven's sake. Still, Talia felt her mind keep playing tricks on her. She sometimes caught certain looks that said Walker wasn't completely against the idea of taking her to bed, always evaporating so quickly they left her wondering if she had imagined them. She often wondered if he felt the pang in his chest when they touched or the need to cross his legs to relieve the pent-up pressure—did men do that? All these thoughts were entirely inappropriate to be having for a friend who had no interest in anything other than platonic coffee-drinking and the occasional dinner party.

The touching was always casual—a light squeeze of her shoulders here, a gentle transfer of a coffee stirrer there. The fact that he noticed she liked to gnaw on the stir sticks and always had one ready for her when they sat together was another on the long list of reasons he made her feel seen. But there was nothing inherently romantic about Walker knowing she wanted to bite down on plastic every morning. Every touch and thoughtful gesture could easily pass as friendly and chaste. It was, in all likelihood, completely platonic.

Only a month had passed since Talia had first felt like slapping Walker across the face in the middle of the street. *Thirty days*. It was amazing what could change in the span of a second, let alone a month. It only took a single moment to turn your entire life on a dime. Meeting Walker felt like one of those occurrences. A thing to label the fractured pieces of your life as "before and after x event happened." She'd had a few of those moments in her lifetime: leaving Archwood when she was a kid, her mother dying, and the doctor's appointment that ripped her dreams out from under her. Today felt like another one of those days. The looming feeling of importance made her muscles stiff with anticipation.

Amala, being her new best friend, was well aware of Talia's habit of head-banging whilst brushing her teeth, cleaning, and basically everything else that involved being alone in her house, so Talia continued her loud rendition of "Welcome to the Black Parade" as she walked toward the door. A gust of wind blew back her disheveled, unstyled hair when she opened the front door, the toothbrush still dangling from her frothing lips. Walker stood on the front porch wearing an amused expression, and Talia quickly pulled the toothbrush out of her mouth with a gasp as she covered her lips with her hand.

"My Chemical Romance?" Walker grinned and pointed into the house, the music blasting away inside. Apparently, everyone her age had had a teen angst phase. Talia's had just never really went away.

"Mm-hmm?" Talia's response was both an affirmation of the music choice and a question that asked *what the hell are you doing here?*

"Amala's car broke down, so she called me to pick you, then her up, since we're all going to the same place," Walker explained, somehow understanding her toothpaste-garbled gibberish.

Talia did her best to hold back a scoff. She could smell the bullshit from a mile away, where Amala was probably looking out her front window at a fully-functioning car and patting herself on the back.

What a—and I mean this in the nicest, most "she's my best friend" way—bitch, Talia thought. Amala's house was closer to Walker's than Talia's was. Talia wouldn't have been shocked if Amala made up an excuse and claimed she wouldn't be ready in time, forcing Walker to drive out to Talia first. He was now a glorified chauffeur, showing up on her doorstep to her unabashedly loud morning anthem. Her half-brushed teeth and frizzy, untamed hair sticking out every which way were nothing short of mortifying.

Perfect.

"Uh, come in?" Talia blanched, and she held her hand firmly over her mouth to protect Walker from seeing the spray of toothpaste that inevitably came out when she spoke.

Nodding, Walker followed her inside, visibly unperturbed by her insanity. He bobbed his head along to the song when it got to the chorus. His reaction gave Talia a bit more insight into his music taste. While he wasn't screaming the lyrics like a deranged howler monkey, he was mumbling them, lips moving with the words.

Stop staring at his lips.

"I'm gonna..." Talia shoved the head of her toothbrush back into her mouth and awkwardly jabbed both thumbs down the hallway.

"Oh, yeah. Take your time. Sorry I'm so early." Walker smiled, his line of sight drifting over Talia's living room, surveying her bohemian wall decor and teal furniture. "I'll just wait here."

He sat on the couch in the same spot Talia had the night before, cramming extra-buttered popcorn into her mouth while she watched a documentary on mall Santa and prolific murderer, Bruce McArthur. There was almost a domesticity in the way Walker took his place in her house, like it was entirely normal for him to be there. She stood near the end of the other couch across the room, engrossed in the way he scanned each wall of her brightly colored living room. All the staring was definitely making her look like the next Bruce McArthur, but she couldn't help it.

"Are you gonna...?" Walker pointed toward the hallway Talia should have already been halfway down. She gave him a firm shake of her head before escaping to her room in embarrassment. The laws of physics said she had to look like a hot mess, minus the hot part, any time she was in Walker's presence. Talia ordered herself to finish getting ready at the speed of light so he wasn't sitting on her couch—which she hadn't double-checked for stray popcorn kernels—for too long.

After quickly pulling her hair into a high ponytail, a hairstyle that was cute but not the attractive beach curls she had been planning on, Talia applied a small amount of makeup and formulated a plan. She was going to walk back into her living room with the confidence of someone who was not at all humiliated that she once found the lead singer of All American Rejects extremely attractive. At least she didn't opt for her boy band playlist that morning and Walker hadn't walked in on a performance of the marionette doll routine from the "Bye Bye Bye" music video. He did not need to know that at one point she had dreams of dating someone with Justin Timberlake's top ramen hair. The playlist she chose that morning made her seem cool, even a little edgy.

You aren't lame, you're a badass. You aren't lame, you're a badass. Talia repeated it to herself like a mantra.

She stepped out of her room with her chin held high, her footsteps matching the drumbeat in the new song. Determined to make it seem like the booming noise level was perfectly ordinary, she refused to lower the volume before strutting back out to Walker. By default, her body had a mind of its own when it came to music. Walker, if the involuntary bouncing of his leg and use of pointer fingers as drumsticks was any indication, was just as into it as she was. He immediately stopped when he saw her and stood up, a grin spreading across his face that was, unfortunately, charming as hell.

"Okay, what is this? Old Fall Out Boy?" Walker asked as "Thnks fr th Mmrs" continued to play in surround sound.

"If you're going to diss Fall Out Boy, you better have a good reason." Talia set her hands on her hips, eyeing Walker sternly.

"I wouldn't dream of it, but I am going to need your Spotify username. I need this playlist in my life," Walker declared. His eyes flicked over her for a moment, lingering near the top of her head before he finally gestured to the door. "Let's go, Ponytail. We can continue to explore your grunge music in the car. What's next?"

Talia did her best not to overanalyze the impromptu nickname as she followed Walker out on the porch. For some odd reason, she liked it. The embarrassment she had felt earlier dissipated with Walker's support of her music taste and last-minute hairstyle.

"Evanescence," Talia recited, looking at the lineup on her phone. "Then Linkin Park."

"Damn," Walker murmured. "When I try to play this stuff at the house, Colin acts like it's death metal, and Pearl requests the newest god-awful pop song that they play on the radio way too much."

"They need to be cultured," Talia retorted, opening the passenger door to Walker's minivan.

"You should come over and teach them a lesson," Walker replied, pressing the button to start the engine.

"I will have to warn you that I also like god-awful pop songs. I'm a smorgasbord of everything good. That sampler meal you get at a restaurant when you have no idea what you want? That's me, but with music. Punk rock is just my current flavor of the day."

"So, you're into Britney Spears and the Backstreet Boys but also Matchbox Twenty, George Strait, 50 Cent, Elton John, and Taylor Swift?"

How the hell he had read her like a light-up neon sign, Talia had no idea. She never once thought of herself as the predictable type. Between studying for the bar exam, wanting to wear a ball cap with expensive clothes, and her love for inappropriate stand-up comedy without downing a lick of alcohol in college, not a single person had figured her out as immediately as Walker. Not even Clifford, and she had spent years of her existence thinking her ex was the only person who truly knew her. Between Amala's innate ability to get her to share the deepest parts of herself and Walker's psychic ability to know everything about her without even asking, Talia was starting to wonder if she ever really had true friendships back in New York.

"Exactly," Talia confirmed with a small smile. "I fuck with some Taylor Swift."

Eleven

TALIA

Roaster's Republic was mostly empty as far as seating went, the majority of the customers there to grab their coffee and slip out the door on the way to their day jobs. The convenience of the shop being deserted on weekdays was that the comfortable couches and lounging chairs were always available. Talia and Walker took their usual spot on a corner couch behind a coffee table, accompanied by a fresh-faced Amala, who had plenty of time to get ready that morning. Death glares and a pretense of innocence was shared between the two best friends, Walker none the wiser to their silent conversation about Amala's little set-up.

Amala had ordered something that was basically a milkshake and ignored all Talia's pointed looks the second her straw hit her lips.

"They say your coffee order has a lot to do with your personality." Amala took a long sip of her frap and sighed for effect.

"Oh, there's actual coffee in that?" Walker chortled and took a purposeful swig of his straight black coffee.

"Semantics." Amala shrugged. "My order says I'm innocent and sweet."

Talia scoffed and shook her head. "I think yours means you're incapable of giving two fucks about anyone's opinion."

"And that you're bold," Walker considered, tilting his head to the side. "Maybe vibrant to the point of a sugar hangover. What's mine say about me?"

"Black? Hmm... you like your coffee like you like your women? I'll remind you that I'm taken." Amala winked and tossed her braids over one of her shoulders.

"I am terrified to answer that," Walker grinned. "Your husband will kill me if I say 'yes' and you will kill me if I say 'no.' Bro code says I should go with the latter."

"I think yours means you're..." Talia curled her lips over her teeth and narrowed her eyes on Walker. "You're simple—"

"Hopefully not a simple*ton*," Walker interrupted.

"Simple with a biting humor. And you're... strong." Talia let her eyes fall to Walker's tattooed arm for only a moment before she hid behind her own coffee, looking over the rim of her mug at Amala, who smirked as she typed something out on her phone. A second later, Talia's phone buzzed in her purse.

"You gonna get that?" Amala asked. "Could be business-related."

Talia strained to not roll her eyes and defiantly pulled out her phone with a jerk of her hand. She tilted the screen away from Walker, unsurprised that the only message glowing up at her was from Amala.

> AMALA 8:32AM
>
> I think if Walker's coffee matched his taste in women, his coffee would be lighter, maybe imported from Israel with a side of New York City branding?

"All good?" Walker's eyebrows rose, and Talia haphazardly tossed her phone back in her purse like it had scorched her skin. She left Amala's text on read and schooled her expression into something bored and unassuming.

"Yep. It's no one important."

"Walker..." Amala scooted out to the edge of her chair, clearly pleased with herself. "What do you think Talia's coffee says about her?"

"If I'm being honest, I think this is like astrological signs, and I think it's all bullshit. It's vague enough to be realistic for anyone."

"But, if I was holding a gun to your head?" Amala pried.

"She's..." Walker drummed his fingers against his leg and cleared his throat after giving Talia a once-over. "She's the perfect mix between the two of us. She's both subdued and will pack a punch if she needs to. Sugary because—well, um, she's sweet. The only thing that doesn't make sense is the vanilla."

"Why?" Talia was now fully invested in his answer and could feel the color rising in her cheeks.

"I just don't picture you as very... vanilla." Walker's eyes flashed momentarily with something Talia couldn't quite place.

The blush crept further up Talia's throat, her mind immediately jumping to the conclusion that he meant she wasn't vanilla in the bedroom. The generalized statement could have easily meant something else, but if it *was* what Walker meant, he wasn't entirely wrong about that. If the books she read had anything to say about it, she wasn't vanilla at all. Technically, the only experience she'd had in the bedroom *was* pretty standard, but that never stopped her imagination from running rampant.

When Walker had asked what book Talia was reading on the car ride over, she was enough of a prude to be embarrassed by her choice of reading material. The cover, luckily, was just a picture of a house that was a bit in disarray with an old deck and chipping paint, so she could easily flash the book at him and get away with calling it a generic romance novel. *Contracted Love* was based off a movie that she'd seen posters for plastered all over the billboards in New York a while back. Given that she always liked books more than movies, she was happy to see that an adaptation had been done, despite the annoying sticker on the front boasting about it being a Netflix Original. Mostly, the movie looked like the plot involved a lot of steamy sex, and that was definitely the type of novel she loved to devour, so she'd impulsively bought the book from a local bookstore the day before.

Sometimes Talia didn't want to think too hard when reading a novel, especially with the rest of her life using up all her brainpower. Was it so bad to occasionally want to be lost in some sappy love story where the sex was not at all realistic and everyone orgasmed at the same time, every time, and multiple times? It occasionally required a little thought to figure out how some of the fictional characters even got into those contorted positions, but, sue her, she was a human trash can feeding herself garbage on occasion, and she was fine with that. Just not really fine with Walker or her grandmother, who had long since been dead, knowing about it.

At least the cover was inconspicuous enough to read in public and didn't have a picture of a shirtless Fabio on the front. Talia reasoned with herself that spicy books might even aid in her efforts to stop thinking of Walker in a sexual way, displacing those thoughts with random book boyfriends that didn't exist. Harmless fantasies. So far they weren't helping at all, but she would persist—mostly because she wanted to continue reading absolute trash and pretend it was somehow for a practical purpose. Instead, more often than not, she pictured Walker as the cover model for one of the books she read on her Kindle, which were more filthy than her paperbacks. White ripped T-shirts, glistening skin, abs for days. She'd already seen him shirtless, so it wasn't hard to conjure an image of him posing seductively in a fireman's uniform, an ax pressed into one bare shoulder. Alternatively, he could be wearing a button-down shirt, mostly unbuttoned, with the sleeves rolled up to the elbows, while he manspreaded across a whole damn couch. It wasn't unlike what he was already doing, sitting next to her and slurping his coffee, one arm casually draped behind her on the couch, his foot crossing over his other knee.

"I guess I'm *not* very vanilla," Talia reasoned. "I just like the flavor." She could tell Amala was about to chime in with inappropriate commentary, so she quickly changed the subject and smacked Walker's knee. "Why do men always take up an unnecessary amount of space?"

"How much space do you need, Your Highness?" Walker joked. He dropped his foot to the floor and scooted to the very far end of the couch, grabbing a nearby throw pillow and fanning her with it.

"Mmm, that's nice, but aren't you also supposed to feed me grapes?"

"Fresh out of those. I need to go grocery shopping again."

"Is that on the roster today?" Amala slumped back in a sofa chair across from Talia and Walker. It was intentionally to force Talia to sit next to Walker, but at least her friend was making good on her promise to alleviate the sexual tension, barring the morning's episode of forced-proximity bonding and one extremely unnecessary text message.

"Yeah, that and writing a crappy romance novel about a guy who finds his long-lost brother and then falls in love with said brother's adoptive sister," Walker grumbled, setting his laptop on the table.

"Sounds... complicated?" Talia peeked at the laptop that Walker had opened to a document with several paragraphs written out. If she didn't need reading glasses to see it, she would have done her best to sneak-read it in her peripherals.

"Trying to find a way to make the main characters appealing when they go behind the other brother's back to do it four times in the movie is difficult. It's all weirdly incestuous, even though it's technically not." Walker grimaced, and Talia choked on the coffee she'd just taken a sip of to cover up her sleuthing. She let out a laugh followed by a bunch of throat-clearing to rid the scratchy feeling in her esophagus.

"Honestly, that sounds like something I would be into." Amala gave an unashamed shrug of her shoulders.

"I'm shocked, truly," Talia drawled. Walker chuckled as Amala forged ahead.

"So, the books you write, do you have to write the sex scenes, or is it like a fade-to-black scenario?"

"Both." Walker lifted his foot to cross over his knee again and reassumed his position, casually draping his arm behind Talia. He was so close, she could feel the heat radiating off his body. "It depends on whether they want it to be an adult novel or a young adult novel. It's not always a romance novel, either. I'm hoping the next one is an action movie or TV show so I can write about explosives."

"And this one? Adult novel or young adult?" Amala pried.

Talia darted her eyes to Amala, hoping she could read her mind. *Worst friendship wing-woman ever.* The last thing she needed right now was for Walker to go into any detail about the sex scenes he wrote.

"I have to write at least two of the four steamy scenes that will be included in the book," Walker answered. "The other two will get written by a female author from the firm, and then they'll either use both or ask one of us to match the other person's writing style. But they're normally pretty mild. The scenes, I mean. I don't have to get super specific or crazy with it."

"And your version of crazy is...?" Amala pressed on. Meanwhile, Talia inwardly cursed herself for bringing her along. *Why* did she think it would be a good idea? Instead of dousing the flames of sexual tension with water, Amala had taken it upon herself to stoke them—dumping gasoline on an already out-of-control fire.

"Um... things I have *not* done? Language that I *don't* use?" Walker said, awkwardly. There was a split second where he glanced over at Talia during his response. Like doing *her* would be one of those crazy things.

Amala rolled her hands over one another. "Like...?"

"Are you going to make me say it?" Walker blushed, a shade

Talia had only seen on his face once before when he was shirtless and had accidentally backed into her.

"No, you don't have to," Talia cut in. "Amala, do you always have to be so... direct? I am one hundred percent sure it is not normal to ask someone what they've done in bed."

"I'm not asking what he's done in bed. I don't want to know that. I want to know his writing process and what makes something too much."

Walker opened and closed his mouth a few times before responding. "The thing about these novels is, I'm a ghostwriter, which means that my publishing house takes credit for everything and I don't have to worry about people reading it and knowing it's me who wrote it. If I wanted to, I could write a bondage scene, and no one would ever know. It's the perfect cover, really. Just like how Talia's book has the perfect cover 'cause it doesn't give away the fact that there are like five sex scenes in it."

He reached over Talia to grab the book from her bag, and she turned beet red.

"You've... read this book?" Talia gaped at him.

"Not exactly..." Walker set Contracted Love down on the coffee table, leaning back against the couch cushions. Amala promptly burst into laughter. Walker crossed his arms over his chest, and Talia looked back and forth between him and Amala, missing whatever the punchline was.

"What? How do you know—?"

"Tal, please tell me that book's based on a terrible rom-com like I think it is." The sparkle of amusement danced behind Amala's eyes.

It hit Talia like a tidal wave to the face. Snapping her attention over to Walker, she adamantly shook her head.

"No. I refuse to believe you wrote this."

"Ghostwrote," Walker corrected, as if that made a single difference.

Talia glared at him. "You're an asshole! You let me just be

embarrassed about the fact that I'm reading this, and you're the one who wrote it?"

"I only wrote two of the sex scenes and like three-fifths of the book!" Walker held up his hands in defense.

"That's basically the whole book! Why didn't you say anything? You just weren't going to tell me that you wrote the freaking book I'm reading?" Talia wasn't sure why she was so angry about the whole thing, but she was. She hated not being the person in the know. Here she was, trying not to think about Walker in a sexual way, and he had written the smut she was reading. Un-freaking believable.

"I didn't want you to know." Walker looked away, playing with his hands.

"Why? Worried I'm gonna judge your ability to write?" Talia asked sarcastically as Amala sat back, watching the encounter with a sly smile pulling at the corner of her lips as she sucked heartily on the straw of her near-empty drink.

"Yes." Walker nodded and reached forward to close his laptop, which Talia was attempting to read again. "I would prefer if you didn't get to critique my writing."

"Oh." Talia fell silent, unsure what to say. Her mind raced, trying to recall what she had read of the book so far. Midway through the book, there had already been two sex scenes. She was suddenly itching to go home and finish it, and possibly go back and reread certain portions.

"See! You're already trying to figure out which sex scenes I wrote, and that's too much pressure!" Walker buried his face in his hands.

"I'm not! I'll stop reading it right now if you want me to," Talia lied. She would definitely be finishing and generally overanalyzing the crap out of the book later.

"No, you won't." Walker sighed. "Just... keep your opinion of my writing to yourself, okay? I don't want to know how bad you think it is."

"Well, I'm reading it, aren't I? I would have put it down if I didn't think it was worth going on," Talia argued.

"You're reading it 'cause you enjoyed the movie and that's it."

"I've never seen the movie."

"Then you're reading it 'cause the price was like two dollars," Walker rebutted.

"It was ten ninety-nine, and I'm frugal! I don't go spending my money on random things I think I won't enjoy."

Walker locked Talia into an unblinking staredown as if he could intimidate her into sudden illiteracy, his jaw twitching in stubborn irritation. The joke was on him, though, because she thought that out of the two of them, *she* was the more intimidating one. The silence between them was loud. Neither of them had to say anything to know what war they were waging, but Talia refused to back down first. She was going to read every single word of *Contracted Love* if it was the last thing she ever did. Amala's cell ringing was eventually what pulled them out of their fixation, and thank God, or they might have both grown old and gray before ever reaching a conclusion to their stalemate.

When Amala picked up the call, her face drained of color. Walker's body went rigid beside Talia, a predisposition for bad news she recognized in herself.

"I'll be right there," Amala muttered and hung up. Their argument forgotten, Talia leaned forward in concern, Walker doing the same as Amala let out a long, frustrated sigh. "My kid punched another kid in the face."

"Oh, Jesus!" Walker let out a puff of air in relief with a short laugh. "I take it you need a ride, then?"

"Yes, please drop me off at the school so that I can read my kid the riot act," Amala said grumpily.

"Could always be worse. Your kid could be doing the drunk walk along the side of the street or forging your signature to skip school," Walker pointed out.

"My kid is eight." Amala rolled her eyes.

A second later, Walker's phone rang, and he looked at the caller ID, blinking in surprise.

"It's Archwood Elementary," he said to Amala before tapping the answer button and putting the phone to his ear. "Walker Hartrick. Mm-hmm. Yep, be there shortly."

"I thought our kids liked each other." Amala furrowed her brow in confusion.

"They do," Talia reasoned. "They both seemed perfectly content to hang out with each other at your house the other day."

"Right... well, they didn't say Jayla punched Coop, so I don't know what's going on. All they said was they need me to come down to the office to discuss 'an incident,'" Walker said, holding his fingers up in a pair of air quotes.

"Only one way to find out what happened." Amala rose from her seat and walked over to the trash can, tossing the remnants of her caramel-soaked frap inside.

"Um, I can... wait here?" Talia asked, wondering how far her walk home was from the coffee shop. It had to be at least a few miles.

"Come with us? Might as well. It's not like you haven't dealt with Hartrick family issues before." Walker gave her a half-hearted smile, and Talia couldn't help herself but to nod yes.

TWELVE

WALKER

The drive to the school was mostly silent, but Walker's brain was anything but. His thoughts were scattered, flicking between anxiety about whatever incident Cooper was involved with and anxiety about Talia reading the terrible romance novel he had contributed to. So, in summary: anxiety.

Cooper was the kind of kid to talk your ear off, so whatever happened at school probably had something to do with his mouth. Truly, the only time Walker had seen Coop at a loss for words was when he was around Jayla, which was why he couldn't imagine that she had punched Cooper considering how stoically silent he was in her presence. The assumption that they were somehow involved in something together made more sense. Walker could see his nephew co-conspiring with Jayla (as long as Jayla was the ringleader).

And then there was Talia. Walker longed to snatch the book from her purse and throw it out the window. He also had the urge to call up his publication company and demand that they not sell his books to any local establishments where Talia could end up purchasing them. Better yet, he could call up all the places that *did* sell those sorry excuses for novels and formally request that they never sell to her. He knew Talia well enough to know she was going to research his publishing company and start working her way through all of the crap they pushed out, trying to guess which ones he had a part in. He should have just kept his mouth shut—let Talia read *Contracted Love* and never mention his involvement.

For the first time in his life, Walker wished he had put a bit more effort into his writing. He'd been mostly content writing stupid, silly stories because he got paid decently and had little stake in the game, but now, knowing Talia was reading them, he was rethinking not pouring every ounce of his abilities into his work. The idea of Talia sitting at home reading the smut scenes he'd written was traumatizing... and maybe a little erotic. He couldn't remember for the life of him what happened in the book she was reading, and he hoped to God it wasn't one of the times he'd gotten a little too creative with his writing. Or maybe he was hoping it was one of the more experimental pieces.

Being self-conscious about his writing hadn't occurred to Walker before since his name was never on the cover. Paisley even read a few of his crappy books, and he wasn't embarrassed about it, even with the sex scenes. It was his job, so why would he be? But Talia, she was a different story. The girl that danced around in the morning to loud music while she brushed her teeth, bantered with him without missing a beat, looked drop-dead gorgeous in both a T-shirt with ripped jeans or a blouse with a skirt and heels, all while being the most kind and genuine person he'd ever met—she deserved to read something worthwhile. She deserved to read a book written by someone who was an expert on love, sex, all of it. All of his previous works were written by a fraud.

When they pulled into the parking lot of Archwood Elementary, Walker took one deep, calming breath to force his anxieties down and prepare for whatever calamity awaited him inside. He would remain cool and collected in the face of any of Cooper's behavioral issues. Whatever had happened, he would deal with it.

Panicking about the unknown wouldn't help anything, so to avoid spiraling into every "what if" scenario, he focused his thoughts on his work ethic, talking himself into trying a hell of a lot harder on the current novel he was writing. Those awful fictional characters who were sleeping around behind their brother's back were going to be the definition of love when he was done with them just in case Talia happened to read the book eventually.

With a sense of purpose, Walker mimicked Amala's confidence as he trudged beside Talia into the school. Amala seemed mostly in control of her kid, the current incident notwithstanding, so he took note of her parental stance, hoping to glean any helpful tips for the future. If he had to bet, whoever Jayla punched probably deserved it, even if it *was* Cooper. After attending to Cooper's possible broken nose, Walker would have to find out what his nephew did to provoke Jayla so much that she felt the need to sock him.

In reality, an entirely different scene awaited them in the principal's office. Cooper was sitting in a chair untouched beside Jayla, who was also unharmed. Roscoe was already standing at the ready behind his daughter and waved politely when the three adults showed up, a look of empathy shot in Cooper's direction that Walker wouldn't entirely understand until later. The other parties in the room included the principal, Cooper's teacher and a woman standing protectively behind a kid with a growing black eye who was holding an ice pack to his face.

"Good, we're all here." Principal Steward stood up from his desk.

"Mind telling us *why* we're here?" Walker took his place behind his nephew, frustrated by the theatrics.

"It's a very delicate situation. I hope you understand," Steward said with an expression that Walker knew all too well: pity. It automatically set his teeth on edge.

"Right, *delicate*," Walker regurgitated, not bothering to hide his annoyance. Talia set her hand on his shoulder for comfort. For once in her presence, Walker had forgotten she was there at all, so focused on Cooper that the realization she *was* forced him into relaxation. He adjusted his stance, finding his calm again. "I apologize. Please continue."

"As you know, we have a zero-tolerance policy for bullying. It has come to my attention that Camden," the principal gestured to Jayla's victim, "has been continually making fun of Cooper."

"I'm sure that's not true!" the woman standing behind the boy chimed in, wielding the classic *my kid never does anything wrong* defense. The calm Talia gave Walker was quickly replaced with anger.

"All of this could have been avoided if you did anything the first time I came to you," Roscoe rebutted Steward, looking just as roused as Walker felt. "You're going to stand there and pretend that I didn't come here two days ago and inform you that Jayla keeps hearing that little asshole bullying Cooper?"

"Officer Winston, we don't use that language to describe children here!" Principal Steward said hastily.

"None of this is true!" the mom of said asshole insisted.

"I'm a little lost here," Walker glared at the mom, then Steward, before looking down at his nephew. "Coop?"

"He," Cooper swallowed and gave a short nod of his head. "Camden keeps saying that Mom and Dad were probably happy to... die so they wouldn't have to talk to me anymore. He said it again today, and Jayla punched him."

"He deserved it!" Jayla shouted, glowering at Camden.

Walker focused his energy on the principal. He could feel Talia's hand on his arm, but his blind fury was too much for it to give him any real peace anymore. Words were coming up his throat with a frightening lack of control, his fist slamming down on Principal Steward's desk.

"Roscoe came to you two days ago and you did *nothing*? I want that kid to stay the fuck away from Cooper from now on," Walker yelled before turning his attention to the offending party, an accusation at the ready for Camden's mom, who was shamefully staring at the floor. "How *dare* you raise your kid to torment other kids whose parents *just* died. Who the hell does that?"

Talia set a hand on his arm. "Walker, maybe just—"

"Mr. Hartrick!" Mrs. Rensie, Cooper's teacher, interrupted, raising both of her hands placatively. "I attempted to reconcile this. I sent a note home with Cooper and a note home with Camden so that we could all discuss this. Mrs. Wylder did respond and was ready to set a meeting."

"I didn't get a note," Walker snapped.

"I didn't give it to you," Cooper murmured, kicking his feet, which were hovering above the ground in discomfort.

"I... why?" Walker blinked stupidly down at Cooper.

"I didn't want to bug you. Piper, Carter, and Colin keep doing things, and I didn't want to..." Cooper trailed off sadly. Walker closed his eyes, letting out a long sigh. He came around the side of Cooper's chair and bent down to his nephew, shaking his head.

"Hey. You are never a burden. *Never.* You hear me? Neither are your siblings." The rising tide of failure washed over Walker again. It was overwhelming, the sensation that no one thought he could do this, that none of his nieces and nephews trusted him enough to tell him exactly what they were dealing with. Here he was, caring about inconsequential things like whether or not Talia was going to read his ridiculous books while everyone around him was in pain. No wonder they didn't deem him good enough.

"And why exactly did you trust an eight-year-old to deliver this information to their guardian?" Talia's question landed on both the teacher and the principal.

"I was going to call him today when I didn't hear back!" Mrs. Rensie defended herself. "I tried calling, but the number we had on file was disconnected. I sent an email, too, but it bounced back, and then I realized I only had his parents' phone number and email, and—"

"You tried to call and send an email to my dead brother and sister-in-law?" Walker let out a puff of laughter in disbelief.

"My list was apparently not updated. When I realized that, I requested the updated contact info from the office. I was trying to get the word out to you! I promise." Mrs. Rensie looked like she was about to break into tears, so Walker didn't say anything further. Educators always had way too much on their plates to be able to keep track of everything, and if he'd been diligent enough, he would have given her his contact info in person.

"My daughter took care of it for you," Amala said with slight pride.

"Took care of it? She punched Camden!" Camden's mom shouted.

"And maybe he finally learned his lesson," Walker bit off.

"Okay, okay," Principal Steward said in the most soothing voice possible. "I can't condone corporal punishment for children, nor can I condone continual harassment. Both Jayla and Camden are suspended from school for two weeks. I take full credit for the office staff not properly updating the records so that Mrs. Rensie could contact you, Mr. Hartrick."

"Jayla shouldn't be punished at all," Walker stated plainly, turning toward Roscoe and Amala. "This is my fault. I'm so sorry."

"No." Amala shook her head sadly. "I was planning on discussing it this morning with you, but I thought you already knew, and then..."

Amala's voice trailed off as the one inside Walker's head grew louder and more bitter. *Great, even Amala is at a loss for words. "I thought you already knew." Right, because you should have known. Try being aware of the stuff going on with the kids you're in charge of for once, Walker.*

"It's fine. It's my fault," Walker repeated, brushing Amala off as he crouched down to Cooper again. "Do you want to go home?'

"No, I'm all right." Cooper gave a half-hearted smile. "Sorry, Uncle Walker."

"None of this is on you. You go back to class with Mrs. Rensie, and I'll deal with this further."

"Here." Talia stepped forward with a slip of paper that looked like it had been torn from the planner she kept in her purse, handing it to Cooper's teacher. "It's Mr. Hartrick's phone number and email address."

"You have my email address?" Walker stood up and looked at Talia curiously.

Talia bit her bottom lip and nodded. "You gave it to me this morning."

The morning felt like eons ago by now, but Walker vaguely remembered her sending him a link to her Spotify punk rock playlist. The recollection only aided in souring his mood further, because of course he could remember to enjoy music but forget to use his email to communicate with teachers like a responsible adult.

"Is there anyone else I can put on file as a backup emergency contact?" Mrs. Rensie asked, picking up a pen off the principal's desk. "I will personally make sure everything is updated."

Right. A backup, for when she can't get ahold of you. Because you're unreliable.

"It's just me," Walker swallowed. The gravity of the statement pulled his eyes to the floor as the sharp sting of salt hit his nose. He tilted his face away from his nephew and dug his fingernails into the palms of his hand in an attempt to drive away the tears that wanted to prick his eyes.

"Wait, Walker, I can..." Talia set her hand on his shoulder again, and he looked over at her with what he was sure was the most pathetic expression he could ever wear. There was no pretending he was in control of anything anymore. He wasn't. Cole and Paisley would be disappointed, and everyone knew it. The most he could do now was hide his reaction well enough so Cooper couldn't see. "I'll be the secondary contact."

Talia reached down to lace her fingers in his. Walker let her, feeling like at any moment if he didn't have her support he was going to faceplant on the ground, which would do nothing to assure Cooper he could tell him anything in the future.

"Put Amala and me down as an option, too." Roscoe raised his hand. Mrs. Rensie scrawled notes on the paper and took Talia's information while Walker stayed silent, everyone else having to pick up his slack. He needed an actual list, not an invisible one in his head. A list of things he had already forgotten and couldn't forget ever again. A list of things he needed to know so he would never make the same mistake twice. A list of things created by someone better than him.

Drive to each of their schools and make sure everyone has your contact info. Check in with each of their teachers. Go grocery shopping. Pick up more tampons and pads. Double-and triple-check on everyone's therapy appointments. See if you can get them in a little earlier. Go grocery shopping (again). Verify all the bills for the house are paid. Visit Cole and Paisley's grave to beg for forgiveness for being such a fuck-up.

When Cooper and Mrs. Rensie left the room, Walker felt lightheaded, tormented by his own self-deprecating thoughts. He turned toward the bully's mom and tried to think of something to say that would prevent this from happening in the future, but, as usual, he came up empty-handed. The fog of unease settled further over him, and he bolted for the door before the walls could close in completely.

"He's going through a lot right now with his dad," Camden's mom shouted after Walker. "I'm sorry."

Ignoring her was the only thing he could think to do. He couldn't spare a thought for anyone else's issues when he couldn't even handle his own. At this point, it wasn't even Camden' fault. Cooper hadn't been his usual self since his parents died, and it was glaringly obvious that he didn't feel comfortable enough to share his struggles.

Screw old girlfriends who don't respond to Cooper's constant questions. It's you. The light is going out in him, and you're the problem.

Talia gripped Walker's hand hard to hold on, pulling herself along behind him as he marched out toward his car. Pissed that he was failing again, he ripped open the door to the driver's side, so unaware of his surroundings the he failed to notice that Talia was standing too close. A loud crack filled his ears, and Talia reeled back, holding the bridge of her nose, eyes watering.

Walker shattered.

The last vestige of control vacated his body as he slid down to the ground, breathing heavily, heart beating so frantically that he thought it might explode from his chest. The sound of the blood pumping through his veins and Talia's nose snapping played on a loop in his head. And the ringing. The ringing was loud. *So loud.*

"I'm sorry," he repeated over and over again through short breaths that weren't giving him nearly enough air. Clawing at his throat, he felt the edges of his vision start to fade to black. Talia thrust herself on the ground next to him, wincing as she swiped the blood away from her nose.

"I'm fine. I'm fine," she repeated in a soothing voice as she wrapped her arms around him. "Breathe. Everything is going to be okay. I'm going to help you."

His breathing steadied and his vision returned minutes later when he focused on her face and her hands gripping him. His face was sopping wet, and he felt so outside of his body that he wondered absentmindedly where the moisture had come from. *Rain?* But it wasn't raining. The only thing grounding him back to reality was Talia and the bruise that was already forming on her nose, the bruise that he had created—another reminder of how reckless he had been with everyone in his life lately.

It didn't even matter how much Walker cared for her—and he was starting to realize just how much he did—he could never be with her. Cole must have sent Talia as some sort of angel to protect his family from his irresponsible brother's care. The kids, they all needed Talia more than he needed to be with her, and he refused to ruin that for them.

He leaned his head into the crook of her neck, taking several deep breaths and closing his eyes as he regained full consciousness, now aware of the tears streaming down his face.

"I'm failing at everything except for becoming friends with you. And I hurt you." His voice cracked, the same way his heart did.

"You aren't failing. This is near impossible to do on your own. You're holding everyone together with your bare hands. You're strong, Walker. You care so much about them that Cooper being bullied made you have a panic attack. And as far as my nose goes, we'll just have to come up with some super far-fetched story as to how I got this bruise. What do you think? Hit by a tiny meteor? I secretly have a night shift as a superhero and defeated several ninjas?"

Walker let out a breathy laugh and pulled his head off Talia's shoulder, peering into dark brown eyes that held all the warmth and strength he needed to get up off the ground. Rising to his feet, he reached a hand out to help Talia up before lightly brushing over her nose and running his thumb under her eyes, which were still watering from the impact, steady tears streaming down her face.

"The second one. You *are* a superhero."

And I'm the stupid, lovesick ninja you defeated.

Thirteen

TALIA

Staring at herself in the mirror, Talia let out a soft groan before again picking up her concealer and wondering why it concealed absolutely nothing. She wasn't normally a heavy makeup wearer, and all the caked-on products looked so out of place on her face that she found herself wiping it off for the second time. The citrusy sting of her grapefruit-scented makeup wipes against the raw skin under her eyes made her wince and suck in a sharp breath through her teeth. When the makeup was finally removed, she examined her battered face, out of curiosity more than anything else.

After giving up on another round of makeup, Talia ultimately decided there was no help for the bruising on her nose and slid her sunglasses over her face to cover the black and blue splotching. It looked atrocious. It didn't matter so much to her and only really hurt when she touched it, but it was still a shock to wake up that morning to see how horrible her face looked. She had the ridiculous notion that her injury would magically heal after Walker gingerly touched it the day before, swiping his fingers over tears that were a mixture of tear-duct-induced trauma from the wound on her nose and the sheer misery of seeing him ripped apart by the events of the day. When Walker broke, Talia broke too, unleashing tears she wasn't aware needed to be shed.

Talia couldn't remember how her mom used to do it, or if she had even attempted to cover the bruises. Being as young as she was when the abuse was going on, Talia couldn't remember much. What she did recall was that her mom always seemed to know how to do everything. This was a woman who had helped Talia practice for the bar exam without ever taking a single law class, leaving her stunned by the amount of information her mom retained. If Talia's mother had been born to a different family, one that had built up her best attributes, then she could have taken over the world. Instead, Lydia focused every ounce of herself on making sure that Talia would succeed in life.

Being the walking Israeli proverb that she was, one of the many pieces of wisdom Lydia gave was the idea that it was everyone's responsibility to raise their children better than their parents before them. Lydia did better than her parents and always told Talia it was her job to continue the healthy cycle, raising her own children better than Lydia had raised her. A stab of pain that had nothing to do with the superficial bruising on her face washed over Talia. The likelihood that children would be in her future was slim to none. The vice grip around her heart was always there, like twine pulling taut, an ever-present reminder in the back of her mind that her body wouldn't allow her to have that joy.

She couldn't have those dreams because she might never be a parent. "To not to have felt pain is not to be human," her mother would say. "The best thing to do when you are down, neshama sheli, is to get out of bed, bathe, use that fancy lotion I got you for your birthday, and put on a bit of makeup—not enough to cover your beautiful face, just enough to enhance the features that you love most about yourself. Nothing will get better unless you first practice self-care."

The "fancy lotion" her mother used to purchase for her wasn't fancy in the New York City sense of the word. It could be purchased at a drugstore for less than twenty-five dollars. Even though Talia's budget was on the higher end now, having saved most of what she made at the law firm, she still continued to purchase lower-end things. It was what she was used to, growing up on a budget. All her clothes were secondhand, even after she could afford to drop three grand on a Chanel purse. The idea of spending that much on a purse was ridiculously frivolous to her. Her well-made purse that cost a fraction of a designer purse was way cuter and more practical, in her opinion. It was professional, yet could still be worn with a laid-back outfit. It matched most of her clothes and had plenty of pockets to carry the standard items: reading glasses, chapstick, tissues, antacid tablets (because being an adult meant having a love-hate relationship with all foods and never knowing when your stomach was going to rise up against you), whatever book she was reading, her planner, and the obligatory wallet. All these things worked for her. If she needed a label to impress a client in the city, eBay was always an option.

What Talia did not have in her purse was a color-correcting palette of various hues. That was what people used, right? Green to correct red... or maybe green to correct yellow? Pulling out her phone, Talia fired off a text to Walker, hoping to postpone their itinerary of planning and scheduling every facet of his life until she had watched a YouTube video on how to cover up the unattractive bruising. Walker would notice she was hiding her injury, no matter how hard she attempted to keep her sunglasses glued to her face, and she didn't think she could handle seeing the pain on his face. It would be worse than getting hit a million times with the door.

TALIA 7:23 AM

Running a bit behind. Can we push this till later?

WALKER 7:24 AM

I'm already outside...

"Shit," Talia hissed out, adjusting the sunglasses carefully to make sure they were properly covering everything. The frames rested painfully against the gash on her nose, but she was too worried about Walker's reaction to face him uncovered.

The knock on the door sounded a second later, and Talia bit her lip as she walked to the front of the house, hoping Walker wouldn't question her on why she was so intent on wearing her sunglasses inside. The thought sent an immediate song into her head, and she quickly flipped to her '80s playlist on her phone and scrolled through until she found quite possibly the worst excuse ever. "Sunglasses At Night" by Corey Hart started to blast in surround sound, and Talia sang along.

You're fucking insane, Tal, but this might just work.

"Hey!" Talia said, entirely too cheerily, when she whipped open the door, ducking out of the way to protect her nose. She was still a bit shell-shocked and on high alert around swinging doors. "You're early."

Walker's eyes immediately landed on her sunglasses, and he transferred the drink carrier with two coffees he was holding to one hand. He was wearing a gray T-shirt, one of the few shirts he cycled through, all muted or monochrome in color, and his black moto jacket, which gave him a dangerous bad boy look she had always avoided before in men.

"It's this new thing I'm trying out called responsibility. What are you doing?" he shouted over the music, cocking his head to the side.

"Just... jamming to some tunes. It's basically a requirement to wear sunglasses with this song!" Talia pointed to the ceiling and wiggled her shoulders to the music like a boppy teenager as Walker stepped into her living room.

"What's your plan after the song ends? Or are you just going to keep it on loop all day?" Walker cut to the chase, eyes honed in on her shades.

Talia silently berated herself. *Nope. That didn't work at all. Of course it didn't. Dumbest idea ever. Never murder anyone, because the second you get put into an interrogation room, your story will fall apart.*

"It's a nice day out! The sun is shining, and—"

"It's overcast and supposed to rain today. How bad is it?" Walker pointed at Talia's face, unamused by her blatant lies. When she didn't respond, he reached up to the rim of her glasses with his free hand, and she shook her head. "Tal..."

"It's not bad at all!" She smiled, hoping her exuberance would soften the blow. Gently, Walker pulled the glasses from her face, and she closed her eyes to avoid seeing his immediate reaction, wishing that, at some point in her life, she had taken a class on makeup artistry. Anything to prevent Walker from feeling guilty.

When there was no shocked gasp or comment from Walker, Talia slowly peeked through her eyelashes. He wasn't standing in front of her anymore. Spinning around, she wondered offhandedly if the sight of her mangled face had made him disintegrate on the spot. A beeping noise in her kitchen put that thought to rest immediately, and she set off in that direction. Walker was leaning against the cabinets, arms crossed over his chest as he stared at something turning inside the microwave.

"My face made you... hungry?" Talia furrowed her brow, flinching from the pain of it. Walker turned to look at her with a slight smirk, and she rolled her eyes. "That's not what I meant."

"I enjoyed The Silence of the Lambs, but I'm not so into that I crave human flesh. I brought a heating pad," he explained as the microwave finished. "You put it over your eyes and it helps heal the bruising. Plus, it feels good. I know how hard I hit you. I came prepared."

"You didn't hit me. The door did. I'm fine, Walker, really. Let's just get started on your list."

"We can do that tomorrow. Let's stay here. We already did the grocery shopping yesterday, and I brought everything I needed from home." He pointed to his laptop satchel, which was bursting at the seams, the flap barely holding together the top. "I can work from anywhere, and today was just going to be organizational anyway. You need Advil, a heating pad, lots of water, and rest."

"Walker—"

"For once in your life, don't argue with me. You know how bad it is! You tried to postpone, then you tried to play a cringey eighties song to hide the fact that you're wearing sunglasses. Why didn't you just say you had a migraine?"

Talia groaned. *Migraine. Yep, that would have been a more believable option.*

"Would that have worked?" she asked.

"No. I know you said you're a human lie detector, but you are also a *terrible* liar." He stepped toward her, holding up the cloth heating pad that had holes cut out for the eyes, and his voice dropped lower. "Stop trying to shield me. You look terrible."

"Wow, thanks! So, not only am I a liar, I'm also ugly," Talia replied sarcastically.

Walker shot her a look of reprimand and reached up to cup her face, gently turning her head from side to side to inspect the damage. The heat radiating from his skin felt good, but the desperation and guilt behind his movements didn't. On an impulse, she leaned forward a little, pressing her cheek harder into his palm, locking eyes with him. Comfort. They both wanted it. She could tell. It would hurt to kiss him when half her face was bruised, but if his touch didn't heal her, maybe his lips would.

The way he was looking at her like she was an injured animal on one of those commercials with Sarah McLachlan was agonizing. And maybe she was looking at him the same way, pathetically begging him with her eyes to use her to take the pain away. His breathing slowed as he continued to take stock of her bruising. She perused every crease on his face, too, every out-of-place tuft of hair atop his head. He must have been anxiously raking his fingers through it before he arrived. The bedhead look made him even more attractive.

It felt like the pivotal moment in a book or movie where the dam broke and the characters ravaged each other like feral animals on the floor. She needed to stop reading the book Walker had written. It was causing a lot of unseemly fantasies to play out in her head, all of which involved herself, Walker, and a lack of clothing.

The book was super problematic, too. That should have been enough to put it down. The male character gave off actual Hannibal Lecter vibes with how stalkery he was toward the female protagonist. The storyline was garbage. The writing, though, was captivating. Walker deserved all the credit, alongside whoever else co-wrote it, for doing their absolute best not to make the supposed sexy contractor, who kept breaking things in the female main character's house so he could come back, not seem like he was going to bottle his victim's sweat as a perfume and pull her used tampons out of the trash can to inhale the scent Joe Goldberg style.

In romance books, there always a fine line between romantic and Ted Bundy. For some reason, Edward Cullen creepily standing in Bella's room to watch her sleep was acceptable, but offering to keep someone from freezing to death by stripping naked and cuddling was not? Teenage Talia had always been firmly Team Jacob, but the adult version of herself no longer cared about the love triangle. On her latest rewatch of the *Twiligh*t movies, post-breakup with Clifford, Talia was too busy thirsting after Charlie and Carlisle to pay attention to the man-children that were Edward and Jacob.

Walker still managed to make the contractor seem cute in a non-off-putting way that was sure to make many men and women swoon, while still maintaining the shitty storyline that involved a lot of sex (quite possibly how the female protagonist was paying for the constant contracting services). Too bad there was no way in hell Talia was going to stop reading it. It would be more likely that she'd buy annotating pens and tabs to mark her favorite parts. Especially after yesterday.

Something felt different after the parking lot incident. Walker had crumpled into her arms, and Talia had clutched onto him for dear life. They held each other like it was the only way either of them would survive. She didn't think he realized just how broken she was, too, the grief and loss of her mother combined with the loss of her dreams overwhelming her at the same time he'd cracked. The shared experience of a mental breakdown was an intimacy she couldn't pull back from. The only person she'd had that kind of a connection with before was her mother, and she'd never experienced anything like it with someone she was physically attracted to. Only Walker.

Every person that Walker cared for got his full attention, and the way he dragged his eyes over the purple sprouting out from the bridge of Talia's nose said she was one of those people. She was spellbound by the longing in his eyes, staring into the sea of dark brown surrounding his slightly dilated pupils, like she would drown if she didn't. The tension between them was a cord about to snap. Walker tucked a strand of her hair back, his fingertips brushing over her ear. She watched the lips she so desperately wanted on hers part ever so slightly, his throat swallowing, she hoped, from arousal. It would've only taken the tiniest of movements to connect with him, to do what she had been trying to convince herself she didn't want and now knew she wanted more than the air in her lungs. The smallest step forward, and she could...

"Uh," Walker coughed loudly and dropped his hand away, quickly thrusting his bag up on the countertop to rifle through it, breaking the trance. He pulled out a bottle of pain reliever, popping off the top and shaking a few pills into his hand. "Where are your glasses at? Over here?" He scurried over to the cabinet to the right of the sink and pulled down a drinking glass, guessing correctly on the first try, and filling it with water at the fridge before walking back over to her. "Here."

"Really, I'm okay," Talia mumbled, but held out her hand anyway for him to drop the pills into. Bringing them into her mouth, she reached for the glass, ghosting over the tips of his fingers when she took it from him. She looked him deliberately in the eyes as she placed the cup to her lips, pulling the cold liquid over her tongue. Walker's Adam's apple dipped low in his throat. It was either guilt from the way her bruised eye sockets looked over the rim of the glass, or maybe lust. She sincerely hoped it was the latter, but given that it was probably impossible to look sexy when her face looked like she got into a fight with a brick wall and lost, guilt was more likely.

"Should we get started, then? I started watching this documentary yesterday and it's really... well, it's a serial killer documentary." Talia gestured to the main teal couch in her living room, wondering why her brain constantly leaned toward murder. "We could watch that in the background while we work on your lists?"

Flipping around, she marched off toward her living room, leaving all sexual thoughts of Walker behind in the kitchen. The blood coursing through her face pulsed under her cheeks, making the sensitive area across her nose throb. If the blush staining her cheeks was any indication, she had to be careful with her friendship with Walker. He continually and unintentionally brought the truth out of her in a way that felt natural. Safe. But sharing too much would be a mistake. What Walker needed wasn't another person fawning over how attractive he was, but someone he could count on. Someone he could be vulnerable about his family with without the assumption that there would be sex involved. Talia had a feeling Walker had been used too often as a good time instead of someone with a dying devotion to his family. Realness. That was what they both needed, and that was what she would give.

"Sounds good. I brought breakfast, too, but they're just the shitty bagels from Roaster's Republic, so don't get too excited." Walker followed her into the living room and sat down next to her on the couch, pulling two crinkled brown paper bags from his satchel, passing her one, then ripping it from her grasp a second later. "You need to wear the heat mask for at least five minutes first, then you can have the bagel."

"What are you, my dad?" Talia huffed and then grimaced,

backtracking. "Okay, not really the right thing to say 'cause my dad was an asshat. You're more like an imaginary dad who took me to the zoo on my birthday, fed me chicken noodle soup when I was sick, and wasn't a sloppy drunk."

"Ugh, don't relate me to a dad at all. That makes me feel like I should be wearing white Shape Ups and khakis with zippers at the knees," Walker complained, still holding out the heating pad.

"Your Shape Ups better have green stains from mowing the lawn, or I don't want it," Talia joked, finally taking the heating pad and laying down on the couch. She propped her head up on a pile of throw pillows and bent her knees so her feet were planted on the cushion a few inches away from Walker's legs. It was best to avoid touching him after the charged moment they'd shared.

"That can't be comfortable. Just stretch your legs out, and I'll use them as a table for my laptop," Walker motioned to his lap. Adjusting carefully, Talia draped her legs over him, feeling the heat rise inside her again. He didn't seem to notice the different kind of discomfort she was enduring as he pulled out his laptop, sliding under her more so that her thighs were ultimately what he used as a tabletop. It was more comfortable than it would have been if he placed the base atop her shins, but the close proximity and her center pressed into his leg made her breathing falter. It took a moment to regain control of herself, fumbling with the heating pad she draped over her face.

"This feels like a warm hug," Talia sighed dreamily. The heat felt amazing. She closed her eyes in ecstasy, not realizing how badly her face had been hurting before until she felt the relief. "How are you so good with black eyes?"

"I've been punched in the face a few times. Why do you think my nose is so crooked?" Walker laughed. Talia fought the urge to ask what the hell he was talking about. His nose was *not* crooked.

"Why were you punched?"

"Let's see... the first time was... there was some kid back in high school who was making fun of Curtis—"

"As in my employee who I just hired, Curtis?" Talia inquired.

"Yeah, I went to school with him, and someone was bullying him for having Down syndrome. I don't think Curtis noticed that they were picking on him, and I probably shouldn't have started a fight, but I was a dumb teenager, ready to take out my anger on unsuspecting assholes." Walker lifted his shoulders slightly.

"And you lost the fight?"

"No, of course not. I'm offended that you would even say that," Walker said pridefully.

"Okay, okay," Talia chuckled. "And the other times?"

"One of them was a random guy at a bar who sucker-punched me when I was a waiter right out of high school because the bartender didn't have a heavy enough pour—yet another reason to swear off alcohol. And the last one was... an ex-girl-friend." Walker looked down at Talia sheepishly then looked away.

Talia jostled her legs in his lap, sitting up a bit more. "Oh? Do tell!"

"I didn't realize we were exclusive 'cause we had only been on two dates. She saw me out with another girl... on her birthday." Walker quickly raised his hands at the widening of Talia's eyes, which shot a zing of pain through her head. "I didn't *know* it was her birthday! I swear! I also maybe forgot that she was an avid kickboxer with a really mean high kick."

"Two dates? That's it. What are you doing to these women to make them so obsessed with you? Was Harper the barista on cloud nine this morning when you came in without me?" Talia teased, a smirk pulling on the corner of her lips despite her attempt to restrain it.

"Uh... I don't know? I just bought our coffee and bagels and left. She only gave me her number that one time. There's no way she's still into me."

"God, you're daft." Talia shook her head in reproach and sat up fully, grabbing the bagel from beside him. "She ogles you like a piece of meat every day."

"No, she doesn't! Plus, you already know that I'm off the

market," Walker stated and then quickly added, "'cause of the nieces and nephews."

"Right." Talia nodded. "Guess that makes two of us."

"You aren't planning on getting out into the dating pool? I'm kinda an expert with Tinder if you want assistance with your profile."

"As appealing as that sounds, I'm not ready," Talia said simply, looking over at him for a moment before pulling her legs off his lap and setting them on the ground. "I was engaged in New York, and that didn't work out, so I'm still... on the mend."

"Oh," Walker swallowed and shifted in his seat. "I'm sorry, I didn't mean to bring up... should I send this guy hate mail?"

"No." Talia forced a smile. "It's just one of those things that I have to get over. It wasn't anything he did."

"He's an idiot," Walker declared.

"Clifford was a lawyer who was the top of his class in law school. He's definitely not an idiot," Talia shot back, not entirely sure why she felt the need to defend her ex, given that they weren't together anymore.

"His name is Clifford?"

"Cliff for short."

"'Cliff' as in I want to throw myself off of one? Terrible name. That's where you went wrong." Talia socked Walker in the shoulder, and he flinched, the devious grin not leaving his face. "I maintain that Clifford is like naming your kid Todd."

"What's wrong with the name Todd?"

"Nothing if you like to drink warm milk at night and get giant stuffed bears, or in Clifford's case, a big red dog, for each of your birthdays because what Clifford doesn't know is that what you really want is good sex for once in your life." Walker flashed his teeth cockily.

"You're literally named after a device people have to use when they throw out their hip."

"I'm more interested in *how* they threw out their hip." Walker winked, and Talia's fist flew out to hit him again. "Ow!"

"No one threw out their hip in the book you ghostwrote so far," she mused. Walker jolted up from his spot on the couch, looking around her living room, his head jerking from left to right. "Jesus, where's the fire?"

"In your trash can when I find the book and burn it," he retorted. "Where is it?"

"I'm not telling you."

"Talia, I looked up which book it was last night, and it's the creepy Bob the Builder one. If you ever dated anyone like that, I would require you to get a state-of-the-art security system!" Walker threw up his hands in frustration and started pacing the room, looking through a basket of blankets next to the couch.

"At least he didn't name his penis 'the hammer' or something," Talia teased, the tail end of her statement cut off by her own laughter.

"Fuck. I hate you. Can you just stop reading it? Please?"

"Why does it bug you so much?" Talia furrowed her brow.

"Because... it just does, okay! There's no way you're enjoying it. You're just going to use it to make fun of me." Walker raked a hand through his hair, and Talia followed the motion, watching the muscles in his forearm flex with the movement.

"Okay, fine. If you want to know my honest opinion—"

"I don't! I don't want to know, Tal. I already know that I don't know anything about what I'm writing, okay? You've been engaged before. I haven't even dated anyone for more than three months. What I write is just a job. I know the sex scenes are lackluster and the romance of it all is bogus—I don't need you to tell me that." He slumped into the spot next to her and massaged his temples.

"That's not at all what I was going to say. The plot isn't great, but the writing *is*. You didn't come up with the plot. The main characters are problematic, sure, but the sex scenes are... not. I would have tossed the book to the side after the first time the contractor purposefully broke one of her pipes if the writing wasn't good. And... wow, I'm now realizing how dirty that sounded. Was that the point?" Talia gaped at him, and Walker burst into laughter, falling back against the cushions.

"No..." he gasped through his laughter. "But I remember thinking the same thing. I mean, the guy was a contractor, *not* a plumber, so why was that even his first choice of things to break? I actually suggested that the tagline be 'he broke her pipes until she broke his.'"

Talia broke into unhinged laughter, not caring about how much it hurt her face. Walker wheezed as he tried to continue the story. "The other... the other author on the job who had been corresponding with me about how ridiculous the book was did an actual spit take during our Zoom meeting. Our supervisor ended the call early because we wouldn't stop with the pipe jokes."

"You're a literal child," Talia giggled until they both gained enough air to calm down. That is, until she thought of a new marketing scheme. "Is the tagline to your new book going to be 'Brother, May I?'"

"Fuck," Walker let out another puff of laughter and wiped under his watering eyes. "I was workshopping something to have to do with sister wives, but that is so much better."

Talia's laughter died down, and she looked at Walker seriously. "Do you ever... think about writing your own book? One you would want to take credit for?"

"I—yes, I do. I just always... I don't know, I have lots of ideas, but the problem is, I can only get a few pages in before the idea seems far-fetched or out of reach." Walker looked away in embarrassment, which only made her more curious.

"Why do you say that?"

"Because I don't understand the topic I'm writing on. Not personally, at least, just from my brother and Paisley," Walker explained.

"So, they're romance novels, then?" Talia pried.

"I... yeah, I guess so."

"Walker?"

"Yeah?"

"You're a bit of a romantic, aren't you?" Talia smiled. She hadn't meant to poke fun at him, but the watercolor pink that splashed onto his cheeks was worth it.

"You never got to meet my brother and sister-in-law. I've never met two people who were more in love, and I guess the reason I don't date for longer than a few months is because I've never..." Clearing his throat, he shook his head, and the normal coloring returned to his face as he pointed at her. "Anyway, I think you and Paisley would have been best friends. I'm sorry she didn't get to know Amala, either."

"I get it," Talia replied quietly, still on track with their original conversation.

Walker had given up so many personal things about himself during their conversation, and she had provided very little. The inequality of that hung thick in the air like molasses. She took more vulnerability than he was willing to share without something in return, and the imbalance of their friendship was clawing at her insides, begging her to tip the scale back. What she needed to say worked its way to the surface, pushing down the fear of saying it out loud and rendering herself unlovable. She had spent so much of her time guarding her heart from thinking about it that her nerves vibrated with terror as she let the words slip from her mouth.

"I thought I knew what love was, but in the end I was just left destitute, wondering if he ever loved me at all. I, um... I thought I was pregnant, and—" Talia choked on her words, and Walker's hand reached out to brush her arm. The comfort of his touch made her feel safe again. "I went to the doctor, and we were so excited. He was really thrilled because we were already planning on getting married, and, sure, it was jumping the gun a little bit, but we were going to be happy, you know? Husband, big family, white picket... apartment," she let out a small puff of air that resembled a laugh through her nose. "But when I went to the doctor, I was instead informed that not only was I not pregnant, but I can't have kids. I have an uninhabitable T-shaped uterus and inoperable blocked fallopian tubes. Apparently, if the block was farther away from my ovaries, or only a partial block, I would have had a slight chance, but, lucky me, I have multiple diagnoses and blocks as close as it can physically get to my ovaries. Cliff would've stayed, I think, if I didn't give him the choice, but... I needed to know. I guess now I do."

"He left you because you can't have kids? What about adoption? What about all the other ways people have kids?" Walker's voice strained with a quiet anger. Talia could tell he was riled up in her defense, and it was sweet, but entirely unnecessary.

"Adoption can take a really long time. I know Carter was adopted under different circumstances, but how long did it take Cole and Paisley to adopt Pearl through an agency?"

Walker bobbed his head, already getting the point. "Five years."

"Other methods can take just as long. People always assume that the answer to infertility is a quick fix, but the solutions are still an agonizing process. Of course I would want to adopt, but it would take years. Clifford always knew exactly what he wanted, and how quickly he wanted it. When everything changed, I could see the light go out of his eyes. Like I'd taken a dream from him." Talia curled her lips over her teeth to keep them from quivering.

"You didn't take anything. Anyone who wouldn't be willing to wait it out through the harder times with you doesn't deserve you." Walker's tone was laced with indignation, and Talia gripped his hand to calm him down. "He had no business even asking you to marry him if he couldn't get through any of the hard stuff. It's 'in sickness and in health,' not 'only in prosperity.'"

"Walker, it's okay. We didn't quite get to the vows." She offered him a soft smile.

"No, it's not. You didn't deserve that. You're going to be a great mom someday. I know it. You've saved my ass so many times with my nieces and nephews. Whoever you fall in love with and whoever gets to be your kid will be lucky." He returned a smile and squeezed her hand, the anger subsiding as his eyes softened on her.

"Thank you. I really hope so. Just gotta find someone to make a petri dish baby with me," Talia jested, trying to bring the conversation back around to something lighter. Walker took her change of tone in stride.

"Is that a real thing?"

"I have no idea. Should we start on your stuff? I was thinking we should sync our phone calendars. That way we can both know what's going on with the von Trapp Family at all times."

"Really?" Walker jumped up from his seat again, but this time in excitement. Confused, Talia stared up at him, wondering if he had become a calendar enthusiast overnight. "Since you said that, I'm gonna go grab something from my car. I was worried it would be too much, but then... hell, I'll just show you." He jogged off toward the front door, leaving Talia looking after him and mumbling something that resembled an "okay?"

When he returned, Walker was carrying a very large dry-erase board under one arm and a bag of multi-colored markers in a Ziploc bag in the other. He flipped it around when he came to stand in front of her with one arm out to the side like he was saying "ta da!" Talia's mouth dropped open. Between the color coding, near-perfect penmanship, and calligraphy titling, it was an organizational wet dream. Instagram moms everywhere would bow down to the chart. It deserved to be on Pinterest at least, if not have its own spotlight on Good Morning America.

"Holy Marie Kondo!" was the only thing Talia could think to say.

"My sister-in-law was nothing if not extremely thorough. It's still got everything from the month that she," Walker paused, swallowing down his emotion, "passed 'cause I couldn't bring myself to erase it." He looked down at the board with the unmistakable far-off look that Talia had come to recognize was how he coped with any and all thoughts about his brother's and sister-in-law's deaths.

"I hope you aren't expecting me to be that good at this. I don't think I could have been friends with Paisley. She would have made me feel extremely inadequate. This is pure art!" Talia exclaimed.

"Yeah, there's no way in hell we'll ever be *this* good, but we can try? I was kinda hoping you would erase it. I've thought about doing it before and almost did once, but..."

"Right," Talia nodded and looked at it again, biting her lip. "I'm going to feel so bad erasing it, though. I'd rather marry it."

"You are such a nerd." Walker grinned. "We can erase it together?"

"After I take a picture of it."

Talia whipped out her phone and took several snapshots of the board laying on the ground before Walker pulled the one eraser from the plastic bag and set it down on top of the flat surface. He removed his dark green jacket and laid it over the arm of the couch before coming to sit on his knees on the ground beside her. The gray T-shirt he was wearing hugged his toned arms, and the tattoos climbing up his left one, disappearing under his short sleeve, drew her attention again.

It felt like one of those things you could stare at forever and still find a detail you'd missed before. Black smoke wrapped around the tree scenery depicted on his forearm like the aftermath of a forest fire, some of the branches half-demolished and seared. The plumes of smoke disappeared into a fine mist as they traveled up to his bicep, where cursive words were scrawled out like multiple pages of a diary or book torn straight from the binding. A large winged bird soared over the carnage of the forest, its feathers draping and covering some of the cursive before it disappeared under the hem.

They sat in silence for a moment as her eyes trailed over every pattern she could see. She should have felt ashamed for outright ogling him, but other than the night of Piper's drunk walk when she was too distracted by his shirtlessness, this was the closest she'd come to seeing each defined detail of the tattoo. She'd seen glimpses here and there, but jackets and clothing were always in the way of appreciating the whole thing.

"A picture would probably last longer for this, too." Walker smirked and pulled up the sleeve on his shoulder to reveal a little more of his arm.

"God, you're annoying." Talia rolled her eyes and reached out a tentative hand out to trace her fingers over his bicep. Heat spread throughout her body, but she couldn't help herself. "What's it all mean?"

Walker's eyes locked on hers as he started off slowly. "The bird is an homage to *One Flew Over the Cuckoo's Nest*. So is most of the writing."

"Why *that* book?"

"It's a battle of rebellion vs. conformity."

"Sounds like you." Talia grinned.

"Oh, I'm definitely a mental patient," he deadpanned. Breaking into a wide smile, he pointed to the top of his shoulder and the end of the tattoo, which revealed a cliff's edge with a small house atop it. "This and the rest of the calligraphy are from *Wuthering Heights*. Catherine was my first fictional girlfriend."

"That's depressing, she dies!"

"But she was stubborn enough to haunt Heathcliff after she died. That's true love."

Talia let her palms fall to the floor and pressed down, straightening her spine to prepare for an argument. "No, that's a tragedy."

"Love *is* a tragedy. Eventually, everyone you ever love will die."

"So, it's not worth it?"

"I never said that. Why do you think I like the idea of people haunting others from the grave? My brother and Paisley haunt me. If I can't have them, then I'll take their ghosts." He brushed the hem of his sleeve back down and gave a sad jerk of his shoulders.

"My mom haunts me," Talia whispered. "Sometimes one of my thoughts will feel like she's talking to me."

"What does she say?"

"She keeps telling me to be nice to you."

"I see you're not taking her advice to heart, then?" Walker cocked an eyebrow and flinched away from her, already expecting a hit to his shoulder.

"What about the rest? The burning trees?" Talia dragged one finger down to the underside of his veiny forearm.

"It's a metaphor for pain and suffering. Forest fires, although they seem very destructive, can sometimes help a forest grow, clearing the brush and producing healthier trees. I regret getting that one now. I can't see how *this* pain and suffering will ever make me stronger. It must be the kind that destroys everything in its wake. Houses. Families... lives." His eyes were heavy with the kind of sadness that was only learned or experienced firsthand. She wanted to piece together all the broken pieces of his heart just so he would smile again.

"Do you hear that?" Talia sat up straighter on her knees and tilted her head to listen. There was nothing to listen to, but she had an idea and was going to run with it. Anything to distract him.

"Hear what?" Walker looked around her living room on high alert.

"Oh, really? He said that?" Talia mimicked talking to someone beside her and watched Walker stare at her in her periphery, at the spot beside her, and back at her again, the puzzled expression never leaving his face. "Mm-hmm, yeah, I figured that much."

"Who the fuck are you talking to?" Walker leaned forward warily to look in the space beside her.

"Shh, don't interrupt." She waved a hand in his direction to get him to stop talking and proceeded to speak to the open air beside her. "He didn't!" She gasped and slapped her hand over her mouth in mock surprise. "That is so gross!"

"Okay, do you need to go to a mental hospital?" Walker

seemed genuinely concerned for her well-being, which only made Talia want to burst into laughter.

"I'm talking to your brother and sister-in-law." Talia watched as Walker's demeanor gained levity. Mission accomplished.

"And what are they saying?" He played along.

"Well, Paisley said you think I'm pretty, and Cole is telling me about the time you shit yourself at an amusement park."

"Okay, how the hell do you know about that?" Walker gaped.

"I just told you!" She gestured to her invisible ghost friends and then the realization hit him.

"Piper told you, didn't she? I swear I'm going to murder your daughter, Cole." Walker glared exaggeratedly at the space beside Talia.

"Actually, you can blame Carter for this one and Colin for giving me every graphic detail about the combinations of food you ate that could have caused your bowels such stress." She gave a full-bodied laugh and fell back to sit on her butt. He shook his head calmly, his cheeks tinged with pink, and scooted to sit next to her.

"And which one of them told you I think you're pretty?" Walker's voice dropped into a husky murmur.

"I look like I fought Conor McGregor. That was just a joke."

"You're very pretty, Talia." Walker reached up and tugged on her ponytail playfully.

"Thanks," she said. Her breath went shallow for a moment, the warm air of his own breath so close to her, caressing her face. The air was charged between them again, and she could have sworn his eyes dropped to her lips until a chill ran up her spine and she shivered, bringing her back to reality. "So... should we erase this beautiful masterpiece, then?"

"Now that Paisley's here to watch us botch the next one?" Walker chuckled and nodded.

They each set their hands on one side of the eraser, pinky and ring fingers overlapping as they slowly removed the top portion, shoulders rubbing together as they leaned forward. Walker's hip nudged hers at the bottom, making her want to cut and run. As they stroked at the lettering with sweeping motions, she imagined it would be similar to how he'd move on top of her. How he'd touch her with long, tentative movements. With a final brush of his hard body hitting her side and his arms flexing beside her, she let out an embarrassingly loud sigh.

"You're *that* depressed it's gone?" Walker asked, mistaking her reaction to the loss of his body heat for something else entirely.

"I—of course I am! Paisley's probably going to send a message to the organization gods that I have severely wronged her and therefore I will be destined to a life inside a hoarder house."

"You don't think you're being just a little bit dramatic?" Walker teased, holding up his thumb and forefinger, pinching the air.

Talia's eyes briefly traced over the arm he suspended in the air before she trained them on his face again. "Not at all."

Fourteen

TALIA

Sprinting back to the house, and more out of breath than usual, Walker slowed when he reached the front door, placing his sweaty palms against it. He leaned forward with his head bent until his breathing returned to normal. The progress he'd made throughout the years with his exercise regimen had regressed drastically in the months following his brother's death. His legs felt like Jell-O, if Jell-O resembled something that had just jogged three miles and was woefully unprepared for how strenuous it would be. Other than deadlifting jugs of milk into a shopping cart, he'd ignored his healthy exercise habits in favor of depression and hauling ass to get everything done.

When Walker was in shape, he had grown so accustomed to his evening run that he barely noticed how much it sucked. One mourning period later, and he was back to realizing that he fucking *hated* running because who actually liked running for running's sake? That kind of behavior was for psychopaths, which he was not, though sometimes he wished he was, so he no longer had to deal with the constant upheaval of his emotions. The sweat that percolated between his shoulder blades and along his fore-

THE ONES WE FIGHT FOR

head was a reminder that everything post-accident was more difficult. He was just the guy scrambling to keep his head above the
pool of anxiety.

A few days ago, he took one look in the mirror when he was
drying off from a shower and decided it was finally time to jump
back on the exercise horse. He was starting to lose muscle tone. It
shouldn't have bothered him so much because he'd already
decided to swear off women and, thus, women seeing him shirtless
for the foreseeable future, but it did. What finally got him out
running again wasn't the idea that he should do it for himself and
for his general health. It was Talia and the sheer amount of times
he kept thinking about the night she dropped Piper off. If he ever
ended up shirtless in front of Talia again—for purely innocent
reasons—he didn't want to have only a flabby stomach to
show her.

The only thing that had made the run better was Talia's
grunge playlist, which he blasted through his wireless earbuds the
whole time. Angry, moody music was the right vibe for how the
run made him feel right up until the end. He had to skip some of
the slow, dramatic songs to avoid his pace turning into a frustrated
strut, but other than that, he enjoyed the emo music declaring all
of the things he felt without having to express a single word
himself.

The truth was, Walker didn't know what he felt. He could,
however, identify the rage that often came out victorious over his
other feelings. He was angry at Clifford for deciding that Talia
wasn't worth every second of possible pain, at the kid who
bullied Cooper, at Piper's ex-boyfriend for being a grade-A
douchebag, at Jeff Cohen, who both killed two of the most
important people in his life and laid hands on the woman Walker
was starting to fall for against his will. At the world. At *himself*.
Then there was the all-consuming sorrow that seemed to spring
up at the most inopportune times. He mourned all of the things
he had lost and all of the things his nieces and nephews would
never have. The heartbreak of knowing that Cole and Paisley

would never get to watch their children fall in love or accomplish all the things they were going to accomplish was almost unbearable sometimes. When Colin's birthday had passed a week ago, Walker just felt guilty for getting to be a part of an important mile marker in Colin's life while Colin's parents were six feet underground.

On top of everything else, it physically pained him that Talia was dealing with her own loss. Out of anyone he'd ever met, Talia should be able to have kids, ones that looked like her, had her smile, her unbreakable spirit. He wanted to be an impenetrable shield, blocking everything that could hurt her. The look on her face when she laid her pain bare in front of him was agonizing. He dreamt of tears and slow, healing kisses that night only to wake up to the disappointment of reality: a world where he could barely even touch her for fear of going too far. It was one or the other lately: unpleasant dreams of Cole and Paisley, or euphoric dreams of Talia. The rollercoaster of his emotions and mental anguish over what he himself couldn't have was yet another loss. His deep-seated longing accompanied by onslaughts of more guilt and more anger made him feel out of sorts. Reckless and pissed that he couldn't control himself or have what he wanted. *Her.*

Any time Talia made him laugh, chewed on one of her coffee stir sticks, helped him organize the chaos of his life, or wore her hair in that goddamned ponytail, the bottomless pit of guilt loomed under Walker, a dark reminder that joy was tainted for him now. The only reason she was in his life at all was because Cole and Paisley died. It was like some sort of sick sacrifice, a game show host pointing at two doors from which he never had the option to choose.

"Through door number one, we have Talia! She's beautiful, kind, and funny, adores your family, and is everything you've ever wanted! But, when you open that door, your family will also be left destitute!" At which point, the live studio audience would gasp in shock at a producer's cue card, telling them to *act surprised.* "Let's see what we have through door number two! It looks like your family will be left intact, but you will never find love."

A sigh of pity from the crowd.

I think I'll take door number two, please.

"I'm sorry, but our producers already decided that door number one would make for better television. Therefore, please enjoy some life-shattering pain and an excruciating run on us!"

Insert the laugh track from any sitcom where the punchline didn't quite hit right.

It was possible Walker hated his evening runs less when they actually took place in the evening instead of at 5:30 a.m., but it was the only time of the day he could be alone. Sleeping in later would result in either no time to shower or no time to make breakfast for the kids. Both options were unappealing and unacceptable. He and Talia had put an extensive amount of effort into coordinating meals and schedules. If he didn't commit to it all, he would've just wasted her time. Plus, he doubted Talia would want to sit next to his dried-on sweaty skin and matted hair during their usual morning coffee. Both a shower and breakfast were mandatory. Usually working out had the perk of relieving sexual frustration, but Walker found that recently, the only things that relieved him were cold showers and masturbation. Unfortunately, the latter heightened his sexual thoughts about Talia first before relief, which added to the stack of guilt he had built up like a teetering Jenga tower. It wasn't enough to keep himself from doing it, though. He wasn't a bad guy. Really, he wasn't! He wasn't so obsessed he planned on stealing away into Talia's house when she wasn't home and rooting through her underwear drawer. His mind was just a jumbled mess of thoughts, and he was having trouble redirecting it to more wholesome pursuits.

That morning, Walker opted for a cold shower because he had satisfied (a poor choice of words considering it hadn't been very satisfying) the other option after a graphic dream woke him up twenty minutes before his alarm went off. Doing *that* twice in one day seemed a bit excessive, not to mention it was a sure-fire way to magnify his guilt to the point where he could bottle it up and sell it. So, he was standing ass-naked in a glass box under a rainwater shower head, surrounded by custom gray tile and already shivering.

Walker found out the hard way a few weeks before that cold showers were not as easy as they seemed. The characters in his novels were always taking cold showers to ward off sexual tension, but the true reason they worked at all was because the ice water made his third leg want to retreat back into his body like a hermit. Anything less drastically cold than freshly melted glacier water on the verge of freezing over again wasn't enough to expel the dirty thoughts from entering his mind, so his shower was set to the coldest setting, causing a slew of curse words to escape his mouth.

"Fuck everything," Walker hissed. He could freeze his dick and snap it off after it became an icicle. Problem solved. "Shit. Shit. Shit."

While becoming a eunuch would solve all his problems, the thought was unappealing. On the bright side, he had conserved a lot of water in the shower recently, speed-washing himself to get the hell out of there. The other happy lining of each polar plunge was that it was even more effective than coffee as far as wake-up calls went. *Ring, ring, you literally have blue balls now, but at least you're wide awake?*

The rest of the morning was devoted to Walker testing out his newfound ability to use the coffee machine. The week before, Talia showed up on his porch with the girl from the coffee shop, *whose name was... something that started with an "H"... Harper,* so she could train him on how to use the coffee maker. Unbeknownst to him, the thing made espressos, too. It was a fine enough lesson, but he could have gone without the brazen flirtation on Harper's end. If she had shown up months before, he would've more than enjoyed her company. He kept trying to convince himself to like Harper just to stop daydreaming of Talia. Harper was very pretty, and dating her wouldn't ruin anything for his nieces and nephews.

She had even laughed at his jokes. Even the stupid one he made about always using the same mug every day even though it looked like Chip from *Beauty and the Beast*. It was mildly funny, but it was also far from his best joke. Nothing to call home about. It definitely wasn't good enough to elicit the forced laugh Harper attempted to pull off as real to make him feel better.

Talia didn't laugh at the joke, just gave Walker a slight smile. She noticed things that Harper did not, such as the reason he was so attached to his favorite mug. The printed picture on the outside, slightly faded after hundreds of washes, was of Walker and his brother when they were younger. Cole won the customized mug online when he was sixteen and they were still broke. It was the best birthday gift Walker had ever received, even after Cole and Paisley's interior design business took off and they bought him more extravagant gifts. It was a time in his life he wasn't expecting to get any gifts other than the donut Cole would always scrounge up a dollar for as a makeshift cake. After all these years, Walker still preferred a donut to cake. It was partially because of nostalgia and partially because maple bars were the shit.

Shoving two slices of bread into the toaster, Walker sipped from his mug and started to prepare eggs. They were supposed to be fried eggs, but because his ability to flip an egg without breaking the yolk was normally a fifty-fifty chance without thoughts of Cole or Talia, they all ended up scrambled. He'd utterly failed in his attempt to daydream about Harper instead.

Walker could barely look at another woman if Talia was standing in the vicinity. The loose ponytail with flyaway strands framing her face and the tight black workout pants she'd shown up in that day didn't help. He wouldn't have been able to notice if Mila Kunis came riding into the room on a freaking unicorn with Talia constantly applying chapstick to her full lips like a hot slow motion scene from a movie.

If her lips are always that chapped, you could help her with that.

Dammit. The cold shower lasted a total of a half-hour. That might be a new record for you.

The toaster popped, and Walker jumped to attention, his daydream rudely interrupted by what turned out to be, upon quick examination, slightly undercooked toast. If he slid the lever down again, the bread was going to inevitably end up burnt like it was every time he attempted a second round. How he could even manage to fuck up toast, he wasn't sure. Sliding in more slices to accommodate the sheer amount of children in the house, he decided undercooked was the lesser of two evils and opened the fridge to pull out a few avocados. Talia taught him a way to remove an avocado peel like a banana, but every time he attempted it, it looked like a rat had chewed up the husk. Learning from his past mistakes, he opted for his normal spoon-and-gauge technique.

Cooper was the first to come down the stairs, rubbing the sleep out of his green eyes as he sat down at the island. Walker automatically slid a plate with buttered toast topped with scrambled eggs and avocado across the counter. Because he was fancy, Walker had even cracked a little salt and pepper over the top of it. Gordon Ramsay would be so proud. Or he would scream at Walker for overcooking the eggs and undercooking the toast, but who the hell cared? Cooper happily chewing away on his breakfast was proof it was at least edible.

One by one, ending with Carter as usual, all of the Hartrick siblings bounded down the stairs in their various moods. Carter and Piper had their first therapy sessions later, and their attitudes toward that fact were night and day. Piper was buzzing with nervous excitement, while Carter gave off a level of doom and gloom that said going to therapy was the equivalent to ripping off a few toenails and he'd rather go the toenail route.

"All right, Carter, I pick you up from school at two forty five, so make sure to actually *be* at school, hm?" Walker made the accusation clear, but Carter just bobbed his head silently and stuffed the last bit of his breakfast, which seemed to have been universally accepted by everyone, into his mouth. "Piper, Talia's going to pick you up at two-thirty for yours."

"You're not picking her up?" Cooper asked.

"I have a meeting at the same time," Walker replied. He technically only had a meeting because he knew he would be free during that time period, but it was a good excuse. He and Talia had specifically planned for Talia to take Piper, deciding that between the two of them, the questions about how well Piper's first session went would be best coming from Talia, the same way Walker, no matter how unprepared he felt for the conversation, was the best person to discuss Carter's therapy session with him. Unless it was urgent, he and Talia planned to reconvene the following morning to debrief.

"When I go to mine next week, can Talia take me, too?" Pearl's hopeful tone made Walker smile behind his own breakfast. Always concerned about the feelings of others, Pearl quickly added, "No offense, Uncle Walker."

"None taken. I'm sure she would be happy to take you."

Talia had already agreed to take Pearl. It was in the schedule on their shared calendar, categorized as the color purple to offset his tasks, which were olive green. Amala was bright yellow and Roscoe blue for the times that they planned to pick Cooper up from school and drop him off on their way back to their house.

Wednesdays were the most chaotic day of the week. It had taken Walker and Talia a full hour to figure out the logistics when they were in their planning stage. While Cooper had therapy, Carter would be at basketball practice (he had agreed to start up again because Roscoe was an assistant coach), Colin would be at mathletes, and Talia would pick up Pearl and Piper for a girls' night, which could only be on Wednesday due to the girls' conflicting schedules. The white board was on display with every appointment, practice, club, work meeting, and dinner night in their future written in Talia's neat script, a silly little reminder of her that Walker looked at more often than not just to remember that she had written it.

"I'm not going to be back today until late." Colin shut the dishwasher and shifted his feet awkwardly.

"Where are you going?" Walker narrowed his eyes to slits and pulled his phone out to put it in the calendar.

"I'm tutoring someone for her science and math finals," Colin said plainly.

"*Her*?" Carter chimed in, a boyish glint behind his dark brown eyes.

Walker had to admit, he was a little curious, too. Colin had one past girlfriend in the entirety of his high school career, a mouse of a girl who barely spoke a word unless it was about something school-related. As if it were a solvable math equation, they had broken up by mutually deciding that the relationship was only beneficial academically and moved on. It was some next-level Sheldon from *The Big Bang Theory* behavior. Sometimes, Walker thought Colin was too smart for his own good. When his nephew did find someone, he hoped they would be Colin's exact opposite. Anyone who could pull the kid out of his comfort zone had Walker's instant approval as long as the relationship didn't involve copious amounts of illicit drugs.

"Yes, *her*," Colin glared at his brother, seeing exactly where Carter's inquiries were headed before they got there. "She's not my type."

"So she's not boring?" Carter cocked his head, one textured ringlet atop his head flopping to the side. Colin ignored him, pulling out his phone and tapping around. Carter looked amused yet determined to get under Colin's skin. "Who is it? You can tell me. Or are you worried that they're going to be more interested in me than you? Is the problem that she is a *she*? I'll support you either way. I have this dude on my basketball team that's super nerdy like you, maybe—"

"I'm not interested in her because high school relationships are pointless. We have virtually nothing in common other than my desire to make a few bucks and her desire to not fail her finals.

Scarlett just wants help in school. That's it." Colin's tone declared an end to the discussion, but Piper cut in anyway.

"Scarlett Wallace? As in crazy good at soccer, red hair—"

"Body of a freaking goddess?" Carter interrupted.

Colin groaned. "Why do I tell you anything? Her body is of no interest to me or you."

"You seem awfully protective of this girl you supposedly don't like."

"Carter," Walker warned. "Reign in the raging hormones, kid. If we could not objectify women first thing in the morning, that would be swell." Considering Walker had objectified Talia that very morning, stroking himself to a lingering erotic dream, he was the epitome of a hypocrite. His own hormones had decided vacations were for chumps and had been holding him hostage now for months.

"So he can objectify them any other time?" Pearl inserted herself into the conversation, swiping her jet-black bangs out of her face and adjusting the circular framed glasses on her nose. The glasses coupled with her long eyelashes almost made her look like a cartoon character, doe-eyed and innocent. Unlike Colin's reading glasses and blond hair, which were always firmly in place, Pearl's frames frequently slipped down the bridge of her nose, and she spent a lot of time in the mirror messing with her pin-straight hair to give it a wave.

Walker sighed and turned to look at his youngest niece, an apology already written on his tongue for Carter's behavior (and, secretly, his own). "No, he can't." He twisted his torso to give Carter a more direct warning. "You can't."

"No one is objectifying anyone," Colin grumbled. "This is strictly a school-sanctioned event. Scarlett is paying me to help her. It's a job." He folded his arms over his chest, giving the conversation an air of finality.

Carter's lips spread across his face in a devilish smirk. The way the apples of his cheeks puffed out in delight over Colin's frustration was a typical occurrence in the house. "A job? Is that what you're calling it these days?"

"Make it stop," Colin huffed under his breath.

"Well, maybe it *could* turn into something more," Walker considered, liking Colin's prior declaration that Scarlett had nothing in common with him. "You never know."

"Is she nice?" Cooper asked.

"I've only talked to her the one time."

"She's a sweetheart!" Piper bobbed her head, and everyone broke out into excited conversation over Colin's prospects. This family had zero boundaries, and Walker figured if he had to deal with years of poking and prodding from Cole and Paisley, Colin would have to take the heat this time. Walker covered his mouth to keep from laughing as a whirlwind of discourse ensued. Colin's eyes flicked back and forth over each of his siblings in a panic, and he covered his ears to block out the noise.

"Guys!" Walker shouted, hands up to put an end to the conversation. "Let Colin talk. You're overwhelming him."

Colin dropped his hands away from his ears and sucked in a deep breath. "I don't like complicated relationships. I like knowing exactly what I'm getting into, and what I'm getting into is a tutoring role. I don't see what the major dilemma is or the need for all this." He waved his hand over all his siblings.

"Try to keep your options open, though," Walker pressed. "You don't have to be so strict with yourself all the time."

"Excuse me if I don't want to take relationship advice from you," Colin muttered.

"What is that supposed to mean?" Walker blinked in surprise, mouth gaping like a fish.

"Nothing," Colin grimaced. "Sorry." He looked over at Piper, whose eyes jutted down to her shoes with the subtlety of a brick wall.

"Piper? Something you want to share with the class?" Walker stared at her until she made hesitant eye contact.

"I just... okay, I can't help but notice that you're really into

Talia, but you're not doing anything about it!" Piper threw up her hands in frustration.

If Walker had been walking during this conversation, he would have faceplanted. Instead, his heart rate kicked up a notch as he floundered for a way to escape the eager look on Piper's face. What was worse than being called out was not realizing that he had been so outwardly obvious about his feelings for Talia. If his niece could tell, who else knew he was carrying a torch for a woman he should never be considering? It was high time to dial it back on his pining and wanting.

"Look." Walker closed his eyelids slowly. "I'm not looking to date anyone right now. I'm looking to get my life and everyone else's life in order."

"So... you aren't denying it, then?" Colin asked, sharing a knowing look with Carter. Both of his nephews looked utterly pleased with themselves. Colin was always excited to know information ahead of the curve, and Carter frequently let his older brother in on the social cues he picked up that Colin was generally oblivious to. It seemed Walker's entire family had been gossiping behind his back for who knew how long.

"I..." Walker swallowed, trying to determine if the best course of action was lying or telling the truth. In the end, he opted for the most amount of truth he could give without explicitly revealing that he couldn't stop thinking about and wanting Talia if he tried. "I am very fond of her. She's helped me out a lot. She's a good friend and a good person. I can't currently be interested in her in any other way than that. Now, that's enough talking about my nonexistent love life. Grab your bags, or we'll be late for school. Colin, take your own car today, since you're staying after school."

The room filled with the sound of shuffling feet as the kids obeyed Walker's request and headed out the front door a minute later.

～

The drop-off went smoothly, with no further conversation of possible love interests. It was a relief, since Walker was already in enough trouble with Talia on his own without the added pressure of his nieces and nephews ganging up on him. When he arrived at the coffee shop, Talia was sitting in her car, on the phone, her face pale like she had seen a ghost. She wasn't talking, but eventually, she pulled the phone away from her ear and stepped out of her newly repaired Lexus wearing an olive green sundress with white lilies printed on it to match her white sandals. Her dress was the same shade as his designated color on the calendar app. It wasn't significant, but it still made his heart flutter, his brain making connections that didn't exist. Her hair was pulled up again, the waves of her ponytail blowing lightly in the breeze. She was wearing coral pink lipstick and a swipe of green eyeshadow. It did nothing to soften the blow of how beautiful he found her. Instead, his eyes trained on her defined cupid's bow, and he imagined what it would be like to kiss her. He could picture her eyes darkening into an even richer brown. Her thick eyelashes fluttered in pleasure as she leaned into him. And when he finally got a taste of her lips, she'd taste the way she smelled, like petrichor and fresh grapefruit. Manna from heaven.

"Hey, Ponytail," Walker bit back his arousal and waved. Talia returned a half-hearted smile as she made her way over to him. "Everything okay?"

"Yeah, it was just a voicemail." Her eye contact was rushed, and any joy in her expression seemed out of place on her face. It made his stomach sink.

"You don't have to tell me, but I'm here if you want to."

He wanted to fix whatever was wrong because he needed her smile to be real. He wanted to be the one to bring it back.

"I'll tell you later. Promise. Today, I just want to celebrate!" A real grin replaced the fake one, the phone call all but forgotten as Talia held out a brown paper sack to him. Walker took it cautiously, peering inside to find a maple bar wrapped in a wax paper divider.

"What are we celebrating?" he asked, already pulling the delicious-looking donut out, mouth watering from both the prospect of sugar and Talia herself.

"Your birthday, duh!"

"But it's not my—" Walker stopped mid-sentence, screwing up his face in thought.

"I sure hope it's your birthday, or last month when we went around to all the schools, you provided a lot of false information about yourself," Talia teased.

The realization dawned on him not a moment later. "Oh, fuck. It *is* my birthday."

"You make that sound like a death sentence." Talia laughed. "Are you going to eat your cake?"

"My... cake? How did you know I would want this?" Walker gaped at her then looked down at the maple bar as if it had appeared as part of a magic trick.

"Piper."

"You didn't get yourself one?" Biting into the donut, Walker closed his eyes in ecstasy. It wasn't Talia's lips, but it was a more appropriate thing to be drooling over.

"No, it's *your* cake. Today's not about me!"

"Don't be ridiculous. What's the point of a cake if you have no one to share it with?" Promptly ripping the bar in half, he passed her a piece. She took it hesitantly, raising it up in front of her face to inspect it. A sexual joke about having her cake and eating it too formulated in Walker's head. If she ended up eating the donut in slow motion and licking her fingers afterward, he would simply pass away.

And now I know how I want to die.

"I'm kind of a donut snob," Talia said sheepishly. "New York City has the best donuts, and I don't want to be disappointed."

"Just try it, and if you hate it, I'll eat your half."

Talia lifted the sweet to her lips and sighed when the sugar touched her tongue.

Holy hell. Happy birthday to me.

"God, this is good!" she finally declared after swallowing her first bite.

"Told you," Walker licked his own lips and forced a smile on his face. "You deserve it after being the only person on the planet who remembered my birthday."

When they made their way to the entrance of the coffee shop, Walker trailed behind so he could hide the sadness that was readily visible on his face. All nostalgic things reminded him of his brother. What was first a saccharine surprise to his morning turned sour in his mouth, and he had to force the rest of the donut down to stop himself from vomiting. The last time he had eaten a maple bar was the morning of the day that Cole and Paisley died. He wondered if he would ever be able to experience simple pleasures again without feeling the immediate pang of loss. For now, even maple bars were tainted by memories.

Fifteen

TALIA

As her knuckles hit the smooth wood of Amala's door, Talia turned the knob without bothering to wait for an answer. Amala was standing in the kitchen with a bag of frosting, frowning at a sheet cake. She gave Talia a nod of acknowledgment at her arrival, but continued to stare down the cake like it had personally offended her in some way.

"Going well, I see?" Talia walked over to her friend expecting to see a frosting disaster, only to find that the cake was entirely blank.

"I'm about to destroy this cake that I spent so much time on with words," Amala sighed.

"How poetic." Talia grinned.

"Can you do it?" A bag of frosting was thrust into Talia's arms before she could protest, and she held it out in front of her like a bomb.

"I'll ruin it!"

"Yeah, but if you do, Walker will still think you hung the moon. Just write something like 'Happy Birthday, Mr. President,'" Amala sang in a breathy voice then squatted down in the classic Marilyn Monroe pose, holding down her blown-up dress.

"Very funny." Talia rolled her eyes and stepped toward the cake.

"How 'bout, 'Happy Birthday, I'm secretly in love with you'?"

"What is wrong with you?"

"You want like a list? It all started in the sixth grade with a kid named—"

"Amala!"

"No, the kid's name was Carl, silly," Amala corrected with a raised finger. "Carl was a racist. And with a name like Carl, his parents were just setting him up for failure. He's in prison now for embezzlement... or maybe it was identity theft? I don't know, whatever white people get arrested for. Anyway, don't worry, I pantsed him in front of the whole class."

"Fuck Carl!" Talia raised her frosting in the air to toast the downfall of her friend's nemesis. "But please tell me you aren't planning on being relentless about the whole Walker thing."

"You honestly think I would give you away?" Amala stared back at her, comedy routine thrown out the window.

"No, I just—he's not looking for anything right now, and I don't want to, I don't know... make his life more complicated?" Talia shrugged, unsure of herself.

"Honey, I think that ship has sailed." Amala set a comforting hand on Talia's arm. "In my very valid and extremely correct opinion, the man is obsessed with you. Even if you make his life a little more complicated, you also make it way better. What would he do without you?"

"And where would I be without *him*?" Talia shot back. "I have you, of course, but..."

"He gave you a family," Amala finished for her.

"He keeps thanking me like I don't adore all his nieces and nephews. I love them. The other week we played Monopoly till two a.m., but I could have told you who would win before we sat down to play," Talia recalled.

"Walker?" Amala asked. Talia shook her head, chuckling.

"No, Walker is terrible at Monopoly. Colin won. Kid is wicked smart and is probably going to go on to be a Fortune 500 million-aire, be published in a medical journal, or discover ancient bones in the Himalayas. And from the second we sat down at the table, Carter was already calling bullshit on the whole thing, wondering what the point was if Colin was just going to win. Pearl was barely paying attention because she was frantically texting a friend about a boy and panicking about him complimenting a beret she wore in her hair at school. Piper was optimistic about the whole thing despite knowing Colin would win, and Cooper asked endless questions about how best to play the game."

"That kid never stops with the questions, does he?" Amala giggled. "Jayla loves it. It gives her endless opportunities to share her opinion on everything. Girl loves to hear herself talk. The other day, Jayla went on a ten-minute rant to him about her silk pillowcase. I think he was too polite to tell her to shut up."

"Half of the questions he asks, I honestly wanted to know the answers to. And Walker... he's present for everything. Every dinner. Every game night. All of Carter's basketball games. Piper said he went to all her soccer games before he was their guardian, too. He knew Colin was going to win at Monopoly but told Carter that winning wasn't the point of playing, even though I could tell he was mildly frustrated when he didn't even come close to winning. He made Pearl put her phone away and told both Piper and Pearl they were too young to be thinking about boys." Amusement played out on Talia's face with her final sentence.

"Isn't Piper sixteen?"

"Almost seventeen. She has *more* than just thought about boys, but there's no way in hell I'm going to tell Walker that unless we want to find those boys floating facedown by the docks. I am one hundred percent sure he would commit crimes to keep her nonexistent virginity intact." Talia looked over both shoulders in case Walker sporadically made an appearance before continuing. "He thinks Piper is the picture of innocence, and I think it's best for his mental health if he continues to think that."

"Mmm," Amala bobbed her head in agreement. "When Jayla gets to that age, I'm not telling Roscoe shit, or he'll start putting anyone she has interest in behind bars."

"Wise woman. I'm sure we're going to have issues when Pearl gets there, too. She's a hopeless romantic."

"'We?'" Eyebrows jumping up her forehead, Amala gave her a knowing smirk.

"I—yes, 'we,' okay?" Talia gave in. "I want to be a part of it. I want her to tell me when she wants to date people. I want Carter to tell me his latest reason for why he thinks his algebra class is a waste of time, and I want Colin to try to explain radioactive decay even though he could explain it a million times and I'd never remember the formula for that."

"You love all of them." Amala smiled and rubbed her protruding stomach thoughtfully. "It's how I feel about Roscoe and Jayla and this little one that hasn't even shown his face yet."

"I love all of them," Talia confirmed. The time she spent with the Hartrick family was her favorite part of every day. When she didn't have an errand to run after work on behalf of Walker and the kids, she would always head straight to Juniper Street. Her own house felt empty and lifeless in comparison without all those people to fill it. Even with the melancholy that often filled the Hartrick house, there was still hope. Feeling emotions, and helping the kids navigate their own, even the hard ones, made her feel alive. She was useful again. All she had at her small bungalow was at best a space to host sleepovers for Piper, Pearl, and Jayla, and at worst a glorified closet, bathroom, and bed. "I didn't realize how much I *needed* them. And Walker... I don't think I've ever— we're not even together, and I feel like he knows me better than anyone ever has."

"Frankly, I'm offended," Amala feigned offense and clutched

at her heart. If Talia couldn't be found at the Hartrick house, the next best bet would be the Winston house. Amala knew well enough that she was high up on the list of people Talia would commit egregious crimes for. If nothing else, at this point, Talia was sure Amala could blackmail her with the video evidence of her horrendous karaoke performance of "Let's Get It On." There were dance moves, and they weren't exactly suitable for the public eye.

"You know I love you," Talia cooed.

"Just not as much as Walker," Amala singsonged back.

"I love you in a different way! I don't feel like ripping your clothes off when I see you."

"Whoa, whose clothes are we ripping off?" Roscoe came into the kitchen, and Talia's face went candy apple red. "You and Walker finally make it official?"

"No, hun. They're both still idiots." Amala wrapped one arm around her husband's waist as he took his place beside her, bending over to kiss the top of her head.

"He doesn't like me like that," Talia explained with a wave of the hand still holding the frosting bag. A glob of white promptly dropped from the tip onto the countertop, and Amala bent forward to swipe it away with her finger, plopping it into her mouth.

"Since when?" Roscoe looked more confused than anything. "You guys have a falling out he didn't tell me about? He spent the entire time talking about you at our bowling night on Tuesday."

"Our schedules are linked 'cause of the kids. That doesn't really mean anything," Talia argued.

"Damn, girl. You oblivious." Roscoe cackled.

"Told you. Idiots," Amala declared.

"Rude. He hasn't said anything, so how would I know?" Talia defended herself, feeling a flush of heat all over her body.

He spent the entire time talking about you.

The statement replayed in her head on a loop as she warred with herself for a suitable explanation. The incapability to find anything worth wanting within herself told her that Walker didn't feel the same. He was just appreciative of her help. All she had ever heard from him was how he wasn't available to date anyone, so surely she was no exception. "He's unavailable," was what she had adamantly told Harper at the coffee shop before inviting her over to help with Walker's coffee machine. An hour of heavy flirting later, Talia was inwardly cursing herself for ever asking for Harper's help. It wasn't jealousy—it was just an extreme amount of touching to witness. Also, Harper was very pretty, which was frustrating because Talia had shown up wearing workout leggings and an oversized sweatshirt to Walker's house (not that she was competing for his attention). If anyone would be the exception to Walker's rule, it would be Harper. And really, Talia couldn't blame Harper for being attracted to him.

"He should say something," Roscoe agreed. "But it's also extremely obvious. He looks at you the way I look at Amala." He shot his wife one of those endearing looks that was so affectionate you could tell in a satellite picture from space that he was head over heels in love with her. "Why do you think I'm okay with him being around her all the time?"

"Because she's literally pregnant with your child and you trust her?"

"That too," Roscoe gave his wife an apologetic look. Amala just grinned, enjoying her husband trying to skate off thin ice. "But also 'cause the dude is infatuated with you, so I know he's not going to go after my wife."

"Walker wouldn't do that anyway. He likes you both," Talia argued.

"Hun, you are missing the point. Walker Hartrick has got it *bad* for you," Amala finally chimed in.

"*Bad*," Roscoe took his wife's side. "And he'd probably have my balls on a platter if he knew I told you that. I'm probably breaking some sort of a bro code."

"If he didn't want her to know, then he should have been better about hiding it," Amala reasoned.

"So... you're sure? You think he likes me?" Talia bit her lip.

"Oh, dear God! What are we, in middle school?" Amala threw up her hands in exasperation. Roscoe turned to his wife and calmly set his hands on her shoulders.

"Honey, sometimes it takes people a while to get there. Not everyone walks up to the person they like and loudly asks 'when are you going to ask me out? Are you interested or not?'" Roscoe mimicked Amala's voice, raising his an octave.

"She did that?" Talia gawked. She'd never heard this exact story before.

"In front of my parents and all of my friends at my basketball game in high school," Roscoe recalled, a dreamy look settling onto his face.

"It worked." Amala leaned into her husband, returning his look from earlier. "You asked me out."

"Never said I wanted you to take it back," Roscoe said in a low, sultry tone that made Talia want to immediately vacate the premises.

"Mmm, I don't think I want to take back what we did on the first *date*, either," Amala's eyelashes fluttered.

"Can you two get a room?" Talia gagged.

"Technically, we own every room in this house." Roscoe gestured with his head toward the hallway, grinning boyishly at Amala, and winked. "I'm free whenever you are."

"You already knocked her up, Roscoe. If you're thinking you can make twins, I'm one hundred percent sure that's not how it works," Talia scoffed.

"And I'm not sure you know that sex isn't just for populating Earth." Amala pointed at Talia. "Why don't *you* get a room, preferably with Walker, but preferably after the birthday party so it's not in my house. As much as I support you, I don't support you that much."

"Wow." Talia blushed and started stuttering over her words. "I'm not even—we're not having... I-I mean, we aren't going to do that."

"Look, babe, I made her all flustered!" Amala raised her hand in the air, and Roscoe returned the high five with a satisfying slap.

"You're just going to keep fucking with them until they end up together, aren't you?" Roscoe was holding onto Amala's waist with both hands now and staring into her face, effectively removing Talia from the conversation.

"Oh, absolutely."

"Guess I should inform you that I told Walker to stop daydreaming about Talia at the bowling alley and he went two shades redder than before?" Roscoe asked.

"Great work," Amala stroked her husband's arm lovingly, like screwing with Talia and Walker was some weird form of foreplay.

"Guys!" Talia shouted. "Can we lay off Walker? I don't want him to feel pressured. He has a lot going on, and... please don't, okay? I don't want him to date me out of obligation for helping him when I would do it regardless of whether he feels the same way."

"We didn't mean..." Amala's face grew serious. "Sorry, we'll stop. It's just hard from the outside looking at you two not seeing what's right in front of you."

"I *know* what's in front of me. Why do you think I'm in love with him? I'd rather have him as a friend than not at all because I ruined it by inserting my feelings into the mix. I can't lose what I already have." When Amala just blinked at her stupidly, Talia sighed loudly, annoyed that she was having to explain herself. "What?"

"That's the first time you've said it out loud." A soft smile settled onto her friend's face, and Roscoe looked just as enthralled. "You are in love with him."

"I..." Talia closed her eyes miserably and took another deep breath. She'd been so careful not to admit to it in the last few weeks and was pissed at herself for falling. Walker was never supposed to be her type. The uncertainty of it all wasn't the kind of self-esteem boost she needed right now. "Okay, fine. I am. A *little* bit. But I'm not gonna go writing it on a cake." Holding up the frosting like a weapon, she pushed her way to the sheet cake and started to squeeze the frosting out over it, eager to leave the conversation in the dust.

It only took ten minutes to destroy the cake. Not only was the writing sloppy and crooked, but Talia ran out of room on one end to write the word "Birthday," so she had to continue writing up the side. It looked like a five-year-old had written it. Walker would make fun of her relentlessly for it. She was never going to live this down.

Distracted by the many declarations made before she went to war with a bag of frosting, Talia couldn't focus on the cake to save her life. Even if she refrosted the whole thing, it would still end up looking atrocious. And maybe she wanted an opportunity to laugh about it with Walker. To see if she could tell for herself whether there was any love behind his smile. The kind that took over his whole face was the most intoxicating, like a drug she would forever be hooked on. Had she self-sabotaged just for an opportunity to see it?

What is wrong with you?

When Walker was around, Talia felt like she could cut the sexual tension with a knife, but she had thought it was one-sided. Her side being the freshly sharpened blade, while his was the dull back of the knife. It still might cut something, but like a butter knife, it required lots of force and a questionable amount of sawing. Walker might be attracted to her like Amala and Roscoe suspected, but not enough to make a move.

Risking everything by telling him how she felt wasn't worth it. At the risk of losing the family she had just found and the companionship of someone who knew her beyond words, she would bottle up her attraction forever. Belonging somewhere, having a seat at a Thanksgiving table and people to buy Hanukkah and Christmas presents for was worth the pain of loving Walker. Would she love to finally feel his lips up against hers? Of course. She could almost feel it, a phantom touch, she'd thought about it so much. Despite the yearning like nothing she had ever felt before, the outright feeling of being known down to her core outweighed the lust. It was more intimate than sex ever could be, although she had a feeling Walker could prove her wrong if they ever crossed that bridge into the bedroom.

The decorating passed in a blur of thoughts and daydreams of what could be. Walker holding her hand at Carter's basketball games. Walker kissing her in the aisle before tossing more Pop-Tarts into the cart as they grocery shopped for all the meals they would eat together. Walker grinning next to Colin at his graduation while Talia snapped the picture, only for him to request that a random passerby take the picture so she could be in it too. *Walker holding a newborn.*

And just like that, the daydreams broke into a billion fractured pieces.

It wasn't real. Some weren't even possible. Not for her. Those dreams belonged to someone else. Someone else was going to make him happy the way that he made her happy.

"Where's your head at?" Amala's voice said from atop the step stool where she was hanging streamers from the ceiling.

"Oh, just torturing myself again." Talia passed a dark-blue-colored roll of streamers up the ladder. "I feel like a middle school girl with all this bullshit floating around in my head all the time. I'm just short of writing 'Talia Hartrick' on a binder and decorating it with a bunch of obnoxious hearts. He's like a... a really hot parasite."

"You don't even need to write his name on a binder. His name is all over the calendar on your phone."

"Shit, what time is it?" Talia frantically whipped out her cell in a panic. Bolting toward her bag, she left Amala standing at the top of the step stool, waving a haphazard goodbye. "I have to take Piper to therapy, and I was supposed to leave five minutes ago! Love you! Thanks for everything! See you tonight!"

SIXTEEN

TALIA

Racing toward the school with a lead foot, Talia found Piper standing out front, a textbook lodged under her arm and a bright smile planted firmly on her face. Piper jogged toward the car and got in, looking as though she wanted nothing more than to spill fun facts about her life to a random stranger with a degree. Walker had mentioned Piper was thrilled about therapy, but this was over the top.

It was a nice idea to be excited about getting help, but Talia couldn't stomach the feeling that Piper was unprepared for the amount of work and thought that would go into it. Therapy was a process—a sometimes harrowing one. The first session wouldn't necessarily involve tears, but it wouldn't be sunshine and roses. Piper reliving her parents' deaths and the lost dreams of having them around in the future wasn't going to be a walk in the park. And so, Talia geared up for a hard discussion about maintaining expectations and the realities Piper would soon face.

"How's everything with the party? Everything set up?" Piper enthusiastically buckled her seatbelt as Talia pulled away from the curb.

"Almost. Are you ready for your appointment?"

"Mm-hmm, I've even got a notebook so I can take notes, and I've been listening to a playlist I made to get me in the therapy mood."

"Oh... that's nice, but, Piper, I hope you know it might not be as fun as you think it is," Talia said gently, trying her best to ease the girl into the conversation.

"I like writing poetry, working on myself, and answering questions that really make you think. This will be good for me." Piper wiggled excitedly in her seat, confirming that she didn't understand the full weight of what she was about to experience.

Finger tapping against the steering wheel, Talia calculated her best move. Therapy wasn't a fun philosophy class; it was a place where one second you were okay, and the next you were broken down, wondering how to put the pieces of your life back together while you mourned the loss of your future. To get the most out of her session, Piper couldn't hide behind her ambition or her routine. She would need to break those walls down.

Walker would be the one to walk Piper down the aisle some day, not Cole. Talia hoped she was at least filling a little of Paisley's role in her daughter's life, but nothing was ever going to make up for that loss. No one could fill the empty spot of a mother who was no longer around. Talia knew from experience. Piper would soon have to face everything that she had lost, and it wouldn't be pretty.

Talia never had a father in the true sense of the word. Her father's death only brought more pain and suffering and a tiny amount of relief, knowing he could no longer hurt anyone else. But Piper, Piper had a father. One who cared and loved her deeply. Talia wasn't sure which one was truly worse: having one to begin with and losing them, or never having one at all.

"Piper," she finally said, her voice cracking with emotion. "It's okay to not be okay. No one is expecting you to be happy all the time. Therapy is going to be a painful place because it's going to be somewhere where you have to confront all your feelings of loss, heartbreak, fear—everything. I don't want you to feel like you have to play the good girl. You're allowed to be sad. You're allowed to be angry. You're allowed to say how you really feel with no consequences, even if it doesn't feel particularly great to say out loud at first."

When there was no response, Talia glanced over at the passenger seat to find Piper's face devoid of color. She was a girl on the edge, holding back tears for everyone else's benefit.

"But that's who I am," Piper murmured softly. "I'm the one that holds everyone together with happiness."

"It's not your job to hold everyone together." Talia shook her head solemnly. "We all love it when you're happy, but I know I would rather see your real smile than the one you try to force on your face to fit a part. You can be vulnerable at your appointment today. You don't have to be perfect. There's no test you have to ace. No one is grading your participation. This is for you, not everyone else. Do you remember the night I met you?"

"Yes," Piper sniffled. "I didn't drink enough to forget."

"How did you feel that night?"

"I...." Piper looked at her feet.

"You don't have to tell me, but these are the kind of hard things you're going to have to face in therapy, and—"

"Alone." The word was rushed, spewing from Piper's mouth in a single syllable. She cleared her throat and tried again. "I felt alone."

"Okay." Talia held back her own tears. The urge to wrap her arms around Piper and rock her like her own mother used to do when she was little was overwhelming. Instead, she settled for reaching for Piper's hand and squeezing it gently so she could still focus on driving.

Alone. That was the best way to describe how Talia felt in New York City every day without her mother. Her new family in Archwood made her feel further from that lost person every single day.

"I know you know this already, but you have me. Always," Talia reminded her.

"I think... never mind, it's stupid," Piper shrugged and looked out the window, her cheeks flushing with embarrassment.

"It's not stupid. What is it?"

"Sometimes I think my mom sent you to help me," Piper whispered as they pulled into a parking spot in front of the therapy office. "She would have done something like that if she knew I needed it."

"*Sometimes*," Talia smiled and unbuckled her seatbelt, "I wonder if your parents knew that I needed you guys, too. You ready for this?"

"I think so."

Seventeen

WALKER

Whatever Walker had been expecting from Carter when he returned from his appointment, it wasn't what he got. When he dropped his nephew off, Carter did his best to break the car door off its hinges when he slammed it shut behind him. After therapy, the car door was spared any drama, and Carter's general attitude was leaps and bounds better.

"So... it went well? You didn't have a hot female therapist or something, did you? I swear I said you needed a guy," Walker teased. In the back of his mind, he really did hope that Carter had gotten someone who wouldn't easily distract him and his raging hormones.

"It was a guy," Carter affirmed.

"And?"

"And what?"

"I want you to tell me how it went. I've never been to therapy, so I have no idea how it works." Walker started the car and looked behind him to back out of the parking space. He allowed Carter to collect his thoughts, pretending to be ultra-cautious of hitting cars that were nowhere near the van. He already knew it would take a bit of prying to get any information; like himself, Carter also took a bit of time to process.

"It was... nice." Carter shrugged noncommittally.

"Nice? You have to give me more than that. I can't keep guessing how you're doing, it's... it's stressing me out." The statement came out a little more frantic than Walker would have liked, and he regretted the second cup of coffee he'd downed earlier with Talia. His coffee consumption lately was getting out of hand.

"Geez, maybe you should go to therapy," Carter grumbled, and Walker shot him down with a look of aggravation. "Okay, fine. He mostly just asked me a bunch of questions about myself. What I like to do, what my home and school environments are like, and what I currently do when I'm feeling... off."

"And what do you do when you're off?"

"Right now... I just kinda... shut down and bolt." His nephew looked at him nervously then quickly added, "but he said that's completely normal."

"Carter, I'm not judging you. I'm just trying to figure out a way to help," Walker explained with a wave of one hand for him to continue.

"He gave me some tips, and it wasn't as bad as I thought it was going to be. We talked about Mom and Dad a little bit, but it was mostly him trying to figure out why I was so uncomfortable being there. I guess I have a hard time letting people see me if I'm... having a moment. I don't like it. It makes whatever I'm feeling at the time worse when everyone is around watching me, ya know?" Carter looked over at him hopefully.

Walker gave a slow nod of his head. He could understand the feeling of wanting to hide. There were only two people he had ever felt comfortable sharing something deeply personal with. One of those people was dead. The other was Talia.

"I'm... different," Carter continued.

"Different?" Walker furrowed his brow, trying to understand. "You mean you're adopted? You look different?"

"I think people look at me and notice I don't exactly fit in at first glance, and then they settle into the fact that I'm there. If I'm having a bad day or something, it just draws more attention to me."

"You are allowed to have bad days, Carter. No one should expect you to—"

"I know that," his nephew interrupted, voice feeble and far away. "I'm the funny guy. If I'm anything other than that, people will notice that I'm different. There are only like five other Black kids in my grade, and I don't fit in with them either 'cause they aren't adopted. I'm just... in the middle. Don't get me wrong, I have friends. People tend to like me, but it's..." The end of the sentence trailed off, Carter looking out the window with a distant, sad look in his eyes.

"They aren't the kind of people you feel you can share personal stuff with," Walker finished for him.

"I already don't belong," Carter agreed, glossed-over irises returning to the present. "I can't add to that. Every guy I know thinks going to therapy means you're weak or crazy. I don't want to be either of those things, so I thought I should be predisposed to hate it. But," he shook his head, "I don't. Dr. Feeny wasn't fazed by anything I said, but I still know that everyone else who isn't getting paid to talk to me would be."

The piece on therapy felt disingenuous for Walker to comment on. Part of the reason he felt so reluctant to go himself was because it made him feel worthless and weak. Frailty wasn't something he could afford to project when the kids were all relying on his strength to pull through. He never once thought his nieces and nephews were weak for getting help and would happily get into a brawl if anyone said otherwise, but the way he thought about himself was an entirely different story. He was the leader of the family now. It would look like he resented the kids or couldn't handle everything if he went to therapy.

Walker tapped his finger against the wheel, mentally calculating different responses, but came up empty-handed. Carter was adopted, and as much as he wanted to relate to him in that way,

Walker would never fully get it. He already knew that whatever he said wouldn't be the right thing to get through to his nephew. There would be no use in explaining all the reasons everyone should want to know even the darkest parts of Carter. Carter would never believe it coming from his uncle.

"What about Roscoe?" Walker perked up, a half-formulated idea springing to the surface.

"What about him?"

"He's adopted."

"I didn't know that." Carter tipped his head to the side in slight interest.

"I'm sure he'd be open to talking to you about it if you wanted to."

"Trying to get rid of me?" Carter's eyebrows rose playfully, but the joke was a sucker punch to Walker's gut.

"No," Walker replied firmly. "I want you to continue talking to me about this, but... I'm not adopted or Black. I wish I could relate to you on that level because you and I typically see eye to eye on most things, but if I'm being honest, it feels like anything I could say on that would be absolute bullshit. Me spouting about how we all love you and don't want you to feel disconnected from us or other people at school is true, but I think you already know that. I can reaffirm that as many times as necessary, but I've realized that maybe I can't be the end-all-be-all of knowledge. If I was, you and the rest of your brothers and sisters would be absolutely screwed. The only reason I'm even remotely organized right now is because Talia stepped up to help me."

"There it is again," Carter laughed.

"What?"

"Talia. Just date her already and stop torturing yourself."

"That's what you got out of that?" Walker huffed in frustration. "Roscoe and Amala also help out with you guys."

"And yet, you forgot to mention them." The smirk Carter gave him was so infuriating, Walker wanted to wipe the smug look right off his nephew's face. Instead, he reverted back to the original conversation, determined to keep on topic.

"Let's just go to Roscoe's right now," Walker decided, pulling onto a side street, flicking his blinker on at the last second.

"No!"

Walker flinched at the panic lacing Carter's voice, expecting to see a deer or something in the road, and slammed on the brakes. When there wasn't anything, he pulled his eyebrows together and jerked his head toward Carter.

"Sorry!" Carter cringed. "I just... shouldn't we notify him that we're coming, at least?"

"He said to come by whenever I felt like it. Now seems as good a time as any."

"Yeah, but I have a lot of homework."

"Homework that you were actually planning on doing?" Suspicious, Walker continued on in the direction of the Winstons' home, putting on the pressure.

Unless Carter flipped the script and became studious in the last hour of therapy, he was lying. If he wasn't, then Dr. Feeny should've been paid more for his magical capability to make kids suddenly care about school. Carter was smart, but not in a stereotypical bury-your-head-in-books way. It was the kind of intelligence that caught people off guard mid-conversation when they realized that the discussion had suddenly taken a deep dive into philosophy. Carter was a critical thinker, but he also deserved an award for procrastination—a medal of honor he would continually put off picking up.

Carter recognized what he was good at and what he would be required to be good at just to survive as an adult. He paid attention to those areas only and deemed anything else a waste of time. Although there were a few things from home economics that Walker wished he paid attention to back when he was in school, he'd had the same study habits as his nephew and couldn't really fault him for his practices. For the most part, Walker's lack of attention in certain departments and extreme focus in others (i.e., English and writing classes), had worked in his favor.

"Yeah, I've got some math homework that I need to start on," Carter declared. Walker's suspicions solidified.

"Bullshit!" Walker called out as if they were playing a round of BS, which, unsurprisingly, was Carter's favorite card game.

"Fuck," Carter hissed.

"Hey, don't say 'fuck!'"

"You literally just said 'bullshit!'" Carter pointed out.

"I'm older than you. The saying 'do as I say, not as I do' applies here. When you move out on your own, you can feel free to do as I do. For now, I want the illusion that I've helped raise someone who's not a heathen," Walker grinned.

"That's BS."

"Yep, and yet, you're following it. I appreciate the acronym. Now, wanna tell me why you're lying to my face right now?"

"I would, but I'm more afraid of Talia than you." Carter folded his arms defiantly, and Walker whipped his head in his nephew's direction at the mention of *her* name.

"Talia? What does she have to do with anything?"

"Careful, Uncle Walker, or you might let on to the fact that you're in love with her." The arrogance took everything just a touch too far for Walker's liking, and his hand flew out to sock his nephew in the shoulder. "Ow!"

"Watch it," Walker warned. "I'm not in love with her."

Shame sparked in his chest. He was a liar caught between wanting to shout from the rooftops that he was in love with her, while also wanting to beat his head against a wall *for* stupidly falling for her regardless of how wrong it was. But, if he could physically beat the guilt into his thick skull, he would have done that already.

"Bullshit," Carter took on the card game tone from earlier, and Walker sighed in frustration, gripping the wheel tighter, too annoyed to correct his nephew's language again.

"We're going to Roscoe's right now, so either tell me what's going on, or I'll find out anyway. Clearly you don't want me to go over there."

"So we're avoiding talking about Talia?" Carter grinned cockily.

"You want to play ball? Let's play ball." Walker straightened his spine. "Are you sexually active?"

"Wh-what?" Carter stammered, blinking like a deer in headlights.

"You heard me."

Nothing but silence filled the car. Walker raised his eyebrows at his nephew menacingly, and Carter wrung his hands together nervously. The answer was written on his face, so Walker really didn't need a response, especially because the week before he'd found a box of opened condoms in the kid's bedroom. At least he was having safe sex?

"Talia's throwing you a surprise birthday party," Carter finally resigned, sounding as though he'd lost a battle.

A birthday party. The last time Walker had one of those, he'd hated every second of it. Birthday parties were an obligation. Between running around trying to split time evenly between all the guests and painstakingly trying to act like he wouldn't rather be sitting alone and reading a book, they were not his thing. The idea of *Talia* throwing him a birthday party, however, was making his heart flutter with a nervous thrill of excitement rather than one of dread.

"Okay, fine." Walker did his best to relax his shoulders.

"Fine?" Carter turned toward him with restored attention.

"I'm in love with her." The frog in his throat barely let Walker say the words aloud. He thought if he admitted to it, the world would collapse in on itself. Instead, his nephew responded with a level of monotone boredom that was mildly insulting.

"No shit, Sherlock."

"Okay, language!" Walker shouted, returning to his earlier rule. Pulling into a random driveway on a side street, he turned the car around, choosing to go home instead of to Roscoe's. He didn't want to ruin Talia's surprise and hoped to at least give her the illusion that he had no idea it was coming.

"So, are you going to date her, then?" Carter ignored the curse reminder.

"No. I can't right now... or ever. I'll screw it up, and I need her help with you guys more than I need to date her."

"That's such a cop-out."

"It's called being responsible. None of my prior relationships have worked out, as you're well aware, and you all need her. Tal's really good with Piper and Pearl. We all need someone stable like that in our lives right now. If I date her and we break up, then I'll be ripping her away from everyone, not just me," Walker explained.

"That makes sense."

"It does."

"It's also bogus as hell, and you're a wuss." Carter lifted his chin stubbornly.

"Think what you want. We're all still in the aftermath of everything, and it would be wrong of me to try to start up a relationship when I'm not... right." Looking away to avoid eye contact, Walker cleared his throat awkwardly.

"You think it's bad to be in a relationship when you aren't right?" Carter was looking away too, the underlying question hanging in the air as Walker pondered if his nephew was experiencing some of the same things he was.

"Are you in one?" Walker started carefully.

"No." Carter shook his head. "Was just thinking about it."

"So... that brings me back to my original question, which you won't deter me from. Are you being safe? I mean, I found condoms in your bedroom, but I still need to make sure. It's not like I can stop you from—"

"Walker!" Carter cut him off, throwing his hands in the air. "I'm not having sex, okay? I mean... I have... done that. Once. But not currently. The condoms are from before Mom and Dad died, and I haven't needed to replenish the one in my wallet, if you catch my drift?"

"That's good. You're too young."

"No, I'm not. And stop snooping through my room!"

"I wasn't snooping!" Walker argued. "I was putting your basketball shoes in your closet. If you put them away instead of leaving them on the floor downstairs, then we wouldn't have had this problem."

"The condoms were inside a bag in my closet. You were snooping."

"The bag was partially open," Walker shrugged. "If you didn't want me to see it, then you should've hidden it better or put your damn shoes away. I was looking for foot spray or something because the inside of your shoes smells like rotting flesh. I *did* snoop after I found the condoms, but the only thing I found was a disturbing amount of dirty socks that I didn't touch with a ten foot pole."

"Yeah, I wouldn't touch those," Carter looked up at the ceiling of the car.

"Teenage boys are disgusting," Walker grumbled, wrinkling his nose. "Wash your freaking laundry."

"You're starting to sound like Mom."

An unexpected swell of pride hit Walker square in the chest. If someone had paid him the comment before everything happened that year, his rebellious personality would have taken it as an insult. Instead, he found himself grinning from ear to ear. Paisley Hartrick was a phenomenal mother, wife, sister-in-law, and everything in between. How the hell she did it all, he would never know, but if he even remotely resembled her, it was something to be proud of.

Talia was like Paisley: organized, down-to-Earth, caring, and attractive. The phrase "MILF" had been uttered in regard to his sister-in-law more than once by Walker's high school friends when she was alive. It always made him want to gag or throw punches. He *did* hit Cole a few times for being too open about their sex life. His brother was always annoyingly chipper after a routine date night with his wife.

Walker couldn't help but want the same thing for himself: a life filled with date nights and mornings after that made him float on cloud nine. No one had ever made him feel that way after sex, but Talia made him feel it after just one conversation. Touching her would be inspired. She did everything with an admirable fervor, and he was sure kissing her would be more of the same. Her lips would move with a purpose against his until both their mouths were raw from biting and licking and tasting everything. And he would die a thousand deaths to taste more than just her lips. If he could drag his tongue over every inch of her naked body and feel the essence of salt hitting his taste buds, he would sell his soul. To feel her soft skin as he explored the curves of her hips and the feel of her plump breasts resting in his hands. If she rocked against him in the middle of the night with that damned ponytail swaying against her bare spine, he would be lost to the world.

"Helloooo?" Carter's voice pulled Walker from his daydream, and he blinked into awareness. "Are you gonna get out?"

Somehow, they ended up parked back at the house. It was one of those times where Walker's body had gone into autopilot, making him wonder who had allowed him to get a license in the first place. He couldn't remember the last five minutes of the drive past the point where they talked about Carter's nonexistent sex life—yet another thing they had in common. It was a miracle they'd gotten home safely.

"Uh, yeah. Sorry." Pressing down on the bright red button to release his seatbelt, Walker glanced back down the road. "When are we supposed to go to the surprise party?"

"Talia's going to text you to pick up Piper at Amala's instead, and then all of us are supposed to just... volunteer to come with," Carter explained.

"And I wasn't supposed to realize that all of you deciding to go on a random outing was weird?" It was ridiculous and wildly amusing that Talia thought that would work. If Carter hadn't told him, he definitely would have thought something was up.

"That's what I said! I suggested that Colin just drive us after you get there, but then Colin took his tutoring job, and he just texted me to tell me he's going to be late. Will you just pretend like you don't know?" His nephew laced his hands together, ready to drop to his knees and beg.

"Talia will never know."

The second his hand touched the handle to exit the vehicle, Walker's phone vibrated in his pocket. Raising his eyebrows, he stretched his legs out under the console and arched his back so he could pull it from his jeans. Unsurprisingly, there was a new notification from Talia. Her name displayed on the screen sent his heart hammering in his chest. Even her text messages consumed his body and had the ability to raise his blood pressure without a moment's notice.

TALIA 4:12 PM

Will you pick Piper up at Amala's? We're watching reruns of the Bachelor and I'm unfortunately very entertained by this. I think one girl is about to curb stomp another girl, and I have to watch that.

WALKER 4:13 PM

I will never understand the appeal. I get sucked into those crazy ER reenactments, though, so no shame. I'll be there shortly. Hope it's enough time for you to witness some girl on girl action. ;)

TALIA 4:13 PM

You're a perv.

WALKER 4:14 PM

Always.

Eighteen

WALKER

"Surprise!"

Walker flinched as he entered Amala's house. There was no need to perform his shock because not only was the volume of Jayla's voice way louder than everyone else's, but she had also jumped out toward him, decked out in full costume. Her face was painted like something straight out of a horror film, down to the fake blood dripping from her mouth and the tattered white fabric she had draped over herself as a dress. She seemed rather pleased with Walker's reaction, immediately breaking into a smile that showed off her fangs as she raised a high five to Cooper.

"Nice! I think you got him." Cooper gave a hearty grin and smacked his hand against Jayla's.

"Jayla, are you wearing vampire teeth and a sheet?" Pearl asked, mid-laugh.

"They said it was a surprise party." Jayla spoke with a lisp, sucking in air to keep her fangs in place.

"What's more surprising than a jumpscare?" Cooper agreed.

Since the first dinner party, Cooper and Jayla had been thick as thieves. Jayla looking like the *Evil Dead* was probably something they had planned together. She was always the ringleader, a firecracker of an eight-year-old who Walker was sure came up with the original plan. It worked, too. He was lucky he didn't piss himself or reactively punch a child. All he really could do was thank their insanity for keeping him from revealing he already knew about the party.

"You got me. Great job!" Walker lifted both hands in defeat, a smile lighting up his face as he looked over to Amala and Roscoe. They grinned maniacally at him, pleased with their spawn's performance.

Talia was laughing and clutching her heart beside Amala. Streamers hung overhead in a straight line leading to her, a guiding path that was completely unnecessary. Walker's internal compass always found Talia at true north. There weren't many people in the room, but even if she were thrust into a *Where's Waldo* book, it would take him two seconds flat to pick her out of the crowd. She was a siren calling him to his death on the open sea.

"Hey," Walker said, the corners of his mouth ticking up as he made his way over to her.

That's all you got? "Hey?" Dumbass.

"Hey," Talia replied. She gestured to the cake on the table beside her. "As it turns out, you also get *real* cake."

"Tal wrote on the top," Amala said quickly.

"Wow, way to throw me under the bus!" Talia complained.

The source of argument was clear when Walker leaned over the table to get a good look at the cake. He tipped his head slowly to read the letters traveling up the side. Even the chicken scratch of Talia's attempt at writing made his insides heat up. It was perfect. The streamers, the cake, and the presents he could see lined up on the table next to the cake made him want to throw his arms around Talia and kiss her senseless. He sent up a silent prayer for her to stop being so thoughtful and sexy before he made a fool of himself. For the time being, his best option was to break the tension by teasing.

"You did *that* all by yourself, did you?"

"It's pure art." Talia nodded, a stubborn look behind her eyes.

Walker grinned. "In that case, we should probably ship this off to the Louvre. I've been hearing talk lately that they're looking for the next great Mona Lisa."

Talia shrugged, the hint of a smile on her lips. "I'm more of an abstract artist."

Walker reached his index finger out to the cake, hesitating for just a moment before he decided he couldn't help himself. Talia gasped when he dipped his finger into the frosting. He dragged it along the top of the cake until a sufficient amount had built up on his fingertip and turned toward Talia. With an innocent expression, he lifted his hand between them, displaying the frosting in all its glory.

"I'm more into pointillism," he stated, quickly tapping his outstretched finger to Talia's nose, where it left a dot of frosting behind.

"You didn't!" Talia's eyes widened as Walker licked the rest off his finger, looking her dead in the eyes as he did it.

"Oh, I did." He gave her a playful lift of one brow to taunt her. *What are you going to do about it?*

That question was answered swiftly when Talia dug her fingers into the side of the cake. Walker stepped back a fraction of a second too late as Talia smeared the cake on his forehead, down his nose, and over his lips. The fiery smirk on her face coupled with the graze of her fingers across his lips was almost too much.

"My cake!" Amala cried, bringing Walker back down to earth. "What is wrong with you two?"

"Daddy issues," Walker announced.

"Mommy issues," Talia added.

"Nice," Walker agreed, tilting his head to the side in thought. "Sometimes I leave my cereal bowl in the sink for a day."

"That's horrible!" Talia covered her mouth in mock horror.

"Sometimes I reenact the *Risky Business* dance. That's definitely a cry for help."

Fuck. Talia in nothing but a white button-up and socks, dancing around her house. God, I need to see that and then "help" her with the buttons.

Walker could not think of a single snarky thing to say in response. All of the blood his brain normally used to create thoughts was rushing down to forbidden areas. He was useless. He shot Roscoe a panicked expression, and like the stellar friend he was, Roscoe jumped forward and grabbed his own handful of cake. The commotion snapped Talia's attention over in that direction, momentarily relieving Walker from nosediving further into lust.

"Don't you dare!" Amala shouted, bolting away from her husband, but Roscoe was too fast. One strong arm wrapped around Amala's back, and he had her firmly pinned to his chest, the cake finding its new home on her face as she squirmed to get free. Then, because Talia was also a good friend, the back of Roscoe's head was suddenly conditioned with Betty Crocker.

All hell broke loose.

"*Cake fight!*" Jayla screamed. Everyone flocked to the cake like vultures, nabbing chunks of birthday surprise in their hands as they launched at each other with flailing limbs.

The next person to deem Walker a target was Carter, an evil grin perched on his lips as he lunged toward him. Maneuvering to the side, Walker avoided contact with his nephew only to run right into Talia, who flipped around and raised her caked fingers. Her eyes danced sinfully until Walker ducked, grabbing her hips with enough force to pick her up and toss her over his shoulder like a sack of potatoes.

"That's not fair!" Talia yelped, writhing underneath his grip.

"I wasn't aware there were rules!" Walker laughed, finding the last portion of the mangled cake and picking it up.

"You're using my height and weight against me!"

Yep, her height and weight is definitely... against you.

"Okay, fine. Truce?" Walker suggested.

"Truce."

As he lowered her to the ground slowly with one hand, Walker met Talia's eyes. He held onto her a touch longer than necessary, reveling in the feeling of her body pressed up against him, his other hand stretched out to the side to avoid smearing cake on her. By the time he let go, they were locked in a heavy gaze, the moment sucking all the air out of the room.

"Tal..." Walker murmured quietly, barely loud enough to be audible over the sounds of the others shrieking around them as the food fight continued.

"Yeah?" Talia's tone was the same, low and breathy, sending a surge of longing down to Walker's groin. The pull. The desire. The absolute need to have her, not just in his bed, but by his side.

"I—"

Whatever Walker was going to say was cut off by the front door opening. All of the shouting came to an abrupt stop as everyone's attention snapped to the front of the house. Colin stood in the doorway, looking so perplexed he might as well have just walked in on a possible alien abduction.

"What the hell is going on?"

A current of suspense ran through the room, everyone connected by the same thought. Walker glanced at Talia, who gave him a short nod just as he caught a glimpse of Carter and Piper having the same silent conversation. The second that Colin shut the door behind him, the room set into motion again. With a fistful of cake, Walker raced toward his only clean nephew. Carter got to Colin first. Roscoe pinned Colin to the door, one forearm braced across his chest, as they descended on him. Whatever amount of cake everyone else had been inflicted with, Colin received tenfold, every inch of his body smeared with frosting as he cursed and tried to break free.

"Why?" Colin jerked his head back and forth to avoid Piper slathering more cake on his face.

"You're late, you're late!" Piper recited in a singsong voice.

"For a very important date!" Walker, Carter, Cooper, and Pearl all finished off Paisley's favorite catchphrase from *Alice in Wonderland*, which she used to repeat endlessly to get them out the door quicker.

"A very merry unbirthday to you," Colin griped at Walker, looking down in disgust at his sugar-coated clothes.

Nineteen

TALIA

The wind whipped around outside, making the trees bend, each limb pliable under its force. It was cold, and yet Talia felt warm from the top of her head down to the very tips of her toes. Walker had been relentlessly flirting with her the entire night, and it was enough to keep all of her extremities from getting frostbite as he walked her to her car. His arm brushed her shoulder, and she had to suck in a sharp breath.

Talia was reveling in the afterglow of an evening spent with her new family. They played a ridiculous round of charades that ended with Amala rolling with laughter and almost peeing herself when her husband had to act out skiing (fittingly, the majority of the guesses involved the use of the restroom). Colin eventually got it after Walker guessed "lift the toilet seat" and Roscoe took the opportunity to go the ski-lift route, constipated facial expressions and squatting abandoned.

Everyone was still covered in cake. Despite a thorough cleanup, Talia found there wasn't really a way to get the sticky film of frosting all the way off her skin without a shower, one of which Talia wouldn't mind taking with a certain tattooed man. His body heat was burning the right side of her body as they finished the trek to her Lexus.

"So..." Walker opened the car door after Talia hit the button on the key fob to unlock it. She moved in front of the opening, leaning against the side of her car.

"So." She gave him her best playful smile, head tipping to the side. He was so close, hanging on the door with his arm draped over the top of it, tapping the metal with his fingers. Was he nervous?

"Thank you," Walker said. He reached his other hand up and touched her shoulder. It felt intimate.

"Are you still going to pretend you didn't know about your surprise party beforehand?" Talia cocked an eyebrow, and Walker winced.

"Dammit, how do you do that?"

"Carter should never pursue a career in acting."

"Kid gave me away after giving me a whole song and dance about how he was scared of you and made me promise to not tell you?" His head shook slowly in feigned disappointment.

"You still had fun, though, right?"

"It was amazing. *You're* amazing."

Talia swallowed thickly, wondering if his comment meant what it made her feel. Her head filled with the consuming thought of what his lips would feel like against hers. There was no doubt in her mind that he would leave her breathless. Just his short glances and soft touches were enough to make her heart pound in her ribcage.

"You deserve even more than this," Talia gestured behind herself, back at the house.

"More..." Walker repeated, his voice husky as he dropped his eyes to her lips.

As it turned out, he could not only make her heart beat out of her chest, but he could also make it skip a beat or stop on a dime. Talia leaned forward a little as an invitation. There was no missing his body language. He was leaning forward, too, electricity charging the air between them. If they didn't touch soon, she thought gravity would snap them together like magnets. The pull was too strong to back away from. Walker's mouth parted slightly, and the tip of his tongue quickly dragged a line of moisture over his bottom lip. Talia could feel his breath mingling with the night breeze, replacing it with a warmth that she desperately wanted to absorb.

"Ponytail..." he murmured, eyes flicking to her pulled-back hair. The nickname he had adopted for her made her feel known. She wasn't just Talia, ex-lawyer, ex-daughter, and ex-fiancée. Her identity wasn't contingent on who she used to be, but on who she was becoming. It was one thing to fall in love with Walker, who was so easy to love, but it was another thing to be taught to love herself. He saw her lazy hairstyle and still found it beautiful. That was what it was—she felt beautiful around him. The best version of herself.

"Walker," Talia whispered, her breath hitching.

Their lips were only separated by an inch or two of unwelcome space, getting smaller, smaller, until they both tore out of the moment when a loud ringtone blared in Talia's pocket. Irritated at the interruption, she smacked her pocket aggressively as she yanked her phone free. Whatever breath Walker hadn't already stolen from her vacated her body on a last exhale when she saw the contact name and picture.

What did he want from her?

Avoiding the voicemail all day had done nothing to make the problem go away like she'd hoped it would, just like avoiding the three missed calls from him earlier that week had turned them into a voicemail. She could ignore it. Should ignore it. Why was he waiting until she was finally happy to rear his head again? She had moved clear across the country to avoid dealing with the aftermath, and he was still haunting her.

"Why do you look like you've seen a ghost? Who is it?" Concern crossed Walker's face, replacing the lust Talia wished would stay put. To reassure him that she was okay, or maybe to confirm that she wasn't, she flipped the phone around to show him. His eyes widened as the phone rang one last time before going to voicemail. "Clifford? What does he want?"

"To talk? I didn't answer him, so I don't know. His voicemail earlier said he needed to 'clear up a few things,' whatever that means."

"Are you going to call him back?"

"I... do you think I should?" Talia waited for his response warily. Some part of her knew that she should call Cliff back, but another, larger, vengeful part of her wanted him to be unnerved that she wasn't. She wished Walker would just tell her that Cliff could go to hell and that they could resume what they were doing before her past came back to bite her in the ass.

"Yeah. I think you should. So you can hear what he has to say, ya know?" His shoulders jerked up to his head in a shrug. "Maybe you can get some closure?"

"Right." Talia didn't want or need closure, but she nodded anyway. The only thing she really wanted now was a future in Archwood. With Amala, Roscoe, the kids. With Walker. "I guess I'll call him when I get to my house, then."

"Great." Walker sounded less than enthusiastic, the word slipping from his mouth like a cheap way of filling the space. "I guess you should go home, then." Stepping forward, his arms came around her, cocooning her in warmth and the scent of sandalwood mixed with a lingering frosting smell.

"I'll see you tomorrow?"

She didn't want to leave at all. She didn't want to hear Cliff out or spend even a second dwelling in the past. At the moment, she was convinced that anything but exploring Walker's lips was a waste of time.

"Yeah, of course." Another space-filler. The sexual tension was gone, leaving nothing salvageable other than an awkward goodbye and a look of discomfort on his face.

When Walker closed the door, shutting her inside her car, Talia gave him a stiff wave through the window that he returned just as uneasily. The funk she was in when he walked away caused her to miss twice when she tried to shove her key into the ignition. Then, even worse, when she flicked her wrist to start it, the car turned over without the engagement of her spark plugs. Embarrassment coursed through her veins as she tried again, begging the car to start. It had to start.

A few tries later, to no avail, Talia let out a groan of frustration, bowing her head over her steering wheel and smacking the dash angrily with the palm of her hand several times.

"Why won't you fucking work, car? Why are you just as broken as me?" Great, now she was yelling at her car as if it would respond with a "sorry, ma'am. That was just a misunderstanding. Of course I'll start for you now."

A loud knock on her window made Talia jump, slamming one of her knees into the underside of her steering wheel. Letting out a small gasp of pain, her head swiveled to look outside, where Walker was standing again. Shooting him a sheepish smile, she opened the door.

"Who the hell sold you this car? I want to have a little discussion with them." His tone had flipped to anger. Her car not working seemed to be an affront to his very being, and maybe it was, considering how they met.

"What are you gonna do? Walker, it's fine. I'll just take it back to the shop, and I'll have them do a full workup." Talia tossed her hand in the air to declare it no big deal.

"When you bought it, they said it was in perfect condition, did they not?"

"Well, yes, but it's a used car, and—"

"I'm going to drive you home, then I'm going to find out who sold you this bucket of bolts and screws and I'm going to give them a piece of my mind. It should be safe for you to drive it. I *need* you to be safe!"

Safe. He was hyper-aware that driving took too many lives, and it felt like a stab of pain to her heart. He shouldn't have to feel that way. He shouldn't have to worry constantly that the people he cared about wouldn't come home. The sudden realization that she was now one of those people struck a chord with her. It gave her even more of a sense of belonging.

"McDanielson's," Talia gave in, providing the name of the dealership.

"Thank you. Now get in my car. I'll drive you home."

TWENTY

TALIA

The drive to Talia's house was uncomfortably silent. Walker looked as though he was wrought with tension, his jaw ticking like he had to physically restrain himself from looking at or touching her. Talia couldn't figure out if it was Cliff's call, the car trouble, or the force that had been pulling them together all night that was putting Walker on edge. She had half a mind to try seducing him when they arrived and was still considering the logistics of that when they pulled up to her house to find another car in the driveway.

"You have guests?" Walker asked.

Talia peered at the unfamiliar black sedan with rental plates in front of her house. "Not that I'm aware of." The strange car was pulled as far off to the side as it could get, as if whoever the vehicle belonged to was leaving her room to pull in beside them. No definitive markers told her who the driver was. Her eyes narrowed into slits as she glanced at her house. A shadow lay in wait by her front door. She latched onto Walker's arm as fear spread through her body, all ideas of getting lucky abandoned. "There's someone on my porch."

Walker saw it, too. His face transformed into something cold and calculated as he turned to position his body closer to her. One arm stretched around her far side to grip her headrest, effectively blocking her exit and the shadowman's direct view of her face. "Stay here. I'll find out what they want."

"Please be careful, okay?" Talia looked into his eyes, clutching onto his arm tighter.

Walker set a gentle hand on her shoulder, and his face softened. "I'll be right back, I promise. You can't get rid of me that easily." She gave him the go-ahead with a jerky bob of her head.

When the driver-side door opened, Talia restrained herself from yanking Walker back down into his seat. This seemed like one of those moments in a horror movie when you scream at the main character for being stupid enough to investigate a too-suspicious noise. Walker slid out of his seat and shut the door, hitting his key fob to lock her inside as he moved around the front of the car. Talia could hear Walker call out a question to whoever was lurking on her porch, too muffled for her to understand. Panic welled up inside her as she realized too late that she should have called Roscoe or 911 before ever allowing Walker out of her sight. She was going to end up on *Dateline* as the girl who made all the wrong choices and ended up at the bottom of a lake beside a man whom she never even got to sleep with.

But then it was over. Walker was already making his way back to her and opening the passenger-side door. Her eyes shifted between the shadowman on her porch and a now very irritated Walker.

"I can get him to leave if you want." Walker's tone was clipped and harsh. He was no longer wearing the cautious expression from earlier. It sounded to Talia like he was looking for an excuse to use the intruder as a punching bag.

"Who is it? What do they want?" Talia cut right to the point.

Walker's nose scrunched as if he had just smelled something foul, and she watched his fists clench harder at his sides. "It's Clifford," he spat. "And I didn't ask him what he wanted."

Talia's eyes went wide in surprise as she flung herself out of the car, scrambling for words. "What? Clifford? Here? You're sure it's him?"

"I saw the contact picture on your phone. Same guy." Walker's boots shuffled along the ground as he made a wall with his body in front of her, preventing Talia's progression toward the house. When she met his eyes with arched brows, Walker grimaced and shoved his hands into his pockets. "Do you want me to stay, or—?"

Talia made a hesitant sound, scrunched her eyes shut, and shook her head. "I should probably talk to him on my own, right?"

A protective hand made its way to the small of her back. "I'm walking you up there, just in case."

The heat of his palm set Talia's insides ablaze with the desire to tell Clifford to get lost so she could have Walker's hands all over the rest of her body. "He won't hurt me," she assured Walker as they started toward her front door. Walker didn't move his hand or respond. If anything, his fingers pressed further into her spine as he walked in step beside her.

"Tal?" Sure enough, a nervous version of the voice from her past lofted into the air as her ex-fiancé's head ducked out of the shadows.

"What are you doing here?" Talia gaped at him, half-expecting Cliff to be a hologram.

Cliff looked just as she had left him—at least, from what she could tell in the dim moonlight. The same short, soft brown hair, clean-shaven jawline, and kind blue eyes stared back at her. His family had good genes. Ones Cliff was hoping to pass on to his kids someday. Until that instant, Talia thought Walker might have gotten it wrong and had been mistaken about who was paying her a visit, but there Cliff was, standing in... *sweatpants*? Well, that was different.

"Nice to see you, too? I tried calling you," Cliff pointed out, stepping closer to her. Talia felt Walker's fingers tilt against her back, guiding and pushing her into his side. The lengths Walker was willing to go to keep her safe. The thought made her lips quirk with a hidden smile. She snuck a small glance up at Walker before responding.

"I was busy. Did I leave something important in New York, or something?"

"No. I need to talk to you. *Alone.*" Cliff's eyes darted to Walker, who didn't so much as move a muscle to retreat.

"You flew all the way from New York to *talk*?" Talia scoffed. It felt like some sort of a weird dream, and she thought briefly about asking Walker to pinch her to confirm it wasn't.

"Well, you wouldn't call me back." Cliff held up his iPhone as proof, the device opened to a screen full of outgoing calls to Talia's contact. "I didn't have much choice."

"Maybe sitting on her porch in the dark wasn't the best option," Walker grumbled, turning his whole body to face Talia. He dragged his hand up her spine and rested it on her shoulder. "I can stay if you want me to, Ponytail."

"No, I'll be okay. You go home and rest. Twenty-seven is getting up there in age. You must be exhausted." She playfully poked Walker's chest to lighten the mood, and his concern transformed into a grin.

"A year wiser than you," he countered, leaning forward and enveloping her in his arms. "Thank you for everything. For *tonight.*" Walker didn't pull away immediately like he usually did. Instead, he pressed a slow kiss into her hairline, his warm lips grazing her forehead. The heat of his breath made her sink into him, her eyelashes fluttering shut.

When Walker dropped his arms from around her and stepped back, Talia's heart was beating frantically. It wasn't a romantic kiss in the slightest, but she couldn't help the spark of excitement that coursed through her veins. Even a chaste kiss from him was enough to make her feel lighter than air.

"Coffee tomorrow?" she asked.

"Always."

Walker offered Talia a wave as he stepped around his car. His eyes were solely focused on her until the last second, when they flicked to Cliff, who was now standing dumbfounded next to her. Walker's soft smile fell away in an instant as his eyes trained on her ex. The glare was a warning. No words were exchanged between the two men, but Talia couldn't help but discern the meaning in Walker's heavy stare, thick in the air that circulated between them.

You hurt her, I hurt you.

The sound of Walker's car door shutting and the minivan starting snapped Talia out of Walkerland, and she begrudgingly turned her attention to her ex.

"Who is that?" Clifford watched with obvious distaste as Walker's car drove down the street and rounded the corner.

"Walker," Talia said simply, giving Cliff nothing in the way of an explanation. Frankly, the massive pissing contest Walker and Cliff had put on was both unnecessary and annoying, but she'd live through the tension again for another moment with Walker.

Clifford's eyebrows bent together. "Are you—is he your boyfriend?"

"He's... a friend," Talia replied, still supplying the bare minimum. She sighed deeply and lifted her shoulders. "Why are you here?"

"I wanted to talk. To discuss us. I don't like the way it ended. It doesn't feel right." Clifford pointed at the wooden bench swing on Talia's porch, which Walker and Roscoe had installed for her earlier that month. "Can we sit?"

"Cliff, I'm not the same person you dated anymore." Talia didn't move to take a seat.

"At least talk to me. You didn't even tell me you were leaving. I found out from a piece of mail with your forwarding address on it that they mistakenly sent to our old address. New York is your home, Tal."

"This is my home now. You broke up with me." Talia remained calm but swallowed when she remembered the reason for their split. "I did what I had to do to move on, to move past it."

"What if I changed my mind?" Cliff looked down at his feet.

There it was, the reason Clifford was there. The reason he had flown across the whole damn country just to see her. Months ago Talia would have wanted that, wanted him. Or rather, she would have wanted the comfort of something easy and stable. There had always been something missing from their relationship, though. She loved him, of course, but she didn't *need* him. When they broke up, it was more the lack of stability, the loss of a friend, and the change of plans that pained her the most.

Clifford always had the same mindset with their relationship as Talia did. A sense of duty to a scripted life outweighed his need for anything involving extreme risk or passion. It was why when they slept together it was more strategic, just one of many on a checklist of things to accomplish. They didn't try new things. They did what worked. When one of them needed release, the other person provided it. Cliff was reliable. He showed up when it was required of him, but this was the first time he had ever shown up unexpectedly. They had never even had any heated arguments. In the time she had known him, the closest they had ever come to a fight was right then, with Cliff standing in front of her with a determined look across his face.

Walker was a different picture. Every time he touched her, Talia felt like she was both bungee jumping and curled up on the couch with hot tea and a blanket, reading her favorite book. He was equal parts comfort and exhilaration. On occasion, she had felt the desire to sleep with Cliff, but it was never the almost animalistic way her body tensed up in Walker's presence, begging to be touched by him and only him. Everything with Walker went past duty and obligation and edged into indescribable need.

"Let's sit down," Talia decided, and made her way over to the front door. "It's cold out. Do you want to come inside?"

"That'd be nice. I've been here for a while."

Clifford followed Talia through the entryway, taking a seat on the couch with an appropriate amount of space between them. He was always respectful and mild-mannered, the type to put most women at ease with his presence. If a woman came across him in an alleyway, she would probably be more likely to hit on him than to cut and run out of fear. Walker's concern earlier was almost laughable, but Talia didn't mind it. She would never mind being forced to stand so intoxicatingly close to Walker.

The two men were so vastly different from one another, it was hard for Talia to justify how she had been attracted to both. Cliff's humor was more dry and calculated. When he overtly laughed at something she said, it always made the moment memorable because his laughter came in moments that were few and far between—not because he didn't find things funny, but, rather, because he never lost control enough to laugh so hard that he peed. Nothing like Roscoe and Amala's relationship, which was filled with the hilarity of everyday life.

"I'm a little confused," Talia finally spoke up after they had sat silently for long enough. "I don't really understand how you could change your mind." She was eager to put it all to rest. There was no way the deal-breaker that had toppled their relationship was no longer a problem. "I still can't have children, Cee. I'll never be able to." Her old nickname for her ex slipped out of her mouth, and she scooted further away from him to set down a solid boundary.

"I still want kids, but we can cross that bridge when we get there." Clifford folded his hands in his lap, a mannerism that reminded Talia of client meetings back in New York. Business as usual. "I miss us."

"That's not the same thing as missing *me*." Talia was pretty certain she didn't even want to get to that bridge, let alone cross it. "Did you take off work to come here?"

"Yeah." Clifford sighed, running a hand through his hair. It was extremely unusual for him to take vacation leave, and he knew it. "I've been doing a lot of things recently that are out of my comfort zone."

It was the first time since his arrival that Talia realized the changes in his appearance. Clifford's hair was disheveled, a far cry from the every-single-hair-in-place look he normally went for. His eyes were lined with dark circles, making his face a portrait of exhaustion: still handsome, but tired. The usual curfew he set for himself, assuming it hadn't changed, was 10:00 p.m. Unless he was working through the night on a case, he typically looked fresh-faced and ready to take on the world. Talia wondered what kind of hell Cliff had been through recently that led him to her door.

"Are you okay? You look... off." Talia touched his shoulder, more of a caretaker's touch than a flirtatious one.

"Sorry, I probably look awful. I haven't gotten much sleep lately." Cliff looked down at the floor with an expression she had never seen on him before. Was that *anxiety*? "Maybe this isn't the best time to have this conversation. I was on a plane for six hours, and I feel like I'm not making any sense right now."

Something was clearly wrong with him. Talia was hard-pressed to believe that his newfound demeanor and disorganized composure had anything to do with her. She had never elicited such weird behavior from him before. If anything, when they were together, she made him even more docile, just as he made *her* calm, cool, and collected. Since moving, she found herself to be more loose-lipped and free. Before, she had been a bird contented in its cage, comforted by the notion that she never had to stretch out her wings.

Level-headed Clifford had taken a hiatus. The new person sitting on her couch was a ball of nervous energy that made an unease crawl up Talia's spine. No real conversations could happen while he was in that state. She had no idea how to settle anything with this version of him. They normally settled disputes with a level of precision most people only dreamt of. Even their breakup had been smooth sailing: heartbreaking, but still smooth.

"There's a mini golfing course on this end of town. We could go tomorrow, if you're up for it?" she suggested. Golf courses were Cliff's happy place. While Talia hadn't paid much attention to where the nearest golf course was, she had seen the old-fashioned sign reading "Par for the Course" several times since moving to the area. Sticking Cliff in an easy environment for him seemed like the best way to pull him out of his strange behavior.

"You are terrible at golf," Cliff chuckled, his hands reaching up to massage his temples.

"*You* are good at it." Talia shrugged, indifferent. Normally she minded losing, but she'd put off her competitive streak to get to the bottom of Clifford's visit. "You can give me some pointers while you explain why you're *really* here."

"I told you why I'm here. I changed my mind," he said with a confidence that was almost convincing. But Talia knew him well enough to know it was fake. It was the same look he gave his overbearing father every time he was asked how things were going at the firm. Overconfidence ran in Clifford's family, and he was expected to live up to his parents' perfect standards. It was also the same look he gave her when she found out she couldn't have children, claiming everything was fine when it wasn't.

"Sure." Talia wasn't buying it, but she decided to let it slide until the following day. "Where are you staying?"

Clifford's eyes widened slightly, and he shook his head. "I haven't figured that out yet. Where's the nearest hotel?"

"You didn't plan for somewhere to stay?" Talia was even more shocked.

"I know, I know. It was irresponsible of me. I panicked and just hopped the first flight here. I'll figure it out."

"Just stay in my guest bedroom. I just changed the sheets a few days ago, and Piper and Pearl aren't spending the night till next weekend."

"Piper and Pearl?" Clifford cocked his head to the side in curiosity.

It dawned on Talia that Cliff knew nothing of her life anymore. He used to know her schedule like the back of his hand. He knew all of her friends. He knew her mother. It was strange to think that someone who used to be such an integral part of her life didn't know who her family was anymore. He'd never met Amala, didn't know Talia spent every possible moment she could with five mostly adolescent kids and their uncle who she'd hopelessly fallen for.

"Uh, Walker, the guy that dropped me off, Piper and Pearl are his nieces. He has three nephews, too. Anyway, the girls spend a lot of time here," Talia offered the SparkNotes version of a long story and got up from her couch.

"You spend a lot of time with his family?" Suspicion laced Cliff's voice.

"Mm-hmm." She wanted to correct him. They weren't just Walker's family anymore, they were hers, too. But she didn't feel like explaining anything to an old flame. She didn't owe him anything but courtesy, and, really, she only felt she owed him courtesy because it was what her mother would have wanted. "Well, I have a long day ahead of me tomorrow. I'm renovating the grocery store I own, and I have to meet my business partner after coffee. I'll spend most of my day at the store, but we'll do mini golfing after that."

"Of course. Sorry." Cliff got up from his seat and looked around her living room. Unlike every time Walker had been there, Cliff looked out of place. Talia didn't miss the touch of surprise in Cliff's voice that said he wasn't expecting her to have much going on after leaving New York, either. Pride swelled in her chest. She had accomplished a lot since she left. She wasn't that same lost girl anymore. She had rebuilt herself into someone better.

"It's fine." She gave him a polite smile. "The guest bedroom is the first door on the right, down the hallway."

TWENTY-ONE

WALKER

A plastic stir stick balanced on top of the to-go cup Walker sat behind. He had positioned himself on the couch so he could see the moment Talia entered Roaster's Republic. It was a bit obsessive and over-the-top, but he was—well, he was both of those things when it came to her. Compulsively, he straightened Talia's morning chew stick atop her drink so it was parallel with the counter, as if she would somehow notice that the stirrer was slightly off-kilter like he was.

He might have been losing it.

What little sleep he had gotten alternated between replays of the night before and his usual recurring nightmare before he jerked awake and settled back down to repeat the process again. Both dreams ended with him drowning somehow. With Talia's, after leaving her house, he'd drive right off the bridge that magically appeared on the road back to pick the kids up from the Winstons'. Once, his brain had even combined the dreams. The second he hit water with his car in the first dream, he was locked in a water chamber again, catapulting him into dream number two.

Occasionally, the replay of the forehead kiss in his dreams transformed into something more sensual, and he'd wake up after drowning again, gasping for air, with a raging hard-on. It was truly a confusing mix of emotions, like his brain couldn't decide what to focus on, so it just threw him everything at once.

What was that forehead kiss, anyway?

Truthfully, Walker knew what it was: a territorial way of telling Clifford Talia was *his*. It was also the closest thing he could do to kissing her without actually taking her inside and throwing her down on her bed, leaving Clifford waiting in the wings. (That may have happened in his dreams once or twice.)

"Creative," Walker muttered to himself, congratulating his overactive brain for yet another round of sleep deprivation. Talia was often up in the middle of the night too, and usually they would wind up talking on the phone or texting until one of them fell asleep, but the night before, Walker thought it best to put up a barrier of space between them after almost demolishing all the rules of what was supposed to be a platonic friendship.

On cue, Talia materialized inside the coffee shop, her hair tied back in her classic ponytail. Walker wanted to take her hair down, watch it fall around her shoulders, lace his fingers through it, and gently pull her head back so he could kiss just under her ear. Then he'd whisper every single dirty thing he did to her in his dreams. But friends didn't do that. Friends didn't usually stay up the majority of the night pissed off that Clifford probably had more of a chance at doing those things with Talia than Walker did, either.

"Hey, I already got your coffee," Walker called out, waving Talia over. He adjusted back in his seat, attempting to play into a relaxed attitude while simultaneously wanting to jump into a game of twenty questions. In his head, the line of questioning was followed by a demand for Clifford to get the hell out of Archwood and go back to the city that stays awake too much. Let *Clifford* be the sleep deprived one for once.

"Thank you!" Talia's eyes lit up as she bounded over to

Walker, dropping onto the couch beside him and picking up the stir stick to twirl it between her fingertips. She took a long sip of her coffee, eyes closing with a soft hum of pleasure.

"I realize the coffee is hot, but it's not supposed to make you *hot and bothered*." Walker grinned stupidly at Talia, cutting his arousal the best way he knew how: with a joke. A light flush of pink dusted her cheeks, and Walker hid his amusement behind his own coffee. "Am I intruding on a personal moment between you and your coffee?"

"I can't help it," Talia said dreamily. She put a flat hand to the side of her mouth like she was sharing a secret, leaning toward Walker and quieting her voice to a whisper. "*I want this coffee inside me.*"

Walker choked. The hot liquid lodged in his throat, a prickly cactus making him cough and beg for air. The term "down the wrong tube" came up short. It felt more like the coffee had taken seven different tubes, all equally painful. His eyes began to water as he hacked up a lung and frantically tried to clear his throat. Talia slapped his back to assist, unaware that touching him would be the opposite of good.

"Probably shouldn't have said that while you were drinking," she said when he calmed down enough to take another sip of coffee.

"Jesus," he huffed under his breath. "Look, I'm sure the coffee wants to be inside you, too, but if you could refrain from making the coffee eject out of my body, that would be fantastic." *Classy, Walker. Very smooth.*

"Sorry, I'm really tired. I didn't get much sleep last night." Talia set her coffee down and got to work chewing on the stir stick while Walker tried to keep himself from imagining why she didn't get any sleep and praying it had nothing to do with her ex-fiancé.

"So. Last night went well, then?"

"If by 'well' you mean Cliff was acting really weird and we both decided that we should talk after a full night's rest, which I did not get, then yes." Talia flopped back against the couch, and it was only then that Walker noticed how bloodshot her eyes were, like she had been rubbing them, or maybe crying.

"What did he want?" Walker asked. He meant to ease into the conversation, but he had become tactless the second Talia walked into the coffee shop.

"He said he wants me to come back to New York."

If Walker didn't know any better, he would have thought he was having a heart attack. If not a heart attack, at least heart palpitations, but he could feel all of his limbs if he focused on them hard enough, which confirmed that it was a panic attack making him feel as though someone was standing on his chest.

Breathe, just breathe. Choose something to focus on. Talia's eyes.

"He said he missed 'us,'" Talia continued, the pressure in Walker's chest bearing down even harder. "I just... I don't want to go back to New York."

Air finally entered Walker's lungs. The vice grip on his heart loosened with Talia's statement, and he found his feet were firmly planted on the ground again. He could wiggle his toes and feel the weight of the to-go coffee he was still clutching in his hand, the paper cup creasing under his grip.

"You don't?" He met her gaze, doing his best not to look pathetic.

"I don't. I like it here. There's nothing for me in New York."

"But you're still going to talk to him later?"

"Yeah, we're going mini golfing at six."

"Like a date?" Walker took another sip of his coffee so Talia wouldn't notice his clear distaste for *that* idea.

Talia let out a sharp laugh. "It's not a date."

"Sounds like one," he rebutted, raising his eyebrows. Mini golfing was a classic romantic comedy move. There was no way Clifford wasn't aware of that.

"Well, it's *not*. I just thought it'd be better to have a conversation outside of my house since I don't know how long he's staying there."

Fuck. He's living with her now? Jealousy swarmed Walker's

brain. He set his cup on the coffee table so he didn't end up squeezing it so hard the lid popped off.

"He's staying in your bedroom?" He was starting to sound like a broken record, repeating half of the things Talia said back at her like she wasn't speaking the same language.

"In my *guest* bedroom. Anyway, I'm going to get to the bottom of it tonight."

"Great," Walker's voice cracked. Saying the word out loud did nothing to help him believe it. It felt more like the ground was about to open up and swallow him whole.

Talia acted as though her ex-fiancé had dropped by for a spot of tea, not to beg for her to come back to New York with him. Walker could tell she was masking the pain that always came up when she spoke of New York. Usually, the sadness had to do with her mother or her medical condition, but Walker was starting to wonder if he had misinterpreted her feelings for Clifford. Maybe she wasn't over him. Maybe she still loved him. The thought made him want to flip the coffee table over.

While Talia talked on about the renovations she and Amala were starting at Lydia's, Walker barely listened. Normally, he hung on her every word, even if it involved light fixtures, signage, shelving, or even menstrual products. While his brain took a vacation from being a good friend and listening to the ups and downs of grocery store ownership, it also took a break from logic. Irrational thoughts led him down a path that ended with him formulating what was probably the dumbest plan he'd ever come up with.

Mini golfing would be the perfect family outing.

Twenty-Two

WALKER

When they pulled into a parking spot at Par for the Course, Walker all but threw himself out of the mom-mobile. It took too long to load up the van with everyone balking at the idea of family bonding. The blatant lie he told his nieces and nephews made him feel a little guilty, but not enough to tell them the truth. The compulsion to insert himself into Talia's date was a childish one, but too persistent to pass up. Torturing himself with the question of how well her conversation with Clifford was going wasn't his idea of a great night. It was going to eat at him alive unless he came to see it for himself. So, really, his only option was to show up to Talia's non-date date under the guise of some much needed quality time with his family.

'Not a date' my ass, Walker thought as he looked around the bougie golf course. No one traveled across the country or invited an ex-fiancé on a mini golfing excursion just "to talk."

"You are *way* too excited to golf," Carter grumbled as all the Hartrick siblings came to stand beside Walker in the equipment line.

"Yeah, well, we haven't done anything fun in a while," Walker replied, distractedly scanning the course over Carter's shoulder for Talia.

"It's supposed to rain," Pearl whined.

"What are the chances?" Cooper asked.

"Eighty percent," Colin chimed in, easily sliding into his role as the resident meteorologist.

"Look, guys, it's going to be awesome!" Fake enthusiasm cracked Walker's voice.

"Is it just going to be awesome because Talia's here?" Piper pointed across the way, and Walker's eyes found who they had been looking for.

Talia was wearing a dark pair of jeans, a deep red blouse, and matching red lipstick that made her and her lips look even more enticing. A juicy red apple, ripe for the picking of... *Clifford*. The man in question was standing beside her dressed in high-class casual wear, smiling as he spoke to her.

Walker feigned ignorance and tried his best not to grind his teeth. "She's here? Didn't realize."

"Mm-hmm," Piper drawled. The accusation that laced his niece's voice was clear as day: Walker wasn't getting away with shit. Carter and Colin stepped off to the side to murmur secretively among themselves. And then, like the bull in a china shop she was, Piper ruined Walker's entire facade with a loud, "Hey, Tal!"

Both Talia and Clifford bounded down the hill toward them, clubs in hand. Walker waved awkwardly and forced a smile that was as close to an *I am here for a family outing* shit-eating grin as he could muster. Talia's eyes locked on him the second she came within spitting distance, and Walker's smile turned into a real one. She was stunning.

And dressed to the nines for someone else.

"Hey." Talia narrowed her eyes. "What are you doing here?"

"When you mentioned mini golfing earlier, it reminded me that we haven't really done a whole lot together as a family lately. I thought you said you were going at seven, though. I didn't mean to interrupt your evening," Walker lied through his teeth.

"Nope, six," Talia stated.

"I can see that." Walker nodded, hoping she wasn't going to pull her human lie detector hat trick out of the bag. "My bad." She'd put her date as an event in her Google calendar, which he was linked to, so he'd have to have been incredibly daft to not know the real time.

"Why don't you join us?" Clifford offered. The man was completely guileless and unaware of any tension between Walker and his ex. He also seemed like the sunshine and roses type of person that Walker hated, and what the fuck did he have to be happy about, exactly? Crawling back to Talia after making the huge mistake of breaking up with her in the first place should be embarrassing. His smiley Cheshire Cat vibe was going to make Walker lose his damn mind.

Wish he would vanish like the Cheshire Cat, too.

"Oh, no," Walker waved his hand in dismissal. "We wouldn't want to intrude."

"Nothing to intrude on," Talia clipped.

"Right." Walker shrugged. "Well, if you don't mind..."

"Not at all! I love kids," Clifford bobbed his head.

"So I've heard," Walker huffed under his breath. "Wouldn't really consider them 'kids,' though. They're mostly teenagers."

Legally, they were all kids, and Walker had called them that plenty of times, but he was feeling a bit combative. He felt like mentioning that Carter and Pearl were adopted, too, just to poke at Cliff's apparent aversion for children who weren't his biological offspring, but Walker wasn't about to use his niece and nephew as bait.

"Sometimes I still consider myself a kid at heart." Clifford beamed.

"I bet you do." Walker flashed his own teeth, hoping they looked less inviting. Talia shot him an angry look, and he ignored her. "Should we get started, then?"

~

They were only two holes in when Walker realized how good at mini golfing Clifford was. It set his teeth on edge. The guy was born with a silver spoon in his mouth and had probably gone golfing every weekend at an elitist country club with his very-present father from the time he knew how to walk. If Walker had to guess, Clifford earned all his high-paying clientele as a lawyer by schmoozing them on the greens, where he received a hole in one every other time he shot. Lucky bastard.

Pearl was easily taking second place and was surprisingly good, completely abandoning her complaints about the possible rain when she realized she could beat out all her siblings. The Hartricks were nothing if not extremely competitive. Carter and Piper were neck and neck and enjoying the competition between them while Cooper and Colin meandered about each hole, arguing about the best tactic to make it in. Cooper questioned Colin's every move, which Colin used as an excuse to explain his strategy in a long-winded way that involved statistics he had researched on the drive over. The rivalry between all of them was comical, and Walker was thankful that at least *they* were getting some enjoyment out of it.

Having been mini golfing all of one singular time before then, and never at a full-fledged golf course, Walker was the epitome of total garbage with a club in his hand. Between the overcorrecting and how it felt to be towering over a tiny ball, it was not going well. Mini golfing required a gentle touch, and Walker was more or less the poster child for all aggressive sports. Give him someone to tackle or wrestle to the ground, and he'd come out with the upper hand, but a golf club? It felt like he should be using the metal-plated stick to smash something, not hunching over it to lightly tap a ball into a decorative windmill.

By the fifth hole, his nieces and nephews were all beating him by a long shot, while Clifford steadily kept the lead. When a dude was trying to win back a girl, the obvious choice would be to show her his strengths, and Clifford had chosen the right sport. The smooth invitation for them all to join Walker deemed another calculated move. Getting in a good impression with Talia's friend —an unfortunate title Walker had bestowed upon himself—was a solid move. It was too bad Walker had no intention to befriend the man who had broken Talia's heart and was acting like he still owned it.

Talia, who Walker had wrongly assumed would be good at golfing given that he had always pictured golf players as people with their shit together, had maxed out at six strokes on every single hole. She was in dead last, just behind Walker. It made him chuckle at first, amused that they could at least enjoy their mutual destruction together, but any ounce of enjoyment he was getting out of failure vanished the second Clifford started to give Talia pointers. Walker had written more than his fair share of romantic comedies—he knew where Clifford's impromptu golf lessons were headed.

It started with a gentle adjustment of Talia's hands here, then a purposeful touch of her hips there, to quote, "fix her stance." It was all Walker could do to not forcefully pry the guy's hands off of her. Talia didn't seem to notice anything amiss. She took Clifford's suggestions in stride, upping her game every time her ex touched her as if he knew how to make her body tick. The thought made Walker dig his nails into his sides, hoping to give himself a physical pain to focus on. All it did was make him wish the pain was coming from *Talia's* nails raking down his back.

"Is that better?" Talia asked, shifting one of her feet forward and looking back over her shoulder at Clifford.

"Yeah, that's good." Cliff nodded and stepped forward, wrapping his arms around her and pressing his front to her backside. The lump in Walker's throat and the pit in his stomach grew two sizes, to the point of suffocation. "Now you just need to hit it with the right amount of force, and you should get pretty close to the hole."

This is straight-up pornographic at this point.

"Like this?" Talia pulled back her arms a little, and Clifford's hands glided over her with an ease that made Walker want to throw up.

"Just like that. You're good at taking suggestions."

It was the last straw. Before he knew what he was even doing, Walker crossed over to them in a flash, ripping Clifford's hand away from Talia's and effectively placing himself in between their bodies to create a cavern of appropriate space.

"You two want to get a room?" Walker growled, glaring at only Clifford, the edge to his voice unmistakable. The fact that he was even able to say a single word with how tight his chest felt was a miracle.

Talia glowered at him. "What the hell, Walker?" He stepped back a little when he felt her seething energy burn his skin, but he wasn't quite ready to give up the fight yet.

"I'm just saying, maybe you want to save the bedroom talk and the rubbing up against each other for another time. There's kids here."

Carter came up on his right side, setting a hand on Walker's arm, a cautionary gesture. "Uh... Walker? I think we should go."

"I actually have a big test tomorrow, and I should really study for it," Colin agreed, finding Walker's other side. "Huge test. Massive. It's life or death, really."

Walker's nephews were like two bouncers about to toss his ass out of a bar, one with a firm grip on his bicep and the other rambling on about the dire consequences of not being prepared for a test that Walker knew Colin had already aced that morning. The test was logged in the calendar that Talia also had access to. Even if she didn't, Colin's acting skills were abysmal.

"What is happening right now?" Clifford turned to Talia, and Walker cut in before she could answer.

"Nothing." Walker clenched his jaw and sucked in a breath. His nephews were right. He needed to get the hell out of there before he dug himself into an even deeper hole. "We were just leaving."

"No, no!" Talia exclaimed with a short, sarcastic laugh, shoving Walker's shoulder harshly. He flinched, recognizing the fire behind her eyes that was zero parts sexual tension and all pure rage. It had been a while since she had been this obviously pissed at him. "You know what? *I'll* go since I need to 'get a room' so badly. I've got a few of those in my house, and I've been thinking all night about how I'm just *dying* to rub my hands all over my Kindle. Is that okay with you? Any objections? Want to stop by and make sure that my book keeps its hands to itself? I know a certain filthy contractor that would probably break my pipes."

"Tal, wait, I—"

"Forget it!" Talia pushed past Walker, shoving her putter into his arms and only looking back over her shoulder when she was halfway down the hill. "Cliff, we'll talk tomorrow."

"Uh, okay, I'll call you," Cliff yelled back, then turned toward Walker in irritation. Clifford the Big, happy Red Dog had apparently left the building. Cliff held up both his arms for Talia's club, balancing his own on the pads of his hands. "I'm going to return our stuff. It looks like it's about to start raining, and I can't imagine that will help your golf game. Good luck with that."

Wordlessly, Walker dropped Talia's putter into Cliff's outstretched hands and raised his fingers to his temples to massage his incoming stress headache. As predicted, it started raining immediately, the clouds decidedly graying alongside Walker's mood. Clifford turned to walk the opposite direction of Talia, toward the rental booth, and Walker watched for a moment before impulsively shouting after him.

"You broke her heart. I'm just protecting her."

Clifford stopped mid-step, but he didn't turn around to face Walker with his response. "If she didn't want to try again, why did she suggest coming here?"

A new wave of hurt socked Walker in the chest as Cliff continued his descent. He had assumed, incorrectly, that Clifford had set up this little shindig, but it was Talia. If she wanted her ex back and Walker ruined another piece of her happiness, he'd never forgive himself.

"Shit," Walker cursed.

"Are you going to go after her, or are you just going to stand here like an idiot?" Piper sighed loudly over the sound of the rain pelting the ground as it started to come down harder. She pointed in the direction Talia had stormed off, and Walker bit his lip, his teeth gliding off it from the moisture. Even the weather seemed to realize he had made a complete ass of himself and had opened up the sky to let him know it. Staring off toward where Talia had made her grand exit, he thought over his options.

It was obvious to everyone else what he felt for her. Talia had to know why he had been such a jerk. Walker could only assume that the reason she was so mad was because she had wanted to rekindle something with Clifford and he'd ruined that. She at least deserved her shot at cutting him down a step for his less-than-stellar behavior.

"Go, dummy!" Pearl yelled. Walker was so shocked that the sweetest of all his nieces and nephews was yelling at him that he really had no option *but* to chase Talia down. Sucking in a decisive breath, he took off in a jog. If nothing else, Talia could yell at him, and it might make him feel less pathetic.

A minute later, Walker found Talia stomping toward her car in a whirlwind of fury, her hair drenched and clumped together in thick strands. Her clothes were sopping wet, clinging to her body like Saran wrap. If he hadn't been so aware that she was livid with him, he might have found the sight of her covered head to toe in fresh rainfall arousing. What he did feel were his waterlogged shoes beginning to soak through into his socks. Oregon weather was always unpredictable. He should have known to wear his boots, but he had opted for tennis shoes earlier, thinking that boots might hinder his mini golf game.

It's mini golf, jackass. You're not Tiger Woods. Literally no one cares if Clifford is better.

When he caught up to Talia, Walker thought he'd either be

turned to stone or burned by lasers from looking into her eyes. It turned out Medusa and Supergirl had nothing on Talia's rage. She jerked open the door of her Lexus when he drew near, as if he was a fly she could easily flick off, which hurt more than plain old anger.

"Tal, wait," Walker reached out, pressing his palm into the door to stop her from leaving. She whipped around to face him, outrage etched into the lines of her beautiful face. He winced, taking a step back, but still shut the door, careful to avoid hitting her. "I'm sorry."

"Why are you being such an asshole?" Talia jabbed his chest with her pointer finger, aggressively stepping into him, toe to toe, just like the first time they met.

"Because he doesn't deserve you!" Walker shouted back, feeling defensive. It was true—no one really deserved Talia—but it wasn't why he had thrown a wrench into the night.

"That can't be the only reason, Walker!" Talia instantly called his bluff, like she always did, and he frustratedly rubbed a hand over his face. For once, he wished Talia would just accept whatever lie he wanted to tell her as fact. "I'm not his to have. I already told you that we weren't on a date."

"Fine!" Walker snapped. "I'm jealous. Is that what you want to hear?" He threw his hands up, relinquishing any illusion of calm.

"Of what? My mini golfing skills?" Talia folded her arms over her chest, defiantly staring him down.

"You are terrible at mini golf and we both know it," he scoffed. There was no way she didn't know what was going on. He was too goddamn obvious. "It was the perfect excuse for that asshole to put his hands all over you with that 'let me show you how' bullshit."

"So why, then?" Talia ignored Walker's cut at Cliff's impromptu (totally planned) golf lesson.

"You're really going to make me say it?" Walker shook his

head slowly. "Come on, you know why. I'm not very good at hiding it."

Talia remained silent, just arched her eyebrows, waiting for him to continue. Refusing to back down.

Walker ran a flustered hand through his rain-matted hair, then down over his damp stubble. He rocked back on his heels as his eyes squeezed shut. When he opened them, he had hoped that she would either be gone or prepared to let the whole thing slide. No such luck. Talia wasn't going to let him off easy, and she wasn't admitting to knowing anything. Walker's walls were starting to crumble around him, his shirt beginning to resemble a napkin thrown into a vat of liquid, suctioning against his body and making the tightness in his chest worse.

"I can't... I don't..." Walker stammered, floundering to find the right words. Any words. Finally, he shuddered in a breath and reached a hand up just in front of Talia, desperate to cradle her face. He hesitated just a moment before letting his hand fall back to his side, deciding he didn't deserve the comfort of her touch while he said what he was about to say.

"I think about you every waking moment of every day, Tal," Walker exhaled. "And I know I shouldn't. I shouldn't want to touch you like that, but I... I even dream about you, and it's— God, it's agonizing when I wake up and it's not real, knowing that I can't have you and I can't be with you."

"Why can't you?" Talia's voice cracked with emotion, a pained expression taking over her face that made Walker want to die on the spot. He had already hurt her with that single admission.

"Because I feel fucking guilty! The only reason you're even here right now is because my brother and sister-in-law died. If they didn't, I would never have met you."

There it was: the truth, or, at least, part of it. And yet, it felt like a lie the second it left his mouth. Maybe he and Talia could have met under different circumstances. Or maybe if Cole and Paisley were still alive,

Walker would have found someone else, someone who would never be as genuine or as beautiful as Talia, but at least he wouldn't have known what he was missing. Picturing a life without her made him want to pull her in and never let go, but he had to stop before it went any further. He had to do what was best for her and for his family.

"You're blaming me for their death again?" A flash of anger passed through Talia's eyes, and her nose twitched.

Walker violently shook his head to dispel the idea. "Of course I'm not! But I'm not going to act like fate threw us together as some sort of fucked-up consolation prize! Even if I did, I'd end up ruining it. I promise you, you don't want me, Tal. Don't you get it? They can't lose one more person. If we dated, I would inevitably screw everything up, and I wouldn't be the only one losing you. They would, too. If fate brought you here, it was to help *them*, not me."

Talia adamantly shook her head and took a step forward. "That's not true."

"Yes, it is." Walker took another step away from her, fearing what might happen if she came any closer. "The only reason I'm doing okay with the kids now is because of you. I'm unreliable. I'm surprised I haven't set the fucking house on fire with the amount of food I burn. And the way I repaid you for helping me was by giving you two black eyes that you've only just healed from. I destroy everything I touch, and I–"

A flash of motion catapulted toward him, and Walker's peripherals picked up on it just in time for him to feel the pressure and sharp pain of a fist cracked against his nose. Reeling back in surprise, he stumbled, feet splashing in the water that had puddled on the ground. He caught his footing a moment later and balled up his hands to defend himself from his assailant. For a second he thought Talia had punched him, and he wouldn't have been surprised. He deserved it. Instead, Clifford stood glowering at him, hands still raised like he was planning on landing another sucker punch.

"Cliff!" Talia gasped. She slapped her hand over her mouth, eyes wide and alert.

"Now, wait just a second." Walker unclenched his fists, flattening and holding them up in front of him in an attempt to defuse the situation. "This is a misunderstanding, I didn't hit—"

Cutting him off again, Clifford swung. Walker side-stepped the flying fist in the nick of time and jutted his hand out to grasp Clifford's arm. He twisted, forcing the arm into compliance behind the idiot's back to restrain him. It was harder than it usually would have been. Walker's hand kept wanting to slip off due to the rain coating everything, but the maneuver was still second nature to him thanks to his wrestling days and the Krav Maga training he'd kept up with until Cole died.

"Walker, don't hurt him!" Talia shouted as Walker strategically pinned Clifford against the side of the car, pressing his face into the window.

"Wasn't planning on it." Walker's voice was strained as he struggled to hold Clifford in place with one arm lodged in between the guy's shoulder blades to keep him from moving. The makeshift straitjacket required his entire body weight to force Clifford into submission. Realizing they had an audience of all his nieces and nephews across the way, who were always too nosy to keep to themselves, Walker leaned forward to growl his demands in Cliff's ear. "Calm down, Rocky. I would prefer to not hurt you. I could easily dislocate your shoulder, and trust me, that hurts like a bitch, but I don't want to have to do that. I can respect why you punched me, but I will have to defend myself if you refuse to settle this civilly."

"Oh, now you're a pacifist?" Cliff hissed back through gritted teeth. "But punching a woman is totally fine with you?"

"It was an accident. I hit her with my car door when I opened it," Walker said coolly.

"They always say it's an accident," Clifford snapped, writhing against the side of the car. He groaned, stopping before Walker could actually pop his shoulder out of its socket.

Talia stepped in with frantic persistence. "It was an accident, Cee, I promise. He even came over afterward and spent a whole day babying my face even though I was fine."

"Cee." She loves him.

Clifford was still squirming, unrelenting in his disbelief, so Walker did the only thing he could think to do: double-checked to make sure Piper and the others were far enough away to not hear him when he admitted the truth.

"I was... having a panic attack, and I wasn't paying attention to my surroundings when I opened the door," he said, his voice dropping in shame. "It was still my fault, but it was an accident."

It was the first time Walker had ever said the words "panic attack" out loud. The only other person who knew about what had happened was Talia, and she wasn't aware that he had at least ten since his brother died and several more when he was younger. It felt degrading to admit it to someone who wasn't her, like he had lost whatever invisible battle of honor he was fighting. Clifford probably didn't cave under pressure. He was probably stable and mentally capable of anything the world threw at him.

"Walker," Talia said. She reached out to touch him, her eyes filling with tears. He moved away, transferring his weight to his left foot and letting go of Clifford's arm.

"Look, man. If you're willing to fight me on her behalf, then you aren't as bad as I originally thought." Walker created even more distance between himself and Talia and only spoke to Clifford, fearing that if he looked at Talia, she would finally realize what a disappointment he was. "I'll back off, okay? I shouldn't have intruded on your date. If she's going to be with anyone, it might as well be you."

"I don't get any say in this?" Talia seethed.

Walker gave a short reply, barely making eye contact. "He's better for you."

"You're taking the easy way out." She shook her head.

This is far from easy, Walker thought.

Clifford looked back and forth between them, massaging the

spot on his arm that was bound to be bruised later. After Walker's admission, he seemed to believe the story. It was either that, or the guy was too confused by the conversation to throw any more unskilled punches. Walker had no idea how much of what he and Talia had said Cliff had heard, since Walker only noticed his presence after being punched in the face. While it wasn't hard enough to break Walker's nose, it *was* enough to break his attention off Talia for a few moments while he tried to get his head on straight again.

"I'm doing the right thing," Walker mumbled a half-hearted response.

"No, you're not. You won't even consider how I feel about it. You're just passing me off. I'm not anyone's property, Walker." Talia was fuming, unperturbed by Cliff still standing between them like a doe-eyed child between two parents fighting.

Walker scoffed, shaking his head. "Like anyone could ever tell you what to do, Tal. If anyone is property here, it's me." Talia opened her mouth to say something, but he steamrolled on. "I will ruin you. I'm right about this. I know I am. And I know you're pissed at me. I should never have said anything, but please just promise me you'll still be there for them. They need you." He looked over to where his nieces and nephews were standing, stock-still on the edge of the parking lot.

"Why would you assume that I would ditch them? The world doesn't revolve around you!" In the time Walker had known her, even after he had accused her of drunk driving and trying to kill him on his motorcycle, Talia had never seemed so offended. She escalated louder, and he closed his eyes, tilting his face toward the sky to feel the sting of her words as he allowed the rain to pelt him. "I can't even believe you right now. You're just going to decide this for the both of us? Ask me what *I* want, Walker!"

He *wanted* to ask her, wanted to know if she felt even remotely the same about him, but he knew it wouldn't make a difference. In the end, he was fighting for his family. She was right: the world didn't revolve around him. It revolved around the five kids he was responsible for, and they deserved to be loved by someone like Talia. If he crossed over the line of friendship, someday she would resent him, and that would impact her relationship with them, whether she wanted to admit it or not. It would do no good to know if she felt the same. If she didn't love him back, he would be crushed. If she did, he would want what he could never have.

"No," Walker decided. He swallowed every declaration of love he wanted to say. "It won't change anything."

The only sound for a long time was the rain beating against Talia's car. Clifford took his place beside Talia, his arm stretching to drape over her shoulders for comfort. A pang of jealousy squeezed Walker's heart, but he knew he had no right to it. He shoved down the feeling, burying it under the responsibility to Cole and Paisley. He was the one who didn't belong, not Cliff.

"I need some space," Talia finally spoke up, a mere whisper. Walker's pupils snapped wide with panic, and she stepped forward, closing the gap between them. Her hand found his shoulder, her warmth burning through his two layers of wet clothing. "From you, not from them. I'll help you grocery shop, plan, and pick up like I always do. I'm not giving up my time with any of them. They're family to me, and I love them, but I need some time away from our friendship for a little while. To think."

"Okay." Walker's throat burned with emotion, his insides feeling as though he'd been shot straight through the heart. Biting back the tears that wanted to flood his eyes, he nodded in agreement and curled his teeth over his lips as he looked away. "That makes sense. That'll be good. For both of us."

It was a lie. At that moment, Walker thought he might simply cease to exist. He'd managed life without Talia before, and yet, the idea of her absence now, even just as his friend, felt like his very soul was being ripped from his body.

"I'll see you on Saturday at the store. I'll make a list of meals," she said, her voice going cold.

"No, um... I can make the list, no worries." He took a few

steps backward. His arm, along with the rest of his body, felt heavy with regret as he raised one hand in a stiff wave. A single hot tear rolled down his face, and he didn't bother to wipe it away. The rain wasn't punishing him, after all. It was helping him hide the pain from her.

"I'll see you then." The words barely crept up his dry throat as he fought the urge to run back to her, cup her face in his hands, and beg her to love him back right in front of her ex-fiancé. He wanted to risk it all, to kiss her until the world fell apart around them. Instead he found what little strength he had left and forcibly turned away, fixing his attention across the way.

For them, you will deny yourself.

He'd obliterate his own heart a thousand times over before he'd ever allow theirs to suffer again.

TWENTY-THREE

TALIA

Two people were making out on her TV screen. Heavily. Talia groaned and hunched over to grab the remote. She had started the movie thirty minutes before and hadn't paid a drop of attention to the plot, characters, or lead-up to the moment where the main characters had apparently decided that clothes were for chumps and ripped each other's shirts clean down the middle. She couldn't decide if she would find that hot or annoying in reality. Was ruining a shirt really worth the two seconds they'd saved? And how many shirts did the actors destroy before the director decided they'd done enough takes?

The display screen blared back at her, a reminder that she had made the poor decision to even watch *Contracted Love* to begin with. The trashy movie was doing nothing to lift her spirits. She had originally deemed it a compromise between the side of her that wanted to reread the book and the more rational side of her that knew that was a terrible idea. Either way, she hadn't been focusing on the movie. Her mind was hell-bent on a torture consisting only of replays of everything that had gone down that night.

For starters, she had gotten nowhere with Cliff. Thanks to Walker's timely appearance and his feelings confession—or, rather, the confession that he regularly thought about sleeping with her, which, while flattering, didn't outright equal love—Talia was permanently stuck in limbo. Her feelings toward Walker were more solid than some vague admission of sexual tension. He was her person. But even if she did want to finally verbalize what she had been keeping mostly to herself, Walker would refuse to listen. That alone hurt more than any old wounds Clifford could bring up.

The fact that Talia had known it was a bad idea to fall for Walker from the get-go simultaneously pissed her off and made her feel worthless. She'd been bamboozled by her own damn self. How could she be so stupid? He was never going to let her in as anything more than a friend, and yet she had still fallen head over heels like a self-sabotaging idiot.

You did this to yourself, Talia thought. This is your fault.

Lack of control always made her hands tremble, and hers were shaking like a leaf. It wasn't quite as bad as the day she found out she couldn't have children, but it was still the same feeling she had high-tailed it out of New York to get away from. Grief and self-hatred were catching up to her again, and she couldn't shake the feeling that this longing for a man she couldn't have was going to be permanent, just like her medical condition and her mother's death. Learning how to unlove Walker wasn't something she could stick on a to-do list and mark off when it was done. She had to somehow train her heart to stop beating out of sync in Walker's presence, had to stop stocking specialty Pop-Tarts for him to try out at Lydia's, and she *definitely* had to stop reading his books.

Beyond everything with Walker's impossibility was the looming reminder of the man who was a possibility. The one who blatantly asked for her to come back to New York with him. The one with no surprises.

The one who never made her feel like her heart was in freefall.

The one who never made her laugh uncontrollably.

The one who was... *boring*.

Would Cliff lay down his life for his family without hesitation like Walker would? A pang of regret for calling Walker selfish took up residence in Talia's brain, another gnawing ache of remorse. He was so blatantly the opposite. The fact that he was denying the obvious attraction they had toward each other just for the sake of his family proved his devotion to everyone. Everyone *but* her. She had mistakenly thought she was a part of their family, but maybe she was just a means to an end, nothing more. Or maybe she really was just there for the kids. She'd had the unfounded belief that for once in her life, she could have it all: a big family and the kind of love that lasted past the grave—and had acted out of childish anger when it was snatched from her grasp. Her mother would be disappointed in her.

Her request for space was a forced and half-hearted one, but Talia didn't regret it. Her mother always said "time is the wisest counselor of all." Lydia had whispered the words of advice enough that Talia could recognize when she needed to take a step back. Tensions were high. She needed to cool off and regroup before she said anything else she would later regret. Nursing a broken heart after giving it to someone who never asked for it in the first place wasn't going to come easy. It would have been easier if Walker had flat-out said he felt nothing for her. Knowing that he had thought about taking her for a roll in the sheets just made everything worse.

By the time midnight hit, Talia was spiraling into an ice-cream-and-popcorn-induced coma with a frenzy of self-destructive thoughts when a knock at her door pulled her back to the present. She wiped her hands on the paper towel she had draped over her lap and brushed her fingers through her hair and over her chest, popcorn particles dropping to the floor. After quickly disposing of the pint of ice cream she'd been spooning into her mouth straight from the container, she took a steadying breath and marched over to her door. She must have resembled a flustered teenager who had just gotten caught watching porn when she swung the door open. Her face fell in disappointment and embarrassment as she wiped at her mouth to clean herself up a bit. Walker wouldn't have minded her disheveled appearance at all, but that wasn't who was at her door.

Clifford stood in front of her, looking handsome in his usual gray slacks and collared shirt. His electric blue eyes were what really sucked her in when they first met. They were somehow both soft and striking. Anyone would find him attractive, and yet, when she waited for the sex appeal to dawn on her, nothing came. There was no incessant need taking over her body, just a mild appreciation for his gym-sculpted body and the thought that whoever he ended up with was going to be a lucky lady. Talia preferred dark brown eyes. Ones that tried to veil their pain and suffering but would always break in her presence. Eyes that stripped her bare when they looked at her but made her feel safe even as she stood metaphorically naked.

"Uh... hi?" Talia managed to get out, forcing an uncomfortable smile onto her face.

"I know you said we'd talk tomorrow, but I need to do this now," Clifford said hurriedly, brushing past her into her living room.

Sure. Come on in.

Talia followed him back over to her couch, and before she even sat down, Clifford launched into a monologue, running a hand through his hair and tapping his foot against the floor.

"I know it's late. I'm sorry, but do you want to get back together, or not? I need to know so I can figure out what to do with my life. I don't have a lot of time to decide. Exactly none, really. I'm going to get chewed out by every single person I know when I get back home."

"I..." Talia bit her lip, thinking for a moment. Not about what her decision was, but how best to explain to Clifford why she couldn't. "I can't," she finally decided on, stating it outright. "Nothing has changed for me, medically speaking, and I think you and I both know we're over."

"You're in love with Walker?" Clifford asked with a tilt of his head. He looked more curious than affronted.

"Yes, but that doesn't matter so much as I care enough about you to let you find what you deserve." Talia reached out to set her hand on Clifford's shoulder, and he slowly bobbed his head.

"I already found it." Clifford sighed as if breathing was an arduous task and closed his eyes.

"Cliff, I really don't think you have. I'm not what you want. I'm not—"

"It's not you, Tal," he cut her off and scrunched his eyes shut harder, shaking his head.

Stunned into silence, Talia blinked at him for a bit. If there was another dimension entirely devoted to men not wanting her, she had obviously stumbled into it. Between Walker and Clifford, she was starting to think there was something wrong with her. Despite the stab of pain at his statement, she could also tell that Clifford was clearly going through something that had reduced him to an anxious mess.

"You're running away, aren't you?" Talia asked. "That's why you're here, hoping we can fix things?"

"I guess so? I don't know what I'm doing anymore. I'm freaking out."

"Who's the girl?"

Cliff let out another shaky breath. "Mary. She's my parents' housekeeper." A second later, his eyes went wide, and he started to ramble and wave his hands about. "That sounds really bad. That really shouldn't have been the first thing I said about her. She's amazing. She actually owns this whole cleaning business, and she's—"

"So you were just using me as a scapegoat?" Talia interrupted, frowning at Clifford as he covered his face with his hands.

"Fuck," Clifford swore, yet another on the long list of things he never did. "I did love you, Tal. I really did." He said it sincerely, taking both of her hands in his and giving them a squeeze. "You were my best friend. Everything is so chaotic right now, and I just thought if I could get back to normal then everything would be okay. We were good together, you and I."

"I *did* love you, too, and yes, we *were* good together, but being good on paper doesn't translate to forever. Whatever you have with Mary sounds risky, but if I went back with you now, you would always wonder what your life could have been like with her, and that's no way to live."

Talia felt oddly confident about the pep talk despite her own love life casually laying on the floor in shambles. There was some strength within her that understood exactly where Cliff was coming from. It would be easier for her to go back, easier to fall right into her usual patterns with him instead of facing the music. Facing the fact that she was never going to love anyone the way that she loved Walker.

"My parents, they're going to disown me. They were both so heartbroken when you and I ended, and now..." Clifford trailed off with a miserable sound escaping his throat. "Giving up my entire life for love is so reckless. It wasn't part of the plan, Tal. My dad got me the job at the firm. You know him. He'll destroy me and burn Mary's business to the ground. But I just... I really love her."

"Is she worth it?"

"She's worth everything, but I don't want her to have to go through that." Clifford resembled a pouting puppy dog begging for food: mildly pathetic, but still adorable.

"So, you thought you'd just take yourself out of the equation and pawn yourself off... on me?" Surprisingly, she wasn't even mad, just entertained. If she couldn't have her own happy ending, then hearing about Clifford's was oddly satisfying. Love was real, and some people could have it. Just not her.

"Yes." It was barely a whisper. "I wouldn't consider it pawning so much as—I just thought it was a logical decision?"

"Is that a question?" Talia chuckled.

Clifford groaned, burying his face in his hands. "I don't fucking know!"

Talia slapped her knees with both hands, and Clifford flinched, looking back up at her. "Cee, who the hell cares what your parents do? If she loves you and you love her, nothing else matters." The tension in his face ebbed away a little as she continued. "You can get through all of the bullshit if you really want to. Sometimes, love is worth whatever pain it comes with. You and I even had a purpose, and I'll try not to be offended that you didn't really come here for me at all. You need to decide on your own if you want to pursue Mary, not because I said so."

"I'm so out of control when I'm around her and I never once felt that way with you. I thought I needed calm, but... I was wrong. And," he swallowed, "I didn't know at the time that I was lying, but I think I lied to you about why we broke up."

"You knew something was missing." Talia nodded, already knowing where he was headed.

"We were just playing a part. The part that everyone else wanted us to play."

"And then the part we were playing splintered," Talia finished for him. "For what it's worth, we were really good at our roles."

"We were," Clifford agreed, with a touch of sadness.

"You were always good to me, Cee. It wasn't either of our faults that our relationship ended. But now that I know what real love feels like, beyond the friendship kind of love we had, I'm not so sad anymore."

"Really? Because you look miserable."

"Right, well, it's been a long night. And I am sad, but knowing that that kind of love exists will have to be enough for me. I'm happy for you, truly." Talia broke eye contact when she could feel the start of tears pricking at her eyes.

"He'll come around," Cliff murmured, his soft hand brushing her arm. She jerked her head back to look at him. "I only caught the back half of the conversation, but that dude is desperately in love with you."

"He didn't say that, and I don't think I've ever heard you use the word 'dude' before." Talia let out a short laugh.

"Mary also got me to eat spicy food." Clifford shrugged. "And I didn't need to hear him say it considering the whole 'get your hands off my girl' thing and how destroyed he looked when he left. I imagine it's how I looked when Mary told me that I could either decide to love her fully or she was breaking up with me."

"I think I like Mary. She sounds like a badass." Talia grinned.

"You would love her. She's terrifying. Assuming that you aren't lying about the whole battered face thing, Walker seems like a good person, too."

"I got into a fight with a car door and lost. Promise."

"I'm not going to apologize for punching him, though. He ruined our date, and letting off some steam felt really good. Like, maybe I should get a membership to a boxing club, *good*."

"That wasn't a date, and where was this Clifford when I was around?"

"Hidden under piles of self-doubt and parental obligation. And it was definitely a date, Tal. We went *mini golfing*. Do you ever watch movies, or do you still just sneak-read sex books?"

"I—were you actually trying to feel me up?" Talia's eyes widened.

"No! You really suck at golfing. I was just trying to help you." Clifford crossed his arms over his chest, clearly offended by the insinuation.

"Fine, then you and Walker are both idiots, and I'm the only sane one." Talia lifted her chin with pride, and Clifford shook his head, chuckling.

They sat quietly for a moment before he set a gentle hand on her shoulder, giving her a soft, appreciative smile. That was their relationship in a nutshell: appreciative, respectful, and easy. Talia could have married Clifford and loved him every day until they died, never knowing what she was missing. He was a good person, kind, committed, and hard-working, but he didn't want to make her lose herself in torrid touch or schedule her entire life around five unruly children. He didn't make her a better person. Clifford belonged to Mary. And she, no matter whether she would get to love him or not, belonged to Walker.

"Friends?" Clifford asked, hand still warming her shoulder.

"Friends," Talia agreed. Cliff kissed her cheek and stood up from the couch, looking much more at ease. That made one of them. "Invite me to your wedding?" She called after him as he walked toward the front door.

"If you invite me to yours."

Talia lifted her shoulders, a failed attempt at indifference. "If I ever have one, you're first on the guest list."

Twenty-Four

TALIA

As expected, Talia spent the entire night tossing and turning in her empty bed, thinking of Walker. Despite the resolution of one of her major problems with Clifford hopping on a red-eye flight back to New York, she was still stuck. The closure offered her no relief because after months spent with Walker, she no longer needed it. She had run from rejection in New York just to run smack-dab into even more, and more painful, rejection.

Talia couldn't just tell her father to go to hell. Her romantic problems with Walker weren't as simple as hopping on a flight and admitting she loved someone like Clifford was doing at that very moment. There was no snapping of her fingers and boom, presto, feud evaporated. The only thing that would resolve the tension rested on her capability to shove her feelings so far into oblivion that she could be content with friendship alone. Having Walker at all was better than not having all of him.

Lydia's was dead silent when Talia arrived. It was pleasant, considering she already had a barrage of overcomplicated thoughts crowding her brain. The three cups of coffee she drank that morning from her own machine at home—which was nowhere near as good as Roaster's Republic—ramped up the chaos in her head. She should have ignored her body's demands for caffeine, but the exhaustion level she had reached was starting to edge into self-deprecation again. It would become an extremely unhealthy pattern if she allowed her degrading thoughts to consume her the way they did after her diagnosis.

"What the hell happened last night?" Amala was eagerly leaning forward in the chair behind the desk when Talia finally made it to their shared office. "You can't just text me saying you need to talk and then go MIA!"

"Sorry, it's been not so fun." Talia slumped into one of the guest seats across from Amala and immediately spewed out the basics: "Walker freaked out when Cliff and I were mini golfing and confessed that he thinks about me as more than a friend, Cliff punched him in the face, Walker said that we can't ever be together, and Cliff ran off to be with his parent's housekeeper—or, I guess, he's probably on a plane right now, it's a long flight."

Amala's lips opened and closed several times before she screwed up her face and blurted, "Woman, was that even English?"

Talia groaned and dramatically laid her head down on the desk between them.

It took twenty minutes to give Amala a proper run-through of the prior day's events. A sweeping declaration of how all men were idiots rattled out of Amala's mouth before she sat back in her chair, crossing her legs with a heavy look of contemplation. Amala's head rocked from side to side, the human embodiment of a bobblehead as Talia waited a long, agonizing five seconds of silence before demanding answers.

"Tell me what to do!"

"Seduce him?" Amala suggested.

Talia rolled her eyes. "You're no help."

"I'm just saying, the whole cake fight thing felt like a euphemism. He clearly wants your cake, or... wants to lick icing off your body?"

"Can we get past your sexual fantasies about cake and be serious for two seconds?" Talia bit off.

"Oh, it's not a fantasy for me. I've already lived that. I'm very into the whipped cream thing."

"I'm so happy for you," Talia drawled, sarcasm dripping off every word.

"Fine, fine. My honest opinion is that Walker's right," Amala stated.

Talia's mouth fell open. "Excuse me? You can't be serious!"

"Look, while I don't agree with Walker's 'I screw everything up' narrative, I understand where he's coming from. I have a kid and one on the way, and I would do anything for them."

"I'm aware that I don't have and won't have kids, Amala, you don't have to remind me." Talia scowled and pulled her arms tight to her chest to hold herself back from exploding on her best friend.

She was twisting Amala's words into something they weren't, and she knew it. Occasionally, bitter resentment for everyone without infertility problems rose to her surface without warning in a very woe-is-me manner. The truth was, she was jealous. There were people out there who *accidentally* got pregnant, let alone tried and succeeded, and Talia would give anything to be one of them. But she wasn't the type to throw herself a pity party, so she immediately regretted trying to make Amala out to be the bad guy. She had allowed anger to win out again. Defeat relaxed her limbs until her arms fell to her sides.

"Sorry," Talia swallowed. "I know that's not what you meant. I didn't mean to get snippy with you."

"Tal," Amala's tone grew softer as she spoke, her dark eyes warming with sincerity. "You may not have your own kids, but the reason Walker feels so strongly about not wanting to screw up your relationship with the kids is because it would be a huge loss for them."

The truth of the words found its way straight into Talia's heart, and she sat up straighter to listen.

"You're not their mom, no, but you are a motherly figure to them, and that's what they need right now. You know I've been on team Tal-Wal since the beginning, and I still am, but for right now, he's right. It's best to focus on healing. I really don't think this will last forever, but am I wrong in thinking that you have some stuff to heal from, too?"

Talia bobbed her head and drummed her fingers on the desktop. "No, you're right."

Amala had a way of always cutting out the bullshit and getting to the root of a problem, and while it was painful for Talia to listen to, she was grateful. It made it easier to put everything into a neat little box with a bow and leave it in New York. Clifford coming to see her out of the blue had opened that box. Even without him, the box would have split out eventually. As it turned out, Talia hadn't left her struggles behind at all. They stowed away on the plane with her to Archwood and chose the most inopportune time to resurface the wreckage of not just her infertility, but her mother's death. The number of times Talia had scolded herself for disappointing her mother just that morning was excessive. Lydia wouldn't have even been disappointed. Instead, she would have had her sit between her legs on the floor so she could calmly brush Talia's hair while offering soft-spoken words of wisdom and helping Talia consume the ice cream and popcorn she had single-handedly gorged on the night prior.

Then there was Talia's father. Surely, her giant sinkhole of daddy issues deserved some attention, too. It was painstakingly obvious, due to her several recent outbursts and the accusations she had thrown at the people she loved, that she might have inherited some of Jeff Cohen's anger issues. It was getting harder and harder to disassociate from someone who had given her half his gene pool, no matter how badly she wanted nothing to do with him. Jeff Cohen was the type of narcissist that was still sucking the life out of Talia beyond the grave. His rage was a part of her, and the trauma he caused was not only still haunting her, but Walker, the kids, and even Amala.

"You don't have to be perfect before you can date someone," Amala's voice called Talia back from her thoughts. "But I do think it would be nice if both of you figured out that you're worth it. Walker needs to realize that it's okay to want something for himself, and you need to realize that you *are* wanted. Not just by Walker, but by all of us."

Wanted. The word knocked the wind out of Talia. All she ever hoped for in any relationship, whether it be platonic or otherwise, was to be wanted. Her lifestyle motto had always been to make herself indispensable so she'd be wanted at her job, wanted in her romantic relationships, and wanted by her friends. Constantly giving quickly led to burnout, which then led to a short temper.

Logically, as an intellectual who'd passed the bar exam with flying colors, Talia knew she wasn't truly unwanted, but making herself feel that way was another story entirely. Walker's admission and refusal to bridge the gap between friendship and more left her tied to a dock: wanted, but not enough to risk being lost on the open sea.

Even after endless rejection, there was still one thing Talia could hold onto: the kids. They *did* want her, needed her, even— she was sure of it. And she would be damned to ever give that up. Her own mental health didn't just affect her anymore. Healing from her own trauma could eventually help them, too.

"Okay," Talia sucked in a steadying breath as she worked over a plan of action. "Therapy would be good for me. And I guess I'll work on figuring out how to be just Walker's friend without hurting myself more than I already have."

"For now," Amala agreed. "Then you're both going to fail miserably at the whole friendship thing and rail each other into next week."

"Is it just the pregnancy making you this horny?"

"I crave pickles, milkshakes, salt and vinegar chips, and sex *constantly*," Amala confirmed with a cheesy grin. "But I'm also too bloated half the time from this baby sitting on all my internal organs and eating all the aforementioned foods to do the last one, so I channel all of my desire for sexcapades into wanting my friends to also get laid."

"What are friends for?" Talia laughed. "I'm not planning on failing, though."

"Failing at what?" A deep voice rasped from behind Talia, sending a shiver up her spine. Walker was leaning against the door frame as he always did. His face quickly edged from concern to discomfort when she met his gaze. "Right, sorry. None of my business."

"Got your shopping list?" Talia inquired with an overly chipper voice. Feigned happiness became even more difficult when Walker displayed the list he'd brought on the colorful stationery she had bought him. She could feel the heat wanting to creep up her chest and neck to her cheeks. Using her phone as an excuse, she picked it up and swiped her finger over the screen to unlock it. "Send me a copy so we can conquer and divide."

They never divided the list, but in order to get through the whole affair, Talia needed to keep her distance from Walker as much as possible. If he was shocked or disappointed with the new tactic, he didn't let on, just pulled out his own phone from his pocket. A second later, a notification appeared on Talia's phone, and she opened it to find a picture of his list, all of the items categorized and laid out exactly the way she had taught him.

"Which categories do you want?" he asked conversationally.

Talia opened her mouth to respond but was interrupted by the sound of foil and air popping like a balloon. She turned to find Amala looking between her and Walker with amusement as she plopped a potato chip—salt and vinegar, of course—into her mouth. Amala crunched loudly as she stared Talia and Walker down, watching them as if they were one of her crappy reality TV shows. Ignoring her, Talia swiveled to face Walker and get down to business.

"I'll take the cosmetics, toiletries, house supplies, and—"

"But you always make *me* grab the tampons," Walker noted and gave her a handsome smile. It was true. Talia teased him relentlessly about it and knew he was barely fazed by the idea of picking up feminine hygiene products anymore, but she usually attempted to find a new way to embarrass him anyway. For the time being, though, their back-and-forth banter and flirting had to stop. It was hard enough with his smile lighting up the room.

"Yeah, well." Talia shrugged noncommittally. "I got it. You do dairy and dry foods. Text me when you're through, and then we'll divide the rest of the list."

"Okay." Walker's mouth twitched, and he moved out of the doorway, pulling his shoulders back like he was preparing for a sock to the stomach. "I'll meet you at the front when I'm done."

Talia tossed Amala a glum look over her shoulder once Walker turned his back to them. She had put on a brave face while he was watching her, but she wasn't sure how long she could keep her broken heart hidden from him. The only hope now was that he'd never ask how she was feeling, or he would easily be able to read it on her face. Amala gave her a thumbs up and a reassuring smile as Talia trudged out of the office, already googling therapists on her phone.

TWENTY-FIVE

WALKER

Nothing worked. Walker could not stop thinking about Talia. She was everywhere, despite also wanting to be nowhere near him. A month had passed since the fight at the mini golf course, and Walker was starting to think that if Talia continued to barely acknowledge his presence, he might start wandering around with a cartoon storm cloud over his head. It felt wrong to see her pick up her coffee at the place where they had sat and talked for hours and only receive a wave in greeting before she promptly left to avoid him. Grocery shopping had become an agonizing torture, knowing Talia was wandering around Lydia's with a cart the same time he was, but separated by several aisles he wasn't allowed to cross. They always stuck to their categories. Walker wanted the feminine hygiene category back so Talia could make fun of him again.

During family dinner nights at Roscoe and Amala's, Walker spent most of his time talking to Roscoe since Talia averted her eyes every second she could. He wondered how much space she needed to forget that he had ever mentioned how obsessed with her he was. She might not ever be his friend again. It was possible she was too worried about his sex dreams of her he had so casually announced like an absolute creep to ever consider sitting down with him for a cup of joe again.

The distance should have been enough to stop what he was feeling or thinking about her, and yet, all it did was make him overanalyze all of her passing glances and yes-or-no responses. The dreams hadn't stopped, either. If anything, his brain had upped its ability to form fantasies because he couldn't create new ones with her, live and in person. Not that he had fulfilled any of his sexual fantasies before, but just talking to Talia on a regular basis like when they were friends now felt like something unreal.

Piper and Pearl still had their weekly sleepovers with Talia, and it had become the only way Walker received any information on her life. Luckily, Pearl was a blabbermouth and was loose-lipped with any information she deemed worthy of talking about. He probably shouldn't have encouraged gossipy behavior, but when it came to Talia, he was desperate. Pearl was how he knew Talia had sent Clifford packing. That, or Cliff had decided to go home? It was unclear to him, but either way, Walker was thrilled that Talia's ex-fiancé was not in the picture anymore. Only light bruising had resulted from the guy's sucker punch, but that wasn't the reason Walker wanted him gone.

He was doing that bullshit "if I can't have her, no one can" thing. It was stupid, considering he had absolutely no claim to Talia, but the primal part of Walker still wailed that if she found someone else, he might just keel over and die. It was possible Pearl got her flair for the dramatic from him.

Thinking about Talia with anyone else at all made him sick to his stomach. It was wrong.

Walker had been ruminating on the idea of Talia in bed with another man for too long, letting his morning eggs go cold, when Pearl announced that Talia's car had broken down again and he would have to take over pickup and drop-off for therapy later. His bad mental state was only heightened by the new information, sending him into a full-blown rage directed at the sleazy car salesman he had already chewed out over the phone once for selling her the damned car to begin with.

"Where are you going?" Piper called after him.

"Looks like he's about to Hulk smash someone's face in," Carter said in amusement.

"Don't do anything illegal!" Colin warned. Walker gave his nephew an annoyed thumbs up before stopping himself with a deep breath next to the front door so he wouldn't rip it off its hinges.

"Colin, take everyone to school. Pearl, I'll pick you up for your appointment later," Walker grumbled, setting a firm hand on the door to pull it open.

Illegal, he decided, did not include speeding. Flying down the road, Walker attempted to calm himself down while he strained to let up on the gas. Getting in a car accident was probably the worst thing that could happen to him. That, or Talia calling him up to say she didn't feel the same and never wanted to be his friend again. Either way, the car salesman would receive the brunt of his frustrations.

Walker made it within a couple hundred feet of the car lot when red and blue lights flashed behind him. Looking back in his rearview mirror, he cursed under his breath at the police cruiser tailing him. He turned on his blinker to maneuver off the road and safely pulled to the side before contemplating his life choices for the thousandth time that day. He had no idea how fast he'd been going when the cop clocked him, but he was too distracted to care. The car lot awaited just out of reach as a way to relieve some of his pent-up disgruntlement.

"Hey, idiot, roll down your window!" Roscoe's voice called out from beyond Walker's car door, his knuckles rapping on the window. Complying immediately, Walker shot his friend a sheepish look.

"How fast was I going?"

"Eleven over," Roscoe said pointedly.

"Damn," Walker cringed. "Sorry."

"I'm not giving you a ticket because I figure telling you that you have five kids who would prefer if you didn't die on the road like their parents did is a worse punishment."

"Jesus, harsh! I wasn't paying attention. I'm a little ramped up at the moment, I guess, which I know is a dumb excuse."

"Where are you going?" Roscoe looked over Walker's hood as if he could magically tell the trajectory of his car by what was ahead.

"You're gonna tell me I'm an idiot again..." Walker started awkwardly, receiving no confirmation from Roscoe that he wasn't an imbecile. "Tal's car broke down again, and I'm going to the dealership to—"

"Assault someone?" Roscoe's eyebrows rose.

"No! I just wanted to fix one of her problems."

"So she'll stop giving you the cold shoulder?"

"She shouldn't be driving something that's going to cause an accident. I know she doesn't care to talk to me right now, or maybe she just doesn't want to ever be friends again, but I can't have her driving around that piece of shit." Walker's hand tightened around the steering wheel, his knuckles going white. Roscoe looked at him for a moment, eyes narrowing like he was trying to decipher a long math equation, before letting out a long sigh.

"The irony of you wanting Talia to be safe in her car and then driving like a bat out of hell. Okay, I'm going to tell you something as your friend, and if you tell anyone, especially my wife, that I told you this, I will deny it."

"I won't tell."

"Talia's not indifferent to you."

Walker gave a sarcastic laugh. "Wow, how exciting."

"Walker, focus." Roscoe snapped his fingers next to Walker's ear, and Walker returned most of his attention back to his friend, still eyeing the car lot in his peripherals. "This whole thing has her coming over to my house constantly to talk to Amala, even though they already spend all day together at work talking about it! I was kicked out of my own living room during a basketball game so they could use the TV to watch some sappy rom-com and talk about you while Amala painted her nails. Again. Talia's going to have to speak to you eventually, and the sooner you two figure out your shit, the sooner I can get back to watching March Madness in peace and stop hearing your name come out of Amala's mouth with some sexual joke attached to the end of it."

The fluttering in Walker's chest was instantaneous, both due to mortification of whatever Amala had to say and because Talia was thinking of him. More than just thinking of him, apparently, she was constantly discussing him with her best friend. That had to mean something. Walker didn't know if it was a good or bad thing, but Talia hating him felt better than her not thinking of him at all. Unless Roscoe was pulling his leg.

"Really? 'Cause every time I see Tal, it's like I'm invisible."

"She's a much better actor than you are. But, honestly, you both suck at pretending. Every time I catch you looking, I feel like I need to leave the room before you jump each other. Now," Roscoe clapped his hands together decisively, "I'm going to follow you to the car dealership to make sure you don't do anything stupid." Briskly turning on his heel, Roscoe stomped back to his car before Walker could protest that he wanted to be a lone wolf for his car salesman altercation.

Roscoe rode Walker's bumper on the way to the lot, lights on, just to be an asshole. Walker caught him grinning in his rearview mirror with a devious expression that said he was taking the affront to his basketball game-watching to heart. Not sure if he wanted to murder his friend or hug him for giving him hope, Walker opted for sporadically turning his blinker on and off at inappropriate times.

They pulled up to the dealership like their own damn parade, and Walker hopped out of the soccer wagon just in time for Roscoe to blast his siren once when he was right in front of the cruiser. Walker flinched and whirled around to glare at his friend, who seemed entirely too amused with himself as he got out of the car.

"Look, I can do this myself. I promise I won't bash his face in." Walker folded his arms over his chest.

"Really? 'Cause you seem kind of jumpy to me." Roscoe smirked. "Plus, maybe I want to make sure that Talia's car gets taken care of, too. The amount of car issues she's been having is ridiculous."

They fell into step side by side, marching toward the glass entrance to the main office without another word.

The receptionist took one look at Walker and Roscoe as they made their way over to her and sat up straighter in her chair, tossing her dark hair over one shoulder, her eyes sparkling with flirtation. She was youngish and pretty, but not Talia pretty— then again, no one could ever be that pretty. Between the woman's smooth, tanned skin and her bright smile, most people would find her extremely attractive. Walker just found himself extremely *uninterested*. Talia had ruined all other women for him, and they weren't even together. He wished he could have some fling to get over her, but he couldn't bring himself to do it. He doubted he would even be able to get it up with anyone but her.

Should've become a eunuch when he had the chance. The receptionist, as it turned out, was way more interested in the man in uniform standing beside Walker. Roscoe definitely screamed stability and kindness, and it also helped that he was tall and handsome, a fact his wife bragged about relentlessly. Of the two of them, Walker wasn't shocked that Roscoe was at the center of the receptionist's attention, but she failed to notice the wedding band on his friend's finger when she traced her eyes over him.

"How can I help you gentlemen?" she asked in a breathy voice.

"He's married," Walker said bluntly. He was friends with Amala, too, and not that Roscoe would ever cheat on his wife— he would be offended by the very implication—but Walker wasn't about to allow the flirtation to go further than one sentence. "We're looking for the asshole who sold Talia Cohen a faulty vehicle that's going to get her or someone else killed. I'd like a copy of her contract, too."

"Oh..." The woman blinked back at him, immediately getting flustered. "We run safety inspections on all vehicles, so I'm sure that—"

"Then tell me who ran the safety inspection. Her brakes went out and got her into an accident, her battery died, the spark plugs went bad, and now the car won't start again. I'd like to know who exactly considers that safe?" Walker snapped, not wanting to deal with the whole song and dance.

"All right, let's just take a chill pill, Walker," Roscoe scolded. "But, ma'am, I have to say, this place could get into some serious legal trouble. We don't want to have to do that. If you could just look up who was in charge of Talia Cohen's safety inspection, we'll get out of your hair." Roscoe set a cautioning hand on Walker's shoulder, and Walker rolled his eyes.

"Of course, officer," the receptionist smiled hesitantly at Roscoe and started to clack away on her keyboard, only looking up briefly at Walker. "And you?"

"And me what?" Walker grumbled.

"Are you married, too?"

Second fiddle. Nice.

"I'm... taken." Walker awkwardly tapped his fingers against his thighs and shifted a glance at Roscoe, regretting his choice of words when he saw the smug look on his friend's face.

"Is Talia Cohen your wife? Because I really can't give out information unless you have a warrant or you're her husb—"

"Yep, we're married!" Walker slipped his brother's wedding band off his middle finger and smoothly transferred it to his ring finger, holding his hand up as proof. Hearing Roscoe cough loudly next to him, Walker slapped his friend's back with a big smile. "This guy here was our best man! We just got married a few months ago, and I've never been happier!"

The girl beamed and wiggled in her seat, the idea of a wedding pulling her out of whatever nervousness she had stammered through just a moment ago. She kept typing on her keyboard, made a few mouse clicks, and pulled a sticky note from her desk, scrawling something on it before she wheeled over to the printer and grabbed a copy of the contract, no questions asked.

"Oh, she's pretty! Even the copy of her license looks good, and that never happens!" the receptionist cooed.

"Yeah, she's beautiful," Walker agreed without hesitation, refusing to look at Roscoe as he accepted the contract from her outstretched hand.

She held the sticky note between her thumb and forefinger. "This has the head mechanic's name on it. He was in charge of the car. Between you and me," she leaned forward and dropped her voice lower, "he's an ass. I was dating him for two whole years before he cheated on me. Wouldn't be surprised if he cheated on *other* things, too."

"That just makes me want to kick his ass more," Walker declared, taking the sticky note and slapping it onto the front page of the contract.

"I can tell that you really love your wife. I'd be thrilled to have someone stand up like that for me. Go straight down the hallway, make a left, and he should be through the first door on your right. Give him hell," the receptionist waved, a vengeful smile pursing her lips.

Walker started down the hallway. He caught a glimpse of Roscoe's amusement out of the corner of his eye as they found the right door. The lie he told about his marital status proved that Walker was absolute shit at hiding how far he'd fallen with Talia, and Roscoe was living it up.

"Stop it," Walker griped.

"I didn't say anything."

"I can hear you thinking."

"Let's just stick to the game plan where you don't beat anyone up and I don't get involved with anything resembling police intimidation."

"Fine."

Throwing open the door, Walker stormed inside the covered garage in search of the head mechanic, Michael Rubio. It wasn't hard to figure out which asshole was the right asshole considering there was a man leaning against the side of a car, blatantly staring at a woman's chest while he spoke to her. Fashioned in a nice dress and heels, the object of his perversion looked to be one of the saleswomen from the main lot. She seemed completely oblivious to Rubio's wandering eyes as she ran through some sort of a list on her clipboard with the creep.

"Classy guy," Roscoe muttered.

"Eyes up here, bud," Walker shouted angrily, stomping over to the pair. The saleswoman backed up, glanced down at herself, and glared at Rubio before turning on her heel to leave. Rubio just shrugged, indifferent to being caught ogling someone who didn't want it.

"What can I help you with?" the mechanic asked dryly, without a hint of remorse. "Don't have a lot of time today."

"You'll make time," Roscoe said plainly.

"Let's see," Walker thumbed through Talia's contract and found the inspection sheet, signed at the bottom by none other than the dipshit in front of him. He flipped it around to face the guy and jabbed a finger at the bottom of the page. "This your signature?"

"Could be." Rubio took a step back, and a flash of fear appeared in his eyes, which, in turn, brought up the corners of Walker's lips.

"Great. You're going to fix this car that you signed off on, run a full inspection, and have two other mechanics sign off on it, free of charge," Walker demanded.

"And why would I do that?"

"Because it's the right thing to do." Roscoe smiled coolly.

"Brakes shouldn't go out if they're inspected properly. Batteries don't stop working after a month of use. If you did your job, her car wouldn't break down every five fucking seconds," Walker bit off.

"And if I don't?" Rubio looked over at Roscoe.

"Don't look at me." Roscoe held up his hands and tipped his head toward Walker. "I'm just here to protect you from him."

"If you don't fix this, then I will make your life a living hell." Walker massaged his knuckles menacingly, which earned him a disapproving look from Roscoe. "In a legal way, of course. I'm quite certain I can get you fired and bring a lawyer in to find out how many other vehicles you've botched. It would be in your best interest to look back through the vehicles you've touched recently and to fix them. While we're at it, I'm also going to escort you to the receptionist at the front of the store so you can apologize for being a lying, cheating scum of the earth."

The mechanic stared back at Walker for a moment before his eyes darted toward the door. His next move was clearly making a run for it like a common criminal, so Walker stepped toward the exit, strategically blocking it off with his body. Rubio's eyes dropped to the floor, and he wrung his hands nervously.

"Fine. I might have rushed through a few inspections or signed off on some I hadn't checked," Rubio murmured, still averting his gaze.

"You better hope that no one gets hurt." Walker scowled and gestured toward the door they had entered through. "After you."

Rubio stiffly led the way back to the front desk, uncomfortably looking over his shoulder at Walker and Roscoe every few seconds. Walker forged a path directly behind the guy to purposefully make him anxious. He had no intention to make this easy on Rubio. In his opinion, the idiot should be fired on the spot, but he'd rather have something to blackmail the guy with so he'd fix Talia's car faster. Rubio was lucky Walker didn't pummel him into a fine dust. Considering his recent lack of self-control, Roscoe's presence was definitely for the best.

The receptionist grinned when the three of them made their way over to her, but completely ignored Rubio when he approached the counter, turning only toward Walker and Roscoe.

Good for her, Walker thought.

"How can I help you?"

"Mr. Rubio would like his records for the last...?" Walker tipped his head toward the mechanic, waiting for him to chime in with the length of his negligence.

"Eight months," Rubio offered up quietly. Walker balked at the number. Maybe after the guy actually fixed Talia's car for good, he should make sure the owners knew about Rubio's misconduct.

"Perfect, I'll print those off. And would you like to schedule an appointment for your wife, sir?" she asked Walker, back to ignoring the mechanic.

"Yes, today would be great. Her address—I mean, our address is correct on the document. The car needs to be towed," Walker stated, hoping the woman didn't catch his slip-up.

"I'll arrange for it to be picked up."

"And one more thing," Walker elbowed Rubio harder than was necessary and cleared his throat, eyebrows raised expectantly. Rubio's face turned a deep shade of red, as if having to apologize was the most embarrassing thing he'd ever endured.

"So, Saanvi." The guy looked at his ex-girlfriend for a split second before dropping his eyes to his clean hands. "I apologize for the way things ended between us."

Walker scoffed. *Way to really sell the apology, dickwad. Shouldn't your hands be covered in grease or dirt from all the work you're supposedly doing?*

"No harm, no foul." Saanvi tilted her head to look at Rubio with a bored expression. "Really, you just saved me from more mediocre sex and," her eyes flicked up and down his figure impassively, "an unimpressive everything else."

Walker let out a puff of laughter at Rubio's expense that he didn't even attempt to hold back. Roscoe didn't laugh, but Walker watched his friend curl his lips over his teeth to keep his composure. If someone had ever declared Walker to be a bad lover and implied he had small equipment, he probably would have dissolved on the spot. No one *had* ever said that about him, however.

And no one ever would, thank you very much.

The mechanic looked pissed. With Walker's hand placed firmly on Dr. Too-Little's shoulder, though, Rubio was very aware that he'd be making no moves to argue or insult Saanvi without retribution. Roscoe was of the same mind, carefully watching Rubio to determine if his aggression would stray past facial expressions. Saanvi was back to sweeping her mouse over the pad on her desk and clicking with a flourish of enthusiasm, not giving her ex the time of day.

"The tow truck should be at your house in thirty minutes," she said cheerfully and looked up from her computer.

"Thanks so much for your help, Saanvi." Walker grinned. "Can I give you my number in case you come across any trouble in the future?" He fixed the mechanic with a hard glare and squeezed his shoulder hard before releasing his grip to make sure it was clear that by "trouble," he meant Rubio would be keeping his hands and eyes to himself on top of actually doing the damn job he was hired to do.

"Sure thing!" Saanvi chirped, slapping a sticky note and a pen atop the counter.

After scrawling out his name and contact info, Walker pointed off toward the hallway that led to the mechanic's quarters and made eye contact with the seething man. "Feel free to go back to your hole now. I look forward to hearing about your new work ethic."

The tail end of Walker's dismissal was interrupted by the vibrating of his phone in his pocket. He assumed it was something work-related—earlier in the week he had submitted a final draft for the novel he was working on—but it wasn't. Talia's contact stared up at him, and his heart did a flip in his chest. Fumbling and almost dropping his phone, he answered the call.

"Tal? Hey, are you oka—"

"Sorry to bug you," Talia cut him off quickly. "But I figured you needed to know. Harden keeps texting Piper, and apparently, he invited her to another party. I told her I wouldn't tell you, but she let me read some of his texts the other night, and—"

"What did they say?" Walker interjected, feeling his blood run cold.

"Without going into too much detail, they were all really sexual and manipulative. Not good. Really, Walker, I swore I wouldn't tell you, so please don't do anything crazy. I just thought you should know, and it's been eating at me for the last twenty-four hours not telling you," Talia rambled, her voice edged with nerves.

"Thank you for calling." Walker's voice was clipped as he tried to reign in his anger.

"What are you going to do? Walker, please don't—"

"I'll take care of it."

"Are you mad at me?"

The pain behind Talia's voice made his stomach drop. "No. I'm mad that this fucker won't leave my niece alone. You did the right thing in telling me. I'll make sure it doesn't get back to you."

Roscoe's eyes widened across the countertop at Walker while Saanvi hung on his every word. Turning his back to both of them, Walker took a deep breath, clutching his phone with a death grip.

"Don't do anything stupid, please," Talia begged.

"Have a great day, Tal," Walker huffed, and he ended the call before she had a chance to convince him not to confront Harden.

Twenty-Six

WALKER

One shoulder leaned against the minivan as Walker waited. His jaw clenched and unclenched, his folded arms growing more tense as the time ticked away. He had parked two cars down from Harden's infamous red Mitsubishi with a spoiler the size of Texas. It was exactly the type of vehicle Walker would expect for a douchey jock with an ego the same size as his spoiler. Harden had parked off campus, which worked in Walker's favor. The car was easy enough to find. All Walker had to do was pay one of the many stoner kids who were skipping school twenty bucks to tell him which car belonged to Piper's ex.

Thirty minutes passed with no sign of Harden, but Walker was determined to wait all day if he had to. Pearl's therapy appointment wasn't until four, and he intended to put an end to Piper's involvement with anyone who gave her an ounce of disrespect. To his surprise, Roscoe let him go at it alone. The fury behind his friend's eyes was enough validation for Walker to know that he wasn't overreacting. Heaven help whoever ended up with Jayla.

By the time lunch rolled around, Walker thought he may have to wait all day, until he finally spotted Harden walking away from the school. He vaguely remembered the way the kid looked from one of Piper's soccer games earlier that year, but the cocky stride and gaggle of other boys surrounding him like his personal entourage gave him away. The Mitsubishi made an unlocking sound when Harden brandished his key fob. Walker immediately jogged over to the car and hopped into the driver seat, leaving the door wide open so Harden could see him clearly.

"What the fuck, man?" Harden yelled and sprinted toward his car, his posse of friends in tow.

Once Harden made it over, Walker pulled the lever on the side of the seat he was sitting in and let it slide back as far as it could go before he kicked his boots up on the dash, propping his arms up behind his head to make himself comfortable.

"Not so nice when people fuck with things they shouldn't, is it?" Walker glowered up at Harden.

"What are you talking about? I'll call the cops, you psycho!" Harden jabbed an aggressive finger in the air.

"Go for it. And while we're waiting for them to show up, let's have a little discussion. Get in the car." Walker pointed to the backseat, then added, "all of you," jerking his head toward Harden's minions.

"Why would we do that?" Harden growled.

"Because you can either get in of your own free will, or I can make you do it." Walker shrugged. "Your choice."

"There's four of us and one of you." Harden puffed up his chest, a clear attempt to look threatening. Walker chuckled to himself.

"I'm not fighting anyone for you, Harden," the only kid in the clan who looked vaguely out of place snapped. He wasn't sporty-looking like the rest of them and was standing off to the side like he would rather not be associated with them.

"Either way, it's a fun challenge for me and nothing I haven't taken on before," Walker replied curtly, blowing his knuckles. "Plus, I could just claim self-defense."

The out-of-place kid, who looked more inclined to give Walker a hand than Harden, grinned and shouted "shotgun!" before he ran over and slid into the passenger seat. Harden and his pitiful gang looked at each other for a second before they all cautiously got into the backseat, terror radiating off their bodies.

"Wise decision." Walker smirked. "Now, let me introduce myself since you don't seem to know who I am. My name's Walker Hartrick." He stared Harden down in the rearview mirror. Harden swallowed, clearly recognizing the name. Walker cracked the knuckles on one hand and nodded. "Yes, that's right, I'm Piper's uncle. So lovely to meet you."

Harden stuttered and shifted in his seat. "I-I don't want any trouble." The other boys in the backseat caught on, their eyes wide with fear.

"Hmm," Walker considered, cracking his neck. "You should have thought of that before you decided to harass my niece. Here's what's going to happen." He kicked his feet down from the dash and started messing with the cigarette lighter on the console. "You will stop texting and speaking to Piper completely. If I hear that you've made a single sexual advance toward her or anyone else who didn't explicitly say 'y-e-s,' I will have things to say about it. That goes for all of you." The broody-looking teenager who had refused to be Harden's backup snorted, and Walker whipped his head toward him. "Something funny?"

"Nope. I firmly agree. I'm only here because Harden's failing Spanish, and his rich-ass parents are paying me to tutor him. Not that it's helping. He can't roll an 'r' to save his life. Piper deserves better. Carry on." The kid waved his hand in the air and leaned back in his seat with a grin, apparently enjoying the show.

"Shut it, Diaz." Harden scrunched his nose in anger.

Before Walker could jump to his passenger's defense, Diaz shot back a quick response. "*Mira, pendejo.* I've got three older brothers. If you think I don't know how to fight, you're sorely mistaken. One of us will come out with the upper hand, and it won't be you."

Harden snapped his mouth shut, smartly choosing not to provoke Diaz further. Diaz raked his fingers over the mop of dark curls on his head and yawned like he was legitimately bored with the conversation.

Amused, Walker continued with his spiel, injecting his voice with the maximum level of condescension. "Just to educate you a bit further, Harden, sex is more fun when all parties involved want to be doing it. And manipulating women who don't want to doesn't make you a god, it makes you a massive fucking creep. So, if you so much as look at Piper wrong again, I'll make sure everyone in school knows that you're in *Ripley's Believe It or Not!* for the world's smallest micropenis. Delete her number from your phone and stick to your right hand. Capiche?" Walker clicked his tongue, and Diaz snickered beside him.

"O-okay," Harden frantically bobbed his head. His comrades mimicked the gesture in unison like the lemmings they were. Diaz raised up a polite hand like he was in class.

"I would love to assist you with that." Diaz glanced into the backseat and cocked his head at Harden with a wide smile.

"Great. And your name is?" Walker asked.

"Leo. It would be my absolute pleasure to help spread the micropenis agenda." Leo stuck out his hand, and Walker gave it a firm shake.

"Perfect. If Harden or any of his friends make any advances toward Piper, feel free to make their lives a living hell. Have a fantastic day, Leo." Walker barely acknowledged the rest of the teenagers as he hopped out of the car and swaggered toward his own vehicle.

By the time Walker started up the minivan and pulled away from the curb, not a single kid but Diaz had gotten out of the douchemobile. Walker watched in his rearview mirror as Leo flipped off the boys sitting in the backseat of the Mitsubishi and strode away from the car, slinging his backpack casually over one shoulder. Apparently, Harden's parents weren't paying the kid enough to deal with their son's shit anymore. Walker chuckled as he flicked on his blinker to turn back home. He had a good feeling that Dickwit would be leaving Piper alone for the foreseeable future.

Twenty-Seven

TALIA

The engine started, and Talia heaved a sigh of relief, her hand dropping away from the ignition to shift into reverse. After her Lexus was towed to the dealership a week before, her car troubles, even small ones like the tiny rattling sound that used to sing with her air conditioning, had taken a hiatus thanks to Walker. She wanted to text and thank him, but she wasn't sure if it was appropriate given that he had told Roscoe to take credit. She wasn't stupid, though; Walker was the only one who knew where she had bought her car. That, and Roscoe let the truth slip about two minutes later under the hard gaze of his wife. Roscoe didn't even need a badge to tell him to uphold his morals when he had Amala to force them out of him.

The sixties playlist Talia had opted for when her Bluetooth auto-connected started off with Etta James' "At Last," and she quickly swapped it out for "Respect" and queued up "Suspicious Minds" and some others just so she wouldn't have to listen to love songs. She would have just put on her punk playlist, but she wasn't in the scream-your-feelings kind of mood. Her heart felt like more of a dull ache, and she was much too tired to attempt any head-banging thanks to her recent lack of sleep.

The dull ache could have also been coming from her feet. It was the first time in months she had pulled a pair of heels out of her closet. The live auction at Archwood High was the perfect excuse to dress up. The tight black cocktail dress she was wearing accentuated her curves in all the right places, and she was relishing the idea of showing it off.

Coincidentally, Walker would be in attendance.

It had felt like such a long time since his eyes had lingered on her the way they used to. Despite the danger it would put her heart in, Talia had pulled the black number out of her closet hoping it would make him look. She craved that look, the one that set her insides aflame. The hunger. It was a terrible, no good, very bad idea that she knew she should have abandoned, but it was too late. The little devil on her shoulder had screamed at her to throw on a bit more makeup and paint her nails and lips candy apple red. Piper had mentioned several times that this was a dress and heels type of event, so Talia figured that was as good an excuse as any.

Colin, Piper, and Carter were all weirdly adamant that Talia come support the school's student organizations and sports. They talked about it constantly in the few weeks leading up to the event, as if she'd somehow forgotten the last eighty times they had mentioned it. Talia didn't need any convincing, though. With Colin's mathletes team fundraising for state, Carter's basketball team fundraising for new jerseys, and Piper's soccer team fundraising for an athletic camp during the summer, there was plenty to support. She had even offered to scrounge up something to auction off—a basket with baked goods from Lydia's, a gift card, something—but all three siblings declined. Multiple times. Talia briefly wondered if they thought she was incapable of making a cool enough basket to show off. The next time there was an auction, she would just show up with an auction item, regardless of their protests.

Since their friend break, Talia and Walker had kept things cordial, but she missed him. Missed the way he could make her laugh and the way his eyes lit up like a menorah when he smiled. She hadn't seen him smile once since their friendship was put on pause, and that pained her more than anything else. The distance had done nothing to stop the swell in her chest when she thought of him. The fact was, Walker made her happy. He made even the most mundane of tasks fun. Talia had finally decided that despite the fact the love hadn't left her like she'd planned, the pain of staying away was becoming worse than the pain of knowing they wouldn't be together. Companionship was going to have to be enough. It would be, because there was no other option. She couldn't stay away anymore. It wasn't helping. Tonight, she would tell Walker that she wanted to drop-kick their pause downfield. Screw her feelings, she needed her friend back.

After lucking out when she found the one parking spot left in the lot, Talia followed the crowd of classily dressed adults into the theater room. When she made it through the door, a hand latched onto her arm and pulled her in the direction of the stage. Her fight-or-flight response let up when she realized it was Piper, wearing the navy blue dress they had picked out a few months ago together. She looked beautiful. To see Piper looking so alive filled Talia with pride.

"You're here!" Piper beamed with nervous excitement

"I told you I was coming," Talia laughed. "Did you really think I wouldn't?"

"No, but I'm presenting one of the auction items with Colin and Carter, and I was hoping you could come onstage with us. We're supposed to have an adult onstage with us," she added, eyes darting to her left.

"Where's your uncle?"

"He's supposed to bid on our item, so he can't be onstage," Piper said, practically spraying the words as fast as she could get them out.

Talia peered out at the audience through the red curtains on the side wing of the stage. "Where's he sitting?"

"He's the one looking extremely bored directly in the center, second row back," Carter said, shuffling over to Talia's other side, joined by Colin.

"I made sure he had a good view." The corner of Colin's mouth ticked up.

"Perfect." Talia's mouth formed the words before she had a second to realize that what she was saying *perfect* to was Walker's ability to see *her*. Carter mumbled something under his breath and received an elbow to the side from his sister, who was playing with her arms, swinging them through the air like she was spinning a pair of yo-yos. Watching her made the nerves spark up Talia's spine. She had led several boardroom meetings when she was a lawyer, so she wasn't so terrified to be presenting. It was more who was in the audience that made her stomach knot.

"You're up first," a high school student, looking very authoritative with a headset and all-black outfit, pointed at Piper. There was a weird undertone to the directive, and Talia swiveled to watch the conversation play out, intrigued. As far as she could remember, Piper hadn't mentioned anyone remotely similar to the guy standing just to the right of her with dark curls sprouting out from under the band of his headset, but he had a certain look about him that felt familiar.

"I know that." Piper rolled her eyes at the newcomer. "I'm not just standing here for fun."

Talia's mouth dropped open in surprise. She'd never heard Piper blatantly be rude to anyone before. She was just about to scold Piper when the guy spoke up instead.

"Just making sure you don't screw this up, *princesita*. Seems to be a habit of yours." The boy offered a slight smirk before promptly turning on his heel to stalk away. Talia followed him with her eyes and wasn't surprised when the guy peeked back over his shoulder at Piper, who had already set her vision straight ahead to the stage.

Interesting.

"Always have to get the last word, don't you?" Piper muttered under her breath.

"What the hell was that?" Talia gestured toward where the kid had disappeared behind a large stage prop.

"Nothing." Piper shook her head like she was trying to clear it and set her shoulders back, lifting her chin. "Just a theater kid who thinks he's better than everyone else."

"He's been Piper's partner in Spanish class for the whole year. She hates him," Colin piped up.

"I don't hate him," Piper protested before quickly backtracking. "He just seems to think his sole purpose in life is to call me 'Peter Piper' or 'Perfect Piper' then rip apart my pronunciations every four seconds 'cause he speaks fluent Spanish."

"What a dick," Carter said. Talia narrowed her eyes at him, assuming the comment was sarcastic, but one look at him said he was actually serious. Talia chuckled and arched her eyebrows at him. Carter constantly called his sister 'Perfect Piper' as an insult, so he knew exactly what her pointed stare meant. He shrugged. "She's my sister. I'm allowed to make fun of her. That asshole isn't."

"Touché." Talia tried to hold back her smile, but she couldn't help it.

"To be fair," Colin raised a correcting finger in the air, "you do suck at Spanish."

"Carter's not good at it, either!" Piper protested.

"I'll admit it. I do suck at Spanish." Carter shrugged, then got a devilish gleam in his eye. Talia waited for the punchline. "I'm really good at speaking with my body, though."

"Ew!" Piper groaned.

"You told Walker you weren't having sex," Talia shifted her tone to a parental one. "Should I inform him otherwise?"

"Oh, he's definitely not sleeping with anyone," Colin interjected.

"Everyone shut up!" Carter buried his face in his hands. "I'm going to kill Walker. I can't believe he told you that!"

Talia figured his embarrassment was punishment enough, but couldn't help but to get one last stab in. "Would you rather he tell me when you *do* start—?"

"Forget I said anything!" Carter groaned. "*Please.*"

Polite applause from the theater announced that the principal's grandiose speech about community and the bond that glued that community together—which was apparently the high school?—was finally finished. That sentiment seemed a bit dramatic, but Carter seemed happy enough to have a change of subject.

"Ready?" Piper asked, gnawing on her bottom lip.

"What are we auctioning? Is it already out there?" Talia peeked onto the stage but saw nothing in the way of something resembling a prize.

"What we are selling is more... the idea of something," Colin said as the principal walked off the stage toward them, passing the mic off to Piper. Piper nodded to both Carter and Colin, who bobbed their heads back like there was some unspoken knowledge between the three of them.

"Too late to turn back now," Carter sighed, motioning to the stage. "We go down together."

"Sorry about this, Tal," Piper cringed.

"Sorry?" Talia whispered back, furrowing her brow.

"I'm not." Carter grinned.

"It's a good idea," Colin insisted under his breath.

"It was *your* idea, Colin," Piper rolled her eyes.

"Exactly," Carter and Colin said at the same time. Talia jerked her head back and forth between the siblings as she tried to follow the conversation.

"You agreed to this, Piper. You orchestrated half of it." Carter nudged his sister.

Piper squeezed her eyes. "You got the donation to go with it!"

"What the hell is going on?" Talia asked.

"Everything is fine." Colin smiled. It was an awkward smile that did not at all reassure her that everything was fine, but the next thing Talia knew, she was practically being pushed out onto the stage by all three of them.

The spotlights on them were bright, but the house lights were still on, so Talia could see the audience. As soon as her eyes adjusted, she found Walker easily. His hands were folded in his lap, and his mouth twitched when she looked at him. He was handsome as always, this time wearing a collared button-down shirt that was tight across his toned chest.

"Thank you for joining us tonight!" Piper spoke into the microphone, an edge of anxiety to her voice. "The first auction item, sponsored by La Truffe Noire Restaurant, is an all-expenses-paid date to the restaurant with this beautiful lady right here!" Piper shoved Talia forward, and Talia stumbled to catch her footing in her stilettos.

What the fuck?

"What the fuck?" Talia's head reeled back in alarm.

"There are people watching," Carter murmured in a low tone only Talia could hear.

Talia found Walker in the audience again. The expression on his face said that he was just as surprised as she was by the turn of events, or, rather, the completely thought-out meddling. One of his fists was clenched, sitting atop his knee, the other gripping his auction paddle like he wanted to hit someone with it.

When his eyes met hers, his head tilted to the side and his eyebrows pulled upward as if to ask *did you volunteer for this?* Talia gave a slight shake of her head to confirm that she had not woken up and decided to shell herself out to the highest bidder. The word his lips formed as his nose scrunched furiously was obvious, although no sound left his mouth. *Fuck.* She mouthed *help* back to him, and Walker adjusted to the edge of his seat with a nod.

Colin took the mic from Piper, avoiding Talia's eye contact as she glared at the side of his head. He was also conveniently not looking at the second row, where his uncle was shooting an unmistakable you-are-all-grounded-until-you-turn-forty look at the three of them. Piper refused eye contact as well, but Talia made it a point to take a turn staring daggers at her, too. Piper chewed on her nails, the picture of guilt.

"We'll start the bidding off at a hundred bucks," Colin's voice announced through the speakers.

Several paddles shot up in the air. Actually, several was an understatement: at least fifteen people had their hands raised, mostly men, but two women as well. While extremely flattered, Talia was planning on ripping the three musketeers a new one the second they were off the stage. She looked down at Walker, who was glancing over both his shoulders to gauge his competition, and his eyes squinted closed in frustration before his paddle also shot into the air. *I got you*, he mouthed, turning back to her. Closing her eyes, Talia sucked in a breath and mouthed back *thank you* before setting her sights on Colin, who was upping the bidding to two hundred dollars.

As the auction continued, Colin and Piper's words from backstage rang in Talia's head.

He's supposed to bid on our item. I made sure he had a good view.

Carter, out of anyone, looked the most confident, standing next to Talia with a smug grin. The only thing that got her through being thrust onstage with every person in the audience ogling her like a prized calf was thinking about how she and Walker were going to appropriately punish the kids.

In the middle of her plotting to force feed them all laxatives, Talia watched the crowd slowly taper off as the price grew to five hundred dollars. *Five hundred fucking dollars.* There were people on Earth who would pay a ridiculous sum just to sit down and have a meal with her. They had to realize that she wasn't about to strip naked and offer herself up, right? *Right?*

"Seven hundred dollars?" Colin asked the audience, his voice more hesitant.

"You are all in huge trouble," Talia said under her breath.

"A risk we were willing to take," Carter whispered.

"We'll see if you still think that after this is all over," Talia challenged. Carter's mouth opened to respond before it quickly snapped shut, and a look of panic passed through his eyes like he didn't quite realize how bad the situation was until confronted with a consequence. Colin was now also nervous, drumming his fingers against his leg as his eyes shifted over the audience. He seemed more off-put by the people in the crowd shouting back at him with higher bids than the predicament of getting in trouble, though. Carter gulped loudly and stepped forward to take over for his brother, probably just to get away from Talia's seething eyes.

Eventually, Talia decided the best course of action was to look as unapproachable as possible, so she fixed her face in a frown that she was hoping would get her pegged as bitchy by every misogynistic guy in the crowd who only wanted to wine and dine a "good girl."

Meanwhile, with each raised hand, Talia could tell Walker was getting more and more pissed off. By the time the bid rose to nine hundred bucks, he and a balding, creeping guy in the back were the last two people stuck in a bidding war. If Talia was planning on feeding the kids laxatives, Walker seemed like he was inclined to bar their windows, bolt their doors, and put them up in fancy lodging resembling a psych ward prison for the rest of eternity.

Talia's attempt to look off-putting to deter the balding man who was probably ten years her senior at least was interrupted by her phone buzzing in her pocket.

WALKER 8:14 PM

Do you want me to stand up and call bullshit on this whole thing? You're not for fucking purchase. I'm going to kill them.

A small smile played across her lips as she glanced down at him. He had his paddle firmly raised in the air the whole time without dropping it, his phone resting on his knee as he looked at her, eyebrows raised.

TALIA 8:14 PM

> I don't want them to get suspended. But they can pay us back every cent. They're just increasing the price on themselves.

"Fifteen hundred dollars!" Walker shouted from his seat, standing at attention. Talia's face split into a wide smile when Mr. Potato Head in the back dropped his paddle with a groan of defeat, thank God.

"Sold!" Piper croaked, looking absolutely terrified.

Walker scowled at his niece, clearly none too pleased with the word "sold," and made his way down his row to the aisle, where he stomped up the side stairs that led backstage. Eyes widening, Carter, Piper, and Colin all slugged their way offstage, Talia practically shoving them toward their uncle, who was waiting in the wings, steam coming out of his ears.

Anger made all of Walker's muscles flex with tension, and Talia found it entirely too attractive for the circumstances. She should be pissed, too, but Walker had just gotten her to smile again, and it was what she had been missing for weeks.

"Get your stuff," Walker snapped at his family when they finally made it over to him. "We're going home to have a family meeting. Now."

"Should I tell Amala to keep Pearl and Coop a bit longer?" Talia offered.

"Already did," Walker grunted. He was getting really good at the parenting thing, and it was yet another on the long list of turn-ons that Talia hadn't been aware could turn her on.

Friends. She could only be his friend.

"Need my checkbook?" Talia asked. Walker's hand shot out to her arm to stop her pulling it from her purse.

"No." He pulled his hand back slowly when her eyes drifted down to it, heat blazing across where his fingers met her bare skin.

"I'll pay it. Meet at the car in five?" He was blatantly ignoring his niece and nephews, and it was only making them more antsy. Standing beside Talia, Piper looked like she was about to shit herself. While Talia wasn't ever actually planning on feeding them stool looseners, it seemed the guilt had the desired effect anyway.

"Sure."

Everyone was sitting at the dining table when Talia walked into the house, shutting the door behind her. Not entirely sure how far into the conversation they had gotten or what she was walking into, she treaded lightly, finding Walker's eyes first. He stood up from his seat and gestured with his head toward the living room.

"Wait here," he said, motioning for Colin, Piper, and Carter to stay put.

Talia followed him back out to the living room, a little nervous herself, wondering if she was going to have to go to bat for the kids to prevent Walker from being too harsh on them. She had a bit of time to think about it during the drive to the house, and after the initial rage wore off, she could see things rationally again. Despite the tone-deaf way they had gone about it, Talia could see the kids' reasoning. It was irrational and incredibly inappropriate, but she did understand why they had done it: they missed her and Walker's old dynamic.

"What are you going to do?" Talia asked when they were out of earshot.

"I figured we could decide that together since the biggest grievance was toward you. Clearly they were trying to—"

"Get us together," Talia finished for him. Walker looked down at his feet, a flush of pink staining his cheeks.

"Yeah," he mumbled back. "That. I'm sorry."

"It's not your fault. I'm the one that made it so they felt they had to."

"Okay, that's ridiculous, and you know it." Walker huffed out a laugh. "Whatever's going on between us doesn't give them a right to sell you to me like a—"

"Prostitute?" Talia interrupted with a slight smile. Walker covered his face with one hand, looking thoroughly embarrassed.

"God. I just fucking paid fifteen hundred bucks for you."

"Does that make me a high-end prostitute or a cheap one? How much do people normally pay for that?"

"Why the hell are you asking me? It's not like we're going to..." he trailed off.

"Have sex?" Talia raised her eyebrows.

"Can you be serious for two seconds?" Walker scrunched his eyes shut.

"Okay. So, obviously, they're all grounded. They are going to pay you back the fifteen hundred bucks, five hundred each, and it's not going to be from their parents' money. They're going to have to work for it."

"Ponytail, that's not good enough. They need to really feel this one. They can't just sell you at an auction and get away with it!" Walker ran a flustered hand through his hair. "Who even let them do that? Someone at the school actually approved this?"

It had been a while since Walker had called her "Ponytail." That, along with the anxious way he'd started to pace, sparked something inside her again. A familiarity that Talia wanted to cling to and never let go of. She knew him well enough to know he was doubting himself to the point of anxiety. He was always so focused on doing the right thing. Decisions like this were the kind that ate away at him and made him wonder if he was doing a bad job as a guardian, letting his brother and sister-in-law down.

"Hey." Talia stepped forward and touched Walker's arm gently. "Look at me." When his worried eyes met hers, her hand slid up to cup his face. She knew she shouldn't be touching him that way, but he looked so broken that she couldn't help herself. "You're a good parent. You're doing a great job, Walker. This isn't a reflection on you. They just miss their parents, and I think that they miss us being a duo. Can't say I don't miss it either."

"You do?" Walker blinked and reached his hand up to encircle her wrist.

"I've been miserable," Talia admitted. "I feel like every coffee I drink is shit and I'm missing a piece of me. You're... you're family."

Walker sighed. "I'm sorry I ruined everything," he said, eyebrows pinching together in a saddened expression that made Talia want to rub the creases away with her thumb.

"You didn't ruin anything." Stepping into him, she buried her face into his chest, wrapping her arms around Walker and breathing him in. There was no hesitation before his arms wrapped around her back, pulling her harder against his torso. She was finally home again, cocooned in the safety of someone who cared so much about her that he was willing to drop fifteen hundred bucks to save her.

"I missed you," he whispered into her hair.

"I missed you, too," Talia breathed.

"Do you want the stupid restaurant ticket?" Walker let out a breathy laugh as he let her go.

"Let's just go together. We might as well get some good food out of this whole debacle. Plus, I'd like to watch you eat escargot," Talia mused.

"Es-car-what?"

"It's snail."

Walker scrunched his nose, smiling. "Gross. Let's do it."

Twenty-Eight

WALKER

Walker nearly catapulted himself out of his car, leaving his door wide open as he sprinted toward the entrance of Roaster's Republic. The sign was already flipped around to read "closed" when he peeked through the glass. Everything was dark inside. Mission failed. Letting out a sigh of defeat, he turned back around. He was midway through convincing himself on the trek back to the car that it was a stupid idea anyway when he heard a rustling coming from the side of the building. Stopping dead in his tracks, he looked around the corner to find Harper dragging a large black trash bag across the ground.

"Hey, let me get that for you." Jogging over to her, he took the garbage from her and heaved it into the dumpster. Harper was surprised by his presence. Either that, or he had scared the shit out of her when he yelled 'hey' like some deranged person hiding in the bushes.

"Oh, Walker." Harper blinked, then offered him a light smile. "What are you doing here? You know we closed fifteen minutes ago, right?"

"Yeah, um..." Walker wiped his hands on his slacks and

cringed at the thought that he was about to go to a nice restaurant and had just dusted his trash hands on his legs. "It's stupid, really. I'm going to dinner with Talia, and she really likes those stir stick things. Well, she likes chewing on them—I'm not sure she's ever actually *stirred* anything with them. Anyway, sorry to bother you. It's dumb."

"Do you want me to go get one for you? I think most girls prefer flowers for a date, but it's not that hard for me to walk back inside and get you a stirrer. At least you're not asking me to make you a coffee," Harper laughed.

"I—it's not a date, but if you could, that would be... I'd owe you. Thanks, Harper," Walker stammered, finishing lamely by looking at his feet. His hands went clammy at the mention of the outing because, if he was being honest, it definitely felt like a date. He and Talia had both been really clear that it wasn't, but he still had the nerves of a sixteen-year-old about to show up to some girl's house with a corsage (stir stick) to take her to the prom (a French restaurant with snail food).

"No problem." Harper smiled genuinely and turned to make her way back inside. She came back a few minutes later holding out a small rectangular box. Walker broke into a wide grin.

"A whole box of them? She's going to love this!"

"Sure thing. You guys really aren't together?" Harper pried.

"Just friends." Walker rolled the box over in his hands.

"Why not?"

He turned to Harper again, confused. "Why not what?"

"I've been watching you and Talia for months, Walker. You're in love with her. She's in love with you. What's the problem?"

"She—" Walker's mouth dropped open. "What?"

The blunt way the barista had just casually declared his love for Talia wasn't *that* shocking. He was starting to get used to everyone blatantly calling him out. What was shocking was Harper's impression that Talia loved him, too. Talia would have to be clinically insane to love him back. She was so out of his league it was laughable. There had been a sexual spark between them

Walker couldn't ignore, but there was no way Talia had conveniently forgotten what a disorganized hot mess he was.

Harper gave him a pitying look, and this time it had nothing to do with Cole or Paisley. "I thought when she invited me over to your house that one time you might have thought I was cute or something and she was trying to set us up, but then Talia gave me this whole song and dance about how you weren't available, and then she looked incredibly jealous when I was showing you how to use the coffee maker, so I figured that she really was just trying to get a demonstration on how to make espressos. You've always been nice to me, Walker, and I'll admit that I think you're very attractive, but I know a lost cause when I see one. That right there," Harper pointed to the box of stir sticks gripped in Walker's hand and shrugged, shaking her head, "lost cause. You're not available. You're taken. If you want my advice, which I'm offering freely because I think you need to pull your head out of your ass, whatever you two are doing, just figure it out already. It's exhausting just watching you beat around the bush from behind that counter. One time, I put soy milk in Talia's drink instead of regular milk just because I was bored and I wanted to see if you would switch with her. You did, by the way."

"Wow." Walker blew out a heavy breath, his face flushed with heat. "She just—she really hates soy milk."

"I know."

The next question slipped from his mouth like an eager child asking for ice cream. "You really think she likes me? I mean, she shouldn't. I don't think she does."

"Ohmigod," Harper groaned, looking up at the sky as if to ask why she had to deal with such an imbecile, and gave a dramatic toss of both hands. "Walker, you're giving me a headache. Talia does not want to be your friend. I promise. You're freaking blind, and I'm going home to eat cold leftover pizza. Have fun on your date, that's not a date, that's definitely a date."

"Thanks for the—" Walker awkwardly lifted the box of stir sticks, and Harper nodded before brushing past him to get to the only other car in the parking lot. "You're very nice!" he called after her. "And for what it's worth, you're also very pretty! I just, Talia's—"

Harper didn't even look over her shoulder as she responded, unimpressed, "Yeah, yeah." She didn't give Walker a second glance before hopping in her car, starting it, and promptly leaving the parking lot. He was definitely one of those annoying people who had overstayed his welcome and kept an employee from ending their work day by being too chatty. Harper just wanted to go home and eat pizza. Why the hell was he still talking? Her observations about him and Talia had made him a blubbering idiot.

Walker's heart was beating a million miles a minute on the way to pick Talia up. The conversation with Harper had him even more nervous than before. It had him wondering what would happen if dinner turned into a real date. What would happen if he acted, just for one night, like they could be together. He didn't have to go overboard. No kissing. No sex. Just a date. While Harper had to be mistaken about Talia's interest in him, Walker couldn't help but want to take everything too far. His former reckless self was asking for it, prodding him to *live a little, to indulge. What's the big deal?* Old Walker taunted him, standing arms crossed in front of his motorcycle like the world was his playground.

Pulling into Talia's driveway and claiming the spot beside her car, Walker killed the engine and turned his attention to his clothes. Gray slacks, brown shoes, brown belt, and a white collared shirt: all his brother's clothes, and all items he used to pick on his brother for wearing when Cole took Paisley out on formal dates. Walker had felt a little strange when he first perused Cole's old belongings, still hanging in the master closet as if Cole were still around, but something inside him said it was okay. Not only okay, but right. Like he was honoring his brother by doing exactly what Cole would have done under the circumstances.

Dress to impress, clean up, pull out all the stops. Paisley would have had an absolute conniption if she knew how dressed-up Walker had gotten for a woman, and the thought made him smile.

When Walker got to the front door, he let himself in, knowing Talia wouldn't mind.

"Ponytail?" he shouted over the loud music Talia always blasted when she was getting ready. Today's music of choice seemed to be '90s boy bands. New Kids on the Block blared through her surround sound, and he grinned when he heard her singing. Unlike Piper, Talia could not hold a tune to save her life. While Piper would at least make it past the first round on *American Idol*, Talia would have definitely ended up one of those viral audition clips everyone laughed at.

Walker chuckled to himself and listened a moment longer before meandering down the hallway in search of Talia. He caught a small glimpse of something in the far right corner of her bedroom when he made it all the way to the end of the hall. The door was wide open, so he stepped through the doorway, ignoring all the warning signs in his head that said he should *never* be alone with her in a room where her bed was always only a few steps away.

"Tal, are you—fuck!"

Standing in front of the mirror was Talia in all her glory, wearing only a black lacy bra and matching lace underwear that left nothing to the imagination. Her cheeky underwear left enough skin showing on her firm, round ass that it made Walker's eyes bulge out of his head, along with another body part that wanted to bulge out of his pants. His traitorous eyes wandered up the smooth curves of her body to her breasts, displayed so prettily in strappy lace. It wasn't enough. Nothing was enough. No matter how fucked up it was, Walker wanted all of Talia's clothes off, to find her standing completely naked and waiting for him.

"Walker! Shit, what time is it? Close your eyes." Talia's body hunched over itself, and her arms wrapped around her torso in an attempt to cover up. Walker flipped around in a panic and imme-diately started counting backwards from ten in his head.

"S-sorry," he breathed, closing his eyes to try to rid the images and thoughts of Talia's body as she rustled around behind him.

"Are you okay?" Her hand touched his shoulder a minute later, and he flinched, eyes still closed. "I'm decent now."

"Please don't touch me," Walker pleaded, shutting his eyes harder. Talia's hand immediately dropped from his arm, and he wanted to take his words back.

Never mind. Keep touching me. Touch me everywhere.

"I thought we said six," Talia finally broke the silence.

"It was five forty-five when I arrived, and I feel like I've been standing here for an eternity, so that makes it six and an eternity," Walker replied.

"I don't think that's how time works."

"Forgive me, my brain short circuited with all of that." Eyes still closed, Walker gestured wildly behind him with one hand, accidentally hitting Talia's arm. He ripped his hand back with a soft groan. "Open your eyes," Talia giggled. "This is ridiculous. It's not like you haven't seen a naked woman before, and I wasn't even naked."

Walker gradually lifted his eyelids, body tense as a skittish horse, ready to cut loose and bolt from the room as he turned slowly to face Talia. He finally allowed his eyes to set on her, mentally screaming at himself to keep his gaze from wandering down her body. He reached up, involuntarily, to the strap of her dress, and heard Talia take a ragged breath. It was his favorite color. The olive green fabric hugged her body like a glove, a hint of what was underneath—what he had just seen. He gently moved the strap to the side, indulging in the feel of her skin under his fingertips. The strap slid off her shoulder, revealing the black strap of her bra, and he instantly regretted it when a pang of need hit his groin. His throat worked to speak, voice coming out like gravel when he finally did. "Do you always wear that? Under your clothes, I mean."

"Sometimes," Talia whispered, eyes blazing. He had missed that spark behind her obsidian eyes that used to always appear when they were alone. The one that he had craved every day since meeting her.

He wanted to ask follow-up questions: was the outfit specifically for him, or was it just coincidence? His gaze lingered on her lips a moment longer, not even realizing the song playing overhead had ended until "I Want It That Way" started up. The new song broke Walker out of his spell enough to make him laugh. It was so ridiculously corny given the circumstances, he couldn't help it. Talia broke into a wide smile, too, laughing with him.

"Ridiculous," Walker muttered, shaking his head. He was both talking about the song and his attraction to Talia. Instead of going dormant like it should have during their break, his desire had apparently ramped up to new heights. How much longer could he go on like this, begging and pleading with his body to settle down?

Walker took one shaky breath to summon the strength he wasn't even sure he had and reached down to grasp Talia's hand, tugging her toward the doorway. "Let's go."

"Ow!" Talia laughed, yanking his arm back. "Wait, I need my shoes!"

"Go barefoot. I don't care. Just get in the car."

If Talia wasn't already aware that he was two seconds from taking her on the floor of her bedroom, then his urgency to get the hell out of her house probably revealed him.

"Walker!" Talia protested when they got halfway down the hall, her feet still bare.

"Fine," Walker grumbled and backtracked to her room, striding straight over to her closet to snatch a pair of gray heels off her shoe rack. "These," he decided, holding them up between them.

"Those work," Talia agreed.

Walker took several hasty steps in her direction and held out one of the heels. Her eyes bore into his as she used his arm as a balance beam, sliding the first shoe on and then the other. He breathed steadily through his nose and wasted no time escaping her bedroom once both shoes were on her feet. Talia practically had to sprint after him in her stilts to catch up. It maybe wasn't the most chivalrous thing to leave her in the dust, but it was either that or doing the most unchivalrous thing and ravaging her against the wall.

The ride to the restaurant was mostly silent apart from Walker tapping his finger against the wheel and the music Talia had turned up—thankfully, not any love songs. He was still doing his best not to imagine her standing in front of her mirror or lying on her back with her hair splayed across a pillow.

It's just a date, it's just a date, it's just a date. The mantra Walker chanted in his head was failing miserably.

"So," Talia interrupted his internal war, cutting through his thoughts like a hot knife in butter. "Should we talk about this, or are you just going to act weird the whole time?"

"I just saw my best friend naked. Excuse me for taking some time to process it." Walker tried to make it sound sarcastic, like *hey, that was a funny little accident back there. No biggie, I'm totally chill.* But he was not, in fact, chill.

"I wasn't naked! And I've seen you mostly naked already. Now we're even."

Walker balked. "What? No you haven't. When?"

Talia raised an eyebrow. "When I brought Piper home and you tried to dive bomb away from her vomit."

Vomit! Walker clung to the word, trying to redirect all thoughts to something disgusting to calm himself down.

"Okay, I was wearing pants," he argued. "Wait, did you check me out?"

"Don't get cocky!" Talia chided. "You were an asshole. I was mostly trying to figure out why God gave you so many muscles when you were such a jerk."

"That's not a 'no,'" Walker pointed out, a smirk growing on

his face as he parked the car outside the restaurant. "Was I really that bad?"

"I believe your exact words when you opened the door to find me and Piper standing there were 'what did you do to her?' as if I'd brought her over to my house for a few keg stands and some night caps."

"Keg stands and night caps have very different vibes," Walker laughed, reaching over to unbuckle Talia's seatbelt for her. "My dad was more into night caps, but scratch the night part and make it the entire day and then pass out at about six-thirty p.m."

"My dad usually passed out after drinking a fifth of Scotch and throwing a tantrum." She said it with a lilt of comedy, but Walker found himself immediately boiling over with rage, the joke falling flat. He released his own seatbelt with an aggressive, stiff-fingered jab. Talia noticed and reached out to touch his arm. "It's okay. I don't need you to protect me. He's gone."

"I know that. I want him to still be alive," Walker seethed.

Talia's hand fell away. "What would you do?"

Walker took a thoughtful breath. "I think I would feel better if I could physically punish him. For you, for Cole, for Paisley. I never want to be like him or like my dad. It's like they were only here to cause destruction and pain." The words flowed easily from his mouth, like they always did when he talked to Talia, but Walker still felt a jolt of guilt for speaking that way about his dad. While it always bothered Walker that his dad never accepted that he had a problem, never fought against his sickness hard enough to be present, he still felt a pang of affection for him. The memories weren't all bad. "Do you ever worry that you'll end up just like him?"

"Like my dad?"

Walker nodded.

"Yes. All the time." Talia gave him a somber head shake. "He was so angry all the time. I don't ever want to be that bitter. Sometimes I feel like I am that bitter, and it terrifies me."

Walker bobbed his head, a simple acknowledgement. He

knew Talia well enough to not contradict or dispute her feelings. She wasn't anything like her father, but Walker understood how it felt to see parts of yourself and wonder where they came from.

"My dad was..." Walker paused. "It was like he just couldn't control himself, ya know? Nothing was ever good enough to pull him out of it. Not me. Not Cole. Sometimes I think I'm like that. Like I can't accomplish what I want to accomplish because I'm in my own way. I used to wish Dad would fall in love or something, and maybe then whoever he fell in love with would be good enough for him to go get some help. It's stupid. I think he might have been in love with my mom, but she was just as sick. Or, at least, I assume so, since she died of an overdose. I never really knew her, but maybe my dad did. Cole always said Dad was broken before Mom died, but maybe he just felt helpless. It's not like we had a lot of money lying around when I was a kid, to send him to rehab, but I just wanted him to snap out of it. I just wanted him to be *there*."

Talia grabbed his hand and squeezed. "You're good enough, Walker. You are. I wish he would have pulled out of it, for you and for Cole."

At least for Walker, the reason for his dad's negligence was understandable. Jeff Cohen was a different story. The anger and aggression that man had to have living just under the surface of his skin to ever be able to look at Talia or any other woman and want to harm her was pure evil. Walker's stomach churned, disgust pricking at the back of his neck. "Where did he hit you?" he asked.

Talia pulled her eyebrows together at the abrupt change in conversation, and Walker winced. Even with the intimacy they had just gained by sharing so much of what made them vulnerable, it was still a heavy question to ask.

"I don't remember." She gave him a sad smile.

He cupped her face with his hand, desperate to touch any stretch of her skin, to heal it. To think that someone could hurt the same beautiful person he had just seen standing in Talia's mirror made Walker sick.

"You can tell me," he whispered, dropping his hand to run it over her shoulder. Talia deserved to be touched with only reverence and appreciation. She chewed on her lower lip, her eyes going distant as she shook her head.

"Sometimes our brains just block out the painful memories, so I actually don't remember. I remember a little bit after and a little before, but I don't remember him hitting me other than knowing it happened. I couldn't even tell you where he left bruises," Talia explained. "I barely remember living here before. I know stories. I remember what he looked like when he was angry. That's about it."

Walker smiled. "I always knew you were smart."

Talia barked out a laugh. "Because my brain hid my trauma?"

"If you think about it, that's kind of amazing." Walker swallowed heavily, tracing over the soft contours of Talia's face with his eyes. "*You're* amazing."

If that was a touch too far, it came across in the silence that fell between them. Walker wanted to be taking Talia on a date that night. If nothing else, just to show her exactly what she deserved. So she would know when she did find the person she was supposed to be with—even if that person wasn't going to be him—how she should be loved. And he could show her that easily enough. Sometimes he felt like he was wearing his love for her right on his sleeve.

"Walker, I'm confused," Talia murmured. "We said this wasn't a date."

"Sorry." Walker shook his head. "You're right. I'm making this weird. Can I just run something by you before we go inside? Please?"

"Anything."

"What if we *do* make it a date?" Walker held up his hand when Talia opened her mouth to protest. "Let me explain. I want to, just for tonight, go on a date with you to show you how you deserve to be treated."

"You mean, like... pretend we're on a date?" Talia asked.

"Sort of, yeah. I'm not going to kiss you good night or anything, but I think, as your friend, I could help show you your worth. You deserve a good date, Tal. Someone should tell you how stunning you look in that dress. Someone should open doors for you and hold your hand," Walker explained. "I can be that for you tonight. Then you'll know how beautiful you should feel when you're with the right person. And when you search for them, you won't settle for anything less than what you deserve."

Talia rolled her bottom lip between her teeth, her long eyelashes fanned out above her flushed cheeks with one slow blink before she nodded and looked down at her hands, like she was imagining what it would feel like to have his fingers entwined with hers. She didn't look at him when she responded with a nervous "okay."

Walker's hand wavered as he lifted it to her face, tucking his index finger under her chin and tipping her head up to meet his eyes straight on. "Are you sure? If you don't want to, we don't have to."

"I want to." Talia nodded, her full lips spreading into a smile. She reached for her door handle, and Walker set a hand on her shoulder to stop her.

"Wait!"

Talia's head reeled back, and she looked at him with her coffee-colored eyes, her irises clouded with uncertainty.

"I got your door," Walker laughed, and he hopped out and rounded the car to Talia's side. The heart on his sleeve was ready for one night in the driver's seat.

TWENTY-NINE

TALIA

"So, what's the verdict?"

They were sitting on the same side of the booth. Talia was wedged so closely to Walker that their legs were touching from thigh to heel.

Walker looked down at his plate and chewed slowly, one hand interlocked with Talia's like they were on a full-fledged date. It made her head spin. It felt so easy to lean into him that if she didn't know any better, she would have thought by the end of the night they would be going home together, not back to being just friends.

"Tastes like weird green chicken." Walker set his fork down and shrugged.

Talia giggled. "That's escargot to a T. It's maybe more rubbery than chicken, too?"

"Not that I know how to cook chicken, either, but I would never make this when I could make actual chicken that doesn't cost a billion dollars."

"Fifteen hundred dollars, to be exact," Talia recalled.

"Mmm." Walker nodded in appreciation and unlaced his

fingers from hers. She impulsively wanted to snatch his hand back, clutch onto it for dear life, but the need morphed into something stronger when he dropped his hand to her leg and set it along the hem of her dress, riding up her thigh. "Is this okay?"

"Yeah." Talia's voice came out huskier than she would have liked. She cleared her throat and adjusted in her seat. "So, this is what you would do on a normal first date?"

"Not really, no." Walker grinned. "Just with you. Other guys probably shouldn't be doing this on a first date with you, either. Should I stop?"

Talia's heart was beating a million miles a minute, her cheeks flushing beet red. There was no use in hiding it. Walker had to know at this point that she was wildly attracted to him. The lines kept getting blurred, and she was starting to wonder if being friends and friends alone would ever feel normal.

She wanted to wake up next to him, curl into his side, and breathe in his scent. She wanted to cook breakfast with him and laugh about whatever silly thing one of his nieces or nephews had said. She wanted to be included in every decision about the kids and watch them grow up. And, dear God, her body was dying to be underneath him, to feel his weight against her, to run her hands over his bare skin like she did in her imagination when she read Contracted Love alone in her room.

I'm only thinking about you, Walker. I don't want anyone else, Talia thought, staring into his eyes. *How can you not see that?*

Talia set her hand over his and, with a light touch, swirled her thumb over his skin. "No, it's... comfortable. If you remove it, I'll just end up being cold."

"Good. So, tell me something I don't already know about you. What's your most embarrassing story?"

"Oh, we're going there?" Talia laughed and picked up her water glass, putting it to her mouth to take a swig before answering. Walker followed her motions, and she could have sworn that his eyes dropped to her lips as she drank. "Let's see... actually, I don't think I can tell you my most embarrassing story."

"What? Why not?" Walker gaped at her. "I'll tell you mine."

"It's too mortifying. I promised myself I would never tell anybody. Except Amala, of course."

"But I'm not just *anybody*. I'm me." Walker gave her the poutiest of faces, sticking out his bottom lip like a literal child. It reduced her to a puddle, and she gave in.

"Okay fine, fine. But you have to promise not to laugh." Talia pointed at him sternly.

"I won't, promise." Walker held up his free hand like a Boy Scout giving an oath, his thumb folded over his palm.

Taking a deep breath first, Talia launched into her story. It was more a series of events that led to the worst embarrassment of her life. It started off with her showing up in her brand new outfit to her first day of school in NYC just after moving. She made it halfway through the school day before running into a kid in the cafeteria who was unfortunately in the middle of drinking a carton of chocolate milk. Her outfit was ruined, a questionable brown stain down the front, and there was nothing to be done. Her mom was at work, and Talia had no spare clothes. It ended up looking like the worst kind of bathroom incident, and it did not go unnoticed by her classmates.

Next was the *actual* bathroom incident. At the time, she was so terrified of being a bother to anyone and so desperate to fit in, she figured asking to use the restroom would only be met with more commentary on the large, brownish stain down the front of her. So, she tried to hold it, as any reasonable person would do. It didn't end well.

"What happened after you peed yourself?" Walker pried, the corners of his lips turning up with a force beyond his control as he attempted to keep from laughing.

"I just sat there in my own pee, waiting for class to end as it ran down my legs. When I got up, that's when Cory Wilkshire—he was actually a nice kid—asked me why I was all wet."

"And you said...?"

"Slipped in a puddle."

"Did he buy it?

"Nope. Especially when a different kid pointed at my ass and yelled 'she peed herself' at the top of his lungs. Anyway..." Talia blushed furiously and averted her eyes in embarrassment before Walker reached his hand up to cup her face.

"Hey, that's not that bad." His thumb brushed over her reddened cheek, and she returned her gaze to him. "And if you ever need to pee during dinner, you just let me know, and I will hop on out of this seat." His face split into a grin, and she nudged her shoulder against his.

"I hate you."

"Do you really?" Walker asked, his voice low and breathy. Talia found his hand again, resting against her leg under the table, and rubbed her thumb over it with slow, methodical circles. His breath hitched, and she liked the sound of it, wishing she could guide his fingers between her legs right then and there.

"No, I don't hate you. You have to tell me *your* story now, though. And it better be worse than mine." She lifted her chin defiantly, and he smiled again, his pearl-white teeth gleaming in the candlelight.

"Um, mine is... not exactly appropriate for dinner." Walker looked away.

"You promised!"

"You're never going to look at me the same."

"How do you want me to look at you?" Talia pried, leaning into him further and finding his eyes.

"Like that," Walker murmured back. She batted her eyelashes for effect. His jaw ticked, his eyes wandering down to her lips for a split second. "Fine, but I warned you. So, just to preface this, I didn't really have someone around to give me 'the talk' about the birds and the bees when I was a kid. Cole never thought to tell me because he was also still a kid. Anyway, I found this... video in my dad's old crap, and I watched it. I was, like, seven or something."

"Oh no!"

"It gets worse. I thought the people were dancing. I guess I thought it was cool? So cool I brought it to show and tell."

"No!" Talia's mouth dropped open. "You didn't."

"Oh, I did. Then I had to have a meeting with my principal, my teacher, the school nurse, and my brother. My dad was too drunk off his ass, as usual, to attend. They all sat me down and explained as a team what the video was and why it wasn't appropriate for seven-year-olds to watch. I'm pretty sure they had to send a letter to all the parents in that class about the porn that I exposed them to."

"That's horrifying but also... kind of adorable?"

"I'm not sure how you reached that conclusion." Walker let out a puff of laughter.

"You were so innocent!" Talia said earnestly.

"I'm not innocent anymore." He fixed her with a hard stare. The seduction behind it made the heat grow between Talia's thighs.

"No, I suppose you aren't," she choked out.

Walker's eyes darkened as they flitted down to her breasts, the scoop neck of her dress revealing a little of the black lacy bra underneath, then back up to her face. "Are *you*?"

"No." Her tongue dipped out of her mouth to drag along her bottom lip. "I don't want to be."

"Here we are!" The waitress appeared out of thin air, and Walker ripped his hand away from Talia's thigh. Talia hadn't realized how close they were, or that his hand had slid a little further up and over on her leg, mere inches from where he could have ruined her in seconds. The waitress set down Walker's plate of steak frites, and he coughed loudly, scooting several inches away from Talia, the boundary set again.

They made idle talk as they ate their meal. Talia tried to break down the invisible wall he had put up as she fiddled with her spoon in her ratatouille, but it was to no avail. The closest she got was holding his hand, but it was from a distance. He was a million miles away.

"Where'd you go?" Talia finally asked when she couldn't take it any longer. Walker blinked the haze from his eyes and twisted his torso to look at her.

"Sorry, I'm just overthinking. Cole's birthday is on Saturday. We used to do something fun, and I just don't feel like celebrating. Then I feel like we *should* be celebrating. But what exactly is there to celebrate? I don't know." He took another bite of his food, which he had admitted ordering solely because it had the word "steak" in the title. After Talia had explained that steak tartare was actually raw ground beef, Walker had grown concerned with the menu items of anything he didn't recognize and opted for the safest option. Talia had mostly been pretending to eat her food, shifting the eggplant and zucchini around to keep herself occupied, so she took his lead and took a bite. It was still warm despite her delay in eating it. It had originally tasted bland when she first tried it, but the opening in her and Walker's conversation had her reconsidering. Now it reminded her a little of the stews her mother used to make when she was sick.

"Maybe you can do both?" she suggested. "What do you normally do?"

"Cole never really had a childhood, so he had this tradition where we would all do something that no one had ever done before. It didn't even have to be big, but it had to be new."

"That sounds fun." It did. Cole should have gotten to live out so many more firsts.

"I think we're just going to hang out this year—eat some cake, maybe," Walker offered with a shrug.

"My mom used to take me shopping to get one full outfit on my birthday. We'd spend all day out, agonizing over every detail of it, then we'd go get ice cream." Talia smiled, glancing down at her stew. "I think you would've liked her. She would've given you so much unwarranted parenting advice."

"If she's anything like you, I'm sure I would've loved her. Cole would've loved you, too, and Paisley—God, you and Paisley would be best friends. She was a force to be reckoned with."

Walker looked up, as if he could see them in a pattern on the ceiling. Talia clasped his hand in hers again, a gesture of comfort, and joined him in looking up.

"And here's your dessert!" The waitress walked straight into another of thier moments with the chocolate lava cake they had ordered. They nodded politely as she set it down in front of them. They agreed on the typical date standard earlier, one that involved sharing a piece together. So much had passed between them that by the time it actually came, they both stared at it in awkward silence, neither of them reaching for a fork.

"You know you're not betraying your brother by eating a piece of cake with me, right?" Talia brushed Walker's shoulder to try to break into his thoughts again. Walker opened his mouth a few times to respond before he clammed up. He snatched a fork off the table, scooted closer to her, and dug the fork carelessly into the middle of the cake before he suspended it between them with a small smile.

"I know. Open?"

Talia obeyed, met with the rich taste of fudge when he lifted the fork to her lips. It mixed into her senses, her nose breathing in Walker's cedar woodsy scent while her mouth worked to swallow. He was staring at her lips again, and she knew her eyes were begging him to kiss hcr.

"You have a little..." Walker wiped at the corner of her mouth and did the most erotic thing she'd ever seen: licked the chocolate off his finger.

Holy shit. Talia had never thought of frosting as sexual before Walker, but this was now the second time frosting felt like foreplay to her.

"You normally make sure I'm covered in frosting, not the opposite," Talia chuckled, opting for a light joke to cut her sexual frustrations. She stabbed into the cake with her fork, shoving a heaping portion into her mouth.

The sooner the cake was gone, the sooner they could leave,

and the sooner she could avoid grabbing Walker by the collar to devour his mouth in front of the whole restaurant.

"Yeah, well, I figured I'd give you a break for once, and—wow, you really like that cake," Walker chuckled as Talia shoved another behemoth of a bite into her mouth.

"Mm-hmm," she mumbled and covered her mouth to prevent any crumbs from spraying out of her mouth. Slicing into the piece once more, she lifted it toward Walker and murmured something resembling "want some?" before practically jamming it into his mouth. Never in a million years did she think she would be forcing Walker to deep-throat cake. After he got over the surprise of her force-feeding him like a toddler, he closed his mouth over the fork and ran his tongue over his lips to get the stray crumbs when she took the fork back.

Fucking hell. Talia had to hold back a groan.

The cake was finished within five minutes, and Talia all but launched out of her seat when the waitress returned with Walker's receipt and he moved to slide out of the booth. He held out his arm naturally for her to grab onto, and she was surprised how when she took it, it made her less nervous. Touching him felt good. Better than good. It was the same when they were eating. Other than her obvious arousal, Walker's hand on her leg and his body so close to hers felt like they belonged there. When he had put space between them, that was when she had been the least sure of herself.

Everything else that followed felt right, too. Walker opened her door and held her hand as she climbed into the passenger seat. He massaged circles into the palm of her hand on the drive back to her house as they made the kind of conversation they always did. It was light and fun, but with an edge of anticipation. A sexual current ran through the air between them. Talia wondered if he could feel it. Could he tell how much she wanted him? Not just his body, but everything else, too?

"I'll walk you to your door." Walker parked the car in her

driveway, hesitating a moment before he hit the button to turn it off.

"Okay."

Talia's heart skipped a beat. Usually, Walker left the car running when he dropped her off places. If he wasn't planning on staying, then pocketing his keys seemed unnecessary. She no longer knew if they were still in fake-date territory or if they had ventured past that. Each touch gave off the vibe that their previous boundaries might have shifted.

When they made it to her porch, Talia stood there for a moment, facing Walker. One of his hands held hers like he didn't want to let go, and the other held something behind his back.

"I had fun tonight." Walker grinned and rocked back on his heels.

Talia bit her bottom lip and smiled back. "Me too."

"I have something for you."

"You do, do you?" Talia hadn't meant for it to come out sounding all salacious, but she wasn't mad at it.

"I do." Walker pulled his hand from behind his back, holding up a small box. It took her a second to make sense of what it was, but when she did, her heart flipped in her chest.

Her voice was almost unrecognizably low and sensual when she finally responded. "You got me stir sticks."

"I did."

Talia blew out a breath, trying to prevent herself from jumping Walker on the spot. Her hand lingered in the air between them, held up to receive her gift. With an agonizingly slow delivery, eyes locked on hers, Walker placed the box in her palm, dragging his fingers unnecessarily down her wrist.

She watched his throat work to speak. "You look really beautiful tonight."

"Which time?" Talia gave him a flirty smirk. "When I was mostly naked, or right now?"

"God," Walker whispered. "Both."

Talia went still, waiting for him to make a move. She could

hear her heartbeat pounding in her ears, a rhythmic chorus of *do it, do it, do it.*

"I guess I should go."

Talia's face fell, and she bobbed her head relentlessly to hide her disappointment."Right, yeah. Totally."

Walker stood unmoving for a moment, before he pressed one hand into the small of Talia's back and pulled her into his torso. His scent enveloped her as she leaned further into him, resting her head against his chest. She succumbed to the feeling of the hard ridges of his body wrapping her in bliss, his warmth protecting her from the biting chill of the evening. She was more at home in his arms than if she were to take two steps inside her actual house. Her eyes closed, and she didn't let go until Walker made a move to leave. When he did, he didn't remove his hands from around her, just pulled back a little to look into her eyes.

The insurmountable tension between them drew her in. Her mouth felt like a magnet to his. She hadn't even realized she had moved toward him, just a centimeter or two from grazing his lips, until the unthinkable happened.

"Oh." Walker dropped his arms, his hands hitting his thighs with a slap as he took a giant step back from her.

Talia's eyes widened in horror from the clear rejection. She whipped her purse off her shoulder and started to dig through the compartments for her keys. She kept doing this to herself, expecting more when there was never going to be more. Walker had done exactly what he said he was going to do, taking her on the most wonderful, amazing date without the expectation of anything more, and now she felt like the world's biggest idiot.

"Wait, Tal! I didn't mean to—"

"It's fine," Talia cut him off. "I don't know what I was thinking. Everything's fine. We're fine."

"If you say 'fine' a few more times, I'll believe you." In her peripherals, she could tell Walker was trying to catch her eyes, dipping his head down to see her face, but she couldn't handle having to meet her embarrassment head-on.

Instead she turned away from him and muttered, "Don't be a jerk."

"I'm not trying to be. But I can't kiss you. It's a terrible idea."

"Got it." Talia flinched and finally glanced up at him. "Kissing me would be terrible."

"That's not—" Walker ran his fingers through his hair and started to pace on the porch. "I'm sorry. I took everything too far tonight, and I shouldn't have. I knew I would, and I did it anyway. This is on me, not you. Please forgive me. I'll stop baiting you, I promise. I don't want to lose you again."

"You won't. Nothing to forgive." Each sentiment came out with a definitive period at the end as Talia continued to flounder for the keys that were evading her grasp. When she finally found them, she maneuvered to frantically unlock the door and twist the knob.

"Tal, *please*. I'm sorry!"

She had no idea what Walker was apologizing for. He had done virtually nothing. She should be apologizing for trying to cross the line. "Like I said, we're good. We're just friends. Thanks for the date. Have a great night, Walker!"

Then Talia did what any rational, sane person would do and slammed the door in his face. She leaned back against the door and let her eyes fall shut as she sank to the floor, dropping her stir sticks and purse haphazardly on the ground. Knees hiked up to her chest and hands covering her face, she waited for what felt like forever for the sound of Walker's car to leave her driveway. When it finally did, her cell phone had found its way into her hand and her fingers had swiftly pulled up Amala's contact.

She picked up after the first ring. "Girl, why are you calling me? I figured you'd be up to your ears in Walker's sheets by now."

"Nope." Talia groaned and let her head fall back against the hard wood of the door. "Instead, I tried to kiss him, and he dodged it. I'm going to slowly crawl into a hole and die now."

Amala gasped. "Oh, he did not!"

"He did. His exact words were 'it's a terrible idea,' and then I freaked out and shut the door in his face. I'm so embarrassed. We already said we weren't going to do that, but he kept looking at me, and then I thought maybe he wanted to kiss me! Please kill me. Or if you don't want to get your hands dirty given your husband's job, maybe you know of a local serial killer I could offer myself up to as tribute? Can people hire hitmen for themselves?"

"Okay, is this really pee-your-pants-at-school-with-a-choco-late-milk-stain-down-the-front-of-you embarrassing?" Amala asked.

"It's worse!" Talia shouted into the phone.

"Um, ow!" Amala yelled back. "Bitch, you're going to blow out my eardrums! Stop spiraling."

"Do you want to go buy a bunch of cats with me? I need to finally accept my role as a lowly spinster."

"You're allergic to cats. Before you go buying a ranch in Texas to hoard all your animals, I'm coming over. Be there in ten."

"I was just going to read and attempt to go to bed," Talia sighed. "You don't have to come."

"And what exactly were you planning on reading, Tal?" The accusation made Talia's face flush.

"*Nothiiiing*," Talia whined. "Definitely not *Contracted Love*."

"You liar." Amala laughed. "I'm coming over, and when I get there, I'm taking that damn book!"

"But I need it!" Talia jumped up from her spot on the floor and jogged to her room.

"I'm pretty sure you can use a vibrator without Walker's book." A car started on the other line as Talia spun around in her room in search of her prized possession.

"I don't know what you're talking about," Talia singsonged.

"Don't you dare hide it, Talia Seraphina Cohen!"

There was no surprise when Talia eventually found the book in her underwear drawer, right next to her *other* prized possession that was rechargeable and bright pink. "I actually lost it. I have no idea where it's at." She lied and slid the book under her mattress like it was a *Playboy* magazine.

"I'm not stupid, Talia! I'll be there in a second." The call ended, and Talia straightened her comforter a few times, examining her bed to make sure the book was fully covered.

Amala arrived a few minutes later, throwing open Talia's front door and stomping straight back to her bedroom. Talia jumped up from her couch, where she was attempting to paint a picture of nonchalance, and followed on Amala's heels. It only took two seconds for Amala to find the book, and when she pulled it out, she held it up with a glare.

"You *annotated* it, you freak!" Amala tossed the colorfully-tabbed book on the bed like it had caught on fire and folded her arms over her chest, letting them rest on her protruding belly. Talia stared back like a deer in headlights, shocked at how easily Amala had found her hiding place.

The staredown was broken up when they simultaneously burst into fits of unhinged laughter. Accusations about Talia acting like a teenage boy and why Amala seemed to know exactly where to hide things were tossed around as they giggled. They were both wiping tears from their eyes and sitting on the carpet with their backs resting against the side of Talia's bed when the laughter finally died down minutes later. One pathetic look in Amala's direction was all it took for her to pull Talia into her side. Talia laid her head down on Amala's shoulder and sniffed back the real tears as she let her eyes fall shut.

THIRTY

WALKER

It was going to be a terrible day—Walker knew it the second his alarm went off. Everything inside him felt sick when his brain came to, awakened from another dream where he was close to drowning. The pressure in his chest felt claustrophobic. He took several rhythmic, deep breaths to ward off the stress that wanted to crash over him. He needed to deter another panic attack from consuming him. *Not today. Please, just not today.*

"Happy Birthday, Cole," he muttered aloud with a sigh, pulling the covers off his body and wandering into the bathroom, thinking a hot shower might do the trick.

It didn't.

When he made his way downstairs, everyone was up already. The normal pleasantries—or, in his family's case, loud arguing and general chaos—were absent. It was dead silent except for the sound of Carter dumping cereal into a bowl. The kids all looked up when Walker entered the kitchen, and he felt the vice tighten its grip on his chest. He knew he should say something. Anything remotely inspiring or nice to get them through the day.

He came up with nothing.

Instead, he remained silent and made his way to the cabinet on autopilot to grab a bowl. He wasn't even hungry. There was no way the cereal was going to slide down his dry, strangled throat.

Get it together, Walker, he berated himself.

"So," Walker stifled his panic enough to speak. "What do you all want to do today?"

Five faces looked up with matching expressions of sadness that made him die inside. The pressure increased. No one responded, so he picked a random person. "Piper?"

"What? You want me to be my happy, joyful self today?" Her unexpected sarcasm smacked him across the face. "Sorry I can't be happy all the time."

"I'm not expecting you to be happy," Walker choked out and turned toward his youngest nephew. "What about you, Coop? Something you want to do today?"

"Nope." Cooper's reply was simple when he normally would have posed a thousand questions about possible activities. The curious sparkle behind his eyes had dulled into a muted haze.

"Anyone?" Walker swiveled to look over at the rest of the siblings, practically begging for someone to respond. His plea was only met with more silence. He tugged on the collar of his shirt, pulling it away from his neck.

"I'm just going to go read a book," Pearl said sweetly after no one coughed up an answer for an agonizingly long time.

"I'm going to a friend's to study for my AP Chem exam." Colin picked his textbook off the counter and displayed it for show.

"Carter?" Walker pried.

"I'm just going to watch TV." Carter shrugged noncommittally.

"I'm going for a walk," Piper announced, shoving her earbuds into her ears and leaving the room with a sour expression.

It was only nine in the morning, and he was already failing them.

Heaving an unsatisfactory breath of air into his lungs, Walker tapped his fingers anxiously on the island before abandoning his empty cereal bowl and grabbing his keys off the hook near the door. He wasn't sure where he was going or what he was going to do, but he needed to get out of the house. Out of the room where he was disappointing everyone. Surely getting some fresh air, windows down and cool air blowing in his face would help relieve the feeling of an elephant sitting on his chest.

Minutes after getting in the car, Walker found himself parked outside of Talia's, fighting the urge to go inside and ask for help. His brain did its due diligence in reminding him that just a couple of nights ago, he had let himself get so wrapped up in Talia and their "date" that he even had her fooled into thinking she liked him back, just in time to reject her and screw everything up. Again. Recalling the look of hurt on Talia's face when he pulled back after almost kissing her only made the pressure in his chest increase.

He didn't deserve her help.

Walker started the car again and kept driving, searching for anywhere else to go. It was a bad idea to drive to the corner of 5th and Pine, but he was hell-bent on punishing himself for being reckless with Talia and failing with his nieces and nephews. What would Cole and Paisley think? The only two people on Earth who ever gave a shit about him were gone, and he was doing nothing to help their kids.

In the past, Cole would have woken up on his birthday to breakfast in bed made by his wife and kids, and Walker would've meandered over to their house to enjoy breakfast with them, free of responsibility. Asking what everyone was doing that day wouldn't have been an imposition. It would have been met with excitement over whatever event Cole had planned for his family that day. One time, Cole got a blow-up kiddie pool and filled it with water and dirt, and it became the great mud-wrestling incident of 2015. Walker never let Cole live down the fact that he beat him, pinning his brother in under a few minutes. Up until the day he died, Cole argued that his back was out and that was why he hadn't won, to which Walker would always reply with. "you keep telling yourself that, old man."

"Except you never got to grow old like you were supposed to, did you?" Walker asked the open air as he slumped down onto the curb. He stared at the streetlight. The cars passing under it became blurred by tears. Everyone was driving over the intersection and going about their day, unaware that two of the most wonderful people to ever walk the Earth had died there. How could everyone just move on? How could the world keep on spinning as if nothing had even happened?

Walker wasn't sure how long he sat there, watching the light turn from green to yellow to red, but the throbbing of his tailbone said it had been a while when he finally got up to leave. The pressure in his chest hadn't subsided at all. He had just been able to zone out on the street for a while to ignore the rising panic. In the end, he couldn't sit on the curb forever. He had a responsibility to make sure his family was okay. But he still needed help.

Something. *Anything* to help him get through the day.

The day dragged on. Everyone in the house moved about like zombies without souls or personalities, just lifeless creatures filled with the pain of loss. Walker desperately tried to take the day in a better direction. He bought cupcakes and attempted to scrounge together a family movie night. All of it was unanimously rejected. The cupcakes sat on the counter untouched, and the TV was stuck on a channel that only played As Seen on TV product commercials. The silence was deafening and becoming too much when Walker finally gave up the fight and retreated to his room, hiding what he had purchased earlier from the kids' sight.

The door to his room barely shut all the way before he crumpled to the ground, the pressure building to a new height as he crawled over to lean his back against the frame of his bed—what used to be their bed.

Breathe. Just breathe.

Focusing on the bag under his arm, he dropped it to the floor and stared at it, trying to regain his sense of self. Tears were starting to fall down his face freely, and he couldn't help but feel the overwhelming desire to give in for once, to let the temptation consume him. He was gasping for air when a knock came at the door and Pearl's voice called from behind it.

"Uncle Walker? Are you all right?"

"Uh... yeah," his voice cracked in response, unable to hold back the emotion through short breaths. "I'll be down in a minute."

No response came from behind the door, so Walker choked back a sob and hit his palm against his forehead repeatedly to try to force his anxiety into submission. Someone might eventually come in, and they couldn't see him like this.

Getting up off the floor, head spinning out of control, Walker grabbed the bag off the ground and stumbled over to his bedside table, tossing it into the drawer and throwing it shut before he fell into a heap on the ground. The edges of his vision were starting to darken with a blurry shadow, sucking him under. He fought to breathe, but the weight of everything was crushing him, his throat too constricted.

The struggle to gain full control over his body felt like it lasted an eternity. It could've been seconds, minutes, or hours of fighting before he was too weak to wrestle with his mind anymore. Too tired of constantly fighting what felt so much stronger than him.

He finally let it win.

And everything went black.

THIRTY-ONE

WALKER

"Walker."

A soft voice called out to him. It was soothing, almost angelic.

Am I dead? He fought to regain consciousness, floating in the dark room behind his eyelids.

"Walker, listen to my voice, okay?"

Someone was stroking his hair. It felt good, comfortable—the same way the new weight draped across his arm felt. It replaced the feeling of his heart being strangled, a good kind of pressure that left a tattoo of warmth across his skin as it drifted up and down in a soothing wave of motion.

"You're in your room. Can you feel the ground beneath you?"

It was Talia's voice, he realized. So he wasn't wrong when he'd thought it was an angel.

The ground solidified when he focused on feeling it below himself, and his eyes fluttered open. He took several long, labored breaths before reaching up to touch Talia's hand. She stopped moving it, and he slowly shifted into a sitting position, placing his head between his knees to get more air.

"I'm sorry," he finally spoke, and the haggard sound that came out felt pathetic. "Who called you?"

"Pearl." Talia tentatively touched his shoulder. "You don't have to be sorry. I know what today is."

"Did they see me like this?"

"No." Talia shook her head, and he let out a small breath of relief. "She just thought you needed somebody. She heard you crying."

"Dammit." Walker ran a hand through his disheveled hair and leaned back into the bed frame. "Thank you."

Talia tucked a strand of hair behind her ear, revealing more of her somber face. "Why didn't you call me?"

"I'm embarrassed that you keep having to deal with me." Walker sighed. "I didn't want to bother you. Especially after I was such an ass on our date."

"You weren't an ass."

"Come on, I fucked up. We both know it. Everyone might as well just get used to me fucking up." Walker glared down at his clenched fists, frustrated with himself.

"Why do you always do that?" Talia snapped. Walker looked over at her, surprised by the edge to her tone. "You always shit on yourself. Do you even realize how great you are?"

"I can prove that I'm a fuck-up, Tal. I did something so unbelievably stupid today."

"What?"

"Look in my nightstand."

Talia slowly rose from the floor and made her way over to the drawer, pulling it open. The contents rolled forward with a thunk, and Walker waited for her to realize that he was broken beyond repair. He'd finally be able to prove why he would never be good enough for her. She'd finally understand.

"Condoms?" Talia faltered.

"What? No!" Walker panicked, ripping his head toward her in explanation. "Not the *unopened* condoms. I don't even know why I have those. I'm not sleeping with anyone."

"Then I assume you're talking about this?" Talia held up the brown bag with a glass bottle of tequila inside. The paper crinkled against her fingertips. He gave a miserable nod of his head. "It's not open either, Walker."

"No, but I bought it." He deflated. "I wanted to numb the pain for a little while."

"But you didn't."

"It doesn't matter. I wanted to." Walker argued and closed his eyes. "I still want to. Can you dump it out?"

"No."

He snapped his eyes open to look up at her with a furrowed brow. "No?"

"You're going to dump it," Talia said.

"I can't—"

"Walker, don't give me that bullshit. I'm not going to do this for you. You're going to dump it yourself. You are capable. Since Cole and Paisley died, I've watched you upend your entire life to help those kids downstairs. You learned how to cook. Well, kind of." Walker let out a shaky chuckle, thankful for the lighter note as Talia edged on. "You know how to make a grocery list and how to use the espresso machine. You signed everyone up for therapy. You've handled every outbreak of teenage rebellion like a champ, so I don't want to hear that you can't do anything. Get up off your ass and dump this out."

"Jesus, you're really bossy today." He grinned, and she smirked back at him, holding her hand out to help him up. "I don't mind it."

Talia shrugged. "You're going to have to get used to it."

"Ponytail, you've done nothing but yell at me since the moment I met you. What makes you think I'm not already used to it?" The punch he received to his shoulder as a warning made him smile wider. "Okay, give me that." He held out his hand to receive the bottle, and Talia passed it over.

Forging ahead, Walker made his way into the bathroom, followed closely by Talia. He stood in front of the toilet for a moment before removing the brown sack and letting it fall to the floor. Talia bent over to compulsively pick it up, and he let out a laugh.

"Saving that for the next time I take a trip to the liquor store?"

"Shut up." She rolled her eyes.

Walker sucked in air through his teeth as he grasped the lid of the bottle and twisted hard, the tabs holding the aluminum cap breaking to release it. The tequila smelled like the cleaner he had made the older kids, due to their most recent misstep, clean the toilets with.

"It smells like rubbing alcohol mixed with bad breath," Walker noted and turned to Talia, who had also scrunched her nose in disgust. "At least I didn't buy the expensive stuff. Here goes nothing."

As the liquor dumped out into the toilet bowl, air bubbled up the bottle with a hollow glugging sound. They both stared intently as the liquid sucked into the drain when Walker flushed it, until all that remained was water.

"See? You did it!" Talia threw her arms around his neck, and Walker dropped the bottle in surprise. He fumbled to catch it, but it was too late—his high school football coach would have reamed him over the coals. The bottle clattered to the floor with a loud crash, shards of glass spraying across the tile.

"Shit!" Walker hissed, holding Talia tight to his body. "Don't move."

"We have to get out of the bathroom at some point." She clutched his middle with stiff arms. His breathing was starting to quicken for an entirely different reason than a panic attack as her body molded to his. He would much rather have Talia's weight sitting on his chest than the weight of all his failures.

"I don't want you to get cut. I'll pick you up, okay?" He squeezed her harder, readying himself.

"All right." Her voice sounded a little breathless and far away. He wondered, with her head pressed up against his chest, if she could tell his heart rate was faster than normal.

"Jump straight up on three and wrap your legs around my waist. Don't sweep your feet. One—"

"Walker, that's a little..." Her hesitancy said everything he was thinking. Talia with her legs wrapped around him would be painfully erotic.

"Can you think of a better option?" Walker asked. "I mean, I can pick you up from your legs, but your crotch or chest will just be in my face, and while that might be better for me, it'll probably be more uncomfortable for you."

"It's going to be weird either way. Let's just get out of this death trap." Talia cackled nervously, and he found himself laughing with her.

Mid-hysteria, Walker managed to call out the numbers, and she jumped, her legs swinging behind his back and arms locking around his neck. Her center pressed up against his stomach made his nerves light on fire, her breasts just a few millimeters away from his face. When his brain finally jump-started again, he hobbled into his room, trying not to rake his socked feet over any glass particles.

"I'm gonna lay you down on my bed. I don't know if any glass got out here," Walker chortled as he shuffled toward his mattress, Talia clinging to him like a sloth on a branch.

"Okay," she agreed, leaning backwards when his knees hit the frame.

Walker held his breath when he carefully laid Talia back, hovering over her, his torso pressed up against hers. He supposed he could have just let her free-fall to the mattress, but that seemed a little harsh. Tossing her around like a rag doll didn't quite fit the rescue mission. Then again, white knights probably moved on after they deposited their damsels into safe territory. He was frozen, his chest rising and falling, each inhale forcing him closer to her.

"I really want to kiss you right now," Walker admitted, all his other thoughts going hazy. He didn't feel so bad about admitting it, considering she could probably feel his erection growing hard against her.

"Didn't you say that was a bad idea?' Talia looked up at him, her eyes wide and dark.

"It *is* a bad idea," he agreed, but made no attempt to move.

"Then don't," she stated. Her body said otherwise. Her eyes drifted down to his lips, her chest heaving to press further into him. His breath hitched.

"I don't think I can stop it this time." A husky exhale left his lungs, the need to have her growing more urgent by the second. Walker could barely contain himself as he leaned forward another inch. "I want you so bad. Please. I can't stand it anymore, Tal. I need you."

"Okay," Talia murmured. Her eyelashes fluttered closed, but she didn't move closer. She waited for him to make the first move.

And he did.

All his self-control snapped the second his lips slanted over hers. It was better than any dream he could ever have combined. Talia's lips were soft just like he knew they would be, and she tasted like the sweet undertones of honey in a calming chamomile tea, the exact way she made him feel when she wasn't setting him alight with desire. Even sweeter than her taste was the soft gasp she let out when their lips finally connected. He couldn't hold back any longer if he tried. Their mouths moved in a frenzied tandem, tongues and limbs tangling like entwined roots. The push and pull had Walker's body begging to rub up against her, his hips pressing Talia down into the mattress, which dipped under their combined weight. The word "desperation" paled in comparison to the way he wanted to consume her, stroke every inch of her skin, taste her melting against his tongue.

"Fuck," Walker panted into Talia's mouth. "Terrible idea." He nipped at her bottom lip, gently pulling it with his teeth. She always bit her lip too much for him to not want to do it himself. The tip of his tongue swept over her swollen lower lip, and she

sighed, happily sinking into his kiss and rolling her chest against
him before dragging her mouth to the shell of his ear.

"Feels pretty good to me," Talia said in a seductive whisper,
gently tugging on Walker's earlobe with her teeth. She lifted her
hips to his with a persistent thrust, and Walker groaned as a rush
of warmth spread down his body to his groin, hardening all his
muscles and making him ache for release.

"So good," he agreed, grinning against her mouth. He pulled
away for a second to kiss up her neck, relishing in the vibrations of
her throat.

The small, strangled sounds Talia was making drove him wild.
Walker sucked at the soft flesh of her throat as her back arched off
the bed. His hand advanced to her chest, grabbing a handful of
one breast and massaging the soft mound with his fingertips. Talia
pushed her chest against his palm, and it took everything in
Walker not to rip her clothes off right then and there. He had
been thinking about the way she looked in her matching set of
black underwear nonstop since seeing her in her bedroom mirror
a few nights before. He wanted to stand her back up in front of
her reflection and do obscene things to her body until they could
both watch her release. She needed to know how beautiful
she was.

The position they were in had Walker half-off the bed. Eventually, he decided he was in the make-out session for the long haul
and crawled up to the headboard, grabbing at her waist to pull her
into his lap as he sat on his knees. Talia straddled him and let her
head loll back with her eyes closed when she started to grind
against him. He pressed into the comforter with his shins to lift
up against her each time she ground down into him. The way she
looked with her ponytail swaying behind her was a dream. No, it
was better than a dream—it was heaven.

You were right. She's a fucking angel.

"Walker," Talia moaned, picking up the pace of her thrusts.

If he wasn't already rock-hard and throbbing for her underneath way too many layers of clothes, hearing her say his name in

that breathless cry of pleasure would have made him grow to his full length in seconds. As it stood, he could feel her heat grinding against him, and if she continued for much longer he was going to end up with an accident in his pants. He didn't even care. Talia would never make him feel embarrassed about it, and he wanted her too bad to slow down. He wanted to make her say his name over and over and over again until she lost her voice from screaming it as she came. No one else was allowed to say his name ever again. Only her.

"Talia." His hands slid up her sides, one finding placement just below a breast, fingers digging into her ribs. His free hand slipped into her hair and cupped the back of her head, gently tipping it back so he could look at her. "I want—" Another buck of her hips made him lose his train of thought, and he pressed his fingers into her ribcage to bring himself back. "I want to watch you chase it."

On command, Talia leaned back a little so he could see the movement of her chest as it rose and fell like a wave crashing onto his shore. Walker's eyes met hers before he dipped forward to kiss her again: a slower, more indulgent kiss than before. He only broke the lip-lock to watch her again.

"I'm so close," Talia moaned, her eyes sliding shut, thighs pressing down harder with each thrust.

"I'm going to get you there." Determination welled up inside Walker's chest as he slid one hand down to cup his fingers against the spot just above where they were grinding against each other. Talia bit back another low moan and he smiled sinfully. "That's it. Ride me, sweetheart. You have no idea how long I've wanted to make you come."

"I'm—oh God, Walker, I'm...." Talia's words were choppy as Walker felt her body start to writhe and clench with the start of her orgasm. She was so pretty losing herself on top of him that he felt his own release start to build low in his abdomen, his muscles stiffening with reckless abandon.

"Hey, are you guys—Whoa!"

"Shit!" Walker jerked his head to the unlocked bedroom door, which was now ajar with a very surprised Carter standing in the doorway, his jaw hanging open. Talia flung herself off Walker at lightning speed, her hand slapping over her face in embarrassment as she curled into a fetal position on his bed. "Don't come in here!" Walker held his hand up in the stop position, eyes darting over the floor in the room.

"I can see why you want me to stay out." Carter's tone quickly transformed from shock to teasing, the hint of a smirk playing on his lips.

"I mean because there's glass all over the floor," Walker explained as he reached behind himself to grab a pillow, setting it carefully over his lap, which was still bearing the evidence of what he had just been doing. At least he hadn't finished.

"Sure it's not because you want to continue doing whatever you were just doing?" Carter raised his eyebrows.

"Oh my God," Talia groaned, and not in the way she'd just been doing moments ago on top of him. Her voice was muffled by the pillow she had her face buried into. It was so adorable that Walker had to laugh.

"I only came in here 'cause I heard something break and nobody went up to check on it," Carter said.

"Cool, well, you came and checked it out. We're fine." Walker looked down to Talia to make sure she really was fine. She was still doing her best to hide her bright red face in the pillow.

"Clearly." Carter's smug expression was enough to make Walker catapult the pillow at his nephew's head, revealing his boner be-damned.

"*Get out!*" Walker yelled.

"Okay, okay!" Carter slammed the door shut behind him, rattling the walls. Walker fell back onto the bed beside Talia, turning on his side to face her.

She stayed silent for a while before she finally emerged, angling her head out from the pillow to peek at him.

"So, that happened." Walker grimaced before seeing her mortified expression made him break into laughter.

"Stop it!" Talia shoved his shoulder. "It's not funny!"

"It's a little funny," he laughed. "I feel like a teenager who just got caught—"

"Dry-humping?" she offered up. "What are we, sixteen?"

"Give or take ten years. Did you finish?" Walker asked hopefully.

"No, and I think I might die from not," Talia sighed dramatically and flopped onto her back.

"I would take care of that for you, but it seems a bit inappropriate to just pick up where we left off."

"Ha. Ha." She reached out a hand and shoved him. When her hand connected, Walker realized he was purposefully trying to antagonize her just so she would touch him again.

"Tal, I..." He swallowed, unsure of where to pick up the conversation. Her face grew serious, and her eyes locked with his as she turned on her side.

"Walker, be honest. Were you only kissing me because you were sad and wanted to feel good?" Hurt plagued her eyes. "Was this just a one-off to you?"

Walker reached out to cup her face, wanting to erase the pain from her beautiful features. "No. I mean, I'm sure that was part of it, but I meant it. I have wanted you for months, Talia. You know how I feel about you."

"I guess I know that you're sexually attracted to me, but even after you said that, all you've done is push me away."

The crack in her voice shot him straight through the heart.

"Talia, you know me better than anyone. Even more than Cole did at this point. You could never be a one-off. But I'm messed up." Walker looked straight into her eyes, unveiling all the pain behind his so she could see just how in love with her he really was. "I'm struggling. I really, *really* like you, but I don't even know how to be normal. I have low energy. Sometimes I can't even function, and the only way to get through it is to be numb.

The worst is when I can't even breathe, like today. I don't know how to fix it, and I don't want to pull you down into my guilt and depression with me. It feels like something I can't get over. I just..."

"You just need a friend right now," Talia finished.

"I do not even kind of want to be *just* your friend." Walker laughed and brushed her arm playfully. "But I do need to get some help, of the non-relationship variety. So, yes. At the moment, I need a friend. *You* specifically."

Until he could figure out to have all of her, if that was even possible, Walker knew things couldn't go further with Talia. Maybe the guilt of being with her was just something he would eventually have to accept, because going on like this, like a half a person, was just as bad as not being with her.

Talia gave him a shy smile, then her expression grew serious. "Have the panic attacks been coming on a lot more recently?"

"Yes," Walker admitted. "There's something wrong with me, Tal. It's like I can't get ahead. I'm always drowning. I dream about drowning constantly if I don't dream about you. It's like I'm trapped and I can't get out, and no matter what I do, it's never enough. I'm not good enough." He didn't realize he was crying again until Talia's hand slipped up to wipe a tear from his face. "I'm sorry. This is not how I envisioned this going. I'm really embarrassed. I'll get help, okay? I'll just accept the fact I'm weak and get help."

"Don't be sorry." Talia shook her head and stroked her fingers through his hair. "Walker, you're not weak for needing help. Do you think I'm weak?"

"I would never think that."

"I've been going to therapy recently, and if you don't think I'm weak, then I don't know why you would think that about yourself."

"You have? But you just seem so put-together."

"More put-together people go to therapy than you think. Plus, it's funny that you even think that considering you know how screwed up I am. Do you think Piper's weak for going to therapy? Carter?"

"No," Walker answered immediately.

"Then maybe it's best you stop holding yourself to some unattainable standard." Sitting up, Talia set her hands on her knees and motioned for him to get up, too. When he did, she set one hand on each of his shoulders and spoke as if directly to his soul. "You're a good parent, Walker, and those kids love you. You're amazing with them. The way that you love is fearless and sacrificial. It's the way I want to love. You're strong, you just don't know it, and I think admitting that you need help and going to therapy only makes you stronger."

"But I want them to know that I'm committed to them. Are they going to think I can't do this if I have to go to therapy? I don't want them thinking they're a burden," Walker said sadly.

"You can't keep hiding your pain from them. It's time that they saw the broken side of you, too. The one that deserves to heal, too. Maybe it'll be better if they knew that you're just as sad and as lost as they are."

Walker sucked in a choppy breath and nodded, the worry already starting to crease his face. "Okay. You're right."

"Hey," Talia's hand gently traced his arm, and he relaxed a little. "You got this. We can figure us out later. Your focus has always been on the kids, but I think it's time that you take care of yourself, too. You gotta give yourself the oxygen mask before you give it to the person next to you."

Walker's mouth twitched. "What?"

"When you're on a plane, they tell you that you need to fasten your own oxygen mask before putting ones on your kids, or you won't be able to help them at all because you'll be passed out," Talia explained. "I was a flight attendant for a hot minute."

"You were?" Walker leaned forward with a glint in his eye. "Flight attendants are on my top ten list of kinks."

"Okay, I'll bite." Talia giggled. "What are the other nine?"

Walker smirked. "Wouldn't you like to know?"

"You're such an asshole." Talia pushed her shoulder against his.

"No, assholes aren't on my list, actually," Walker teased, then immediately jumped off his bed before Talia had the chance to hit him again. "Now, let's go get a dustpan and tell everyone I need therapy!"

Thirty-Two

TALIA

If there was a way to force herself to stop looking at Walker, Talia would have found one already. Distracting herself was the closest she was able to get, but the problem with that was that she distracted herself by imagining Walker pinning her to the bed again. He was standing so close to her that she could feel the heat radiating off his skin, and she wanted more of it. Her hands wanted to press into his skin and absorb the heat. She barely noticed when all his nieces and nephews congregated in front of them for the family meeting that she vaguely remembered calling to order with Walker.

When Walker's hand reached down to hold hers, Talia pulled her head back up to look at him. The confusion behind his sudden show of intimacy dissipated along with her residual desire when she saw the look on his face. He was nervous, his eyes pleading for her support. She gave it with a firm squeeze of her hand and tucked herself into his side. He leaned into her and cleared his throat.

"So, I have something that I need to tell all of you." Walker straightened his shoulders with a forced rigidity. Talia let go of his hand, and he shot her a panicked look before she set it on his back and started to rub back and forth, the way she did when he had been in the thick of his panic attack.

"Well, finally!" Piper clapped her hands, a wide smile displaying her straight, white teeth. "Took you two long enough."

"What?" Talia glanced between Piper and Walker for an explanation. The realization dawned on her a second later when she watched Carter lean toward Colin to say something in his ear. "Oh! We aren't... I... I mean—"

"We aren't dating," Walker cut in, saving Talia from the awkwardness as her hand fell away from his back, only to return a moment later when he gave her another pleading look.

"So, just friends with benefits, then?" Colin inquired.

"What's that?" Cooper lifted his hand like he was in class.

"It's when—"

"No!" Walker loudly interrupted. "Just friends. No benefits. Colin, that information is not appropriate for Coop."

"Oh," Colin nodded, seeming unfazed by talking about sex at all.

"There were definitely some benefits," Carter stated smugly.

She should have known that Carter would call bullshit immediately. Out of everyone who could possibly walk in on her makeout session with Walker, Talia couldn't decide if Carter was the worst or best option. She honestly might have liked for Carter to just explain to her what she and Walker were, because after their bedroom rendezvous, she could still feel an electric current running in the small space that divided her and Walker. She had to fight to stop herself from closing the gap.

"Watch it," Walker scolded his nephew with a stern look, then dropped his eyes to the floor. "What I have to tell all of you has nothing to do with Tal. It has more to do with all of you."

"Are you okay?" Pearl's voice was sweet and full of concern. Her emotional intelligence far outweighed that of someone her age and even some adults. The fact that she even called Talia to come in the first place proved that.

"I will be," Walker smiled softly at Pearl. "I've been having trouble for a while now, and I've been trying really hard to keep it hidden from all of you, but I'm starting to realize that maybe that isn't the best way to go about this." Walker glanced over at Talia again, and she moved her hand down from his back, lacing her fingers easily with his. He continued on, his voice steadying. "I get panic attacks. I had them before when I was younger, and your dad used to help me with them, but since he died, they've been uncontrollable."

"What's a panic attack?" Cooper inquired.

"It's an episode of extreme anxiety that can give you increased heart rate, shortness of breath, and nausea if it's really bad," Colin explained.

"How do you know? Do you get them?" Carter asked Colin.

"No. I saw Walker have one last week, and I researched it," Colin stated offhandedly.

"You saw Walker have a panic attack and didn't do anything about it?" Piper glared at Colin.

"You saw me?" Walker's mouth opened slightly in surprise.

"I *did* do something. I got him a book. It's supposed to be here on Tuesday," Colin said.

"Okay." Walker dropped Talia's hand, and she returned to her original spot, brushing his back softly with her fingertips while he massaged his temples. "Colin, I appreciate that, but I'm going to need a little more help than a book. I don't want any of you to think that being your guardian is too much for me, because I would do anything for you guys, but I do need to see someone so I can be better. *Do* better. We're going to have to become a therapy-going family."

"Then Talia has to go to therapy, too," Pearl chimed in. "She's family."

It was one thing for Talia to feel like she'd found her family and quite another for them to declare it wasn't all in her head, that they thought of her as family, too. The remaining heads in the room bobbed in unison, like they didn't have to think twice about including her in the decisions that impacted all of them, like she was meant to be there. A tear slipped down Talia's face, and Walker reached his hand up to swipe it away.

"I, um," Talia sniffed. "I actually started going a few weeks ago."

"Good." Colin nodded. "Therapy was a suggestion in that book that I got for Walker," he said matter-of-factly. "It's a lot of going over feelings and stuff, but it's pretty helpful. It's a quick read. I got through it in one sitting with the e-version, but I thought you'd want a hard copy. Tal, do you want one, too? I can order you one."

"I—sure, that'd be great, Colin." Talia smiled.

"Is there something we can do to make it better for you?" Piper directed her question to Walker as she moved her butt to the edge of the couch, ready to spring out of her seat at his request.

"No." Walker shook his head. "For now, I just need to go get some help. Everything that happened after the accident was so traumatic that I don't think I got to really grieve them, ya know? And I don't want any of you to feel like you don't have the space to feel sad or feel whatever you want to feel just because I've been shoving my own feelings down. You can help me by working on your own healing. I don't want to fail any of you, and I feel like that's all I've been doing. If I'm being honest... I still have no idea what I'm doing."

"Neither do we," Carter said.

"So, maybe it's time we just all admit that no one in life really knows what they're doing," Talia suggested. "But we can walk through all of that together."

"Does that mean you're going to start helping us clean the house now?" Carter smiled hopefully.

"No. Absolutely not," Walker replied in amusement. "Nice try. You tried to sell Talia to a crowd of people at an auction. Your punishment stands."

"When they go to clean Jayla's tomorrow, can I go, too?"

Cooper bounced in his seat. "She's going to teach me how to do a backflip off a swing."

"Sounds... dangerous," Walker considered. "Go for it."

"Is that going to be your 'thing that you've never done before' that dad always made us do?" Piper patted Cooper's back with a smile.

"I guess so. Just not on his birthday." Cooper nodded sadly.

"What if we did something new today?" Talia suggested

"What would we do? We didn't really think of anything ahead of time," Colin pointed out. Walker looked over at her curiously, and Talia bit her lip, not exactly sure where she was going with the idea. She couldn't think of anything on the spot.

"Tal, remember those kids at Lydia's with the carts last week?" Walker's eyes lit up with excitement, and Talia tilted her head to the side in thought before she remembered what he was talking about.

"You want to race shopping carts?" She laughed, considering the idea for a moment before turning to face the rest of the Hartricks. "We could do teams? A relay? Has anyone done that before?" Five heads all shook at the same time. "All right. I'll warn you now, then. You're all going down!"

Laced metal dug into Talia's butt as she wiggled around to get comfortable in the bucket of the cart, feet hanging over the front. Her hands gripped the sides in anticipation as she looked next to her, where Amala was sitting criss-cross applesauce in her own cart. Roscoe stood at the ready behind his wife, his hands gripping the bar. Piper waited next to her siblings in the parking lot, a stopwatch in hand as Jayla and the rest of the Hartrick siblings lined up along the outer edges of the path they had created, complete with several of Piper's soccer cones for weaving and doubling back.

"We have to win, or Amala will never let me live this down."

Talia tipped her head back to look up at Walker, who was gripping the push bar of her cart and staring down the way with pure determination.

"You still think our idea's a good one? What if you get hurt?'" Walker's eyes raked over her as if she was already injured.

"If I get hurt, you'll just end up taking care of me." Talia smiled playfully, and Walker lightly shoved her shoulder.

"This is insane."

"Insane enough to work. You know the biggest issue everyone's been having. This could solve that. Look at the way she's sitting," Talia mumbled under her breath and nodded her head at Amala. Walker followed her gaze and grinned. None of them were dumb enough to think Amala couldn't be in the relay because of her massive pregnant belly, but what *did* seem to be a problem with everyone thus far was getting out of the seat to switch with a relay partner.

"We got this," Walker whispered, brushing a strand of hair out of Talia's face. "*You* got this. Just land on your feet."

"I'll do my best." Talia sighed, trying not to read too much into every touch.

"Everyone ready?" Carter asked, making his way to the front, where he stood directly between the two shopping carts.

"We're ready to win!" Amala shouted.

"You wish!" Talia called back.

"Roscoe, let's make this interesting. Fifty bucks says that team Ponytail-Walker wins," Walker said, and lightly tugged on Talia's hair. Talia grinned excitedly, leaning forward a little in preparation for takeoff. He had faith in their abilities as a team, and she couldn't help but feel a twinge of pride. Just hearing him use her nickname in combination with his own like they were an unstoppable duo made her feel powerful.

"You're on," Roscoe retorted.

"On your mark," Carter yelled, holding a white shop rag in the air like a raceway flag. "Get set..." Carter dropped the makeshift flag, "Go!"

The grates shook underneath Talia as the cart flew forward, Walker sprinting toward the first fluorescent orange cone. Talia focused on leaning when they came up on the cone so they wouldn't tip at the high speed they were cruising at. Roscoe and Amala were neck and neck with them on the other side, flying through the turns with ease. She and Walker hadn't yet made it to the part of the course that would hopefully put them in the lead, but Talia was ready. It was silly how determined she was to win, but she couldn't help the feeling that if she did win, it would be proof that she and Walker could do anything if they were together.

"Okay!" Walker shouted as they came to the end of the lot. "Three... two... one!"

The back of the cart lifted off the ground, and Talia pushed off the sides, launching into the air. There was a moment of panic and flight before her feet hit the ground, but it vanished when she touched down safely. Quickly, she ran around to the back of the cart as Walker flung himself into the basket, and they were off again. Her shoes hit the pavement hard as she bolted toward the finish line with Walker in tow. She had no idea how close Roscoe and Amala were but feared that looking back would only hinder her capability to push forward. Zoning in on the bar vibrating in her hands and the sound of the cart shaking against the ground, Talia pushed herself harder.

"And time!" Piper announced when they crossed the chalk line on the ground. Both Talia and Walker jerked their heads around to find Roscoe and Amala flying into the finish line mere seconds behind them. "It's a new record, beating Colin and Cooper's previous time by two-point-six seconds!"

"You did it!" Walker heaved himself out of the cart and ran around the back, picking Talia up off the ground and hugging her torso tightly as he spun her around. It felt like flying. Her heart and her body felt lighter than air in his arms as he gently set her back on her feet.

"We did it!" Talia corrected when Walker pulled away slightly to look into her face. His smile spread even further, and he dipped his head down beside her ear, pulling her into his chest again.

"I'm going to get help, Tal. And when I do, you're going to know exactly what you mean to me. I've never wanted anything more than I want you. I'm going to figure out how to have you and how to prove to you that you're worth it." The hot air of his breath tickled the shell of her ear, and a shiver ran down her spine as his voice grew raspier. "Then, if you'll let me, I'm going to make sure you finish next time. I'll watch you fall apart in my hands until you're begging for it again, because the way you looked on top of me tonight was the most beautiful thing I've ever seen. I won't let clothes get in the way next time. There will be nothing separating you from me, and I'm going to have you moaning my name so loud you won't be able to breathe. Until then, I'll be thinking about that black set you were wearing on our date and how badly I want it to be on the floor of my bedroom."

"Walker," Talia felt her face flush, her breathing going shallow. *Want.* She was wanted. *Walker* wanted her.

"Shh, not yet. I'd rather hear you say my name when it's time," Walker murmured. "I promise you're going to know when." Then he let go, turning around to face the rest of the group, who were none the wiser to his arousing speech or the way her underwear felt suddenly slick with lust as he said, "Who's ready for cupcakes?"

Thirty-Three

WALKER

Walker slumped into his usual seat on the couch at Roaster's Republic and groaned. Talia looked up from her spot beside him and blissfully took another sip of her coffee. Her eyes met his with an air of confidence that made him desperate to kiss her again. The flirtation since their encounter was a never-ending stream of innuendos and charged brushing of fingertips. Two months was entirely too long to not have Talia splayed out on his bed, and the sexual frustration was actually starting to chafe, like maybe he was breaking out into hives from lack of touching her. Was that possible?

No, it's not possible, Walker chided himself. *Idiot.*

"You're doing it on purpose," he finally complained, staring at Talia's lips as she sucked at the rim of her latte.

"I'm literally just drinking my coffee like I usually do." Talia smirked. Yeah, she knew exactly what she was doing.

"When you drink things, you usually lean forward a little bit so I have a straight shot down your shirt, and you sound like you're performing oral on your coffee?" All Walker got in response was a shrug accompanied by a faint dusting of pink in

Talia's cheeks. He sighed overdramatically, leaning back into the armrest of the couch as she breathed in the scent of her coffee again, closing her eyes. "For the love of God. Just send me to Guantanamo Bay to be tortured the normal way." His eyes wandered back up to her face after spending an inappropriate amount of time in other places.

Talia gave him a cocky grin. "Typical male, acting as though everything I do is about him."

"You're wearing a ponytail."

"And?"

"And, I like it. You know that." Walker couldn't help the stubborn smile from drifting onto his face. What he really wanted to do was wrap Talia's hair around his hand like a bandage and guide her everywhere he wanted her to go. To his mouth. Backwards a little, so he could drag his tongue along her neck again and watch the rise of her chest. Pull her down and lay her on a bed of pillows, one under her hips so he could lift her legs over his shoulders at the perfect angle to—

"I do?" Talia's voice played into a touch of innocence, but she was anything but. "Anyway, how's therapy going?"

"Nice segue," Walker barked out and took a sip of his coffee. "It's going. I have another appointment today. My sixth. I wish it was going faster, so I could..." He flourished a hand in the air between them to encompass every possible ending to his sentence. Saying "so we can fuck like bunnies" outright would just lead into another flirty conversation, and he did not think he could handle that without losing his damn mind. "I still have zero clue what I'm doing. You?"

"I mean, I haven't delved into all my dad stuff yet, mostly just my own anger, but we're working up to it. We're starting off with one of my many other issues first," Talia said with false pride.

"And then you'll get to the enigma that is Jeff Cohen not loving you the way everyone should?" Walker asked. He almost regretted saying it, but not enough to take it back. Talia's dad was a poor excuse for a parent, man, human, and everything in between. How anyone could know Talia and not love her was asinine. How anyone could hurt her the way her father did when she was just a child made Walker grind his teeth just thinking about it.

"At some point." Talia gave him a timid smile and reached out to touch his hand. She was clearly used to his anger when it came to her father by then.

"I'm serious, Tal," Walker griped. "I'm two seconds from digging up his grave and ripping a corpse in half with my bare hands."

"Well, he was cremated, Hercules, so that'd be a bit hard." Her smile turned playful, and he rolled his eyes. "Or at least I think he was. I highly doubt he had a proper Jewish burial given that I sure as hell wasn't going to give it to him."

"You know what I mean. I hate him. I really do. It feels completely useless to hate someone who's dead, but I do. He hurt my family and he hurt you, and you are my family. And it pisses me off that there's not a single thing I can do about it."

"You deserve it, too, you know?" Talia's voice was soft and genuine, but Walker's immediate impulse was to divert the attention off himself.

"To be cremated?"

"Walker." It was her turn to roll her eyes. "I mean you deserve a parent who loves you, too. I know you had Cole and then Paisley, but it was never supposed to be their job to raise you. Your dad should have done that. I know he's sick, but it's not an excuse for what he did to you."

"Do you think either one of us will ever grow into a fully functioning adult?" Walker joked again, still trying to steer the conversation away from himself.

"I think that the adults we think have it the most together are still out there wandering around, trying to figure it out just like we are," Talia offered, her ponytail swaying over one shoulder. Walker's eyes caught the motion for a moment before returning to her face.

"I guess the therapy is helping, at least with the panic attacks, I just—" He looked down at his feet. "I don't know."

"Tell me what you're thinking." Talia leaned toward him, and Walker scooted so he was flush to her side. She knew every time he needed comfort and that her touch gave it to him. He relaxed a little against her and thought about how natural it would feel to set his hand on her knee, not in an altogether sexual way, but in the way people do when they are so tuned in to someone that it feels like the only appropriate thing to do.

"It's not like I thought going to therapy would bring Cole and Paisley back, but I thought it would help me get over it. It hasn't."

"I don't think that's how it works." Talia laced her hand in his and squeezed in solidarity, bridging the gap he had wanted to cross earlier. "The goal isn't to get over it. The goal is to learn how to keep moving forward through the grief. You're a little behind the starting line, trying to make up for lost time because you never allowed yourself to grieve. You skipped a step or two."

"But what was I supposed to do? Someone had to—"

"Hey," Talia interrupted calmly. "You did what you had to. I get it. My mom shut away the injured part of herself for years after she left my dad and only started to fix it when things felt like they were crumbling."

"Really? But she was still good to you?" Walker flexed a perplexed brow.

"She was amazing. But she worked herself to the bone. You're a lot like her." Walker grimaced, and Talia gave a light-hearted roll of her eyes. "I mean that she would have sold both of her kidneys just to make sure I was okay. I loved her endlessly, but I didn't need her to do that for me. Sometimes I wished she would've allowed herself to be sad instead of making sure that I wasn't."

"Wow, maybe *you* should be my therapist." Walker pointed at Talia, and she laughed, a sound he was sure could restore all his hope in life.

"I think there would be a conflict of interest there."

"Feeling a little conflicted, are we?" he taunted, brushing his thumb over the back of her hand.

"I think we should maybe not touch." Talia slipped her hand out of his and maneuvered to the other side of the couch, clasping her hands in her lap.

Walker winced. "Sorry. I didn't mean to make it weird."

Talia bit her lip and slowly shook her head. She didn't realize the lip biting thing always made everything so much worse. She was completely unaware of how adorable it was. No, screw adorable–it was sexy as hell, and Walker wished he was right back in that bedroom with Talia before Carter had rudely interrupted them. It was truly shocking how fast his brain could go from thinking about therapy to picturing Talia on her hands and knees. He should probably dive into his morals and lack of common decency at therapy, too.

"It's not that it's weird to touch you, I just can't really deal with that when we aren't allowed to go there. It feels like you're messing with me." Talia looked down at her feet.

"I'm not meaning to!" Walker said at a decibel too loud for intimate conversation. Awkwardly clearing his throat, he looked around the coffee house to see if he had disturbed anyone. A few people had looked up from their drinks, but they returned to their mundane Monday mornings a second later. "I just don't want to lose you, but I realize that trying to hold onto you like you're mine to begin with is fucked up, so I'm not expecting you to wait for me while I figure it out."

"You don't get it, do you?" Talia stood up from her seat.

"Tal, I'm just saying you don't have to wait!"

"God, Walker! This is ridiculous. We're friends, right? So that means I can tell you when you're blind as a bat. Because you are! The best part is, you won't even let me say it! It's like you don't want me to!" Talia walked over to the trash can and shoved her chewed stir stick through the opening, setting her used mug on the rack full of dirty dishes. Walker watched in stunned confusion as she gathered her purse and sweater from the coffee table. "Let me know when you figure it out. I've got a lot of work to do today. I'll see you tomorrow?" Without another word or even waiting for a confirmation, she turned on her heel and left him staring after her.

Walker pinched the bridge of his nose, trying to figure out where exactly he had gone wrong. Aggressively flirting with Talia was a start, but he had a hard time not doing that when he knew what it felt like to have her moving against him. Even though they were fully clothed at the time, it was enough to make his brain work in overdrive, calculating the time it would take him to be right for her so they could do it again. He knew by the way her body reacted to his that she was attracted to him, so he might have been laying it on a little thick. Holding on to that attraction was his only move. Eventually, Talia was going to move on when he couldn't figure out his life. He couldn't blame her. She had a right to.

"More shit to talk about in therapy, I guess," Walker grumbled and threw back his coffee mug, draining the rest of it with one swallow.

THIRTY-FOUR

WALKER

Walker sat in a cracked-leather armchair across from another one that looked like it belonged in a library from the 1800s. The cherry oak desk to his right, in front of a bay window lined with green potted plants, was piled with neat stacks of rainbow-colored file folders, each stack color-coded. Walker attributed the different colors to indicate the severity of the case, ranging from red (this person may actually end up murdering someone in cold blood at some point) and green (all clear of debilitating diseases and the propensity to murder). He always wondered which color labeled him as stressed, depressed, and an all-around mess. Blue seemed like a likely option.

Unfortunately, by the time Walker arrived, Dr. Thomlinson usually had everything set up already, his usual heavy weighted pen in his weathered left hand and a metal clipboard perched on his knee, no colored folder in sight. Walker swallowed his nerves, drying his sweaty hands on his knees. He thought at some point he would get used to coming after a session or two, but every time, he had to slowly ease back into the conversation or his fight-or-flight response would scream at him to cut and run.

Dr. Thomlinson wrote something down on his clipboard and glanced down at his watch before looking up to meet Walker's gaze. Dr. Thomlinson's eyes were always kind and understanding. After six sessions of dealing with Walker's bullshit, he knew the state of duress Walker was under just by being there.

"You seem a bit more on edge than usual today, Mr. Hartrick." When Dr. Thomlinson spoke, it felt like Walker was talking to someone who held him in the highest regard. From minute one, he had addressed Walker by his last name, with an air of respect that matched the doctor's Southern drawl and inviting personality. It felt a bit strange, given that Dr. Thomlinson had degrees and awards framed on the walls of his office while all Walker had was anxiety.

"I guess I am," Walker admitted, the frog in his throat bogging down.

"Did something happen to cause this? Or is there something I can do to make you feel more relaxed?"

Walker thought for a moment, debating how much he wanted to share. "I got in a dispute with my—with a friend."

"Am I right in assuming that this friend is Talia?" Dr. Thomlinson looked through his reading glasses at his clipboard as if to check Walker's admission against notes from prior sessions.

"Yes."

"The one you're in love with?"

"Oh." Walker blinked. "Uh, yeah, technically." He was mildly embarrassed to admit to being in love with someone of whom he was unworthy.

"All right, let's circle back to that." Dr. Thomlinson set his clipboard on the arm of his chair and crossed one leg over the other, folding his hands in his lap. "You seem a little uncomfortable with that topic of conversation at the moment, and I don't want to pry it out of you. What about your anxiety? Have you been practicing the breathing and grounding techniques we talked about? Taking your medication?"

"Yeah, I have. They work." Walker nodded, loosening up in his seat a little at the thought of having accomplished something.

"Any panic attacks since the last session?"

"No. I had a brief attack once when I was at a PTA meeting for Pearl's school and everyone kept looking at me with pity eyes, but then I used the grounding techniques, and Talia came and sat next to me. It helped."

Dr. Thomlinson hummed appreciatively. "Good, good. I do have some questions if you're ready for them. We previously talked about your relationship with your father and how that has impacted your self-worth, correct?"

Walker nodded noncommittally, wondering where the conversation was going. He could recall the details of the last session, but they didn't make it far past the general assessment that his father's alcoholism and his shaky childhood *did* have a major impact on who Walker had become.

"Why do you love Talia?" Dr. Thomlinson asked.

Walker startled in his seat at the abrupt change of subject.

"I'm sorry, what does this have to do with my dad? Didn't you literally just say we weren't going to talk about her?"

"Just trust me here, we're working toward that. Everything is connected, so I decided that we do have to get into your relationship with her a little bit."

"You decided that just now? Two seconds after deciding not to?" Walker raised his eyebrows.

"Yep. I'm not perfect. I don't always know where I'm headed with things until an idea comes to me. We don't all know the right path all the time. I decided—yes, in the last two seconds—that you aren't going to break if I ask you some hard questions, even if you're a bit uncomfortable. You said it filled you with anxiety when people were pitying you, so I'm doing the opposite of that. I'm not going to feel sorry for you. I'm taking the bull by the horns because you came here for a reason, and we aren't going to get to the healing if I can't ask hard questions and challenge the way you think." Dr. Thomlinson leaned back in his chair with a confident shrug.

Walker stared at his therapist for a hard moment before feeling the weight of the words sink in. The person with a medical degree who was sitting in front of him, whose job was to help other people figure it all out, was freely admitting to not being perfect. Normal people struggled with decisions, too, and that gave Walker a modicum of solace, releasing the tension in his shoulders. His respect for his therapist suddenly skyrocketed with this newfound, no-bullshit approach.

This might actually help.

"Okay. Let's do this, then." Walker leaned forward and set his forearms on his knees. "I love Talia because she's beautiful, and I'm not talking about on the outside—I mean, she's that, too, she's the most physically attractive woman I've ever met—but she's beautiful in the way that she's selfless. She cares about everyone she meets. The way she treats my family like they're her own kids even though she didn't have to is amazing. It's not fake, either, unlike all the people who look at us with pity or the ones who brought us casseroles out of obligation after Cole and Paisley died. She wants to help because she loves them.

"I love that she trusts me enough to have deep conversations and that I feel comfortable telling her about my issues. It feels wrong to say, but I've told her more about myself than I ever told Cole, and he was the only person who really knew me. And she's not just serious, either, she's fun. This woman makes *grocery shopping* fun." Walker grinned stupidly like the lovesick fool he was before continuing, "One time we spent an hour cleaning bathrooms in my house, and she danced around the whole time to some loud playlist, so much so that she splashed bleach on my shirt. I still have it because it makes me smile to see the stain. And it's always different—the playlist—one day, she's in the mood for doom and gloom rock bands, and the next she's listening to Disney's greatest hits.

"She's chaotic, but organized," Walker chuckled, looking up

at the ceiling to form his thoughts. "It's hard to explain, but she's both. She gets the same drink every time we get coffee, but compulsively chews on the stir sticks. She mostly reads smutty romance novels and would never touch a nonfiction book by choice, but she also passed the bar exam on the first try. And I know she would do anything for her best friend. I mean, she inherited a grocery store from her father and then just gave half her stake to Amala without second-guessing it. Her employees love her. Hell, I think even the guy she hit with her car probably loves her. She's funny and complicated. She refuses to put up with my shit, and she... she makes me want to be a better person."

"She sounds wonderful." Dr. Thomlinson nodded. "And what does she think about you?"

"Me?" Walker repeated blankly. "I don't know."

"She must think something. She's around you enough to have formed an opinion, I would think."

"Probably. I guess I know she's attracted to me physically. I don't really know what she thinks otherwise. She's said I was a good parent a few times."

"But she confides in you about her personal stuff?" Dr. Thomlinson picked up his clipboard again.

"Yeah, I guess so."

"Have you asked her if she feels the same way about you?" The doctor clicked his pen twice before scrawling out a note on the page.

"No. I just figured I needed to get my act together before I try to win her over," Walker explained it away logically with a wave of his hand.

"You may never be perfect enough for her," Dr. Thomlinson concluded. It was a sucker punch to the gut far worse than Clifford's actual punch to his face.

"I know that," Walker bit off.

"But what if you don't have to be?"

"What?" The anger faded, and Walker stared at his therapist in incomprehension.

"You seem to think you aren't worthy of love, Mr. Hartrick. Your father didn't show you that compassion when you were in his household, so you've placed that mindset on others. All you've given out is love: to your family, to Talia. Do you think that they deserve all that love?" Thomlinson cocked his head to the side.

"I see what you're doing. You're saying because I don't think my family has to earn my love that I don't have to earn theirs? But it's not the same thing. I've been screwing up since the second I became their guardian and since meeting Talia," Walker maintained.

"But have your nieces and nephews not been screwing up, too? You've had multiple incidents where they have failed to do what they're supposed to."

"They're kids!" Walker blurted, protective hands clenched over the arms of his chair. "I'm their guardian. That's all on me."

"What about Talia? Surely she's taken some missteps. She ruined one of your shirts."

"I was in the way!"

"Or, if she hasn't made any mistakes, if she did mess up, do you think that she wouldn't be worthy of your love?"

The question sunk into Walker's chest, and he swallowed hard.

"No," Walker murmured. "I would love her regardless." The fact that Talia was incapable of decorating a cake and that she was a pushover when it came to car salesmen only made him love her more.

"Good." Dr. Thomlinson tapped his pen against his clipboard, set it on his desk, and leaned forward to rest his hands on his thighs. "I think you should consider that people might love you regardless of your faults, too, and it's unfair of you to act as though everyone will treat you the way your father did unless you're perfect. No one on Earth is flawless. I have proven to you that *I* am not. Unfortunately, if you hold yourself to this unattainable standard, you will find yourself swimming upriver, wondering when you can stop to take a breath."

It was possible in all the times Walker had the opportunity to ask Talia if she felt the same way that he had avoided the question. Between knowing that she was way out of his league, being so wrapped up in grief, and fulfilling his parental duties, he had been focused on ways to win her over. He had never once considered that she might already like him back, and for more than just sex. He kept thinking that when he fixed himself, sex would be the only thing she wanted from him, and he was just hoping that the physical attraction would be enough to keep her around.

"Okay," Walker sighed. "Maybe you're right."

"Maybe?" Dr. Thomlinson grinned.

Walker let out a puff of indignant laughter through his nose. "Someone's a little cocky today."

"I'm just matching your energy. How am I doing?"

"It's working, but you don't have to call me 'Mr. Hartrick.' That feels weird. Mr. Hartrick was my brother. Walker's fine."

"Alright, then, we're getting somewhere, Walker!" Dr. Thomlinson clicked his pen twice, reached for his clipboard, and scribbled something.

Walker slid out to the edge of his chair. "Can I ask you a question?"

"Sure, why the hell not?" Dr. Thomlinson gave a short jerk of his shoulders and gestured for Walker to continue.

"It's wrong for me to want her."

Dr. Thomlinson stared at Walker like he was waiting for something further. "Is there a question in there somewhere?"

Walker's response was a garbled mess. "I-I mean, right? It's wrong, right? She's my brother's murderer's daughter, and I only met her because Cole and Paisley are dead."

"So what?" Dr. Thomlinson challenged.

Irritation bunched Walker's eyebrows together. It was frustrating that no one seemed to get it. "I don't want that!" Walker groaned. "I don't want to be in love with someone who I only met because the worst thing ever happened to me. I feel like I'm betraying Cole and Paisley by being happy with Talia. By *loving* her. I even feel guilty for not feeling guilty when I don't! And I feel guilty that she makes me feel better about losing my family. Nothing should make me feel better about losing them, especially not someone who I only met *because* they died!"

Dr. Thomlinson tapped his pen to his lips. "So, let's say, for argument's sake, you only met Talia because your brother and sister-in-law died. Now, logic says that her father was on the fast-track to death regardless of the accident, so Talia would have inherited the grocery store eventually, but even if that was not the case, every single facet of our lives is interwoven by cause and effect. You and your brother growing up the way you did influenced your brother to go after Paisley as a wife. Sitting here with me right now will influence your future decisions and hopefully help you regulate your anxiety disorder, an anxiety disorder you had *prior* to the accident. So you could even say the accident led you to get help, which is a positive thing. Holding onto guilt about gaining something that's good for you doesn't help you heal."

"That's not quite the same," Walker argued.

"What you are experiencing, Walker, is a roundabout version of survivor's guilt. It's intrinsically ingrained in you to put your brother on a pedestal because he was your hero. The mere fact that you are alive and well while he and Paisley aren't bothers you. Gaining anything from their death, even miniscule things, bothers you."

The words caught in Walker's throat as he said, "I wish it was me that died."

"But it wasn't." Dr. Thomlinson leaned forward, his eyes softening. "And you can't change that. What you can do is live for them. What would Cole and Paisley say if they were around? What would Cole tell you to do about Talia?"

A grin broke out on Walker's face, and he let out a breathy laugh, wiping under his watering eyes. "He'd tell me to stop being an idiot and go get the girl. Then Paisley would throw a party on my behalf for finally wanting to settle down."

Dr. Thomlinson bobbed his head, returning the smile. "You've said before that you thought Cole and Paisley sent Talia to help you with their kids. What if it wasn't just for their kids, but for you as well? Assuming that Talia wants to move forward with you, too, make your brother and sister-in-law happy, Walker. Live. Be in love like they were. Love their kids like they did: imperfectly, but in abundance. The only way you can fail is if you don't try. And being here, right now, in this office is trying. It's not weak. It's placing your own health as a priority so you can continue to live, laugh, and—"

"Please don't say 'love,'" Walker groaned.

Dr. Thomlinson raised a finger. "*Thrive* in your romantic exploits."

"That's literally the same thing as love."

"Listen, I don't want to hang up a cliche sign in my office that broadcasts it, but the saying is sort of all-encompassing." Dr. Thomlinson set his clipboard to the side once again and flashed his slightly crooked teeth as he pointed to the certificate framed on the wall. "Years of schooling and all this can be summed up by a series of cliche phrases. Carpe diem, Mr. Hartrick," he joked.

"Walker."

"Eh, whatever," the therapist laughed and tossed his hand in the air. "You win some, you lose some."

Walker shook his head in admonishment at the use of yet another common phrase and chuckled to himself. "You're killing me."

The rest of the therapy session flew by, with additional tips on breathing and anxiety as well as an adjustment to the medication Walker had started. What Walker liked the most about Dr. Thomlison was not his bedside manner but, rather, his blatant honesty. Walker appreciated people who didn't walk on eggshells around him. Dr. Thomlinson called Walker twice on his distractibility during the rest of the session, but all Walker could think about was wanting to know whether Talia felt the same way about him as he did about her.

What if he really didn't have to have it all figured out? What if it wasn't wrong to be in love with her? What if it was *right*?

The month prior, when Dr. Thomlinson had asked him to write down the places he felt comfortable and the places he enjoyed the most, Walker only wrote down a few examples: the docks, Roscoe and Amala's backyard, in the dining room playing board games with the kids, and Roaster's Republic all made the list. But compared to the number one item on his list, none of his other options mattered. The first rendered all the other options miniscule:

Anywhere with Talia.

Thirty-Five

WALKER

Walker drummed each beat of Sister Sledge's "We Are Family" into the dining room table as he ran the lyrics through his head. He waited impatiently for his nieces and nephews to take their seats, unable to sit still in his chair. The dining room was where Cole and Paisley used to hold all their family meetings. It was where Cole had sat Walker down a few times to get the status of his relationship prospects, which made it the perfect spot for Walker to announce his plans.

After his therapy appointment, he had mulled over several things, coming to the conclusion that he needed to know how Talia felt about him. His body, mind, and soul were already hers, and if she said she was his, he could no longer wait to be with her. There was that squeezing fear in his chest that a relationship with Talia could only crash and burn, but he wanted to try at forever with her. But regardless of how either he or Talia felt, he wouldn't go there unless he knew for a fact that his nieces and nephews were okay with it. There was always his family to think about, and Walker knew he would fight for them until his dying breath, even if it meant fighting himself forever.

"Are we in trouble?" Cooper asked nervously once everyone was seated.

Carter raised his hand. "Whatever it is, I didn't do it."

"No one's in trouble," Walker reassured them, then reconsidered. "Or, I guess, *I'm* kind of in trouble, just in a different way." He waited for any of the kids to respond, but no one said a word, so he charged ahead while he continued tapping the table with his fingertips. "I was wondering, and I won't do it if any of you feel like it'll hinder your relationship with her, but—"

"You want to date Talia," Piper interrupted.

"Yes, I want to date Talia," Walker confirmed. He immediately scanned each one of the kids' faces for any sign of discomfort. He found none. "What do you think?"

"I thought you were already dating Talia," Colin stated, sounding quite bored by the entire conversation.

"I—no, not currently. I don't want any of you to think that her relationship with me is more important than her relationships with you. And I want you to know that it does bug me that she's Jeff Cohen's daughter. Not because she did anything wrong, but because I don't like the idea of gaining anything from your parents' death," Walker explained.

"Dad and Mom wanted you to be in love," Pearl chirped. "They would be so happy!"

"Do you even know how many times Mom tried to talk Dad into setting you up with random people she met through work?" Piper asked. "They wanted you to have what they did."

"Talia makes you smile a lot," Colin chimed in. "And Dad made Mom smile a lot."

"If you're dating her, then that'll just mean she hangs out with us more, right?" The excitement in Cooper's voice made Walker smile.

"I suppose so." Walker nodded. "Relationships don't always work, though, and I am worried about the potential impact on her relationship with all of you if it doesn't. I would never want to ruin anything for you guys, so I need you all to really think about this."

"Just don't break up." Carter looked at Walker like he was the world's biggest idiot. "You guys can barely keep your hands off each other as it is. Seems like not dating would be worse for our relationship with her 'cause neither one of you can focus on us when you're thinking about—"

"Carter!" Walker cut him off with a loud shout to block out the end of the sentence.

"*Each other*," Carter finished with a wide grin. "Get your head out of the gutter, Walker. What did you think I was going to say?"

"When are you going to ask her to be your girlfriend?" Pearl wiggled with excitement in her seat and pushed her glasses up on her nose.

"I hadn't thought that far ahead yet."

"You should tell her now!" Piper slapped the table, the sound cracking in Walker's ears like a war drum call to action.

"Right this second?" Walker's voice went up a few octaves, and he cleared his throat awkwardly. Now was not the time to go through a second round of puberty.

"Yes! That would be so romantic!" Pearl squeaked.

"You should probably do it before you chicken out," Carter teased, receiving bobs of heads all around the table.

"But just to make sure, you all are fine with this?" Walker glanced around the kids' faces again to double-check.

Piper got up from the table and shooed him—actually shooed him—out of his seat while gesturing for only Carter and Colin to follow her and Walker out into the foyer. "Colin, Carter and I are fully capable of taking care of Pearl and Coop for a night. See you tomorrow."

"Okay, I don't like the insinuation. I'm just going to go talk to her," Walker said. He was definitely hoping that turned out to be a lie, because he had been craving Talia's body for months.

"Mm-hmm, sure." Carter chortled.

"Do you need to borrow my duffle as an overnight bag? It has tons of pockets," Colin offered. Walker felt his face start to heat up.

"Uh, no. Nope! That's not necessary. Thanks, though. I'm not packing a bag. That's—"

"Do you need protection?" Piper asked.

"Protection? From what, my own feelings?" Walker stared at her in defiance.

"Condoms," Colin explained unnecessarily.

"I know what she meant, I'm just not entertaining this conversation," Walker said. "I am your guardian, not the other way around. I know what safe sex is."

"Yeah, yeah. I'll give you some of mine for the cause," Carter said.

"I do not fucking need your condoms, Carter! Jesus Christ." Walker raked through the mess atop his head with a flustered hand.

"There aren't any left, anyway," Colin said. Everyone turned to him with equally aghast facial expressions.

"*Why* exactly aren't there any left?" Carter's eyebrows lifted. "I didn't use them."

"I'll buy you another box." Colin shrugged.

"Okay, wow." Walker massaged his temples. "We will address *that* later. For now, everyone get away from me." He marched toward the stairs and batted the air behind him as if the teenagers were going to follow him around to further explain the birds and the bees. Halfway up the stairs, Carter shouted after Walker in a suggestive tone.

"Whatcha doin'? Getting an overnight bag?"

Ignoring the echoes of laughter with a smiling shake of his head, Walker made his way to his bedroom and slipped a toothbrush, toothpaste, solid cologne, deodorant, and six of his own condoms into his jacket pocket. He hadn't been back to his apartment in almost a year, but most of his stuff was still there. Packing clothes wasn't necessary when he could just root through his old closet later. His current closet still contained mostly Cole and

Paisley's clothes. At some point, he would have to claim the space as his own, but for the time being, his procrastination ended up working in his favor.

If things went well, Walker was hoping to end up at his apartment or Talia's house. If he really needed clothes that badly, they could swing by his apartment to grab some. Either way, he'd be damned to walk down the stairs with an overnight bag, his perceptive family, and one apparently extremely sexually active nephew lying in wait for him like vultures.

Who the hell is Colin sleeping with? Walker thought. There were at least twenty condoms in Carter's box the last time he had checked. *Twenty!*

Pulling out his phone as he walked back down the stairs with pockets full of hopeful toiletries, Walker managed to make it to the door before being accosted by the triplets again.

"Have fun!" Carter said cheerily.

"You'll call me if anything happens." Firmly ignoring Carter, Walker pointed to his phone. "And I mean *anything*. If someone so much as stubs their toe, I want to know about it. Make sure Pearl and Cooper are in bed by nine-thirty. It's a school night, and Coop has a social studies test tomorrow. I'll probably be back tonight anyway."

"No, you won't," Piper said in a singsong voice. Walker glared at her and turned toward Colin.

"I can get everyone to school tomorrow. Don't worry about it." Colin passed the keys to his Audi over to Walker, clearly having already thought through needing the minivan to lug all of his siblings around. Or maybe it was just that Colin was apparently always thinking about the logistics of getting laid (see: twenty missing condoms).

"Thank you." Walker twisted the knob to the front door. "I'll see you... at some point," he finished lamely, already halfway to the car Colin had gotten for his seventeenth birthday when he called back over his shoulder.

After depositing all of his toiletries in the backseat, Walker nervously tapped his fingers against the wheel the entire way to Talia's house while he formulated a speech in his head. He was either going to burst at the seams with hope or vomit—one of the two.

Hi, so... what do you think about possibly... maybe... going steady with me? Going steady? Why the fuck do you sound like a Pleasantville high schooler or one of those Duggar siblings?

Hey, Talia. I would like it very much if you'd be my main squeeze. Fuck, this is getting worse by the second. Who even are you?

Tal, I'm kind of obsessed with you. Nope, that sounds really creepy. Why don't you just tie her to the radiator in your basement and feed her through a tiny slot in the wall while you're at it?

Talia you are... incredibly hot. Can I please, for the love of God, take your clothes off now? I'm also in love with you, so there's that. Nice. Real smooth.

Saved by the nonexistent bell, Walker pulled up to Talia's driveway. It was empty. She wasn't there. He let out a slow breath and pulled back out, turning in the direction of Lydia's. Between the store and Amala's, there were only two places Talia frequented when she wasn't with him.

The second time was the charm when Walker found Talia's Lexus in the grocery store parking lot and pulled into the spot next to hers.

Lydia's was closed, and the door was locked when Walker tried to pull it open. He peered inside of the dimly lit store and spotted Talia standing in an aisle, looking at the wooden clipboard he recognized as the one she used to track inventory. She had head-phones over her ears, in true Talia fashion. Walker was more surprised she didn't have the music playing over the intercom. He pounded against the glass to grab her attention, but she didn't hear. Her head was bobbing back and forth to whatever song she was blaring into her ears. Adorable, but irritating.

"Talia!" Walker shouted. "Let me in!" He continued beating his fist against the glass for a while and watched, defeated, as she walked to her office with her back turned toward him. "You can't hear me, but you really need to be able to hear something! What if someone broke in while you were here and you had those damned headphones on? That's really fucking dangerous, Tal!"

There was no response, of course. Walker was just berating the door. If anyone passed by, he'd resemble someone on drugs, strung out and having a full-on conversation with themself.

Frustrated, he yanked out his phone and dialed Talia's number. No response.

"You have got to be kidding me. She *would* make it impossible to tell her I love her," Walker muttered.

Amala's number was next. He tapped the call button and pressed the phone into his ear to wait for the dial tone. It rang once before someone picked up, and not the voice he was expecting to hear.

"Walker!" Jayla screeched.

"Hi, Jay, I really, *really* need to talk to your mom. Can you please pass the phone to her?"

"*Mom!*" Jayla shouted even louder than the first time, and Walker flinched, pulling the speaker away from his face so he didn't permanently damage his hearing.

"Hello? Who—?" Amala started, but Walker cut her off, getting right to the point.

"I need you to let me into the store."

"Going late night shopping, Walker?" Amala asked, sounding patently amused.

"No. Talia's in there, and she can't hear me, even though I'm pounding on the door," Walker explained. "You guys have some sort of alarm system, right? Because she wouldn't even notice if someone broke the freaking glass when she has her headphones up that loud."

"Yes, we have an alarm system. Why do you need to talk to her right now?"

"I need to—" Walker swallowed before restarting with confidence, "I need to tell her that I'm in love with her and I want to be with her."

"I'll be there in a minute." The phone call ended before he had a chance to say anything more, and he started to pace in front of the door, occasionally peeking inside to see if he could spot Talia. She wasn't visible anymore, which probably meant that she was still in her office.

It bothered him that when Talia was out in the main section of the store, he could clearly watch her while she was none the wiser. Anyone could see her if they were passing by, realize she was alone, and take advantage of the situation. As usual, Walker's head ran through a list of possible disasters ranging from robbery to much, much worse. Next time Talia planned on staying at Lydia's late with her music cranked up to a hundred, he was going to park his ass out front and wait for her.

Amala showed up a few minutes later and hopped out of her car wearing an obvious smirk. Without saying a word, she walked up to the front door and stuck her keys in the lock.

"You're not going to say anything?" Walker pried. Amala was never silent.

"What do you want me to say? It wasn't like I didn't know you were in love with her. You're not so slick about it. Plus, Tal and I are joined at the hip. She told me all the dirty things you whispered in her ear." Amala grinned, and Walker's mouth fell open.

"She told you that?" he hissed, looking over both shoulders as if anyone was there to eavesdrop. "Jesus."

"No, I don't think Jesus would have approved of that," Amala joked.

"Are you any less annoying when you're not pregnant? You look like you're about to pop. I'm hoping this baby reels you in a bit," Walker retorted.

"Not less annoying, just more tired." Amala laughed and pulled her key back from the door. "Go get your girl."

"Thank you." Walker reached over and pulled the woman into a hug, one separated by her large, protruding belly. "I'm going to buy your kid so many obnoxious toys."

"And I'm going to make sure Cooper goes home with them," Amala said snidely, giving him a wink. "Good luck, Walker. I'm sure I'll hear about this tomorrow."

Walker nodded and sucked in a breath as he pushed through the door. The second he was inside, Amala locked him in. His nerves were screaming with anxiety, but it was time for Talia to have the truth. His feet somehow started moving, carrying him to his fate across the store.

When he finally made it back to her office, his skin flushed at the sight of her. She was filing some papers away into a cabinet in the back. Judging by the quiet sound coming from her headphones, she was listening to her grunge playlist. Talia's voice belted out lyrics as her body swayed, back turned to him. She was a horrendous vocalist, so he couldn't tell what song it was, but, God, she was so beautiful.

"Hey, Ponytail," Walker called out, setting one hand on her shoulder. Talia jumped and flung herself around to face him, fists raised and ready to start throwing punches. He stepped back and held up his hands in a gesture of peace. Talia shoved her headphones down to her shoulders when she realized who he was.

"You scared the shit out of me, Walker! I thought you were a serial killer or something!" As usual, her attitude came out with a fling of her fist, hitting him in the shoulder.

"If you're expecting a serial killer, you should probably not listen to your music so loud you literally can't hear your surroundings." Walker poked her headphones with a lopsided smile that fell serious. "I've been pounding on the door for the last five minutes, Talia. Do you know how unsafe that is?"

"How'd you get in?" Talia crossed her arms, blatantly ignoring his occupational safety suggestions.

"Amala."

"And... are you just here to tell me to turn down my music, or—"

"I figured it out," Walker started hastily. When Talia just stared back at him, he forged ahead, starting to pace the length of her office. "You told me to let you know when I figured it out, and I did."

"Okay?" Talia warily set her headphones down on her desk. "What did you figure out?"

"I haven't asked you what you want because I'm scared." Walker searched Talia's face for any sign that she might reciprocate his feelings, but her features were frozen.

"Are you going to ask now?" She took a step toward him, and he froze.

"First, I need to tell you exactly how I feel."

"Okay."

"Okay." Walker cleared his throat and shifted his stance, playing with his hands to divert some of his pent-up anxiety. "I can't go an hour, let alone two minutes without thinking about you. You've completely ruined me for anyone else. I love you, and not just as a friend, Tal. I'm in love with you." He watched her face soften before he continued, growing more confident, "I want you so badly, and not just underneath me, but *with* me. I love that you chew those coffee stir sticks. I love that your organization skills are borderline sociopathic. I *love* your fucking ponytails. I even love that you were blasting your music so loud it was downright dangerous and that you made it damn near impossible for me to come in here and tell you that I love you.

"I can breathe around you, Talia. I can just fucking *breathe*." Walker let out a small puff of air, shaking his head. "The pain of everything doesn't go away completely, but it dulls a little bit when I look at you. I don't feel so damn alone when I'm with you. It's like I don't have to try so hard just to survive anymore because you're breathing for me when I can't do it. I'm not hopeless when I'm with you. I'm not worthless when I'm with you, because sometimes I think I breathe for you too when you can't do it yourself. Sometimes I think that... maybe you love me, too."

"Walker," Talia said, her voice low and breathy. Her dark, honey-colored eyes shined back at him. "Ask me what I want."

"Ponytail," Walker gulped. "What do you want? And please

tell me that it's me, or I guess let me down easy if you don't want me, but I need to know because—"

"Walker." Stopping him mid-ramble, Talia closed the distance between them, cupping his face with one hand and looking deep into his eyes. "It's you. You breathe for me, too."

"Thank God," Walker sighed in relief and dipped his head down, crushing his mouth to hers.

Their lips moved against each other with a fire that was even more consuming than the last time. Walker placed one hand on the small of Talia's back to press her further into him, his desperation fully unleashed. He groaned against her mouth and pushed her backwards until his hand hit the filing cabinet, guiding her back to safely lay against it. The desire spread through his body like the wildfire on his forearm, the good kind of wildfire that burnt away the unnecessary foliage that suffocated a forest. He could feel it in her body too in the heat of her torso pressed to his. She was wound so tight that every swipe of his tongue made her let out a soft moan.

Walker smiled against Talia's mouth when she rolled her chest into him and granted him access to cup one of her breasts, grabbing his hand and guiding it there while he dragged his lips over her neck, kissing down to her collarbone.

"I," Talia panted, thrusting her hips against his. "I love you, too, in case that wasn't obvious." Walker paused for a moment, reaching up to cradle the back of her head to kiss her again with one slow smack of his lips before letting go and giving her a playful grin.

"Show me?" he challenged, spreading her legs with his knee and shoving his thigh up between them. Talia gasped, her eyes snapping shut, head falling into the cold metal of the filing cabinet.

"I need you," she whispered, rocking herself against his leg. "Walker, please. All this talk about breathing and you're making it so I *can't* breathe."

"That was the plan. I was hoping to take your breath away."
He grimaced and let out a laugh. "That was corny as fuck."

"I liked it," Talia giggled. "But I'd like it more if you followed
through." She bore down hard onto his thigh and bit her lower lip
to hold back a groan. Walker leaned forward, swiping his tongue
over her mouth and the flash of teeth embedded in her lower lip.

"You know what you're doing every time you do that, don't
you? When you bite your lip. You know I want to bite it for you."
He tugged on her bottom lip with his teeth, and Talia chuckled.

"Yes." Her response got him to push his knee harder into her,
eliciting another choked sob from low in her throat. He was so
hard for her under his jeans that it was starting to hurt, pushing
against the fabric near his groin and begging to come out.

"That's a bit manipulative, Ponytail," Walker teased. "You'll
have to be punished for torturing me. Did you also know that
every time you do your hair like this, I want to pull it?" Reaching
a hand up, he encircled his palm around Talia's ponytail, wrapping it and tugging backward with a firm yet gentle grasp. Her
head tipped obediently, and his mouth landed on her neck,
sucking hard to mark her as his. When he was done, he pulled her
head back further still using her hair, so she could see how serious
he was when he made his next statement. "I gave you that nickname because I want to fuck you. I imagine you on your hands
and knees, screaming when I pull your hair. Every. Single. Time
you wear your hair like this. Would you like that?"

"*Yes,*" Talia cried out, bucking her hips forward. "Please." She
reached down and pulled on the hem of Walker's shirt, and he
chuckled, kissing her again.

"Sweetheart, we can't do it here," he rasped, his voice and
body screaming at him to say the exact opposite.

"Why? We've waited long enough. I want you, you want me.
Take your clothes off."

"Tal, you need a bed to properly feel me inside you." Walker
crowded his knee into the sensitive spot between her legs to give

her a taste of what was to come. Her eyelashes fluttered with pleasure. "But don't worry. I'm not going to leave you hanging this time. You're going to finish right now, and then we're going to go to my apartment, and I'm going to spend the entire night exploring your body and learning all the ways that make you tick." He traced his fingertips down her chest and beneath the fabric of her black V-neck shirt, finding one raised nipple and pinching it between two fingers. Liking the jerky reaction he got from her body, he set his mouth near her ear. "Do you like it when I do that?"

"Please don't stop," Talia whispered. With a roll of her hips again, they started a rhythm of grinding and pressing that Walker could tell was getting her to the end quickly. Her hands reached under his shirt and clawed at his back as every sound she made had his body aching for release. But he was too determined to get her off first. He wanted to know if she looked the same coming undone in reality as she did in his dreams.

A moment later, Walker could feel Talia's muscles clenching with the start of an orgasm as he continued to massage her chest and work her over with his knee. She was shaking with the strain of it when he decided his knee wasn't good enough and shoved his fingers against the seam of her jeans to aid in the pressure against her clit. She came forcefully, legs wrapping like a vice around his thigh. It lasted several long seconds before her body became putty in his hands, limp and spent.

"Walker," Talia whispered with a shaky breath and reached down to feel him through his pants.

"Tal." His eyes closed on a moan, and he attempted to reign in his self-control to make good on his promise to explore her body on a bed. When he summoned enough self-restraint, he took one step back from Talia and reached for her hand. "Let's go. You have to drive, because I don't think it's safe to drive when I'm this turned on."

Talia giggled and nodded in approval, snatching her purse from the back of a chair as he pulled her from the room. She looked over at him with a gleam that made him stop in his tracks to kiss her again.

"Best I've ever had." Walker smiled when he pulled away.

"You haven't even had me yet," Talia pointed out, grinning at him with narrowed eyes.

"I don't care. Watching you let go was enough to know that nothing is better."

"Just you wait."

The seductive lilt in her voice had his eyes widening before he immediately started toward the exit.

They started off with a fast-paced walk to the door, which quickly devolved into a full-on laughing sprint, Walker dragging Talia toward the door as quickly as they could get out of there. He kissed her neck impatiently as she locked the door behind them, and she reached in front of him to pat around his front once the storefront was closed up.

"Where are your keys?" Talia purred, touching nowhere near his pockets.

"Fuck," Walker mumbled under his breath. "You're getting really... warm." He liked her version of "hot or cold" better than the original. Even if Talia wasn't hot on the trail of his keys, she was making her own fire. When she circled her thumb over his swelled tip, it required every ounce of willpower he could muster to not pull her back inside the store and take her against her desk.

"They're in my back pocket. Get in the car."

Thirty-Six

TALIA

Trying to focus on the drive to Walker's apartment was more difficult than Talia would have thought. Walker was so distracted with twisting his fingers through her ponytail, mouth slanted in a permanent smirk, that he kept forgetting to give her the directions. They ended up passing the street twice and laughing hysterically about it. Talia was already directionally challenged, but it didn't help that at every red light they made out like horny teenagers. She had been craving him for so long that every opportunity there was to kiss him, she was going to take it.

Walker's hand rested on her thigh, never breaking contact, and Talia couldn't wait to go somewhere where his hands could travel everywhere else. It was never like that with anyone else, the absolute need to be as close as possible. She wanted Walker flowing through her veins, her heartbeat paced by the beating of his. She'd had sex before—with Cliff, with other men in college and in high school—but Walker was right: even just finding her pleasure against his knee with all of her clothes on was better than anything she'd experienced before. And the things he said when he touched her made her want to live under the sheets for several days, wondering how long one could survive off sex alone.

"Red light!" Walker called out when Talia came to a stop at the next intersection. He turned toward her with a devilish grin, pulling her to his mouth. His tongue swiped over her kiss-swollen lips, and she sighed into him. "It's the next right," he murmured against her jaw. "Before I forget to tell you and we miss it again."

"The next right," Talia repeated, her head feeling light and heady as she toyed with the hair at the nape of Walker's neck, pressing her foot down on the brake harder so she wouldn't accidentally roll forward. A car honked behind them, and they broke apart, Talia lifting her hand to wave sheepishly through the back window when she noticed the light was green. "Sorry," she mumbled.

Walker chuckled beside her, a gloating expression spreading over his face as she let off the brake.

"You don't have to be so smug about it." Talia giggled.

"I like making my own green lights." Walker winked, then pointed out the window. "Turn here."

She had almost forgotten the turn already, and it had only been thirty seconds since the last time Walker had given her the direction. Her mind was a rollercoaster of arousal, waiting impatiently at the top of a steep incline to tip over.

"I'm about to spend a whole night with the sexiest person on the planet. How can I possibly not be smug about that?" Walker shrugged and squeezed Talia's thigh, circling his thumb over her jeans the way he did earlier against the filing cabinet.

"The entire planet, hmm?" Talia's grin widened as they traveled down the street, Walker indicating the large apartment building at the end of the road as their destination.

"Not just this planet. You know those crazy sci-fi smut books with weird alien sex? You're hotter than them, too."

"I'm familiar."

"How familiar?" Walker narrowed his eyes at her, and Talia

blushed instantly, feeling horrifically embarrassed. "No way, you read those?"

"Maybe?" her voice cracked, and Walker gaped at her.

"Is now a good time to tell you that I don't have a double-headed dick? If you're expecting mind-blowing blue alien sex, I'm afraid I might disappoint," Walker teased. Talia's fist flung out and socked his shoulder. He flinched, but his shit-eating grin was unwavering. "Who knew you were so freaky?"

"Do you want to get laid or not?" Talia warned.

"Oh, I definitely do. Even more so now. I'm eager to show up every fictional man and extraterrestrial in your books." Walker's eyes swept down her body as she pulled into the apartment complex, and Talia felt a pang of heat bloom between her legs. "It's apartment one-sixty-nine."

"Nice." Talia laughed.

"I know, right?"

The excitement in her chest was spiraling out of control when she finally pulled the car into a parking spot in front of the building. Walker read her mind, and the second she threw the car in park, they frantically unbuckled their seatbelts, and his lips were back on hers, his hand cupping her face as his mouth took possession of hers. It was intoxicating. Talia couldn't move, didn't want to move, trapped in a limbo where all she could do was kiss Walker back.

You can't straddle him in the car, Talia berated herself. They had to get upstairs and into a bed at some point.

"We should go inside." Walker upped the pressure of his fingertips into her back.

"Or we could do it here," Talia suggested, abandoning her earlier plan. *Hoe Talia has entered the chat, apparently?*

"Too restraining," he snorted, sliding his hands down her sides. "I need to be able to move."

"Then stop kissing me," she countered, dipping her tongue out of her mouth to toy with his.

"I'm trying," Walker groaned.

She didn't want to stop, she really didn't, but the idea of tangling in bed with Walker was even more enticing than taking him in a parking lot. Car sex, from what Talia recalled, was not as fun as it was cracked out to be. It would definitely be fun with Walker, but he was right: she didn't want the constraints of an enclosed space their first time. Summoning every ounce of self-restraint she could, she pulled away from him and threw her car door open. Taking the cue, Walker got out and met her around the front for one full-bodied kiss before entwining his fingers in hers and pulling her toward a staircase.

The apartment complex looked to have been newly painted a light gray color, given the cans of paint and tarping laid carelessly on the ground by the dumpster in the parking lot, but was as cheap and as basic as they came. The apartments themselves seemed just big enough for one person to live in. It was exactly the type of seedy place Talia expected Walker would have lived in before he took guardianship over the kids. Concrete slab steps and black metal railing led them up past two landings to the top floor before Talia could see the silver one-six-nine on the red door to Walker's apartment. He had a plant, or what used to be a plant, sitting in a big clay pot on his porch. This plant looked like it had had several mid-life crises only to finally give in to the elements, withering away into a crumbly dust. Talia had a feeling if she bought Walker a cactus, he'd kill it. Paisley and Cole had hired a landscaper that maintained the yard at the house, and Walker had smartly chosen to keep that going instead of trying to take it on himself.

"Walker? You're back?" a weathered voice called out from the bottom of the steps when they made it to the top. Walker closed his eyes with a pained grimace before turning around to face whoever it was.

"Just for a night," he stated, glancing down at the stranger, who looked to be at least seventy years old with skin like worn leather.

"Just don't be too loud," the crotchety old man grumbled.

"I don't think it's me he's going to have to worry about," Walker said under his breath, the hint of a smirk on his lips. Talia glared at him, her cheeks burning at the insinuation, but she knew that he might technically be right. Walker looked over at her with an attempt at innocence but utterly failed at it. Raising his voice, Walker called back down to the old man, "Why? You gonna call the cops on me if I walk around in my apartment? For someone so old, you have the hearing of a freaking bat."

"Walker!" Talia protested, her jaw falling open in shock.

"Your boyfriend is a menace to society," the old man frowned his wrinkly face and pointed at Walker with one crooked finger. The confrontation probably should have made Talia nervous or angry, but instead, her heart fluttered at the sound of someone referring to Walker as her boyfriend.

"That's a lot of heat coming from someone whose main contribution to society is being a homophobic hoarder. Wear some ear plugs. I'm going to be as loud as I want to be tonight. My friend at the police station says that you call routinely with noise complaints anyway, regardless of me not being here. I hope you got a bunch of fines for making them come out here for absolutely no reason." Walker's nose wrinkled in frustration, and he tightened his grip on Talia's hand. "And if you so much as speak to my girlfriend in any other way than with the utmost politeness in the future, there will be hell to pay. You can be a jackass to me all you want, but the second you say a word against her, I'll finally have a good enough reason to show you some manners. How's that for menacing?"

Damn. Talia bit the inside of her lip. *Why am I so turned on by this?*

Without another word, Rumplestiltskin hobbled back inside his hole of an apartment, grumbling to himself. She couldn't hear him, but she assumed it was something resembling "*my precious*" as he stroked a replica of the Ruling Ring.

Talia was still reeling from how attractive Walker had looked defending her and the fact that he'd called her his *girlfriend*, so by the time he unlocked his door and pulled it open, it took her nose a second to catch wind of the god-awful smell inside. When it did, her arm flew up to her face in hopes of blocking out the fumes.

"What the—" Walker plugged his nose and gagged, backing out of the entryway.

"You haven't been back here at all?" Talia asked, trying to think through the fog of the rancid smell that was setting off every alarm bell in her head.

"Not since a month or two after they died, no." Walker shook his head and coughed. "It smells like they fucking died in *here*!"

Whatever dumpster fire was inside had been making its home in the apartment for almost a year. It was so bad that Talia could almost taste it in her mouth, and she found herself in a fit of coughing.

"Did you clean out the fridge before you left?" she asked in a nasally voice, her nostrils firmly plugged. "I need a freaking hazmat suit."

"Shit!" Walker groaned, shaking his head. "That's probably what the rotting corpse smell is. Tal, I gotta deal with this. I'll take you home really quick, and then—"

"No," Talia interrupted, barging inside. "*We'll* take care of it."

Walker followed in after her, leaving the door wide open.

"You aren't helping me clean my fridge!" He pointed back toward the door, indicating for her to leave. "It's disgusting, and it's not your fault I didn't think to do that before moving out. I should have come back here at some point. Most of my clothes are still here. I haven't cleared out anything, and I haven't even tried that hard to get out of the lease."

"I can get you out of the lease. Are you forgetting that I was a lawyer? And I *am* going to help you clean it. We're a team." Pinching her nostrils harder, Talia walked over to Walker and reached for his free hand.

"God, why do you even like me? I'm a human disaster," Walker said miserably. Talia let go of her nose and buried her face in his chest, wrapping her arms around him. She breathed in his scent.

"I *love* you," she corrected. Walker blew out a breath, and she could feel his tense muscles relax a little. "And I love you because you're more genuine than any other person I've ever met. You fiercely love your family, and you were even willing to work with me, the daughter of the man who ruined your life, to make sure they had what they needed. Despite everything that's happened to you, you still find humor in everything. You make me laugh. You know most of the songs on my playlists. You're strong and protective and sometimes overly jealous. You literally just threatened to beat up a pruney old man if he was ever mean to me. You're going to therapy, not just for me, but for yourself and your family."

"All of that?" he asked quietly, murmuring into her hair.

"All of that." Talia nodded. "Plus, you're also really hot."

Walker kissed the top of her head and pulled back to look into her eyes, which Talia fixed on him with the sheer confidence of knowing exactly how she felt about him.

"I love you, too. You're it for me," he whispered. "And it helps that you look like sex personified."

"Mmm, the words of a writer," Talia cooed.

Walker leaned down to peck her lips, then pulled back.

"I want to hold you forever, but my apartment smells like gangrene."

"Let's take care of that, and then we can shower." Grinning up at him, Talia cocked her head to the side, her thoughts heavy with innuendo. "Together."

"Together as in the shower, or the cleaning of my fridge?" Walker's eyebrows rose, and he brushed his fingertips down her back, sending a shiver up her spine.

"Both."

"I'm suddenly grateful that it smells like crusty feet in here." He gave her a lopsided kiss on the corner of her mouth and pulled away, plugging his nose as he marched over to his old kitchen. A second later, he had a large plastic cup in hand, running under the faucet in his sink. Talia watched in stunned silence as he made his way back out to the front patio and carefully tipped the cup of water over the rim of the potted plant that seemed beyond help. She said nothing when she met him back out on the porch, and he looked up with a sheepish smile as if he knew what she was thinking, the cup still half full in his hand. "Paisley gave me this," Walker offered as explanation, nodding toward the plant. "And I figure nothing is too far gone if I'm not."

Without hesitation, Talia stooped down beside Walker and put her hand over his on the cup, guiding it to dump the rest of the water into the pot. He was right. If she wasn't too far gone, either, then maybe nothing was.

Thirty-Seven

TALIA

While her phone blasted Bowling for Soup, Talia held up her long, purple, rubber-gloved hands and gestured like Vanna White to the large trash bin in front of her. They had spent the last half hour at Lydia's, grabbing all the things they would need to attack whatever demon from the Upside Down was living in Walker's fridge. In addition to makeshift respirator masks complete with clothespins pinching the hell out of their noses over their N95 masks, they also wore snorkeling goggles. Walker had opted for the yellow version of the rubber gloves, which made him look like an evil scientist mixed with a Minion. They'd spent a good few minutes just laughing at how ridiculous the pair of them looked.

"Ready?" Walker spoke through his nose, gripping the fridge door handle.

Talia nodded, mentally preparing herself to be taken out by a radioactive substance the second he opened the door.

"One... two... three!" Walker flung open the door.

They both started gagging.

It became very clear that the smell was not just coming from one thing, but the combination of a dilapidated melon, sunken in where it was rotting from the top with liquidy mold seeping from its pores, and a leaky plastic-wrapped hunk that was barely recognizable as meat. Walker tossed the melon in the bin first, and Talia jumped backwards with a scream, fearing the juices would splash on her. After a brief pause to laugh at her reaction, Walker tossed the meat next, and Talia brandished the spray bottle of bleach cleaner like a weapon.

A half hour later, every crevice of the fridge was clean, and it gave off the scent of a sterile hospital instead of a murder shed. Walker disposed of the garbage in the large communal dumpster in the parking lot, and they spent the next ten minutes airing the room out and plugging air fresheners into every available outlet. Talia pranced around with her spray bottle, filled with the same flowery scent, inhaling the air as she danced to her grunge playlist. She'd probably get cancer from whatever chemicals were in the bottle, but at least her nostrils wouldn't have to be cauterized to get rid of the rancid stench from *Labyrinth* that had taken over Walker's apartment.

When they finally sat down on the ground in the kitchen, breaking into fits of laughter about the fact that they came there for sex only to end up doing the most unsexy thing ever, Talia leaned her head against Walker's shoulder and sighed.

"I didn't even know that you liked honeydew."

"No one likes honeydew. That was a watermelon." Walker grinned, trying to hold back another laugh.

Talia's eyes went wide with disgust. "It was light green! And bumpy!"

"You have no idea. When I picked it up, it kind of fell apart in my hands a little bit."

The only viable response to that was the gagging sound that left Talia's mouth as she grabbed her phone to shut off the music. A new message from Amala happily looked up at her on her home screen, and she tapped it open to read the whole thing.

AMALA: 10:36 PM

I'm going to assume that I should not look at
the recent security footage tomorrow?

Grinning, Talia started to type back her response.

"Who is it?" Walker leaned his head over his shoulder and smirked at the message. "Is there any way I could get a copy of that video before you delete it? For research purposes, of course."

"Right." Her eyes flashed over to him. "For research."

TALIA: 10:37 PM

I wouldn't, unless you want to see me having
the time of my life. I'll swing by tomorrow to
get a copy of it before I delete it from the
server.

"The time of your life, huh?" Walker asked, seductively running his hand up Talia's arm. Three dots appeared on her phone, and they waited impatiently for Amala to finish typing back.

AMALA: 10:37 PM

Nope. I don't want to see that. And a copy?
Dirty. I approve. Have fun. Tell Walker if he
doesn't treat you well, I'll kill him.

"She's so aggressive." Walker shook his head. "But at least we have her approval. You can tell her that I'm not so sure I'll be alive tomorrow."

"Mm-hmm." Talia laughed, typing out a reply before pocketing her phone. "God, I need a shower." She patted the bag of toiletries they'd picked up from her house on the way back from their late night shopping session at Lydia's. "I have like ten pounds of bleach on my skin, and I don't even want to know what other substances could possibly be on me."

"I'll show you where the bathroom's at." Walker hopped to

his feet and held out his hand. "Stupid question, but are we—do you still want to...?"

"You're coming with me, if that's what you're asking." Talia gave Walker a flirtatious smile, and his eyes darkened as they made their way down the hallway.

The bathroom was simple, nothing like the extravagance of the Hartrick house. The tile floor and the laminate countertops made Talia feel safe. Immaculate houses, with their perfect furniture and all-white carpets, made her feel naked, though the Hartrick house had a way of making her feel at home despite its expensive furniture and fixtures. Paisley was clearly a master at interior design. At her old apartment with Clifford in New York, she always felt like her bathroom was prettier than she was undressed.

"So, the question is, do you like your water to burn like the fiery rivers of hell, or be lukewarm like... I can't think of anything that's lukewarm." Walker turned on the faucet in the glass shower and turned to face Talia with his head cocked.

"Definitely hell. I like to burn my skin off."

"Makes sense." He grinned boyishly at her, and she narrowed her eyes for an explanation. Was he alluding to the fact that she was a Satan worshiper? "You're really hot."

"Oh." Talia blinked.

"You don't believe me?"

She didn't respond, unsure of what to say.

"Hmm," Walker hummed and turned the knob higher to test the heat of the water before pulling up on the switch to the showerhead. The crashing sound of the water against the clear glass and white tile made Talia's nerves sting with anticipation. Walker slipped Cole's wedding band off his left middle finger and carefully set it on the edge of the sink, striding over to her. Her body was begging for him by the time he came to stand in front of her.

"Tal, how come you don't know you're beautiful?"

"That's a One Direction song," she joked, avoiding the question. Walker shook his head.

"I want to show you," he whispered, brushing past her awkward song trivia.

"Show me what?"

"How your body deserves to be looked at. Touched," Walker said simply, reaching for the hem of her shirt. "Can I take this off?"

Talia nodded nervously, and he slowly pulled her shirt over her head, dropping it to the floor at their feet. His eyes traced over her torso with a reverence that made her heart beat out of her chest. Wordlessly, she reached forward to his shirt, and Walker lifted his arms so she could pull it off. Faced with his bare chest again, she dragged her hand down his tattooed arm the way she had always wanted to, tracing over a tendril of smoke from the cliff's edge on his shoulder all the way to the floor of the charred forest at his wrist before snaking her fingers into his.

Walker let out a shaky breath as Talia guided his hand to her chest. His palm lightly cupped her, and then he ghosted the pads of his fingertips between the valley of her breasts and continued a path down her stomach to her jeans. "And this?"

"Yes," she confirmed, feeling a bit more confident.

Walker didn't break eye contact while he unfastened her pants, like he didn't want to miss a single flutter of her eyelashes. Talia could feel every notch of the zipper let loose as he pulled it down, her breath becoming more and more unsteady as he progressed. His hand slid over her hips, and he bent into a squatting position to pull her pants down her legs, kissing just below her belly button and across the lace hem of her underwear. She might have changed when she grabbed spare clothes at the house, and it obviously wasn't lost on Walker when he stood back up and offered her his arm for support while she kicked out of her pants.

"You're wearing..." He was breathing heavily, which made Talia flush with pride about her decision to wear the black set he had seen on her once before.

"I figured you'd want to take it off this time." Talia smirked.

"Fuck." Walker set one hand on each of her shoulders, resting his forehead against hers and closing his eyes as he slid his fingers down and up her arms. "You're perfect."

Talia took the opportunity to slide Walker's black joggers down his legs, dipping her head forward to kiss the bulge growing in his underwear. The strangled sound he let out made her want to stay down there forever, but they had to make it into the shower at some point. Standing back up, Talia met Walker's lips with a deep kiss before he reached behind her to unclasp her bra with one deft flick of his wrist.

"Holy shit! You just did that with one hand?" Talia gaped. Walker's eyes raked down her body again as he reached up to cup one of her breasts.

"I know how to take a bra off, yes." He regained his composure a bit, but his voice was still rough with pent-up tension, sounding about ready to explode. "I don't plan on taking anyone's but yours off ever again. I'm a ruined man."

"I've barely done anything yet," Talia cackled.

"No, *I've* barely done anything yet," Walker corrected. "You have been torturing me since the second you got out of your car to yell at me nine months ago."

"Turned on by belligerent women, are you?" Talia teased, sneaking her fingers inside the waistband of her underwear and dropping them to the puddle of clothes.

"I'm turned on by just about everything you do," Walker retorted, his palm tightening its grasp on her breast.

"I can see that." She dipped her index finger under the elastic of his boxer briefs and pulled down, his erection springing free. Walker grunted and took a step back, his darkened eyes scouring every inch of her body. Talia was gripped by a sudden self-conscious urge to cover herself. One arm wrapped around her chest, while the other draped across her middle, hiding all the parts of her she had only let anyone see close up so they couldn't examine her.

"Tal," Walker whispered, his voice taking on an edge of

sadness. "Am I making you uncomfortable? Do you want to stop?"

"No." She shook her head quickly.

"You shouldn't feel like you need to hide yourself from me. If I haven't made it clear what I think of your body, I need to."

"You don't have to do that," Talia said in a hushed breath.

"Yes, I do." Stepping closer to her, Walker reached out to gently pull away one of her arms. "I told you that I was going to show you how your body deserves to be treated, and I fully plan on proving it to you over and over and over again until you realize how beautiful you are." He pulled her other arm away and set each of them at her sides. Talia didn't try to go back into hiding, wanting to know what Walker meant and to relinquish control for once. "You have nothing to be ashamed of." Self-consciously, she touched the small, lopsided scar from when she had to get her appendix removed in high school. "Beautiful," he murmured, bending down to press his lips to it.

"I haven't shaved my legs in two days. They're really pokey."

"If you think I care about that, then you've got me all wrong." Walker dragged one slow hand up Talia's leg as he stood up, chuckling. "More friction. Probably feels a little like my beard. I don't mind a little bit of pain, but we aren't going to get there just yet."

"We're not?" Talia's voice wavered, cracking under the anticipation.

"Later. Right now, we're going to take a shower, and I'm going to use it as an excuse to touch you. Everywhere." Fixing her with a hard look of determination, Walker continued. "I want you wet, soapy, and relaxed first. I want *all* of you. Every place you've been hurt in the past, by your father or anyone else, I know I can't erase it, but I want you to feel safe."

"It's not just that, it's me," Talia said sheepishly.

"What do you mean?"

"When your body doesn't work the way it's supposed to, the way every body is designed to, you start to think that maybe everything is just as dysfunctional and... ugly." Talia looked down at herself in slight disgust.

"Look at me," Walker urged. When she did, the expression behind his eyes was so soft and pleading it was almost agonizing. "Do you see what you do to me? What your body does to me?" He took her hand and brought it to his erection, wrapping it around him. The corner of Talia's mouth pulled up a little at the silk feeling of him in her palm. "God, if you want me on my knees, or if you want me to beg to touch you, I will do anything, because you are," Walker shook his head, as if he was still trying to convince himself that she was real, "stunning. I knew you would look beautiful naked, but this so, so much better than I thought. You're fucking breathtaking. And I think..." he reached out a tentative hand until his fingers were a mere centimeter from touching her between her legs. Walker met her eyes with a heated question, and Talia silently gave her consent with a nod. His fingers curled under and swept across her seam, easily sliding over her wet entrance. When she groaned, he grinned to himself and lowered his voice, dipping his mouth to breathe into her ear. "I think your body is working just fine. It's doing everything I hoped it would. You're soaked, and we haven't made it in the shower yet. Now, I'm going to take my time making sure that every single inch of you is christened with a memory of pleasure and only pleasure. I don't care if it takes me forever, Talia. I need to. I want to. I don't think I'll ever be good enough for you, but I'm going to try my damndest to prove to you I am."

"Walker." A tear slipped down Talia's cheek, and he kissed it away, the warmth of his mouth making her close her eyes in bliss. "You were always good enough for me."

"Then we both have things to learn." He brushed his thumb over her cheek and smiled down at her.

The moisture from the steam made his torso glisten. Talia's mouth watered just looking at him, naked and saying everything she had ever wanted to hear him say. Carefully, she pressed her breasts into his chest. His hands gripped her sides suddenly, and he slung her over his shoulder like she weighed as much as a paper clip. Talia yelped in surprise before she found herself thrust into the shower, Walker setting her down with careful precision before climbing in himself, wincing when the water hit him.

"It's not that hot!" Talia stepped under the stream of water, her eyelashes fluttering shut thoughtfully as she let the heat soak into her skin.

"It feels like lava," Walker complained, recoiling from the water wherever it touched him. "I don't want to melt my extremities off." Talia looked down between his legs at the mention of "extremities," and he smirked at her.

"We can turn it down a little bit, but you're going to have to make up for the lack of heat," she teased, reaching behind herself to twist the knob a bit colder.

"That can be arranged. Turn around," Walker ordered with a circular motion of his finger. Talia complied, turning her back toward him, her breath shuddering with anticipation.

When his hand started to slowly and methodically touch her shoulders, her eyes closed on reflex. He pumped the body wash that was balanced on the edge of the shower into one hand and then massaged it across her back, drawing an involuntary groan from Talia's throat.

"Is this good?" he breathed.

"Better than good." Her voice came out drowsy.

When Walker said to expect pleasure, Talia assumed he meant purely sexual pleasure—and it was that, too—but it also lessened the tension in all her muscles. She felt no need to cover herself or hide from him anymore. His fingers said everything his words did: he wanted her, not just physically, but as a partner. He loved her enough to want to make her feel good. Being told you were beautiful was one thing; being shown it was another entirely.

Walker continued to work his way down her backside with the soap, cleaning everything she was sure never even came close to being dirty. There was an absorbent and purposeful amount of time spent with his hands sliding over and cupping her ass with a few light smacks of his palm. She only realized when he was done rubbing the suds over her legs that she hadn't even thought twice about the fact that she hadn't shaved.

"I think your front needs some attention," Walker finally spoke, his voice gravelly. "I have to warn you that I don't think I can go slow anymore. I've never been so turned on in my entire life."

Whipping around to face him, Talia eagerly crushed her mouth against his, kissing him as if her life depended on it. If she was planning to breathe at all while the water drowned her, she might have needed to steal the breath from his lungs. Walker's hands picked up the pace, quickly running the soap suds over the both of them as their tongues intertwined and limbs groped for purchase.

"I want to get out," Talia whined when they had both been sufficiently lathered up, her lips swollen from his mouth and nipples hardened into peaks that she pressed firmly into his chest to get her point across. "I need you."

The fiery look Walker gave her said he needed her, too. He cupped his palms under the water a few times and ran his hands along her skin, the suds melting away to the floor. He lathered her hair next with a shampoo that smelled like grapefruit, eliciting more groans of ecstacy from her throat as his hands massaged her scalp. She sudsed up her hands with the shampoo from her hair and rubbed it into his scalp, and Walker closed his eyes to breathe in the scent. The conditioner he pumped into his hand and distributed into her hair next was the same scent, fresh and citrusy.

"You smell edible." He licked up the column of her throat as the conditioner soaked into her hair. She slid one hand down his chest and across the V of his lower abdomen until she gripped him between the legs, testing out the feel and weight of him in her hand again.

"You're even bigger than I thought you'd be." She stroked him thoughtfully. Walker's hand slapped the wall of the shower hard, his mouth opening with an inaudible gasp, eyes scrunched shut.

The dam broke a second later, and all Talia's patience went out the window. She lunged at his lips as he met her in the middle, shoving one hand between her thighs, the moisture allowing him to easily slide several fingers inside her. She panted and stroked him faster, her body slipping and arching against him.

"We have to—" Walker stopped mid-sentence to moan when Talia swept her thumb over his head. "We have to get out. You have to stop touching me, or I'm going to come." He thrust into her hand and shoved his fingers deeper inside her, like he was unable to control himself.

Quickly shutting off the water and shoving open the glass shower door with such a force that it shook, Talia threw herself over the ledge as quickly as possible, hell-bent on making it to a bed.

"I get to dry you off." Walker hopped out after her. "And we are not putting clothes back on." Talia raised both hands in mock defeat. She made no attempt to hide the fact that she was blatantly taking in his glistening body as Walker caged her against the wall, kissing her neck as he pulled down a towel from the rack mounted next to her. "Hope you like the view."

"You said that to me the first time we met, do you remember?" Talia recalled and watched in amusement as Walker unfolded the towel with a flick of his hand, cracking it like a whip. "Show-off."

"You were staring at my ass," he said offhandedly, taking Talia back to the moment of their meet-cute that was the opposite of cute. She wanted to both kiss him and slap him.

"I was not staring at your ass!" Talia argued, folding her arms over her chest as Walker draped a towel around her.

"Really? I definitely checked you out when you got out of the car." Walker's eyes scanned her body, putting on a reenactment.

"You did?"

"You said I didn't make sure that you were okay before I got mad at you—which I did, by the way—so I double-checked. I *did* like the view, in case you were wondering, but I like the view even more now." Walker took Talia's towel and swiped it over her arms and chest, crouching down as he continued soaking up the moisture clinging to her body. When he reached her feet, he slid the towel up between her legs from the floor, pressing harder when he got to his destination at the apex of her thighs. The rough cloth made a jolt of pleasure shoot through her that she hoped would go even further in just a few minutes.

"Okay," Talia conceded, arousal flushing her cheeks. "I did look at your ass, and I did like what I saw."

"Mmm." Walker nodded. "And what else do you like?"

"What do I *like*?" Talia repeated, not entirely getting the question.

"Yes." He stood to his full height and dried himself off quickly with the same towel. All Talia could do was stare. Her mind was completely blank and her body completely still, apart from the way her eyes shamelessly wandered over every hard ridge of muscle on Walker's body as they flexed to wipe away the trickling water. "What do you like in bed?"

"Oh. No one's ever asked me that before." Talia shivered, her nerves getting the best of her again. "I guess I'm just surprised by the question. Most people just go with the flow, right?"

"Tal." Walker gripped her shoulders firmly and leaned forward to kiss her. "Are you cold?" His fingers ran over the goosebumps on her arms, and he smiled against her mouth as she bobbed her head, leaning into him. "Guess we better get under the covers, then."

He backed her into his old bedroom, cupping the back of her neck to guide her through the unfamiliar space while he kissed her senseless. Talia was relieved that he seemed to be going with her suggestion to ride the wave as it came. She rolled her breasts into him to encourage his mouth.

When the backs of her knees hit the bed, she lay down and wrapped her arms behind his head to pull him on top of her.

"Wait!" Gasping, Walker rolled off of her, and Talia shot up in embarrassment.

"Are we not? You said you wanted to."

"Hey," he whispered, reaching a hand out to cradle her face. With a short laugh, he looked down at himself to his, to put it lightly, raging erection. "Just look. I more than want to. I'm just very serious about wanting to know what you like, and you're distracting me. I want to get this right. I've never straight-up asked either, and sure, I could guess. I'd probably get pretty close. Or," he leaned forward and peppered light kisses up her neck, bringing his lips to the hollow of her ear, "you could tell me exactly what you need, and I could spend all night bringing you in and out of orgasms till you're too weak to move. Do you like edging? Is that what you want?"

"I don't know. I've never..." Talia trailed off, feeling the red creep up her neck. Frustrated by how flustered she was, she pulled her shoulders back to sit straighter. She wanted Walker to take her roughly. Fully. To have every part of him wedged up against her and inside her until they became one person.

"For now, we'll stick to things you do know," Walker continued. "And we'll leave the experimenting for later. I already know you like it when I touch here." He moved his hand up to one of her breasts, pinching her between the knuckles of two of his fingers. She sighed in response, and he nodded a congratulations to himself before kissing her temple and dropping his mouth to her ear. "Do you want me to be sweet or demanding? Should I whisper words of adoration or take what's mine?"

"Both," Talia answered and bit down on the pillow of her bottom lip. Her past experiences had always been gentle, straight-up efficient to the point of boredom, or uncomfortable. The idea of Walker manhandling her a little bit while telling her how much he liked it made the pang between her legs almost unbearable.

"Mmm, good." He swatted her ass with enough force to sting a little, then rubbed the pain away with his palm, taking to her suggestions like he already had her body fine-tuned. "I want you to completely lose control. How do I do that?"

"I-I can't, um," Talia made eye contact for a split second, then her eyes dropped to the pillows. "I've never gotten off from just…"

Walker's fingers slowly tipped her chin up so she was looking into his lust-glazed eyes. "Eighty percent of women can't climax from penetration alone, if that's what you're nervous to say. It's completely normal."

"How do you know the statistics?" Her mouth dropped open in surprise.

"It's not because I've slept with enough women for a case study, if that's what you're thinking. I researched it for work. If I'm writing sex scenes, they may as well be somewhat accurate."

The sex scenes she had reread a thousand times, replacing the characters with herself and Walker in her head, had suddenly become even hotter.

"I know which scenes you wrote!" Clapping her hands in excitement, she bounced in her spot, her breasts bobbing with the motion. Walker flinched at her outsized reaction and then dropped his gaze to her chest to admire her still very naked body. It was amazing that she had relaxed enough to feel comfortable just sitting, completely devoid of clothes, in front of him for that long, but she was even more than comfortable. He had already touched and caressed her entire body. If she wasn't dying to be pinned underneath him, then she could spend hours laying naked next to him talking about everything under the sun.

"Well." It was apparently Walker's turn to be embarrassed. Talia watched his Adam's apple dip lower on a swallow. "I just figured everyone else could write the scenes where the woman gets off within fifteen seconds of the guy being inside her, and I could write—"

"The ones I think about when I touch myself." Talia's voice cracked with the low octave. Walker's eyes flashed a deep, dark brown, enlarged pupils staring back at her, waiting to suck her under. Eager to get to the main attraction, she changed up who was torturing who and leaned forward to murmur against his neck, lips barely brushing his skin, "I want your fingers inside me while you use your mouth for everything else. And then, when that's done, I want you inside me. When you do, tell me how good it feels." Reaching down, she cupped his balls, and he cursed, his eyes snapping shut. "Now, tell me what you want. Is it this?"

"Yes," Walker choked. "Specifically during. Normally, I want your mouth and your hand at the same time before then, too, but for now, I want to skip that part after I'm done tasting you."

"And?" Talia coaxed.

"And I want you to touch yourself while I'm doing all of it."

To test it out, Talia slowly dragged one hand down her chest, and Walker's tongue slipped out of his mouth to wet his lower lip, his erection twitching.

"No more planning," he ordered, finding her lips with his hard mouth and laying her back on the pillows. "I'd rather hear you moan my name and beg me for more."

"Fuck," Talia huffed out as he started to kiss down her chest.

"That works, too," he chuckled, the warmth of his breath ghosting over her skin.

"Walker, *please*," Talia relinquished her control, writhing under his touch.

"That's it. Ask again. But this time, convince me." His tongue came out to play, dipping into her navel, and she jolted, her body tensing up and screaming for release.

"Walker, if you don't soon, I'm going to *die*," Talia yelped. It was dramatic, but it felt like a based reaction to his torture.

"Good girl. Remember who you belong to when I make you lose yourself again." Walker looked up from his spot, hovering just above her entrance, and reached an arm out to grab one of the pillows against his headboard. "Lift your hips." Talia did as told, and he set the pillow underneath her. It made everything just that much more comfortable when he lifted her legs to drape them over his shoulders. "I've been dreaming of this for months, and I

mean to make it good." And he wasted no time, diving forward
with a rough swipe of his tongue.

Walker didn't hold back.

Talia could have sworn she blacked out for a few seconds
when his tongue finally met her swollen clit. The circular motions
he was using were already set to make her lose herself within a
minute. His stubble scraped and pricked against her thighs, the
friction of it painfully erotic. She couldn't remember ever rising
to her breaking point so quickly before, but then again, at that
particular moment, she could barely remember her own name.
Only his. Only Walker. It was the only word she could say other
than expletives, but it didn't matter, because he liked it.

Walker's eyes locked on her as he worked, her body arching
into his mouth. It took her a second to remember what he had
requested before she moved her hands to her chest. She slid one
up and down her stomach as he lapped at her faster. His hands
gripped her hips. Hard. She liked the reaction she got from him
when she groped her own breasts. He groaned, his mouth
vibrating against her as one of his fingers found her center,
pushing in and stroking at the same pace as his tongue.

Oh my fucking God. Yes. The thought was voiced with a loud
moan and a buck of her hips.

It wasn't just his fingers or his tongue that brought her so
close to release. She enjoyed touching herself, too. Feeling the way
her body moved in response to his touch, the empowerment of it
—it sent her recklessly close to soaring over the edge.

"More," Talia begged. Walker shoved another finger inside
her, spreading her wider just for her walls to tighten with the rise
of her release. It was exactly what she needed to succumb to the
growing heat pooling in her lower abdomen. She moaned his
name like a prayer as he worked her down from the high.

The rest of the words she said were unintelligible—a mixture
of cursing, praise, and gasping. Every muscle in her body tightened furiously, her body shaking for so long she thought she

might combust or implode from the almost painful levels of pleasure.

Finally, when the last of her climax left her limp and lifeless, Walker's head emerged from between her legs with a smug expression that she normally would have chastised him for. This time, however, he deserved to boast a little, considering he had rendered her speechless.

Her body felt useless and weak, but she knew she needed to summon the strength to keep going. This was not over.

Thirty-Eight

WALKER

There was nothing quite like watching and feeling Talia's body collapse in on itself. The dazed expression on her face told Walker all he needed to know. Faking an orgasm of that magnitude would have required some serious acting skills. If Talia had that kind of talent, what was she doing in his bed when she could be sleeping with the likes of Chris Evans? But she was in his bed. Finally laying on top of his comforter, her breasts heaving as her lungs fought to catch air, a sight Walker wanted imprinted on his brain forever.

The feeling deep in Walker's chest was nothing short of pure joy. And the best part was, when he waited for the guilt or sorrow to overtake his happiness, it never came.

Walker moved toward the head of the bed, where Talia rolled onto her side, propping her head up on her palm to look at him. She looked so peaceful, her eyes glossed over with a mirth that had him grinning even wider. On the other hand, he was still so far into his arousal that if she wanted to take the next step, it would be comically short.

"You look so damn hot right now," Walker said. The words

didn't even feel sufficient to describe Talia in her afterglow. There needed to be a new word for the sated look in her eyes as she traced her fingertips in circles along his chest, toying with the smattering of hair there.

"That was—*wow*." Talia let out a happy sigh.

"Wow," Walker parroted, leaning over Talia to smooth her hair out of her face. He held her jaw to kiss her again. "You have no idea how long I've wanted to taste you. I'd be happy just to stay between your legs for the rest of my life." He nipped playfully at her lower lip and stroked her cheek with his thumb.

She was a siren that could easily lure him to his death, and he would thank her for it. He was under her spell. Talia's kissing grew more persistent, and with the first roll of her chest, he was already lost at sea, unable to break away even if he wanted to. And he did not want to.

"Walker." Talia tipped her hips toward him, her pelvis pistoning against his erection. "I want all of you."

"Oh, you'll have me." Walker snapped his eyes shut and groaned, meeting each of her thrusts with his own. His mind was too heated with illicit thoughts to come up with a coherent sentence, but he did his best. "Should we—condoms?"

"We don't need it." Talia froze, her body going stiff underneath him. She shook her head sadly, and Walker bent to capture her lips again. Anything to take away her pain. His mouth was slow and purposeful, more caresses than kisses. Talia ran her fingertips up and down his arms. They moved in quiet unison, as if being as intimate as possible could heal both of their hurt.

"You're going to be a mom someday," Walker whispered. He leaned back on his knees to meet Talia's eyes more directly. "You'll be the best one out there. For now, all this means is that we get to feel all of each other, okay? And I *really* want to feel all of you."

Talia smiled genuinely, something Walker would never get tired of, and silently wrapped her fingers around his pulsing base to tug him on top of her again. Once his skin was flush up against hers, he could feel her heartbeat hammering in her breasts. He supposed it could also have been his own heart, trying to rip free from his chest to join Talia's, but either way, the intense need to be with her had his body wound so tight that he was quickly losing control.

"I don't think this will last long," Walker apologized, sliding one hand under her to palm her ass. "I haven't slept with anyone since before meeting you. And then, after I met you, there was no chance I'd be anyone's but yours."

Talia bucked her hips into his again. "I don't care how long it lasts as long as you're inside me soon."

A low, animalistic growl ripped from Walker's throat. "I fucking adore you, Tal. But I'm going to let you know right now that I'm not going to treat you like you're fragile. I've wanted you for too long for this to be gentle."

"I won't break. Don't you dare be gentle." She dug her short nails into his back, further proof of how serious she was.

Positioning himself at her entrance, Walker gripped himself and slid his head over her wet folds until Talia was panting again, her body keyed up and ready to be taken roughly. The rapturous sounds she made encouraged him to go faster, but he waited. He wanted her to beg for it. He knew that when she did, the whine in her voice would make him that much more turned on.

Talia let out a frustrated cry, raked her fingers down his back, and grabbed at his hips, pulling as if she could force him to sink into her.

"Ah, ah, ah," Walker chastised, his voice coming out like sandpaper. "You're not being very compliant, sweetheart. I want you to beg."

"If you aren't inside me in the next ten seconds, I'm going to lose it." Talia shifted underneath him, her hips jerking upward, a demand for him to enter.

"I'm going to torture you for those ten seconds," Walker decided, a devilish smile curling his lips. Somehow, he was able to withstand her a little longer while he shoved his swelled tip against her clit. "Be a good girl and tell me you want this."

"*I want this,*" Talia whimpered, rocking her body toward him with each glide.

Finally Walker's sense of resolve shattered, and he could no longer find the strength to keep up the game. He jerked forward, pushing his cock halfway in. Talia's breathing faltered for a moment as he let her adjust to the feel of him. The warmth of her tight walls encircling him already made him want to release.

"More?" Walker croaked.

"All of you," Talia begged. "Please."

The plea had barely left her mouth before Walker lurched forward, hips grinding down against hers as he filled her completely. His eyes rolled into the back of his head with the onslaught of pleasure. He trained his sights back on Talia's face a moment later when he had gained a minuscule amount of control.

"You feel amazing," Walker said, pulling out a little and pushing back in until he was fully seated inside her. "So perfect for me. So tight."

"Walker," Talia cried out, moving with him. "Feels s'good."

"I love you." He stifled a moan. "So damn much."

"I love you, too." Her lashes fluttered as she looked up at him through half-lidded eyes, her teeth indenting her bottom lip. Beautiful.

Walker increased his pace, thrusting with even more fervor. Balancing on his tattooed forearm, he tangled one hand in her hair, his other hand massaging one of her full breasts as they found a steady rhythm. He pounded into her with such a force that her body rocked with each thrust, the wooden headboard smacking against the wall in a series of dull thuds. They absorbed each other's sounds with their mouths, Talia's moans of ecstasy shooting directly into his soul as he bottomed out each time.

A few rounds of frenzied thrusting and desperate clashing of tongues later, Walker felt Talia strain to reach under where they were joined. She pulled back when she couldn't quite make it there.

"Roll over," she ordered, shoving his chest hard and flipping him onto his back. Walker blinked in surprise and slight disappointment when they disconnected. That is, until she climbed on top, straddling him with her legs and hovering over him for only a second before she sank onto his cock.

Walker frantically grabbed her hips to hold on as she lifted off of him then dropped down to sheath him, over and over and over again. Her eyes closed, Talia threw her head back and felt around behind her to cup his balls with a firm, groping touch.

"*Holy shit*," Walker panted.

The coiling pressure in his lower abdomen crescendoed as he soared closer to the finish line. He shoved his thumb above where they were joined, finding her clit, and stroked it harshly. Her rhythmic riding became more erratic.

"Don't stop," Walker grunted as Talia tightened around him and took him as deep as he could go. "I'm so close, Tal."

"Right there." Talia sucked in a breath and released his balls to lace her fingers in the hand he had clutching at her chest. With her guidance, he placed his hand at the base of her throat. "Make it so I can't breathe, Mr. Hartrick," she demanded.

Mr. Hartrick.

"Fuck. I'll do whatever you want if you keep calling me that." He gripped her throat harder. "You want to wear my hand as a choker, sweetheart?" She nodded and pressed his fingers more solidly into the delicate flesh on her neck. "Tap my chest if it's too much, okay?"

The sated smile and moan that Walker could feel vibrating against his palm were answer enough. He tightened his hand again, and Talia gasped, her eyes rolling back into her head. Her hand returned to massage his balls a second later, and a new, hurried pace started.

The sounds in the room were obscene. Skin slapped together. The rhythmic boom of the bed smacking the drywall echoed. Strangled sobs of gratification rang out. Walker had only lasted so long because he was desperate for Talia to jump off the ledge with him.

The second he felt her walls clench around him and her body start to shake under the chokehold he had around her neck, his release cascaded through him with a rushing flurry of satisfaction. His muscles were so taut with tension that when he finally poured into her, it felt like a thousand-pound weight that had been crushing his chest for years had finally been removed.

After laying on top of him for who knows how long, the both of them struggling to recover, Talia flopped onto the pillows beside Walker with a breathy giggle that said everything he couldn't even begin to say. Walker heaved air into his chest, finally finding his voice as he turned onto his side with a lazy smile.

"I knew you weren't vanilla."

"That was new, but I really liked it." Talia bit her lip and touched her neck gingerly.

"It's 'I really liked it, *Mr. Hartrick*,'" Walker corrected, getting up from the bed to bare-ass jog over to the bathroom.

"Oh, sorry," Talia laughed, calling out to him as he turned on the faucet. She dropped her voice to a low, sexy rasp. "*Mr. Hartrick*, that was the best sex of my life." He returned with a warm washcloth and a toothy grin, basking in her words.

When the pride dwindled away, Walker climbed onto the bed and tapped the inside of one of her knees. "*Open.*"

Talia blushed. "I can clean myself."

"No one asked you if you could do it." He gave her a stern look. "This isn't a request. I've never been raw with anyone else. I want to see me dripping down your legs and clean it myself. *Open.*"

She obeyed, her knees falling to either side of her.

"Attagirl," he said, adjusting on the bed to get a better angle.

"Just be gentle, it's sensitive now."

Walker pressed the warm rag into Talia, and her eyelashes fluttered. "This okay?"

"Yes." Her dreamy tone made him smile. "It feels nice."

"Good."

Carefully, Walker swept over her folds and the insides of her thighs, ridding the evidence of his desire. He could still smell himself on her skin, though. He could still taste her on his tongue. He wanted to take a picture, half expecting that anything good was bound to be ripped from his grasp before he could hold onto it. The trauma response evaporated when Talia lightly traced her hands over his tattoos, leaving her lingering warmth behind. A new thought replaced it.

This love was permanent.

It would be there long after they were both ghosts. In music that blasted from speakers. In the whirlpool of coffee, swishing around in a mug. In laughter and in sorrow.

Talia brushed her hand across his chest as he finished cleaning her of his release. With joyous triumph, he raised the damp washcloth into the air and shouted "Kobe!" as he catapulted it towards the laundry basket in the corner of his old room. He made it in without a hitch and fist pumped the air in celebration. Talia mumbled "dork" under her breath as he lay down beside her, his eyes softening to take her in again.

"You're always hot, but holy *fuck* you're sexy when you come." Walker dragged his thumb over her bottom lip. "I can't wait to see that again."

Talia lifted her hand to her hair, her cheeks flushing as she tried to comb out her tangles.

"Leave it." Walker caught her wrist mid-brush and pulled it away, setting it on his chest. "You're beautiful."

"You just like knowing that you made it this way." Talia shoved him playfully, and he chuckled, bobbing his head in agreement.

"You're not wrong. But neither am I." He tucked a strand of hair behind Talia's ear and leaned forward to kiss the top of her head. "You're gorgeous. Especially naked and in my bed." His grin stretched over his face, and she rolled her eyes, laughing as she wiggled closer to him and set her head on his chest.

"Your heart is still beating really fast," she murmured.

"It's always beating fast around you."

Looking up at him, Talia tipped her mouth toward Walker, and he brought his lips down to her. The sexual tension had been relieved, and all that was left was Talia. Her sweet citrus scent. Her soft skin glowing in the moonlight that spilled in from the crack in the curtains. The way she sounded sighing against his lips. He continued to drowsily kiss her until he felt the goosebumps spring up on her arms again.

"Here." Walker pulled up the comforter, covering them both as she wiggled into his side and curled up in his arms again, her eyes falling shut. They both stayed silent, relaxing into each other as the bedding warmed over them. Peace was something Walker didn't have much of since the accident, but he had it then, holding Talia in his arms and whispering a "good night" into her hair.

It wasn't long after that her body went completely slack with sleep. Walker was tired, too, but he forced his eyes open just a little longer to watch Talia sleep and to listen to her breathe. The overwhelming sensation that he had finally found someone who knew him fully—every facet and every fault—and still loved him washed over his spent limbs as he smiled down at the top of Talia's head and settled in for the night. The last coherent thought he had before succumbing to exhaustion was one that he had pushed down many times before. This time, the thought rose to the surface with so much certainty that he didn't question it.

You're going to marry her.

Thirty-Nine

WALKER

Walker dreamt about Cole and Paisley, and this time, he wasn't drowning. Instead, he was in the dining room, sitting at the table with his brother, sister-in-law, all the kids, the Winstons, and Talia. It was family dinner night. Paisley's hand was entwined in Cole's, and the kids were all bickering about Colin's latest Monopoly win. Talia, Amala, and Paisley had their own side conversation going about interior design at Lydia's as Cole and Roscoe traded horrendous dad jokes. Walker said nothing. He took in the faces around the table with a soft smile as he set his arm on the back of Talia's chair, leaning into her side. Cole noticed and grinned stupidly at him, tossing Walker a knowing wink before he turned to plant a kiss on his wife's cheek.

The light pouring in through the window was unwelcome. The warm body beside him, however, was heaven. Walker scooted closer to it, basking in the heat, still half awake. The second his consciousness returned to him, he realized what the warmth was, or, rather, who it was. Talia. He was the luckiest son of a bitch to have ever lived.

His attempt to move away from her just a smidge to grab his phone from his nightstand to check for any notifications from the kids proved pointless. His arm was a deadweight under his sleeping girlfriend. There was no blood left in it, but there was no way in hell he was waking Talia up.

I'll just have to amputate it, he decided.

As Walker groggily contemplated how best to make love with one arm, he was interrupted by a dreamy sigh from the heap next to him. Talia's eyelashes fluttered, and her mouth parted with a wide yawn. When her dark brown eyes finally met his, he smiled and stooped to kiss the tip of her nose, arm still firmly pinned under her.

"Morning, Ponytail," Walker murmured through his own yawn.

"Coffee," Talia grumbled. Laughing, Walker brushed her hair out of her face.

"I guess that second or third round really took it out of you, huh?"

They had woken up in the middle of the night the first time to glide against each other in a slow, silent plea for release, which they both reached, and promptly fell back into restful sleep. For Walker, the second time was more of an insatiable need to have her. Talia had started it by pressing her ass into his groin when she crawled back into bed after a midnight bathroom break. Walker had woken up seconds later with a raging hard-on. Within minutes he had Talia on her hands and knees, a fistful of her hair in his grasp that he pulled from the roots each time he thrust into her from behind. He was going to remember the way she looked grabbing the headboard with her head tipped back and mouth parted in an "o" forever. He'd remember the entire damn night, because she was the best thing that ever happened to him. And he was okay with admitting that now.

"No more touching me today." Talia's hand moved under the

covers, landing somewhere in between her legs, and she winced. "I'm sore."

"And I'm devoid of blood. Can you get off my arm?" Walker poked at her ribs, and she launched away from him, more of a reaction than he was expecting. "You're ticklish?"

Talia jumped out of bed, taking the sheet with her and wrapping it around herself. "No." She adamantly shook her head. "I'm not."

"Then come back to bed," Walker challenged, testing the fingers of his right hand as they slowly started to circulate with blood, tingling with the sensation of a thousand tiny needles pricking his skin.

Talia stayed put, narrowing her eyes at his wiggling fingers.

"You're lying." Walker smirked, his eyes dancing over her.

"Don't you dare." Talia backed up as he flipped off the covers, hurtling himself out of bed to slip on his underwear and chase after her.

Talia was fast, but Walker was faster and stronger. His old apartment was also tiny. There was really nowhere to go where he couldn't corner her. Within a few seconds, he had her pinned against the front door, dragging his mouth over her neck as he prodded her ribs and hips with his fingers. She yelped and writhed under him, jerking back and forth in an attempt to get away. When she managed to wiggle most of her body free, he reached up to the adjacent wall to block her exit, palm pressing against the smooth surface.

"Planning on leaving out the front door without any clothes on?" Walker laughed.

"Maybe," Talia replied with a stubborn lift of her chin.

Walker was about to respond with another snide remark when the feeling of his hand on the smooth wall stopped him in his tracks. He turned toward the wall and stared at it in confusion, his eyebrows pulling together.

"What? What's wrong?" Talia asked, following his gaze to the wall

"Nothing, just—this wall is supposed to have a hole in it." He pointed at the spot as if that would make the fist-sized cavity reappear.

"From when Roscoe came to get you after the accident?" Talia asked.

Walker bobbed his head in acknowledgment. "Other than you, and maybe Amala because she's married to him, Roscoe was the only one who knew about it."

She smiled. "He fixed your wall."

"He fixed my wall."

Talia laced her fingers through his, and they stared at the repaired wall in awe. "I'm not the only one who loves and cares about you, Walker."

"I'm starting to realize that. And you're the one that brought them all into my life." He squeezed her hand.

"They would have loved you regardless, but..." Talia let the sheet slide a little lower on her arms with a provocative shake of her shoulders, "I think I have a way I can show you how much I do." She dropped to her knees before Walker could ask what she meant, the sheet pooling on the floor around her naked body as she hooked her finger in the band of his underwear and yanked it down.

"What are you—?" He smacked both hands against the front door when the warmth of her mouth encircled his head, all questions lost to the wind. "Oh God."

Her sudden show of appreciation was unexpected, but it was the morning, and he'd woken up to Talia in his bed, so he was already semi-hard. When her tongue licked the vein traveling up the side of his shaft, his cock stood at full attention. "Fuck yes," Walker panted, dropping his head to watch her work.

Talia's hand stroked his base as she sucked him off, spreading her spit to help her hand glide up and down. Walker mussed up her hair, massaging her scalp but not pressing hard enough to force himself into her mouth. He wanted her to go at her own pace. Her tongue swirled over his tip, and her mouth sucked lightly before she leaned forward, looking up to meet his heavy-lidded gaze as she took him fully into her mouth.

"Talia," Walker moaned when he hit the back of her throat. "That's—fuck, that's so good. You're getting me there so fast, sweetheart."

His eyes kept fluttering shut, but he forced them open to watch her. She continued sucking his tip while her hand worked him over faster. Each time she made blatant eye contact, he knew she was about to do it again. Each time she sucked him deep into her mouth, her tight lips sheathing and ruining every inch of him, he was that much closer to reckless abandon.

"You look so pretty with my dick in your mouth," Walker crooned after the third time, fighting to stay upright. "Where do you want me?"

Talia ignored his question and continued sucking and stroking him.

"I'm gonna come," he warned. Talia looked up at him one last time, eyes focused and determined. "Tell me where you—" His cock hit the back of her throat again. The sound that escaped him was inhuman, a low growl that ripped from his chest. He came forcefully, shuddering and pouring himself into her mouth. There was no other option when he was too deep inside to pull away. Talia swallowed, her tongue pulsing slightly over his sensitive head, and he sucked in a sharp breath through his teeth.

When she released him with a wet popping sound, Walker slumped to the floor opposite her and pulled his knees up into his chest like he did when he had panic attacks. Blowjobs from Talia's hot mouth, he decided, were a much better way to lose all his faculties.

"You good?" Talia looked utterly pleased with herself, resting her back against the front door and watching in amusement as he steadied himself.

"You're trying to kill me, I swear," Walker wheezed, letting his head fall back into the newly repaired wall. "Come here." He grabbed her hand and scooted over to make room as he pulled her in, wrapping his arm around her and kissing the top of her head. "You didn't need to do that, but thank you."

"I wanted to." Talia smiled and burrowed her head into his chest, wiggling to get closer to him. Walker took the discarded bedsheet and draped it over the both of them when she shivered.

"I love you," he whispered into her hair.

"I love you, too."

"I'll never get tired of hearing you say that," he pressed a kiss into her hairline. Go get in bed. I'll go get us coffee and breakfast."

Talia tilted her face up to him, her cheeks tinged with the pink of exertion, plump lips pulled into an adorable smile that gave her that little crinkle in her nose he loved so much. Love practically poured out of her coffee-colored eyes as she stared back at him. It was so obvious that he wondered how stupidly in his own head he had to have been to have never noticed it. He dipped forward and kissed her again. Their mouths were lazy, movements that came naturally. Neither one of them guided the other. Walker just let his lips fall where they may, calm and sure. When Talia didn't make a move to go back to bed, he slowly pulled away and hoisted himself into a crouched position. He reached forward, sliding his arms under her legs and behind her back to lift her off the ground. Talia squeaked at the contact but wrapped her arms around his neck when he stood to his full height. He hugged her against his chest, cradling her body as he walked back to the bedroom.

Forty

TALIA

Talia jogged, borderline skipped her way down the aisle and over to Walker with a small blue box in tow.

"You stocked the Eggo ones!" Walker beamed, taking the Pop-Tarts from her outstretched hand and tossing them into the cart.

"They're your favorite." Talia smiled.

"God, I love you." Walker ducked his head to press a soft kiss onto her lips. "I hate grocery shopping without you." Talia huffed out a laugh. "Seriously, it's boring. How do people not just constantly eat takeout?"

"I think some people do. I don't like to encourage that kind of behavior because I literally own this store, but can I tell you something?"

"Always."

Talia held a stiff hand up to one side of her mouth and leaned forward to spill her secret. "I also hate grocery shopping."

Walker chuckled and pulled her back into his chest. "That feels a little sacrilegious, Ponytail."

"Mmm, but, see, I really hated it in New York. Here, I kind of like it." Talia pulled her head back to look up at him.

"Is that because New York has really shitty grocery stores, or is it because a certain someone frequently likes to bug the owner of this fine establishment?" Walker asked with a distinct overtone of flirtation in his voice.

"New York had phenomenal grocery stores," Talia informed him, standing on her tiptoes to kiss him again. He set his hand on her neck, fingers curling along her throat with a soft touch as he deepened the kiss. There was not a single time in her life she'd ever been happier. Well, maybe the night before, but all those orgasms aside, she was content to be lost in Walker's touch in the middle of the cereal aisle forever.

Someone cleared their throat loudly behind them, and Talia flung herself away from Walker. She had no idea why she was so jumpy, considering she wasn't a sixteen-year-old hiding from her parents. It was probably the residual mortification of getting caught a few months prior. Carter walking in on her and Walker in a compromised position was forever going to be one of those things burned into her brain that she replayed endlessly just to torture herself. With her luck, she would get to her deathbed and her brain would still be whispering, "Hey, remember that time you were dry-humping on a bed and Carter walked in? That was a fun time."

Amala stood with her hands on her hips, eyes sparkling with amusement. "Please tell me this means we can go on double dates."

"Sure," Walker replied and looked over at Talia, giving her a smile that was crooked with innuendo. "As long as we can leave *immediately* after."

"Walker!" Talia balled up her fists, and he took a step away to dodge her. He was getting a little too good at side-stepping her punches. She'd have to get more sneaky about them.

"You could just do what Roscoe and I do and bang before the date." Amala shrugged with the suggestion as if they were talking about the weather.

"Or, and hear me out..." Walker raised one finger and cocked his head at Talia, who could already feel her eyes rolling. "We could boink before and after."

"If you say the word 'boink' in my presence again, you're going to remain celibate."

"Never again," Walker promised, laughing. "Can you blame me for wanting more, though?" He stepped between Talia's legs and slid his hand down from her shoulder, staring into her eyes with such affection that she thought about cutting and running right then to—well, boink.

"You two are making me sick to my stomach," Amala complained.

Talia pointed at Amala's massive belly. "I think that's the baby."

"You might be right." Amala let out a long, exasperated breath and rubbed her stomach. "I gave him his eviction notice several days ago, and he still refuses to vacate my body. Talia, you were a lawyer. Is there any legal action I can take?"

"Legal? No. But sex is supposed to help induce you. I'm sure Roscoe wouldn't mind."

"I can confirm that he would not." Walker winked.

"Listen, if you think I haven't already tried that several times, you don't even know me." Amala waddled over to the shopping cart and pulled out the Pop-Tarts. She opened the box and removed one of the foil-wrapped bags, tearing into it with her teeth. "They're inducing me on Tuesday, but I'm hoping he decides to get out sooner."

"Ooh!" Talia bounced excitedly on the balls of her feet. "I can't wait to meet him."

"Me too." Walker squeezed Talia's hand before shooting Amala an admonishing look and snatching the box of Pop-Tarts out of her hand. "For now, can we distract you, Roscoe, and Jayla with a game night?"

Amala was probably the most competitive person Talia had ever met, and her eyes lit up at the offer. "Yes, I would love to slaughter both of you at charades, even ten months pregnant."

"You're nine months pregnant," Talia pointed out.

"Really? Because it feels like eleven," Amala whined.

"Six o'clock? Tal and I are going to make one of her mom's recipes. And by 'Tal and I,' I mean she's going to make it and I'm going to stir a few things." Walker mimed stirring a pot, and Amala nodded appreciatively.

"On the other hand," Amala considered. "Food poisoning may make the baby come quicker."

"You're losing it." Talia bent forward and spoke directly to Amala's stomach. "Hi, this is your Auntie Tal. If you come out of your mom's belly before Tuesday, I'll give you lots and lots of ice cream!"

Amala shook her head. "Because newborns can definitely have ice cream."

"Shh, this is a private conversation. I'm talking to your spawn." Talia waved Amala off and continued her spiel to her future honorary nephew. "Anyways, I'll give you ice cream at whatever appropriate age you can eat that, and I'm going to spoil you rotten the rest of the time. Just please come soon, because I'm dying to hold you. Colin—you'll meet him soon enough—says your Uncle Walker really loves babies, too, and has a closet full of stuff he keeps buying you."

"Colin ratted me out?" Walker gave an overexaggerated gasp. "That's it. No dinner for him!"

"What on earth did you buy him?" Amala groaned.

"A bunch of clothes, a rattle, a blanket with tiny dinosaurs on it, some binkies, a playmat because I assume he'll be over a lot, a pack n' play so he can nap at my house when you guys come over or if you want to go on a date or whatever, a tiny foam football, a tiny foam soccer ball, a tiny foam basketball, a tiny foam—"

"Is the ending of this list just a bunch of foam?" Amala asked, cutting him off. Talia was busy gawking at Walker, who was even more attractive to her now after the baby shopping spree had come to light. It was all for a baby that wasn't even his. The sincerity behind that thought made her head swirl with hope.

When Walker said that adoption was always an option, he had been serious. Not serious in the way that everyone always told women who couldn't have children to stop complaining because it was an option, but in a way like he had been planning to adopt regardless. Just like his brother. Walker took care of his nieces and nephews like they were his own and was already in love with his honorary nephew before he even came out of the womb. Adoption was something that came as second nature to him. Paisley and Cole had raised him as if he were their kid. It didn't make a difference to Walker whether Talia could conceive on her own; he loved kids regardless of where they came from.

You're going to be a mom someday. Walker had said it so many times, but for the first time since hearing it, Talia believed him. Not only believed him, but wanted him right beside her when she became a mom. Part of the reason she'd fallen so hard for Walker was his heart for his family. She had always wanted a full house. Toddlers screaming as they ran around the house buck naked, teenagers pretending like dropping them off was the most embarrassing thing you could do, and a packed Thanksgiving table—she wanted it all. For the first time since her diagnosis, it felt like she could have it.

"Yes, the rest of the list is a bunch of foam and a few miscellaneous toys thrown in there," Walker confirmed. "Wait, Tal, we should probably get some bottles, right?" Talia's heart fluttered in her chest, and she opened her mouth to respond, just for Walker to continue on. "And I think he needs a stuffed dog. Dogs are man's best friend. Not a big red one, though."

"That's really sweet, Walker. Really, you didn't need to do all that."

"Yes, I did."

"He did," Talia agreed, holding onto the crook of Walker's elbow.

Amala smiled. "Well, I'll leave you lovebirds to your shopping, then. Roscoe and I are very happy for you."

"Roscoe finally gets his TV back," Walker mused.

"What did he say about the TV?" Amala narrowed her eyes.

"What? Who said anything about a TV?" Walker stumbled over his words, latching onto the shopping cart and Talia's arm as he backed away from Amala. He dragged Talia along, and she shrugged at Amala, waving as he bolted down the aisle yelling over his shoulder, "See you at six!"

Forty-One

TALIA

The minivan eased into the pickup lane at Archwood Elementary, and Walker threw the car in park. Talia squeezed his hand, resting casually on her thigh, and smiled at him excitedly. It was the first time they were picking up any of the kids together, as a couple. This was a declaration. One that said Talia was here to stay, both for them and for Walker.

Cooper and Jayla bounded down the sidewalk side by side, Cooper with both their backpacks slung over his shoulders. Given that Jayla was coming to the house in a few hours anyway, Talia had offered to take her off Amala's hands so she could relax, or relax as much as one who was that exceedingly pregnant could.

Pulling open the door for Jayla, Cooper waited for her to hop in first before climbing into his seat, the little gentleman that he was. His eyes landed on Talia's and Walker's now intertwined hands, and he smiled. The nerves flowing through her veins vanished instantly.

"You guys are getting married?" Jayla squealed.

"Uh, not yet." Walker shook his head with a short puff of laughter.

Not yet. Talia's heart flipped.

"But you're together? Tal, are you gonna come stay with us?" Cooper clicked his seatbelt in.

"Sometimes." Talia nodded. "Is that okay with you?"

"Yeah, that'd be cool," Cooper affirmed, wiggling happily in his seat.

The rest of the pickups went similarly. Pearl and Piper chattered endlessly, wanting to know all the details of how Talia and Walker had finally gotten together (Talia left out the majority, her face burning when she thought about Walker throwing her up against the filing cabinet in her office). Colin asked a series of questions in regards to if his car was okay and whether or not this meant that Talia would be cooking more, informing her that Walker had somehow burnt frozen pizza the other night. Carter slapped Walker on the back with congratulations before turning to Talia.

"I'm sorry it took him so long," he joked.

"He had a good reason," Talia responded, looking back at the kids with a soft smile.

When they made it to the Hartrick house, a place that felt like home just as much as, if not more than, Talia's actual home, Walker held her hand as they walked up to the door and followed everyone inside. The shawarma she had planned to make took a few hours to prep and bake, so she made her way into the kitchen first thing, finding one of Paisley's white aprons and tying it around herself.

More than once, Talia had wished she could have met Cole and Paisley. Walker and the kids had an entire life with these people she never knew and could never really know. People who were important to them. More than anything, Talia wished she could tell them how their kids were doing. How Walker was doing.

"They're okay. I'm sticking around, I promise," Talia murmured as she pulled a large cookie sheet out from one of the lower cabinets.

"Who are you talking to?"

"Oh!" Talia jumped at the sound of Walker's voice, thinking she had been alone in the room. "Um... no one."

"I talk to them, too, sometimes," Walker said quietly, looking up at the ceiling and twisting his brother's gold wedding band around his middle finger.

"How did you know I was..." Talia trailed off, and Walker shrugged, coming to hug her from behind.

"I don't know. I was just thinking about how much I wish I could've met your mom and that Cole and Paisley could've met you, and I thought maybe you were thinking along the same lines. They would have adored you, Tal. And they both would have been on my ass about when I plan on proposing." Walker took the tray from Talia's hand and set it on the stove as she turned around in his arms, eyebrows raised.

"Proposing? We started dating yesterday," Talia cackled. It was the logical thing to say, though her heart took a nosedive in her chest at the thought of marrying Walker. If he asked her right then and there, she would have said "yes." No matter how ridiculously quick it was.

"I've been dating you for months." Walker peered into her eyes and brushed her arm with the pads of his fingertips. "Every coffee date. Every time I came to you for help with the kids. I was just too stupid to realize it. So, yes, proposing. I don't want anyone else but you, and it's going to happen. It's not going to be immediate because I want to give the kids time to acclimate to this version of us, but I'd be lying if I said that I haven't thought about wanting you to be my wife multiple times since yesterday and even before then. I want to be clear that that's where this is headed for me. Is that okay with you?"

"Yes." Talia swallowed and blinked back her emotions. "I'm ready when you are. And Walker?"

"Yeah?" He grinned.

"My mom would have loved you."

"Even though I can't cook her recipes?"

"Oh, you're going to learn." Talia retrieved another apron from the bottom drawer that said "Grill Master" on it, and barked out a laugh. "Your brother was a giant dork."

"He was," Walker confirmed.

"Should we see if anyone else wants to help?"

"*Hey*!" Walker shouted into the hallway. "Everyone come to the kitchen! We're learning how to cook."

Half an hour later, Piper and Colin were up to their ears in flour as they rolled out the laffa. Carter was using a blend of cardamom, cinnamon, cumin, and coriander to spice the lamb shoulders, which Talia had already drizzled with olive oil. He seemed the most enthusiastic out of all his siblings, hovering over Cooper, Pearl, and Jayla to make sure they got the red onion sumac salad right, while Talia and Walker watched from barstools at the island, Talia calling out orders and offering help when necessary.

By six, the flatbread was baked, and the lamb was out of the oven, filling the room with the mouthwatering aroma of spiced meat. Amala and Roscoe waltzed into the house without knocking, Roscoe looking like he might die if he didn't have a mouth full of shawarma as soon as possible. Plates were dished out, and soon the dining table was packed with the chaos of the two families scarfing down their food, talking with their mouths full, and relentlessly tormenting each other, a frenzy of food and conversation.

"What do you think? Could you get used to this?" Walker squeezed Talia's knee under the table, and she looked over the table thoughtfully. Cooper was in the middle of telling the story of how he and Jayla had become friends with Camden. He was interrupted many times, as every single person at the table was well aware that Camden was the kid Jayla had punched in the face earlier that year, and they all felt the need to insert their opinions on the matter.

"I already am." Talia nodded at Walker and then said a little louder, "I personally think it's a great idea."

"You do?" Carter balked at the same time Amala did.

"Yes," Talia said clearly. "His mother mentioned he had been going through some stuff. I think that everyone needs a friend. Camden was projecting his own insecurities about himself onto Cooper when they were both struggling. He just needs someone to care about him. My mother always used to say, 'Neshama sheli, you must learn to be the picture of kindness and grace.' Sometimes your enemy isn't your enemy at all, but rather someone you could miss out on knowing." Talia looked over to Walker, who brushed his thumb over her leg in understanding.

"I agree," Walker announced, pushing his chair back as he stood up. "I also think it's time to clean all this up and get to charades. I plan on winning this time."

The table erupted with a chorus of arguments over who would actually win, the consensus being that Colin would *not*. He won everything else, so everyone was happy to point out the one thing he was terrible at.

"I get to go next!" Amala called out as she hobbled over from the bathroom, where she had excused herself to pee four times since the start of the game.

"We just got 'goalie,' and we're in the lead now!" Roscoe informed his wife as she came to stand in the middle, pulling a piece of paper from the hat that sat on the coffee table. Amala barely glanced at the slip of paper as she held up the number three. Walker, Talia, Colin, Pearl, and Carter sat on the other couch, while Piper, Cooper, and Jayla all shouted out the obvious: Amala's phrase was three words. Talia narrowed her eyes as Amala scrunched her face a little, holding her hand out in a horizontal "c" shape like she was holding a glass.

"Drink!" Jayla shouted. Amala motioned for everyone to continue guessing.

Water. It has to be water, Talia thought.

'Water?" Piper asked. Amala touched her nose and held up the number two. "Okay, the second word is water."

Holding her hands out like she was gripping handlebars or a rod of some sort, Amala repeatedly proceeded to snap the invisible object over her knee like a stick.

"Ninja!" Cooper shouted.

"Kung fu?" Roscoe said doubtfully.

Break? Breaking? Talia's eyes widened as the realization hit her. *Holy shit!*

Jumping off the couch, Talia grabbed Walker's hand and yanked him up. He followed her in alarm, wildly looking around the room for whatever was amiss as she snatched the minivan keys off the hook by the door.

"Whoa, where's the fire?" Roscoe joked.

"Amala's water broke! We're going to the hospital," Talia announced.

"What? No, her water didn't..." The end of Roscoe's statement faded as he looked at his wife, who was clearly in the middle of a contraction. "What the hell? Why would you try to tell me that via charades, Amala?"

"Thought it would be fun," she winced, waddling over to Roscoe as he catapulted from his seat to help her. "You're not very good at charades, though."

"Let's just get you in the car, you party animal." Roscoe helped his wife walk to the front door, which Walker held wide open for them.

"I'm getting a baby brother!" Jayla bunny-hopped up after her parents, her arms flailing with excitement.

"Sweetie, we need you to go with Aunt Tal, okay?" Roscoe looked up at Talia to confirm. She opened her mouth, but Walker cut in before she could agree.

"Just go, Roscoe, we'll meet you at the hospital," Walker said, pointing out the door. "Go have a baby!"

Forty-Two

WALKER

The chairs in the waiting room were uncomfortable, rigid-backed and too small for Walker's large body. Waiting was exhausting, especially with two kids, one preteen, and three teenagers in tow. Talia was back in the delivery room with Amala, so all that was left for Walker to do was sit and wait. Pearl, Carter, and Piper all had their phones out, locked into their screens as they wasted the hours away. Jayla and Cooper were hunched over one of those children's Highlights magazines that haunted waiting rooms, open to a hidden-objects puzzle that they pointed at excitedly when they found something. Colin was enamored with a chart he was building on graph paper, carefully drawing lines with a ruler and intently filling in boxes before he crumpled it into a ball and started all over again. He seemed a bit more on edge than usual lately, but Walker couldn't pry any information out of him despite Colin usually being a wealth of information. Walker had already made a physical note to himself in his planner to sic Carter on him later since Carter seemed to be the only one who could get his brother to dole out his feelings.

After flipping through the calendar notes for the next month, adding scheduled days for him and Talia to grocery shop, and organizing an entire family road trip to visit Colin at Johns Hopkins University that worked around everyone's schedule, there was nothing else for Walker to do. He took a hint from the older kids and pulled out his phone, flipping through his social media pages that he never checked. He had already stalked Talia's pages within an inch of their life, but he did so again, tapping on the picture of her with her mother on Mother's Day a few years ago. Lydia had a kind face and eyes that seemed capable of both reprimand and love. If Walker could thank anyone for helping Talia become the wonderful person she was, it would be Lydia.

Another hour passed with no word of how Amala was doing, and Walker felt the rising panic of one of his episodes starting to pull him under. The anxiety screamed at him that there was something wrong, that he would lose another person he loved. Curling his toes to better feel the ground under his feet, he breathed in and out slowly to keep the panic at bay.

Amala is okay. The baby is fine. Amala is okay. The baby is fine, Walker chanted in his head. His therapist's voice came next. *Find something relaxing to do.*

Walker opened a new tab in his search engine and typed in the first thing that came to mind—*engagement rings*. He was met with an onslaught of pictures that normally would have felt overwhelming. They didn't. Scrolling through different styles, he clicked on a simple-looking ring, just a thin gold band with one circular-cut diamond. It screamed Talia, wearable with heels and a dress or a sweater and a ponytail. He hit the Add to Cart button before even thinking twice about it.

"He's here!" Talia burst through the swinging doors into the waiting room, and Walker snapped his head up from his phone, shoving it quickly into his pocket. "We can only have a few people in the room at once. So, Jayla and Walker, do you want to go first?"

"He's okay?" Walker asked, hopping up from his seat, the anxiety of possible loss still vibrating in his veins.

Talia gave him a knowing smile and set a comforting hand on his shoulder when she made it to his side. "He's beautiful."

"Amala?"

"She's tired, but happy."

The tension in his shoulders slackened a little.

They made their way down the hall, Talia's hand laced in Walker's and Jayla's pigtail puffs bobbing as she practically bounced off the walls in excitement. Walker tapped the fingers of his free hand against his thigh, still worried. Until he could see with his own eyes that both Amala and the baby were okay, the pit in his stomach wasn't going to go away. He believed Talia when she said they were okay, but his mind had already irrationally jumped to the idea of something tragic happening in the time it took Talia to leave Amala's bedside to retrieve him and Jayla.

The door to Room 215 was closed when they arrived, and Walker swallowed in preparation. Talia knocked and received a lofty response from Roscoe inside.

"Come in."

When Walker's eyes landed on Amala, relief washed over him. She was okay. *They* were okay. Amala looked thoroughly depleted, laying in her upright hospital bed with a tiny bundle in her arms, but she had a smile on her face that made her look as though she was glowing from within.

Newborns were so little. So fragile-looking. Walker remembered that being his first thought when he held Colin in his arms eighteen years ago, and then each and every time a new kid came into the fold after. Pearl was a week old when he finally got to meet her, but she was just as small, with slender fingers and a strong grip. Amala's and Roscoe's son was no different, all pudgy and wrinkly, but so peacefully asleep on his mom's chest that it was one of the most adorable things Walker had ever witnessed.

"Jayla, do you want to meet your brother?" Amala asked, patting the sliver of space beside her. "Come sit with me."

Roscoe picked up his daughter and set her on the bed with her mom. Jayla was always a giant ball of sunshine, but her grin was even bigger and brighter than usual. Walker held Talia's hand still, hovering beside the bed as he watched Jayla croon over her baby brother. She was going to be a fantastic older sister. Hell, if her brother was ever in trouble, Jayla would come out swinging, just like she did for Cooper.

"Walker, do you want to hold him?" Amala asked after a while.

"May I?" Walker stepped forward hesitantly as she nodded.

Roscoe scooped the baby out of his daughter's hands and neatly transferred him into the crook of Walker's cradled arms. The warm blanket revealed a sleeping newborn whose little eyelids were firmly shut, one pudgy hand escaping the confinements of his swaddle. Walker's eyes watered as he smiled down at the baby and placed an index finger near his little palm. The petite fingers twitched before they latched onto Walker.

"He's perfect," Walker murmured.

"Do you want to tell him?" Amala pointed to her husband, and Walker lifted his head in confusion as Roscoe patted his back with a wide grin.

"His name is Marcel Walker Winston."

Epilogue

8 months later

WALKER

"Piper, I swear to God. Let me in right now!"

Walker pounded on the door, and the knob finally twisted, Piper poking her head out at the same time as Pearl.

"You aren't supposed to see her," Piper chastised.

"Blindfold me, then," Walker said.

"Why do you need to get in here so bad?" Pearl asked.

"Because I need to talk to my fiancée! Alone. Here." Walker undid his necktie and held it out to Piper as a blindfold. She stepped out of the room and walked around behind him, holding up the tie in front of his face to secure it snuggly around his head. Walker stepped forward when she finished, his hands shooting out to feel his way around and hitting the partially open door. "Tal?"

"Here," her voice called out in front of him, and he continued into the room a few steps before a sharp pain hit his shin.

"Ow!"

"Well, if I'd known there was gonna be a blindfolded man in

here, I would have moved my chair out of your way," Amala said from somewhere off to the left.

"Everyone out!" Walker pointed behind him to where he hoped the door still was.

"Okay, bossy," Jayla giggled from the same direction her mother's voice had come from.

"We're going, we're going. But don't take that blindfold off, Walker Colin Hartrick. I will scalp you if you do," Amala warned, brushing his shoulder on her way past.

Walker heard the door shut shortly after, the room falling completely silent apart from his heavy breathing.

"Tal, where are you?" he asked, swinging his hands around in front of him to search for her.

"I'm right here," Talia said, stepping into him. "What's wrong? Are you okay?" His hands found the fabric of her dress. It felt smooth and lacy, and he was dying to take his blindfold off and say to hell with traditions.

"I'm okay. Promise. I just–I'm so excited that I'm nervous, and it's making me all jittery. I needed to see—well, hear you, I guess," Walker explained, pulling her into his chest. "Feel you."

"I'm right here," Talia repeated calmly. The warmth of her fingers stroked his cheek. He sighed deeply, closing his eyes behind the blindfold to revel in the feeling of her.

"I wish they were here," Walker whispered.

"Me too," Talia murmured back, brushing her hand up his arm to where the *Wuthering Heights* house was inked onto his shoulder. "But they are here."

"Their ghosts, you mean?"

"They left traces in their kids. Piper has the same smile as Paisley. Carter has told me Cole's duck buttcrack joke way too many times. Pearl's romantic heart is just like her father's."

"Colin has Cole's nose," Walker took over the list. "Coop makes the same ticking noise that Paisley used to make with her teeth when she'd think about something. And you, you have your mother's eyes and her smile. I wish I could see them." He slid his palm along Talia's shoulder and up to the nape of her neck. Her hair felt like it was in an updo, which made his heart flip. "Kiss me."

"You're going to ruin my makeup!" Talia giggled, squirming out of his grasp.

"Then I'll kiss everywhere but your face," Walker decided. Feeling around, he hit the wall next to him and set his hand against Talia's chest to slowly push her against it, dipping his head down until he eventually found the column of her throat. Talia gasped as if she was scandalized by his boldness. He knew her well enough to know she wasn't going to actually protest a rendezvous, even if it was right before she walked down the aisle. "I'm going to make you come now."

"Walker, you're the one who's anxious!" Talia protested, her hips thrusting against him, body clearly ignoring her plea and singing against his touch.

"This will help," Walker breathed in her ear, pulling on the material of her dress to hike it up as he spoke. "You know I don't like being the center of attention, and my therapist suggested I relieve stress when I'm feeling anxious." He dropped his voice into a deep rasp. "I'm *so* anxious, sweetheart. Are you going to help me?" he teased, sliding his hand up her leg and finding her garter. Talia squawked when he gave it a light snap before he groped up to her surprisingly bare ass. Walker tsked. "Talia almost-Hartrick, you aren't wearing any underwear."

"I was roasting, so I took them off." Talia's explanation was breathless, chest heaving into his as her thigh lifted to prop against Walker's hip, spreading herself for him. "I was gonna put them back on before the ceremony, I swear. I've had a fan blowing up my dress for the last hour."

"And you think *I'm* the scandalous one." He nibbled her earlobe, eliciting a moan when he slipped a finger inside her, his thumb already stroking circles above her entrance. "You want to know what I think?" When Talia gave a muffled sound of plea-sure, he continued, dropping his mouth to the hollow of her ear as he spoke in a low, sultry tone. "I think you were hoping I would want to touch you like this before we made it down the aisle. You wanted to be ready for me to take you, Tal. Don't even pretend you don't want this."

"Walker, we can't," Talia huffed. A slapping sound echoed off the wall next to him. He reached out to find what the noise was, still working her over with his other hand, and found one of Talia's hands against the wall, fingers curled in, a sure sign that she was aroused if he didn't already know by how slick she was for him.

"Hmm." Walker flicked his thumb harder over her clit, her hips bucking toward him, then dropped his hand away. "Well, I guess if you don't want to..."

"Dammit, Walker, don't stop!" Talia complained.

Walker obliged, returning his fingers to her entrance, slipping two inside her this time. "That's my girl." It was a tight fit, and Talia gasped, following up her desperation with a slew of curse words. He chuckled. "Such a filthy mouth for someone wearing all white."

"For all you know, I could be wearing blood red," Talia scoffed, a soft whimper ringing out when he drove his fingers deeper.

"Are you?"

"I'll only tell you if you fuck me right now." Walker's desire was further spurred on by the feeling of Talia yanking on his belt to loosen it. It came undone quickly, the button and zipper following in its wake.

"I'll do it whether you tell me the color of your dress or not." Walker pulled his hand from between Talia's legs and slid his underwear down enough to free himself. "You're going to have to jump a little. And I still can't see anything, so be careful."

"On three," Talia breathed. "One... two... three!" Her legs wrapped around Walker's waist, and he pushed her against the wall more firmly to regain his balance. "Ugh! This freaking dress is in the way!" Talia whined as Walker pawed at the fabric. "Don't rip it!"

"I'm not responsible for what I do when I'm blindfolded," Walker laughed, the dress finally pulled up enough to where he could feel her bare skin.

"Oh, is that how it works?" Talia drawled. Her eyebrows were probably arched, the way they always were when he said something truly outrageous.

"Mm-hmm."

Talia pulled him to her entrance with a practiced hand, and she sank down on him. Walker gripped her hips and thrust upward at the same time. She bounced on his cock, her dress swishing against the wall as she slid up and down.

"Fuck, I love you," Walker groaned.

"Then marry me," Talia panted, sheathing him again and rolling her hips forward.

"I think I will. Just as soon as we're done here."

"What if I told you I was only marrying you for your kitchen?" Talia teased and ground down hard.

"I'm just going to pretend that's a euphemism." Walker grinned and leaned forward to lick up the side of her neck. Talia's muffled sob was exactly the response he was looking for.

They fell into a sloppy and somewhat balanced rhythm, their breaths synced.

"I finished reading your book," Talia exhaled, digging her fingers into his back on another thrust.

"Which one?" Walker asked, shoving himself in her to the hilt.

"The one that'll have your name on it, Mr. Hartrick."

"What'd you think?"

"So good," she moaned.

"The book, or this?" he growled in her ear, increasing his pace and force.

"*Both*," Talia cried out, writhing against him.

"I like it when you call me Mr. Hartrick. Can't wait to make it your last name. Everyone will know you're *mine*."

"I'm already yours." Talia bit his lip, and Walker sighed into the pleasant pain of it, amused that in their frantic lovemaking, she forgot to avoid kissing him.

"And don't forget it." Each word was interrupted with a slam of his hips as he buried himself in her.

"As long as you remember you're mine." Her heels dug into his back, forcing him even deeper as he felt her hand reach between them to stroke herself where she needed more. The image of her touching herself in his head was enough to get him close to finishing.

"Always."

Walker found her mouth again, claiming Talia and letting her take what she was entitled to. Him. *All* of him. Teeming with every impassioned desire, he poured his soul into every thrust, wanting her to know exactly what she was getting by marrying him. Someone who constantly felt he was a disappointment. Someone grieving. Someone broken and still healing. But beyond every other cry of his body, the most urgent one covered all the rest: someone who would never stop loving her.

Talia's body responded with its own declarations. Walker knew her heart so well by then that each statement her body made was clear as day, even behind a blindfold. He was marrying someone bruised by her past. Someone who needed to be reminded that she was beautiful. And, above all, someone who would never stop loving him.

"I'm so close," he grunted as he reached the cusp of release.

"Me too," Talia whispered. Walker could tell she was from the way her thigh muscles were tightening with a shaky tension, her walls squeezing around him. It was the final surge that sent him careening into orgasm.

They both fell over the edge together, working each other down as Walker slid his fingers into Talia's mouth to smother the sound of her moan. There were still people in the vicinity, people who would probably be none too thrilled that he and Talia couldn't keep their hands off each other until after the ceremony

—her maid of honor, for one, who had just promised to skin Walker alive if he so much as looked at his future wife before she walked down the aisle.

The feeling of Talia's legs unwrapping from around his hips was immediately followed by the thudding sound of her feet hitting the floor.

"You ruined my lipstick," she scolded.

"You kissed me first," Walker said and reached for her, slowly running his hand down her chest. "So, what color is your dress?"

"You'll find out in ten minutes." Talia stepped away from him, and he stuck out his bottom lip in a pout. She giggled. "You're pathetic."

"I can't help it," Walker said, feeling his way to the door. When he found it, he paused, blindly turning his head in what he thought was Talia's direction. "Do me a favor and leave your underwear off. I like being the only one who knows you aren't wearing them. See you out there."

Adjusting his tie back into position, Walker shifted in place under the lattice arch draped with white wisteria, peach roses, and silver dollar eucalyptus in his backyard. He was standing next to the officiant, Marty (yes, the man Talia hit with her car—he had been surprised by the request but more than happy to fulfill the role), who was holding a Bible and none the wiser that Walker had just fucked his future wife up against the wall in her dressing room, which was also their bedroom. Roscoe stood in a gray suit on Walker's left after having walked his wife down the aisle. Amala was all dolled up in a blush pink floor-length gown beside Piper and Pearl, who both looked as beautiful as ever. The pure joy radiating off their faces was already starting to make tears well in Walker's eyes.

The yard was filled with their closest friends and also Clifford and his wife, Mary. Walker originally objected to inviting Talia's ex at all, but, apparently, Talia and Cliff had made some sort of weird pact because two months earlier Walker and Talia had flown out to New York to attend his and Mary's wedding, which was so elaborate it was almost indecent. Walker much preferred the low-key, laid-back version he and Talia had organized. It was a family affair.

Twinkle lights hung from the wood fencing in preparation for the sun to set on a perfect evening. The main aisle between the chairs that Talia would soon be walking down was littered with a tasteful amount of white flower petals, even more so after Jayla walked down with her flower girl basket, tossing more petals about as she spun in her flowy dress like the princess she was. Baby Marcel was sleeping in Roscoe's mom's arms out in the first row as the old woman rocked her grandbaby with blissful glee.

Cooper followed after Jayla down the aisle, the rings perched on a handcrafted pillow made by Curtis, who was still cheerfully in Talia's employ and beaming from the third row back. The head butcher from Lydia's, Mateo, and his wife Lucia, who now did all the inventory for the store, were holding hands and looking at each other fondly beside Curtis. The romance of a wedding seemed to be sweeping everyone away into their own memories. Walker's bachelor friends, Liam and Oliver, who'd joked before the ceremony about texting him incessantly while he was on his honeymoon, sat in the back row, cheesy grins on their faces. They thought they were in their glory days, no idea that singledom was nowhere near as good as being with the love of your life.

Even Walker's father was there, three months sober, sitting in the second row, with a smile on his face that almost resembled pride. It wasn't a fix, but it was a start. Dennis was trying. He wanted to know his grandkids and had finally realized that he'd already missed out on so much time he could never get back. Directly in front of Walker's dad sat three picture frames, one for each chair remaining in the front row. Pictures of Cole, Paisley, and Lydia, their smiling faces looking up at him from their seats. The ghosts he forever wanted to be haunted by.

Everyone was there.

When a piano version of "I Will Follow You Into the Dark" by Death Cab for Cutie started playing through a nearby speaker, Walker focused on the sliding glass door where Talia was supposed to be exiting the house.

Then, she did.

Emerging from behind the door, accompanied by Carter on one side and Colin on the other, Talia made her way down the steps from the wooden deck to the narrow, flower-lined walkway, holding her heels in her hand. She was a dream in her white dress. He was right about the lace, too. It was both classy and sexy, hugging her curves and showing off just the right amount of cleavage. She was drop-dead gorgeous. If Walker didn't want to live out the rest of his life with her, he might have keeled over, happily dying on the spot. Wiping at his eyes as they spilled over with joy, he watched her curled, flower-adorned ponytail sway gently in the breeze against the criss-crossed ribbon straps at the back of her dress. Her gown pooled at her bare feet, sewn flower petals traveling down the A-line dress to the bottom of her lace-hemmed skirt. Stunning.

Talia moved with grace down the aisle as every eye fell upon her, the way every eye should when she walked into a room. The way Walker's eyes did every time she was beside him. He could feel the hot tears sliding down his face, but he no longer cared to wipe them away. By some stroke of luck, or by Cole and Paisley's persistent pleading with whatever powers that be, he was about to marry the woman of his dreams. Walker Hartrick, doomed to be alone, unloved, and a stress case forever, was going to be married to the most beautiful person he'd ever met.

Walker inhaled a deep, shaky breath to regain his composure when Talia came to stand in front of him.

"Who gives this woman to marry this man?" Marty asked.

All of his nieces and nephews shouted a smattering of "we do"s. They had practiced beforehand in an attempt to say it simultaneously, but they utterly failed, which only made Walker smile wider, holding his hand out to Talia, who was biting back a laugh at their lack of unanimity. Her firm grip when he took her palm in his propelled him to stand tall instead of melting into a puddle on the ground at her feet. Colin and Carter found their spots beside Cooper and Roscoe as Talia met Walker under the arch, her thumbs rubbing circles into the backs of his hands.

"Ready, Ponytail?" Walker asked.

"Born ready." Talia nodded. Marty cleared his throat, adjusting his glasses on his long nose as he looked down at his notes.

"We begin with the purchase of a very questionable vehicle."

Was it wrong to completely tune out your entire wedding ceremony? Walker could barely remember a second of it, but he could recall the twinkling of Talia's eyes and the way the sun hit her dress and skin just right so she looked like a glowing goddess. He barely cared what Marty was saying, entirely focused on the soft curls of Talia's ponytail and every "I do" that parted her coral-colored lips. When Walker repeated his own vows, it was a struggle not to shout the "I do"s from the rooftops.

Other than his decision to take over guardianship of his five nieces and nephews, he had never been so sure of a decision in his entire life.

The wedding band Walker slipped on Talia's ring finger gleamed in the sunlight. It matched the engagement ring next to it, which he had purchased on his phone in the hospital the night Marcel was born. It had only been a day after they agreed to go for it when he decided that forever with Talia wasn't going to be nearly enough. If he was honest, he had probably known she was the one a month into knowing her, but the thing about his stubborn heart was that it needed to break down before he could build it up again and realize that it was okay to be happy. To want for himself. To feel love.

Cole's gold wedding band stared up at Walker from his ring finger, and he smiled down at it, twisting it around with his thumb to get the feel of the new location on his hand. It felt right.

"By the power vested in me by the State of Oregon, I now pronounce you man and wife. You may now kiss the bride."

In one fell swoop, Walker pulled Talia in and dipped her back over his arm, his mouth landing on hers as he suspended her above the ground. She held onto his face with both hands and kissed him back like she wanted nothing more than to be his forever. Like she was just as in love with him as he was with her and she wanted to spend the rest of her life with him and his unruly nieces and nephews.

The best way to fight for his family was to make her a part of it.

THE END

ACKNOWLEDGMENTS

People always say it takes a village to raise a child. Similarly, it takes a village to write and publish a book. The amount of people I have to thank for this is endless. To my daughter, thank you for giving up some of your time with me so I could write this story. I wish I was as outgoing or had the same level of self-confidence and positive energy as you do. To my husband, thank you for supporting my dream and being more confident that I could do it than I was myself.

To Crystal, thank you for being that constant person in my life. The one who lifts me up and chose to be my friend when I thought no one wanted to be. Thank you to Taylor and Mackenzie for getting sucked under Crystal's spell and believing her when she said I was cool. You three inspire me every day.

To my editor, Maryarita, I am your biggest fan. You made this book ten thousand times better than I could have ever done on my own. Someday, when you're taking over the world, I'll get to point to my TV and say "I know her!" Thank you for putting in the work! I know it was a lot considering I can't use a comma properly to save my life. You're a star. To my betas and sensitivity readers, Charise, Selah, Lauren, Lauren Brooke, Alexis, Danielle, Riley, Leif, Allie, Ali, and Yashika, thank you so much for your honest input. I appreciate all your diverse perspectives, and I'm so grateful for a community of people to bounce ideas off of. You helped make these characters feel real.

To authors Kennedy Ryan, Tarah DeWitt, Hannah Bonam-Young, Julie Olivia, Rachel Lynn Solomon, Amanda Gambill, and so many more who built me up and broke me down with the written word, thank you for being an inspiration.

Last but not least, to Zoey's Extraordinary Playlist. (This is my book, so, yes, I'm going to thank a TV show.) At some point, Austin Winsberg sat down with a grieving heart and wrote the most inspiring show I will ever watch. He chose to channel his grief and love for his father through music, through art, and through love, and it impacted many. It's everything I want to do with my own writing. To the group of people I met through our shared obsession with the story this show told, thank you for your constant support! In turn, I promise to never disclose to anyone what the group chat name "DRPC" stands for.

All my love,
Katie

Dicktionary

Whether you wish to skip the smut entirely or return to it, that content can be found in these chapters:

Stay Tuned

Piper and Leo's story - The Ones We Hate - Coming Spring 2024
Colin and Scarlett's story - Coming Soon

About the Author

Katie Golightly is an Oregon girl who thrives on chaos. She lives happily with her husband, daughter, and overflowing bookshelf. In addition to getting serotonin from the outdoors and well-organized spreadsheets, she has always been drawn to the art of storytelling. Eventually, the endless emotional, funny, and spicy stories she fabricated in her head had to be written down somewhere.

Stay connected:
www.katiegolightlybooks.com

instagram.com/katiegowritely

threads.net/@katiegowritely

x.com/katiegowritely

tiktok.com/@katiegowritely

Printed in the USA
CPSIA information can be obtained
at www.ICGtesting.com
LVHW090330200824
788678LV00002B/182

9 798889 924616